The

Max Hennessy was the pen-name of John Harris. He had a wide variety of jobs from sailor to cartoonist and became a highly inventive, versatile writer. In addition to crime fiction, Hennessy was a master of the war novel and drew heavily on his experiences in both the navy and air force, serving in the Second World War. His novels reflect the reality of war mixed with a heavy dose of conflict and adventure.

Also by Max Hennessy

The RAF Trilogy

The Bright Blue Sky
The Challenging Heights
Once More the Hawks

The Captain Kelly Maguire Trilogy

The Lion at Sea
The Dangerous Years
Back to Battle

The WWII Naval Thrillers

The Sea Shall Not Have Them
Ride Out the Storm
Cotton's War
North Strike

The Flying Ace Thrillers

The Mustering of the Hawks
The Mercenaries
The Courtney Entry

The WWII Collection

Take or Destroy
Swordpoint
The Fox From His Lair
Army of Shadows

THE LION AT SEA

MAX HENNESSY

San Diego, California

 Canelo US
An imprint of Printers Row Publishing Group
9717 Pacific Heights Blvd, San Diego, CA 92121
www.canelobooksus.com

Printers Row Publishing Group is a division of Readerlink Distribution
Services, LLC. Canelo US is a registered trademark of Readerlink
Distribution Services, LLC.

First published in Great Britain in 1977 by Hamish Hamilton. This
edition originally published in the United Kingdom in 2020 by Canelo.

Published in partnership with Canelo.

Correspondence regarding the content of this book should be sent to Canelo
US, Editorial Department, at the above address. Author inquiries should be
sent to Canelo, Unit 9, 5th Floor, Cargo Works, 1–2 Hatfields, London SE1
9PG, United Kingdom, www.canelo.co.

Publisher: Peter Norton • Associate Publisher: Ana Parker
Art Director: Charles McStravick
Senior Developmental Editor: April Graham
Editor: Angela Garcia
Production Team: Beno Chan, Julie Greene

Design: Brianna Lewis

Library of Congress Control Number: 2022945094

ISBN: 978-1-6672-0379-9

Printed in India

27 26 25 24 23   1 2 3 4 5

Part One

One

It just wasn't possible!

There weren't that many ships in the whole world!

In a patchy but warm sun, they stretched as far as the eye could see – 250 of them, 170 of them British. They formed a parallelogram six miles long by two miles wide, yet not a single man and not a single ship had been brought home from abroad for this tremendous display of that principal instrument of Pax Britannica, the Royal Navy.

The great vessels, many wearing admirals' flags, were drawn up in two columns, first of all the dreadnoughts and super-dreadnoughts – *Collingwood*, *St Vincent*, *Superb*, *Vanguard* and others – great angular towering grey fortresses of floating steel sharp against the pearl-grey sky; then the battle cruisers – *Indefatigable*, *Indomitable*, *Inflexible*, *Implacable* – a whole array of them, only slightly less formidable than the dreadnoughts. Then came the armoured cruisers, light cruisers, destroyers, submarines and torpedo boats, and all the ancillary vessels, representing every aspect of naval preparedness, the sea between them covered by darting cutters and picket boats like maybugs on a pond. Finally came the foreign battleships, the German *Von der Tann*, the French *Danton*, the American *Delaware*, and fifteen others, and the foreign potentates' yachts, aflutter with flags – whole strings and windrows of them, all caught by the south-westerly breeze that poppled the grey water.

It was an awe-inspiring sight. Even to British eyes well used to the pomp and majesty of the navy. Even to the somewhat indifferent gaze of Midshipman George Kelly Maguire, on the

2

deck of the armoured cruiser, *Huguenot*. A solid phalanx of machinery and armour manned by thousands of the most skilled seamen in the world, the Coronation Review lay broodingly across the entrance to the Solent, one of the most vulnerable waterways in the British Isles, like a solid bulwark against aggression. A vast new fleet that was the brainchild of that dogmatic, difficult and spiteful volcano of a man, Admiral Sir John Fisher, the great ships belonged to a navy that he had transformed almost overnight – from the antiquated collection of Victorian men-o'-war that had previously graced naval reviews, to a twentieth century instrument fit to meet its first challenge for a hundred years and counter anything the Germans, whom Fisher had long since seen as the enemy, could throw against it.

With its stupefying dimensions and potential, it had been assembled to pay tribute to the newly-crowned monarch, George the Fifth, by the Grace of God King of England, Emperor of India and Defender of the Faith. And, staring from *Huguenot* over the ruffled grey water, untouched by the political overtones that lay behind the review and by the need in an atmosphere of growing European tension for a show of strength, Midshipman Maguire sincerely hoped in his unyielding youthful judgement that George the Fifth, King of England, Emperor of India and Defender of the Faith, appreciated what was being done for him. Because God alone knew how many gallons of paint had been slapped on by bored sailors, how many hundredweights of brass polish and holystone had been used to bring the great vessels up to the standard of cleanliness and beauty they now represented, how much sweat had been wasted, how much cursing uttered, how many hours sleep lost by officers from captains down to midshipmen like himself.

All morning sight-seeing steamers had been leaving for the broad waters of the Solent, and the King, wearing the uniform of an admiral of the fleet, had arrived at the South Railway jetty to the crack of guns from Portsmouth harbour as *Victory*,

Nelson's flagship at Trafalgar, had fired a salute. Then, accompanied by the Trinity House yacht and other vessels – every one of them stuffed to the bulkheads with dignitaries and officials – and escorted by torpedo boats whose task it was to ensure that wayward shipping was kept well clear of the review area which picket boats had previously emptied of pleasure craft, the royal yacht, *Victoria and Albert*, left harbour to the din of cheers from people lining the walls of the old port.

As Kelly Maguire watched, the clouds turned the sea to an iron darkness that caught only occasional glimpses of light, and the great ships, sombre and black-looking with their great batteries of guns, steel turrets and ram bows, suddenly seemed less ceremonial than threatening, less decorative than purposeful. He drew a deep breath. He'd got out of the wrong side of his hammock that morning and, his boyish cheeks shaved to the bone, scrubbed, brushed and polished to within an inch of his life, he was in a questioning state of mind as he stared at all the splendour, and came to the conclusion that in recent years, despite Jacky Fisher, despite the reforms that had been made, naval pomp seemed to have become badly confused with power.

Aboard *Huguenot*, for example, the captain, the Honourable Basil Acheson, was known – without too much effort of imagination either – as God. It was normal enough, of course, for the captain of any ship to be referred to and even regarded as God, but there was always an element of jesting in it, yet on Kelly's first morning aboard, Captain Acheson had summoned to his spacious quarters aft his three newest and youngest officers, Midshipmen Maguire, Verschoyle and Kimister, and let them know exactly where they stood in the order of things.

'Aboard *Huguenot*,' he had announced, 'I am God Almighty, and you are not even junior archangels. Indeed, gentlemen, if there were dogsbodies in Heaven, then that is what you would be, so that now that you've been promoted from cadets to midshipmen, take care that you don't let it go to your heads.

One thing more: It is not advisable to say "Good morning" to the captain of this ship before lunch. This is not a "good morning" ship.'

Even granting that Captain Acheson was unusual – a 'character', one of the last of the Victorian eccentrics, with a tendency to enjoy displaying his eccentricities – it had hardly been encouraging.

His youthful eyes narrowed, Kelly Maguire stared again at the assembled fleet. A splash of colour fluttered from *Lord Nelson*'s yardarm and there was a scuffle of feet behind him, then the whole fleet seemed to burst into a riot of vivid flags as it dressed over-all. What had been a grey and sombre scene was transformed at once with gay bunting, and, as though in response, the sun appeared, picking up the brasswork and white paint, the bulges of the turrets and the lines of the guns. It was as if someone had turned a floodlight on the fleet.

'They're coming!'

To Kelly Maguire, a rebel by nature and particularly a rebel this day because he had suffered his share of lost sleep and sweat, it all seemed an awful waste of effort. Not, of course, that anyone in that year of grace, 1911, gave a fig for the opinions of George Kelly Maguire or would do for many years to come. At the age of nineteen, he was nothing more than a mere cog in a huge wheel, all bony wrists and ankles as he grew out of a uniform he was too impoverished to replace at this late stage of waiting for his translation from the humiliating rank of midshipman to the glory of his first stripe.

'It's normal enough, of course, for the very young to be rebellious at what they consider unnecessary fuss,' Midshipman Verschoyle, standing just to his left, murmured. 'If you're not a socialist at twenty, you've no heart; if you're still one at forty, you've no head.'

Kelly Maguire frowned. The view that all men should be equal seemed at the moment to make very sound sense to a downtrodden snotty. His seniors, however, were doubtless

Tories to a man and regarded egalitarianism as a dangerous new form of politics. Even James Caspar Verschoyle, Kelly's immediate senior in the List, despite his cynical evaluations, was without doubt a hardened Tory who never suffered the slightest qualms of conscience.

'But then, of course,' Verschoyle often pointed out, 'I'm stinking rich.'

And, unlike Kelly Maguire, who, apart from a shock of red hair, was shortish, squarish and indifferent as to colouring and features, he was also tall, patrician and intelligent. Kelly Maguire envied him not only for his airs and graces but also because Verschoyle was an excellent boxer who had had his own way with people all his young life, for no other reason than that he'd always had too much money and too many good looks. The fact that Kelly's father was a rear admiral and a baronet made no difference whatsoever, and Verschoyle, who knew everything about everybody, was quick to point out why. 'He's a rear admiral because he retired as a captain and commodore,' he said, 'and he's a baronet only because his elder brother died of enteric in Bloemfontein during the Boer War. And since the title carries no wealth, young Ginger, you're really just a lot of bog-trotters, aren't you? – as poor as church mice and obliged to live in Ireland, unlike my family which has a town house in London.'

Kelly scowled, far from unaware of the circumstances that made up his background. His grandfather, Colonel Seamus Aloysius Kelly – together with his younger brother, Kelly's Uncle Patrick, lately a major in the Royal Irish Fusiliers but now retired and existing largely on his elder brother's charity – had had to live for years off the rundown remains of the family estate, so that it had seemed wise at the time to get rid of his daughter, Kelly's mother, as quickly as possible to the first bidder, Kelly's father. Instead of getting rid of his daughter, however, Colonel Kelly had merely acquired another hanger-on. The only taste of glory in the long career of Admiral

6

Maguire had been the day when he'd put up his admiral's stripe just in time to discard it again on settling down in retirement, to wipe out by scrimping and saving some of the debts he'd incurred in a lifetime of enjoying himself at sea.

There had never been much love lost between the two sides of the family, and no advantages whatsoever for Kelly from his father's rank. Not even when he'd gone none too willingly to Dartmouth. It had been bitterly cold and an elderly petty officer with a nose like a ripe cherry had lined them all up, even the sobbing Kimister, who'd been brought by his mother – something that had taken a lot of living down – and let them know exactly where they stood.

'You'd better get it into your 'eads 'ere and now, young gentlemen,' he'd said, 'You've got very varied backgrounds, and some of you even 'ave important fathers. Here we're all equal and you at the moment are on the lowest rung of the naval ladder.'

Kelly had hated it. Even his six months at sea in the training cruiser, *Cumberland*, where, if nothing else, he'd learned to be sick over the lee side, hadn't seemed terribly full of promise, while his arrival in *Huguenot* had positively failed to warm his heart.

'You are a wart,' the sub-lieutenant of the gunroom had told him firmly. 'An excrescence. An ullage. A growth. You probably imagine that when signalled "House your topmast", you should reply, "fine, how's yours?" and doubtless the only time you'll show any enthusiasm for the navy will be on full-belly nights when we're entertaining visitors.'

It seemed just then to Kelly Maguire that the navy was not only single-minded but also a touch narrow-minded, too.

He came back to the present with a jerk. Over the lap of the water, he could hear the drone of an engine. In the line of seamen drawn up on deck behind him with the submissiveness of a herd of cows at milking time, there were a few murmurs of interest, and he saw a seaplane moving down the line of dreadnoughts, spidery, ungainly, but somehow a pointer to a different future.

The sun had gone again and the sparkling water had become grey and sombre once more. The seaplane had disappeared now beyond the dreadnoughts and, as the wind grew keener, Kelly began to wonder how much longer they were all going to have to line the decks. He glanced to his left. Verschoyle was waiting with his own group of bearded, heavy-handed men. He seemed quite at ease, and Kelly could never imagine him seething inside with envy and humiliation. He was a tall young man, pale-faced, fair-haired, but lean-bodied with strong shoulders. Kelly disliked him, and disliked him even more because Verschoyle was clever. It would have been so much more satisfactory to be able to feel that Verschoyle would never get anywhere in the navy, or that, if he did, he would do it only through influence and wealth. Unfortunately, this was not so and never would be. Certain he'd dislike Verschoyle until the day he died, Kelly was equally certain that Verschoyle would never be a failure, and that one day he'd be an admiral while Kelly was still trailing behind among the passed-over captains.

On his right was Albert Edward Kimister, the other midshipman who had joined with him. Kimister was a born victim. Small, slight, not as clever as Verschoyle nor as tough-minded as Kelly, he had suffered from bullying all through Dartmouth and still suffered in the gunroom of *Huguenot*, and Kelly had had more than one good hiding from Verschoyle for standing up for him.

'I wonder—' Verschoyle's low voice came over the drum of the signal halyards and the slap of water alongside '—how many senior officers there are still afloat to whom naval history is nothing but posturing heroics gleaming in an eternal empire of brass and new paint. Good at seamanship and having the whitest decks in the fleet, and entirely satisfied because they know how to blacklead their projectiles and paint a gun.'

8

Certain to a T what to use, Kelly thought. 'A foot of grey, an inch of black and the rest white makes a damn good colour,' his father had often said.

'Sad lack of imagination among 'em,' Verschoyle murmured. 'Outlook limited to *The Sporting Times*, *Country Life* and *The Illustrated London News*, shouldn't wonder. I'm finding all this rather a bore, you know, young Ginger. I think I'll get out of it.'

'How?' Kelly's head half-turned as he spoke out of the corner of his mouth.

'Fall in a fit.'

'They'll know you're faking.'

'Not they!' Verschoyle looked smugly self-confident. 'I took the precaution of reporting sick this morning. Of course, they suggested I stood down, but I heroically insisted on carrying on.'

Kelly tried to ignore Verschoyle's sly comments and kept his eyes ahead. Beyond the surface ships, he could see the low hulls of submarines. Despite his father's attitude that they were a 'damned un-English weapon,' he had a feeling that when war came, like aeroplanes, they might prove highly important. He had argued it out many times – admittedly not with his father who, brought up to believe the big gun was the only gentleman's weapon, could never be persuaded to listen to such blasphemy. Not even with his mother who, being Irish and an ardent follower of hounds, was far more concerned with his unfortunate habit of falling off the horses she gave him to ride. But with Charlotte Upfold, who lived two miles away across the fields from Balmero House where Kelly lived, and was a good listener and always had been. Admittedly she was still only a schoolgirl, but she could ride – better than Kelly himself – knew how to shoot and could handle ferrets with the best of them. She was forthright, intelligent and no-nonsense, and they had been friends all their lives. It had been to her that he had bewailed having to go to Dartmouth and poured out his woes about bullying. 'The sub-lieutenant's left-handed—' he could clearly remember his conversation with her '—and Verschoyle's right-handed, so that when they go at you with a dirk scabbard, they make cross patterns on your bum. We had a look in the midshipmen's bathroom.'

Charley Upfold never questioned his assertions, because she expected her whole life to lead towards marriage with him. She told him so when she was barely out of the nursery and had repeated the announcement regularly since.

Bored, he shifted from one foot to the other. Somewhere to his left he could see a group of senior officers in heavy dress coats and glittering epaulettes.

'Discussing the racing at Goodwood, shouldn't wonder,' Verschoyle murmured, and Kelly had to admit he was probably, right. With their intense concentration on gunnery and torpedoes, while they excelled at technical details, they rarely appeared to think about strategy, let alone pass it on to their juniors. Only a few of them had done the course at the war college, and the very idea of lesser beings being interested seemed to be enough to take their breath away.

As the breeze increased, the flags began to snap in the wind and the water slapped more heavily against the side of the ship. Kelly shivered and began to wish he'd put on something warmer under his uniform.

'Probably rain before long,' Verschoyle observed quietly. 'Then we'll all get wet and the fireworks will be spoiled.'

Certainly the sun had not reappeared and a long low bank of cloud, the forerunner of rain, was moving up from the south-west, like the vanguard of an advancing army. The popple and slap of water increased and a sudden gust set the halyards thrumming and the flags clattering noisily. Verschoyle had been growing more and more restless in the increasing cold and Kelly finally heard him give a deep sigh.

'I suppose I shouldn't have joined if I couldn't take a joke,' he muttered, and before Kelly realised what had happened, he had slid to the deck.

There was an immediate scuffle and a murmur of voices and the divisional officer turned, scowling at Kelly and Kimister.

'You two! Get him below!'

Picking up Verschoyle's shoulders while Kimister grabbed his feet, Kelly bundled the limp figure out of sight. Below deck Verschoyle pushed them away with a smile.

'That's all right, chaps,' he said. 'I can manage on my own now. I think I'll go and have a fag in my hammock.'

'But it's the King!' Kimister's face was shocked. 'God, you are a swine, Verschoyle!'

Verschoyle smiled. 'Yes,' he said. 'I've often thought so myself.' His smile died. 'But at least I'm not a wretched little bore like you, Kimister. Now, shove off back to mummy on deck and leave yours truly to enjoy the first bit of peace he's had on this bloody ship since he joined.'

Kimister bolted, terrified he'd miss the chance to salute his sovereign. 'It's so beastly unpatriotic,' he said in a high, indignant voice and Kelly grinned. Although Verschoyle was a rotter, he thought, at least he was a rotter with style.

He had barely taken up his place again in the division when there was a stir on his left.

'Here she comes!'

A petty officer – in fore and aft rig with a made-up bow tie – spoke sharply, the words carrying down the line on the breeze, then he saw the royal yacht, small and gay-looking among the preponderance of grey paint, and there was a sudden bang that made him jump, as *Lord Nelson* fired the first gun of the royal salute. It was taken up at once by the rest of the fleet, and for a few noisy minutes Kelly had a rough idea of what a battle might sound like. As the royal yacht drew nearer, old-fashioned and civilian among the angular shapes of the battleships, he saw groups of people standing on her deck, and the bright colours of women's clothes. The water was white under her forefoot and her flags were streaming in the wind, and she was near enough now for him to see her seamen with their jumpers tucked into cloth trousers, even the silver badges on their arms. *Huguenot*'s band burst into the National Anthem, a little unsteady at first but picking up quickly into an uneven blare of sound. Then somewhere behind him there was a clatter of blocks as flags rose to the yardarm and, as the royal yacht came abeam, the high twittering of bosuns' pipes. Someone called for three cheers, and suddenly, bewilderingly, it all seemed worthwhile. After all, the little man just across the water represented in his person the strength, the power and the dignity of the British Empire, and like Nelson himself, he'd always been noted for his kindness. Into the bargain, he *was* a sailor king. He'd served at sea and loved the navy. And he *was* their commander-in-chief and, if it came to a pinch, could even lead them into battle. His very smallness, even his pop eyes and knock knees, seemed to lend him a sort of homeliness.

There was a crash of cheering all round Kelly and caps were lifted. As he caught sight of the star-studded figure in blue and gold on *Victoria and Albert*'s bridge acknowledging the cheers, he decided that if the King's heart was as full of pride as his own was at that moment, then his throat probably also felt choked and his eyes were probably dim with moisture.

Some fool was screaming his enthusiasm and to his surprise Kelly realised it was himself. Verschoyle, he decided impulsively, didn't know what he was missing.

Two

The fleet was dispersing. The royal yacht had gone, followed by the German Emperor's yacht and all the other foreign ships. All the bunfights ashore had finished, all the gatherings marked by splendid uniforms, champagne and caviar; with the heads of state and their ministers, all splashed with ribbons and decorations, all being cautious and diplomatic as they tried to be enthusiastic, while their womenfolk fought to outdo each other for colour and style and poise.

Presumably, the affair had been a success. Receptions had been held for the principal British and foreign officers on board *Victoria and Albert*, then she had left for harbour, followed by the thuddings and bangings and the drifting blue smoke of a farewell salute. The firework display ashore had not reached expectations because of the rain, and even the illumination of the fleet had not come up to scratch because the downpour had caused fuses to blow in lighting circuits. One great ship was able only to illuminate its admiral's flag, and when Kelly had arrived in *Huguenot*'s steam pinnace with a message for her captain, he had found the commander, with a face like an old seaboot, storming up and down the foredeck looking for someone to throw overboard.

There had also been a few alarms and excursions. *Achilles'* cutter had been swamped after a collision with a picket boat off Clarence Pier, and a steam pinnace from *Implacable*, taking guests ashore to see the George Hotel, where Nelson had spent his last hours in England before Trafalgar, had been rammed by a pinnace from another ship and dumped a party of naval ladies in the water – fortunately without much damage except to dresses and hair styles. A few officers had attended a daring new farce at the Theatre Royal but only one-fifth of ships' companies had been granted leave so that, apart from senior officers and a few favoured juniors, nobody had profited greatly from the affair, a fact which had prompted a letter in *The Portsmouth Evening News* attacking the social conditions in the fleet and suggesting the ultimate horror of a trade union for all naval personnel to improve hours, wages, leave and food.

The weather had grown considerably colder now and the wind rippled the surface of the grey-green sea between the Isle of Wight and the mainland, and sent up little showering cascades of spray as waves broke against the hulls of those ships still gathered in the anchorage. The wild screeching of birds gave the day a feeling of heaviness, and the sky, pearl-coloured with overcast, arched bleakly overhead, its sombreness reflected in the waters of the Solent.

A sprinkle of rain came on the wind as Kelly took his boat away from *Huguenot*'s side, its polished brass winking, its stanchions decorated with turks' heads and other tiddly items of cordwork. 'A ship is judged by her boats,' he'd been told very early in his career. 'So tend to your boat's wants as carefully as you would to your mistress'. And see to it that to your eyes she is just as beautiful, because a mid who cares for his boat and manoeuvres it satisfactorily will invariably behave with equal credit on the bridge of a ship.' He had remembered it well.

In the distance, he could see the dreadnoughts of the Third Battle Squadron beginning to move away in line ahead, great steel fortresses, powerful and swift but, because of their sheer weight, so ungainly in the turn they were known as the Wobbly Eights. It was said they needed all of a mile to change course and Kelly stared at them from the pinnace, hoping he'd never have to serve in one. The spit and polish were said to be formidable.

Jacky Fisher had built them during his years as First Lord. He had wanted a big ship of over 17,000 tons, capable of twenty-five knots with twelve inches of armour plate and twelve twelve-inch guns, and there they were, right in front of him. In fact, they'd turned out to be somewhat heavier than Fisher had wished, had only eleven inches of armour plate and ten twelve-inchers instead of twelve, and could do only twenty-one knots, but at least no one had wasted time. From the laying down of the keel to the launching of the first one, it had taken only a matter of months.

While most of jingoistic Britain thought them masterpieces, however, the people who served in them were not so sure. They threw too much smoke over the gun control and above all they were wet in rough weather. It was even claimed that they'd been too hurriedly thrown together and that all that had been done was produce a new kind of ship on which all the other powers were now improving. Admiral Beresford argued that Britain had declared herself to be the bully of the seas, while others had noted that to pay for the super-ships Fisher had sent 150 lesser vessels to the breakers on the grounds that they were old and outdated and could neither fight nor run away, seeing naval warfare, his critics said, only as a fleet action and forgetting that in places as far away as the Pacific, India and Australia, even old tubs would be useful if there were trouble. Only Verschoyle was eager to be posted to a dreadnought – and preferably to the flagship, spit, polish and all. 'That's where a chap will be noticed,' he said.

Kelly frowned. He didn't see himself in a dreadnought or a battle cruiser. Destroyers probably. Sleek, swift, black-painted little ships that in bad weather were hell to be in, uncomfortable little ships in which even a mere lop on the ocean made eating and drinking difficult, and bad weather could dump the whole wardroom – officers, chairs, fiddles, crockery, glass, stewards and everything – underneath the table in a swill of soup and sea water. They were cramped little vessels where cabins were like rabbit hutches so filled with pipes it was almost impossible to stand upright, but they were also always the hounds when it came to a chase, always the first into action and last out; and a destroyer captain was noticed not for his manners but for his initiative and skill with a ship, while his very duties placed him as far as possible from interfering senior officers.

The wind was cold, punching into Kelly's face and sending spray over the canopy to clatter against the funnel. Just ahead of him he could see Verschoyle in the petrol pinnace bumping in the swell. Verschoyle, being Verschoyle, had been carrying personal messages to the admiral all day while Kelly Maguire, being Kelly Maguire, was merely carrying mail.

Thick smoke was pouring from the pinnace's funnel and the stoker put his head out of the hatch to sniff the wind before dumping a bucketful of ash overboard. The wind caught it, to scatter it over a wide area on the lee side of the boat in a greasy grey patch.

'Any more of that?' Kelly demanded.

'No sir.' The stoker looked as if butter wouldn't melt in his mouth.

'Well, if there is, save it for the return journey. I wouldn't like any to drift through the admiral's scuttles.'

A ship in the distance was flashing a signal and Kelly read it carefully for practice, then another slash of cold water came over and he realised his attention had wandered and he was not watching the boat's head.

Perhaps no one's thoughts were entirely on the job in hand. The fleet review was still too much in the mind. It was the biggest thing that had ever happened to Kelly Maguire and he had happily ditched his complaints in a wave of enthusiasm and patriotism. It was uncomplicated, unsophisticated, probably even unintelligent, and with his mother's rebellious Irish blood coursing through his veins, perhaps even treacherous.

Being the son of Catherine de la Trouve Kelly, it had taken him a long time to feel at ease with the unquestioning royalism of the navy. And even more so to feel at one with its strange attitude of putting the ceremonial before efficiency. He had been brought up to believe that the navy was a weapon, but it hadn't taken him long to realise that the chief concern of many of the senior officers was less how to learn how to use that weapon in time of war than to hold to the Victorian ideal of keeping it spotless. 'Cleanliness is next to Godliness' seemed to be the motto of most admirals, and he had once heard his father boast how he'd made a habit of tossing practice shells overboard rather than spoil the paintwork by firing the guns.

It was at that moment, in fact, that he realised for the first time why his father had never flown his flag as an admiral. He belonged to that old navy Fisher had tried to change. He was a great believer in the fact that so long as the navy simply existed, Britain need never tremble, and with the great fleet dispersing in the increasing rain, he suddenly seemed to Kelly as out-of-date as the dodo. He was probably even the reason why Kelly had never had any particular desire to go to sea. At thirteen, when it had all started, in fact, he'd had no particular wish to go anywhere at all, but, because his father had finally managed to scrape home to flag rank and because his elder brother, Gerald, had followed his grandfather into the army, the step had become inevitable. He had spent hours when the move had been announced sulking in a bitter resentment against an institution which had seemed in the past to add little to his life or even to that of his mother, who had always resented his father's absences and the fact that he was undoubtedly enjoying his life in foreign ports while she had to bear the burden of the debts he ran up. Kelly had long since even suspected there had been other women in his father's background – though they were never mentioned – and for some reason had always blamed this on the fact that his father was a sailor and took his pleasures where he found them.

The rain was heavy now and Kelly spat it from his lips as he saw the water round the flagship crowded with boats. With nothing more urgent than the mail, they might have to wait a long time, and he saw one of the seamen in front of him cursing their ill-luck.

Kelly frowned. He was due before long at Greenwich to sit his sub-lieutenant's examinations. After that he might call himself a fully-fledged officer and a grown man. The fact that London was no place to have handy when you were trying to concentrate on getting good marks was always a little disconcerting. On the other hand, it meant a good feed at the Upfolds' town house. Charley's family always moved from Ireland to London for the season with a view to finding Charley's elder sister, Mabel, a husband; and since Brigadier-General Upfold was not short of money there was always plenty to eat, something that held a considerable appeal to a growing young man kept short of food in his own mess and lacking the wherewithal to buy anything to supplement it.

The boats were queuing up round the stern of the flagship flow, spray leaping up between them from the trapped waves. In front of him a boat from *Argonaut* was jockeying for position and doing it none too successfully, then he saw Verschoyle alongside him, skilful, languid, handsome as the devil and apparently indifferent to the weather.

'I'm going to take a chance and try the starboard ladder,' Verschoyle called out as the two boats bounced alongside each other. 'This way, we'll wait until Doomsday.'

Kelly nodded and, considering it might be good idea to do Verschoyle in the eye by getting there first, increased revolutions and pushed in front of him, the funnel spouting smoke and cinders.

A wave slopped on board, heavier and wetter than he'd expected, but at least there was no one ahead of him, and his attention fully occupied, he headed for the flagship's side. A sailor on the gangway made a warning gesture with his hand but, occupied with outdoing Verschoyle, Kelly took no notice and the Marine corporal with the mailbag moved towards the bows.

Well aft, the flagship's ladder was a good twenty degrees outside the line of the ship. But Kelly wasn't worried because he knew from experience that when he ran his engine astern his bows would kick to port. Unfortunately, the battleship was yawing to starboard on her cable and, overconfident of his ability, he put his engine into reverse just too late. The swell lifted the boat and he saw the sailor on the gangway run for his life, then the lower platform of the ladder crumpled as it holed the port bow of the pinnace. With a crash it spread itself outwards with what seemed a horrifying slowness that Kelly felt he might have halted if he'd thought of it in time; then the treads flew apart and came down on him in a shower. One of them hit him on the head and a second went down the funnel with a clatter and a puff of soot, and he heard a heavy voice from below yell in alarm, 'What the effing Christ was that?' and he became aware of the Marine corporal hanging like grim death to the ladder falls, the strap of the mailbag between his teeth and his eyes sticking out at the devastation, like prawns on a plate.

'That's fucked it,' someone said.

His face pink with shame, Kelly bowed to the furious signals of the figure on the deck wearing three gold stripes and a heavy frown and moved ahead to the ship's derrick. The wreckage of the accommodation ladder was lowered none too gently to the roof of the pinnace's cabin and the commander shouted down in a voice that rasped like a file across the corner of an anvil.

'That ought to trim you up a bit, young feller-me-lad. Ask your commander to return it to us when it's repaired. And, while you're at it, I would suggest also that you report to your sub-lieutenant for six of the best for shoving your nose in where it isn't wanted.'

His eyes down, and silent with self-disgust, Kelly put the boat astern, the foredeck cluttered with the remains of the gangway. There would be a highly dramatic arrival aboard *Huguenot*, he knew, with reports of what had happened preceding him at full speed. By this time, he was certain that Verschoyle, who'd been several times to the flagship that morning, had been well aware of the conditions and had encouraged him deliberately. But that wouldn't let him off six of the best with his leave probably stopped for donkey's years into the bargain. His mind full of the horrors of the next few weeks, he was barely aware of what was happening and, in his desire to get away from the scene of his disgrace, he forgot to look astern.

'Oh, Christ!' the stern sheetsman said and, swinging round, with the hull quivering and shaking as the engine turned at full power in his efforts to back away from his crime, he realised he was heading stern-first right across the blue and white bows of the admiral's barge which was heading at speed for the starboard ladder. For one ghastly second, he caught a glimpse of the shining brass and paintwork and rigidly-held boathooks covered with tiddly cordwork, and of the tall figure of the admiral just stepping from the cabin to climb aboard his ship as his boat came alongside. The look of fury he received, the startled stare of the sailors, and beyond them Verschoyle's gleeful grin, would remain, he felt certain, in his mind until his last breath.

A bluejacket leapt to the bow of the barge with a heavy cork and coir fender, while another made a despairing jab with one of the magnificent boathooks, missed and scored a deep groove all the way down the side of the pinnace; then the barge banged hard into the beam of the pinnace with a thump like the crack of doom. The fender had been dropped into place just in time, but the speed of the barge as it headed in at a brisk canter across the waves to the flagship burst it like a bomb. Kelly saw the admiral stagger off-balance and sit down heavily, then he was being showered with ground cork that scattered all over the pinnace, the barge, and the whole surface of the sea like confetti at a wedding.

–

Both boats had come to a standstill, grinding against each other in the lop of the sea, the spray leaping up between them like fountains gone mad. A livid face lifted above the canopy, eyebrows working, gold-encrusted cap lopsided over one eye, and a furious voice bellowed out.

'Report to my cabin at once!'

Sick with shame, humiliation and dread, convinced that his naval career had come to an end even before it had properly started, Kelly backed off to allow the admiral's barge to proceed. The admiral, his beak of a nose in the air, his face dark with anger, sailed past and Kelly saw him stamping up the steps of the newly-replaced starboard ladder to the deck. The twitter of bosun's pipes sounded like the moaning of banshees.

For a long time not one of the bobbing boats moved. It seemed as if they were all petrified with horror.

'Made a right cock of that one, sir,' the bowman observed quietly as Kelly, red-faced and miserable, went ahead again. Verschoyle appeared alongside, grinning.

'I think you've just blighted your career for ever, old boy,' he said. 'I hope you're good at market gardening because after today I suspect that's what you'll end up doing.'

There were grins from Verschoyle's crew and, keeping his eyes ahead, trying hard not to look anyone in the face, Kelly was aware of sailors lining the decks of the flagship to stare down at him, awestruck by what had happened, and the shocked looks of the men on the boom. As they edged into place, a rope was thrown and Kelly stepped aboard.

'Take it easy, youngster,' a pink-faced lieutenant advised quietly as he passed. 'The old boy's got a kind heart even if he's also got a very short fuse.'

Trying to pluck up courage, Kelly glanced miserably behind him, quite certain that he'd forgotten to see the picket boat moored properly so that at that moment it was more than likely drifting astern, probably even unmanned. The rain was beginning to come down in sheets now, so that oilskins had begun to appear to add to the general gloom. In a short career full of disaster, nothing like this had ever happened to Kelly Maguire and he found himself looking forward to returning home to a future containing nothing more dramatic than falling regularly off the horses his mother provided for him to ride. What lay ahead seemed as empty as the inside of a drum, and the dreams he'd nurtured of becoming another Nelson disappeared in a puff of sea mist as he saw himself with all his bags and baggage being put firmly ashore at Portsmouth without even a by-your-leave or a word of thanks for past services.

He was still wondering what he could do with his life and whether he really ought to go in for market gardening or put an end to it quickly with a rifle borrowed from a Marine, when he heard shouts and sounds of alarm. A seaman on the boom had lost his balance and, even in his misery, Kelly became aware of the sudden appearance of disaster. The sailor, a squarely-built youngster with red hair like himself, had made a wild grab at the lifeline, missed and was falling with whirling arms and legs. His head hit the boom and, as he splashed into the grey sea, the man nearest the lifebelt stood gaping as if he'd been bereft of reason. Below, the boats trying to cast off were only getting in each other's way as they endeavoured to manoeuvre, and the young seaman, swept astern on the tide, seemed to have been overlooked in the stern business of boat handling difficulties.

Snatching at his jacket and cap, Kelly ran for the side. In his misery, the disaster seemed to be something that had arrived fortuitously to distract all the staring eyes that had been resting on him. He took the rail at a jump and the cold and shock of hitting the water took his breath away. As he came to the surface, spluttering and gasping, he saw a pair of arms flailing wildly nearby in an attempt to keep afloat.

The boats, all adrift at the same time, were lying in a confusion of different angles and the drowning man was being carried past them at speed. Kelly set off after him in a strong, awkward stroke. As he reached him, the sailor was going down for the last time, still frantically beating with his arms at the sea, and, grabbing him by his hair as he disappeared, Kelly hoisted him up, treading water, to be immediately grasped round the neck as the sailor panicked.

'Let go, you ass!' The frightened yelp came out like the hiccup of a pup. 'You'll drown me as well!'

A flailing fist caught him on the nose, making him see stars and bringing tears to his eyes, then he felt himself being dragged down once more. Spitting out sea water and drawing his arm back, he thumped the sailor at the side of the head and felt his grasp loosen.

'Now do as I tell you,' he shouted furiously above the drenching crash of the waves which, now that he was among them, sounded twice as loud as they had from the picket boat. 'Just lie still.'

Manoeuvring the sailor on to his back, he grabbed him by the shoulders and began to kick his way back to the side of the flagship. But the sailor was bigger than Kelly was, and he wasn't sure he was going to make it because most of the time his head was underwater and he was convinced they were going to drown together.

Swallowing another mouthful of water that made him choke and cough, he had just decided that the picket boats, which a moment before had seemed to be in the area in dozens, were deliberately letting him sink because of his lack of value to the navy, when a lifebelt dropped on his head, half-stunning him. With one hand he grabbed at it, still hanging on to the sailor's oilskin collar with the other. Then he heard the thump of an engine and a great fist covered with tattoos reached down to grab him.

Dragged into a boat, more dead than alive, he sprawled on the bottom boards, and a second later the man he'd saved landed on top of him. A booted foot stood on his fingers and someone said 'It's that little bastard who knocked the admiral for six,' and then he remembered why he was there and pretended to be unconscious so that he wouldn't have to sit up and face people.

'I think the little bugger's dead,' a gruff voice observed, and an irritable snarl gave a testy reply. 'Then give him artificial respiration, man, and look slippy.'

Heavy hands landed on Kelly's ribs so that he felt every bit of breath in his body was being squeezed out.

'Let go, please,' he moaned, wriggling away, the only thought in his mind the feeling that the ordeal of meeting the admiral was likely to be infinitely worse if he was going to have to meet him wet through. There were a few curious stares as he struggled to a sitting position, but no one said anything and, as the boat bumped against the gangway, someone hoisted him upright.

He went up the steps with dragging feet and, watching the man he'd saved being carried below, he decided he'd better see if he was still alive.

In the sick bay, he found the sailor sitting on a bench, looking green, a thickset youngster with a face like a potato.

'Ordinary Seaman Rumbelo, sir,' he mumbled between heaves of nausea. 'You saved my life.'

'It was nothing,' Kelly said.

'It wasn't nothing to me, sir. I can't swim, so it was a hell of a lot.'

Still soaked and shivering, Kelly became aware of an officer standing alongside him.

'Admiral says you're to report to him at once,' he was told. 'And I think he means "at once."' The officer grinned. 'But, take it easy, he's got a soft spot for the young. Great-grandfather was Archbishop of Canterbury or something and he believes in suffer little children.'

Stumbling below, aware of his shoes squelching a long trail of dark drips along the corridor to ruin the carpet with salt water, Kelly heard a harsh, resonant voice shout.

'No further, boy! You're dribbling all over my furnishings!'

Miserably, his face peaked with anxiety and blue with cold, Kelly stiffened to attention.

'Name?'

'Maguire, sir.'

24

'There can't be so many people with such a bloody silly name!' The admiral was stooping to peer at him under thick eyebrows. 'You Teddy Maguire's boy?'

'Yes, sir.'

'You're obviously as stupid as he was. Do you realise you smashed up my barge and sent me on my backside, boy? And what was all that damned flotsam you were carrying round on your bows?'

Kelly gulped. 'It was the starboard ladder, sir.'

'Whose starboard ladder?'

'Yours, sir.'

The admiral stared. 'Was it, by God? How did it come to be there?'

'I'm afraid I smashed it, sir. I was taking it back to *Huguenot* to be repaired. That's why I wasn't looking where I was going. I was a bit upset.'

As he stiffened for the monumental ticking off he guessed was coming, Kelly became aware of the admiral straightening up. He was a very tall, broad-shouldered man, his face hidden by a heavy beard, and he seemed to be smothered in gold braid and medal ribbons. The deep voice boomed again at Kelly.

'They tell me you've just been in the water. Saved a man's life while everybody else was flapping around like wet hens wondering what to do.'

'It was nothing, sir.'

The admiral's voice rose. 'Of course it wasn't "nothing," you little prig! If you do something brave, admit it like a man. All this bloody nonsense about modesty! Lot of rubbish! Stiff upper lip, straight back, clear eye, honour to the flag! Tripe! And onions! Did a bit of life saving meself once.' The tone changed abruptly. 'Where the devil were you? They were looking all over the ship for you.'

Kelly drew a deep breath, 'I was in the sick bay, sir. I went to see if the man I fished out was all right.'

The admiral peered at him with narrowed eyes. 'Well, that's no bad thing,' he admitted. 'Shows the right attitude. After all if we didn't have sailors we shouldn't have officers, should we, and if we didn't have officers we shouldn't have admirals – and then where would I be? You're Irish, aren't you?'

'Yes, sir.'

'Got a bit of Irish blood meself, I've heard. The Irish usually manage to bring a breath of fresh air into stuffy corners.'

There was a long silence while Kelly waited, still dripping water in a pool at his feet. The admiral stared at it petulantly, then he turned, his hands behind his back, and spoke over his shoulder. 'If you do something like this, Mr Maguire, every time you're up for a reprimand by a senior officer, you should have no difficulty whatsoever in ending up as an admiral.'

Suddenly aware of a change of tone and atmosphere, Kelly's eyes lifted and he was conscious that the rock-hard sternness of the admiral's face had softened a little.

'You, Mr Maguire,' he was saying, 'are wet through, and I have a bruised behind because you cut across my bows – something you should never do with a feller's bows, especially if he's an admiral and you're only a snotty. For knocking your admiral on his backside and reducing his flagship to matchwood, I'm inclined to think you must be a bloody fool. But it's also quite clear that you're a quick-thinking bloody fool and also even a brave bloody fool. I shall therefore recommend you for the Royal Humane Society's medal for saying life at sea. But—' the heavy voice deepened '—so that you shall not completely undermine the discipline of the fleet, you will return to your ship and request the sub-lieutenant in charge of the gunroom to give you six of the best with a dirk scabbard for breaking my flagship and discommoding me. And now, steward, you'd better give him a sherry to warm him up. He looks frozen. And then, for God's sake get rid of him before he completely ruins my carpet.'

Three

'I say, Kelly! How ripping! A medal before you're even a sub-lieutenant!'

Kelly shrugged, trying to look unconcerned. 'It's only a tidgy one,' he said. 'Nobody in *Huguenot* seems very impressed.'

If the reaction of his own messmates in the gunroom had varied from the frank incredulity of Kimister to the disgusted cynicism of Verschoyle, however, there was no doubting the genuine enthusiasm of Charlotte Upfold. Her eyes shone and her excitement was intense. Even her elder sister, Mabel, absorbed as she was with parties, hair styles, dresses and the attentions of the young Guards subalterns who were forever on the doorstep, found time to congratulate him.

'Tell me again!' Charley said, bouncing up and down on the settee in her eagerness. 'Tell me what you did!'

Kelly grinned. 'I knocked the admiral on his backside.'

'I say!' Charley's large blue eyes opened wide. 'What did they do to you?'

'Ordered me six of the best, watch and watch about until both the boat and the ladder were repaired, and stopped my shore leave for seven years. But the surgeon persuaded the captain to cut the punishment, and the seven years' stoppage came to an end because they found I was using it to dodge compulsory cross-country runs ashore.'

Charley drew the deep satisfied breath of an everlasting admirer. 'It was jolly brave of you,' she said. 'I think it's absolutely spiffing. When will you be able to wear it?'

'You don't *wear* medals. They clank too much and put the admiral off. You wear a bit of ribbon. You ought to know that.'

'I thought it might be different in the navy. All our lot are army. Can I sew it on for you?'

'I didn't know you could sew.'

Charley blushed, 'Well, I can't. My stitches look as though they were intended for a horse blanket. But I'd be very careful.' She looked daring. 'I think we ought to wet its head, don't you?'

'What with?'

'We could have a go at the sherry wine.'

'What'll your father say?'

'He's with mother at the theatre. But if he knew I think he'd agree.'

Kelly didn't argue. While the sherry at Balmero House, the home of the Maguires, was always the cheapest possible brand, it was well known that General Upfold kept a good cellar. It was proving profitable being at Greenwich for his examinations, because he was often hungry and had to meet his mess bills and all his expenses out of a mere pittance. Only the occasional postal orders from elderly aunts and the generosity of an Indian prince who was on the same course and could always be openly and unashamedly wangled into providing a dinner ashore made a break in the habit of constant retrenchment, and it was useful to have the Upfolds' town house at 17, Bessborough Terrace as a pied-à-terre.

Charley poured out two glasses and offered him one. 'I think it's absolutely terrific,' she said. 'I shall tell all my friends about it.'

'It's only a teeny little thing really,' Kelly insisted. 'And in any case I got six of the best afterwards. They call me Six-of-the-Best Maguire now. I'm jolly lucky really, ain't I? If that chap Rumbelo hadn't decided to use that moment to fall in the sea, all I'd have got would have been a reprimand. As it happened, I didn't really get a reprimand and I did get a medal.'

Charley gazed at him with shining eyes. From the first day she could remember she had adored Kelly. Notwithstanding his red hair and blunt homely features, to Charley he had always been a Burne-Jones knight in shining armour and she'd never had much difficulty understanding the appeal of people like Sir Galahad and other leftovers from Victorian emotionalism. Yet there was no sentiment about her regard. It was factual, straightforward and no-nonsense. She could think of no better future than to grow into an adult and marry him.

'Will it make any difference to you?' she asked.

'In what way?'

'Promotion, of course.'

'Shouldn't think so. People are always jumping into the sea to pull people out.'

Charley emptied her glass at a gulp and gazed at him with shining eyes. Her cheeks were faintly flushed and there was a strand of dark hair that fell across her nose which she kept having to blow away. Even to Kelly, occupied with the stern business of approaching manhood, it was obvious she was going to be a beauty – and a sight more intelligent than Mabel, for all her airs and graces.

She began to refill his glass and he gestured. 'Steady on with the sherry, old thing. You shouldn't really gulp it down like that, you know.'

She giggled at him. 'I know. But today I feel like it. Drink it up and we'll have another.'

'No fear. I've got to sit my exams tomorrow and I'll need a clear head.'

'Another one won't do us any harm.'

Kelly took the decanter from her and put it firmly back on the sideboard. After a glass and a half she was already looking bright-eyed and not quite under control.

'Perhaps not me,' he said importantly. 'I'm a bit older and more used to the stuff. But you're still a kid. You've got to be careful. Your mother'll throw me out of the house if she comes home and finds her youngest lying under the table blotto.'

As it happened, Mrs Upfold was none too pleased, anyway. She had long since decided that the impoverished son of an impoverished father was not the best bet in the land for one of her daughters. Even the medal for saving life at sea didn't change things much. It just showed how impulsive Kelly was, and Mrs Upfold liked steady men like her husband, who had advanced from subaltern to brigadier-general without ever really putting his neck at risk, even in the recent vulgar scuffle with the Boers.

Since Kelly was there, however, there was nothing she could do but invite him to stay the night and give him supper, and they were joined by Mabel and her latest admirer, a lieutenant in the Fifth Dragoon Guards whom Kelly considered must look a little like his own horse.

Charley waded in at once. 'Kelly's just won a medal,' she announced. 'He saved a sailor's life.'

'Oh?' The dragoon seemed to consider winning a medal a little like being involved in a rough-house.

Supper could hardly be called riotous with Mrs Upfold sitting at her end of the table disapproving of the cavalryman for not showing enough attention to her elder daughter and of Kelly for showing too much to her younger.

'When will you be going to sea again?' She asked pointedly.

'As soon as I'm through my examinations, Mrs Upfold. When I've got them – *if* I get them – I'll be a sub-lieutenant and then I'll be posted to a ship again.'

'What sort of ship do you want?' Mabel asked, her shoulders gleaming in the candlelight, a tantalising glimpse of her bosom presenting itself as she leaned forward.

'Dreadnoughts, shouldn't wonder,' the dragoon said. 'Under the admiral's nose.'

'Not for me,' Kelly said. 'I want destroyers. Perhaps even submarines.'

'Sneaky things, submarines.' General Upfold sat up with a jerk. 'Bit like hitting a man when he's not looking.'

Kelly thought he was joking. 'Well, that's a good way to fight war, isn't it, sir?' he said cheerfully. 'Saves getting hurt.'

General Upfold's face tightened and Kelly realised to his amazement that he had meant every word he'd said.

'Didn't fight that way in South Africa,' he snorted.

Kelly stared at him. Perhaps the army was as out-of-date in thinking as the navy, he decided. The little he could recall of the Boer War consisted chiefly of battles lost by mid-Victorian tactics and thousands of men dead of disease caused by indifference and lack of knowledge. He looked quickly at Charley and as she gazed back at him, troubled, her loyalties divided but nevertheless firm, he swallowed and gathered his courage.

'Perhaps that's why it took us so long to win,' he said brusquely. 'After all, that's what the Boers did to us, and they seem to have been jolly good at it, too.'

There was a frozen silence. Clearly, in the Upfold household one didn't recommend wars where men didn't stand up to each other face to face like gentlemen.

'After all,' Kelly went on, aware that he was making things worse but perversely enjoying his defiance, 'that nonsense they went in for at Fontenoy's a bit out-dated these days.'

'What nonsense was that?' Mrs Upfold asked.

'The French saying to the English, "You fire first," and the English saying, "No, thanks, you." If I'd been the English general I'd have said "Thanks very much" and let go with everything I'd got. That's how things'll be when the war comes.'

'Wasn't aware war was coming,' the dragoon said, and Kelly decided he not only looked like a horse but probably also thought like one, because there'd been a smell of war in the air ever since the Agadir crisis just after the Coronation Review, when the Germans had faced the French with their teeth snapping and their sabres rattling in their scabbards. If the noise hadn't reached the Horse Guards, it had certainly reached the Admiralty and had passed through every ship in the fleet. Every midshipman and snot-nosed ship's boy knew that the Kaiser resented the size of the Royal Navy and wanted one equally large.

'It's bound to come sooner or later,' he said. 'The Germans are getting far too big for their boots, and the Kaiser's half-wit enough to go off at half-cock. I'll bet Jacky Fisher thinks it's coming. That's why he's been building bigger ships than everybody else.'

He looked about him, sure of support this time. After all everybody quoted Fisher – even the most junior midshipman who considered it made him sound modern, up-to-date and go-ahead. But Fisher's pronouncement that the navy was a drowsy, inefficient, moth-eaten organisation filled with splendid seamen but not many men of vision had split the fleet into two camps – the 'Fishpond' versus the Rest – and so, it seemed, the whole of London, so that Kelly's enthusiasm wasn't reflected in the faces of the others.

'Man's a menace,' General Upfold said. 'Don't know how he got the Admiralty.'

'I heard,' Mrs Upfold said firmly, 'that there's something very odd about him. Mad on dancing, they say.'

'Well—' Kelly grinned '—they do say the midshipmen of the Mediterranean Fleet used to get a bit annoyed when he pinched their girls – and even more when they found the girls actually *enjoyed* dancing with him.'

'Sounds like some rather unpleasant parvenu,' Mrs Upfold decided.

'It'll be a land war anyway,' General Upfold said. 'The Germans would never accept battle at sea. Never risk it. Not with our navy.'

Mrs Upfold sniffed. 'I don't think there'll be a war at all,' she said. 'War's grown far too serious these days for anyone to take the risk.'

'What if some bright spark starts something in the Balkans, Mrs Upfold?' Kelly leaned forward eagerly. 'Between Austria and Serbia, say. Russia would have to go to the help of the Serbs because she has an agreement to look after Slav interests, and then Germany would come in because she's got a treaty with

Austria. Then France would have to come in because she's got a treaty with Russia, then England—'

Mrs Upfold stared at him. Clearly she considered him a troublemaker. 'You seem to know a great deal about European politics, Mr Maguire.'

Kelly shrugged. A few days before, with the joyous indifference of youth, he hadn't known a damn thing about them, but with the possibility of war looming on the horizon, the instructor at Greenwich had seen fit to include in the curriculum a short discourse on international affairs and he'd suddenly become aware of what was going on in the world around him.

Mrs Upfold had clearly decided that the discussion had been going on too long, and she put down her napkin and brought it to an end like a conductor bringing his baton down for the last firm beat. 'I don't think England would come in,' she said and began to rise, as if certain that no government would ever dare defy her.

They all trailed weakly after her and, over coffee, Kelly sat on one side with Charley, conscious that he'd probably put his foot in it and done himself a lot of no good in the matter of free meals. Charley squeezed his hand. 'It doesn't matter,' she whispered. 'Truly it doesn't. *I*'m sure you're right.'

It seemed a good idea to go to bed early and Charley went too. Outside his bedroom door, she stopped, close to him, her face raised to his.

'Don't worry about them, Kelly,' she said. 'I shan't take any notice of them when we get married.'

'Marry a sailor, marry trouble,' Kelly said.

She looked faintly embarrassed. 'Mother thinks you're not good enough.'

Kelly grinned. 'She's probably right.'

Charley's eyes widened. 'Oh, no, Kelly! Not for a minute.'

'Did you tell *them* we were going to get married?'

33

'But of course!' That possibility to Charley was as natural as breathing. Getting married to Kelly was as inevitable to her as the sun coming up the following day.

Kelly pulled a face. 'No wonder they weren't very friendly. I expect they think I'm getting you in dark corners. At your age, no mother's going to welcome that.'

There was an awkward pause. Charley was standing very close to him and he could smell the perfume she'd been allowed to put on for the occasion. She'd also been permitted to put her hair up and looked surprisingly grown-up with the white column of her neck rising from the ruched frill round the top of her dress. He knew she was itching to fling her arms round him. It was something she'd never done before, though they'd often exchanged friendly kisses of greeting or goodbye, and he felt that perhaps the perfume had gone to her head.

As her hands fluttered and she gazed at him, her face close to his, he thought of all the free meals he was jeopardising.

Her body sagged with disappointment as he didn't clutch her to him. There seemed a faint odour of treachery about his indifference. Their previous kisses at parties had always been with someone else looking on and, with her hair carefully arranged by Mabel and the perfume she had lathered on until its scent seemed overpowering, she had hoped he might be overwhelmed.

'What's wrong?' she demanded unhappily.

'Nothing,' he said briskly as he opened his door. 'It's just that it's getting late.'

–

The examinations were taken in sub-zero temperatures and Kelly was so cold he sat them wearing a greatcoat in the pockets of which he secreted ginger beer bottles full of hot water. Despite what he'd said at the Upfolds, he had no real fear of failing. He'd had his head crammed with mathematics, applied mechanics, physics, chemistry, nautical astronomy and navigation, surveying, meteorology, naval architecture and foreign languages, and behind all that was the stolid and steady work of years, watch keeping and the hard facts he'd learned about gunnery and torpedoes. Even the boatwork with cutters and picket boats with seamen twice his age who'd nursed him from the day he'd first appeared, sometimes even finding cocoa for him, or fried bread and eggs when he was at his hungriest, their faces always bland and uninformative. 'Well, you know that canteen stuff we took aboard, sir. One of the crates was a bit damaged so we got an egg or two for nothing.'

While he waited for the results, he wrote to Their Lordships of the Admiralty, suggesting that he might be considered for the submarine service. As a sub-lieutenant on five shillings a day it was going to be hard to make ends meet and the extra few shillings he would get as a submariner were a big inducement. The only thing he didn't want was a battle cruiser, and a request for submarines, even if it didn't bring a posting, might at least convince Their Lordships that he had a preference for small craft.

He had no sooner been confirmed as a sub-lieutenant, however, than he was informed that there was no lack of volunteers for the submarine service and he had, therefore, been posted instead to HMS *Clarendon*, part of the Second Cruiser Squadron. Since some sort of celebration seemed to be called for, he borrowed a couple of pounds and took Charley out to lunch at the cheapest place he could find. She turned up wearing half of Mabel's finery and looking such a sight in high-heeled shoes, large hat, make-up and too many beads he felt vaguely ashamed of her.

It wasn't the happiest of meals, with Charley trying not very successfully to be grown-up and Kelly trying not to be big brotherly. Afterwards, outside the restaurant, he put her into a taxi and was startled to see her begin to take off her make-up, hat and beads, miserably aware that her ploy to overcome

Kelly with the charm and sophistication of an older woman had somehow not come off. She had wanted with all her heart for him to be enraptured at the sight of her and she was very conscious that not only was he not very impressed, he probably even actively disapproved.

'Mother will kill me if she sees me in this lot,' she said gloomily. 'She doesn't like me trying to look older than I am.'

Aware that she was hurt, he tried to put things right. 'I don't know that I do either,' he said. 'You're much nicer as Charley than as Charlotte.'

She gave him a grateful look but, realising he was being charged waiting time for the taxi and that the driver was looking at his watch, Kelly kissed her hurriedly. She tried to cling to him, her mouth following his eagerly as he backed away and turned to the driver. 'Bessborough Terrace,' he said. 'I'd like to pay now. How much?'

'With the waiting time, sir, that'll be two bob.'

'Two bob?' Kelly's jaw dropped. He had to join his ship at Chatham and he had a long way to go on the three shillings he had left. Despite the fact that he'd chosen the cheapest wine and eaten the cheapest dish on the menu, his calculations had not been careful enough.

The driver grinned. 'That too much, sir?'

'No.' Kelly's pride was touched. 'No, that's all right.'

'Make it one and nine, sir. I'll see the young lady home safe.'

Blurting his thanks, Kelly handed over the money and closed the door, and the cab drew away with Charley gazing at him with lost eyes through the rear window. Staring after her for a second, Kelly drew a deep breath and headed for the station where he'd left his luggage, aware that he had barely enough for a tip to the porter.

Within two days, he found himself heading with the squadron for Halifax, Nova Scotia, on a cruise to show the flag in

Canadian and American ports. The crossing of the Atlantic was made in a full gale, with the ship battened down and everything below deck swimming in water. Clothing hung at odd angles from the bulkheads as it swung in jerky arcs to the corkscrewing of the ship, and the atmosphere was so damp the deckheads ran with moisture and the seamen's messes were awash with grey suds that sluiced wet clothing and mess traps about the decks.

The greater moments included a dash up the Hudson in close line ahead at seventeen knots which, while it was a fine sight, was a little unnerving to the ferries and small craft that scuttled for their lives from the sharp steel bows. There was also the ruination of a dance they gave in New York when fifteen degrees of frost so froze the hearts of the American heiresses they'd hoped to attract, they remained quite impervious to the charms of *Clarendon*'s impecunious officers.

New York was kind to them, however; almost too kind, because when the New Yorkers took them to their homes, Kelly found himself adopted by the over-eager daughter of a well-heeled businesswoman who, twice divorced, left them alone in her apartment while she went about her own affairs. Finding himself fighting off the girl across a vast bed in the early hours of the morning, he decided it wasn't worth trying to remain a virgin.

As he woke the next morning, dazzled and a little startled by what had happened, and unable to avoid a feeling that was arrogant, bold and self-satisfied all at the same time, the girl appeared in the doorway, holding his shoes and a bottle of beer. 'Only trouble with this, I guess,' she said with a grin, 'it gives you such a thirst. Better push off now because if Mother finds out she'll start the War of Independence all over again.'

Back in England, feeling himself weather-beaten – if not as a seaman, at least as a lover – he realised that his Irish accent had almost gone and that in its place the indefinable but undeniable signs of a seafaring life that were common to all sailors were already beginning to show. For three weeks, he had written almost daily to the girl in New York, but love affairs for sub-lieutenants were pretty deathless affairs, full of adoration, broken hearts and sudden partings, with a new girl and a new broken heart in every port. At the end of it he had found he couldn't even remember what she looked like and he began now to make plans to use his leave to visit Ireland. He was looking forward, if not to seeing his parents, at least to seeing Charley. She had never failed to write to him even when his own family had found other business more pressing, and he was feeling a strange sort of elation at the thought that she would be sixteen now, a mature young lady and, surely to God, too old to be watched day and night by her mother. Kimister, who had always known of his affection for her and had been in love with her himself since he'd met her as a cadet at Dartmouth, called it romantic. Verschoyle called it cradle-snatching. But Kimister was somewhere in the north of England now, with Verschoyle, in destroyers, something that had become a sore point with Kelly since Verschoyle had wanted a battleship and Kimister had never been sure what he wanted.

As he was brooding on it, a head appeared round the ward-room door. It was the navigator, a breezy young man called Fanshawe who was built like a house-side and had once played rugby for England. 'Hope you've not made any plans, Maguire,' he said.

Kelly turned. 'Why not?'

'Leave's cancelled. Everything's changed. We're going to Kiel as part of a banzai party for the German naval review. You'd better survey your uniform, and if you can afford it buy full dress and a ball gown. I've got the order here – "Whilst in German waters, uniform will be worn ashore; for the purposes of sport, flannels will be permitted, but it is hoped that officers will see that the latter are of an immaculate nature."'

They sailed for Kiel in a dense fog. Off the Jutland coast they had a harmless and entertaining dodging match with a group of German fishing smacks and that afternoon rehearsed cheering ship for when the Kaiser appeared. Rounding the Skaw, at the northern tip of Denmark, they made passage for the Belt and arrived at the northern limit of Kiel Bay at dusk two days later.

Kelly was on watch as they anchored and Fanshawe indicated the sky. 'Believe in omens?' he asked.

Above their heads was a cloud shaped like a snake, its head erect and about to strike.

'Looking directly towards England,' Fanshawe pointed out, and as he spoke the sun set, tingeing the cloud with red.

'And that,' he added portentously, 'is probably blood.'

The stay in Kiel was a round of official receptions, banquets and dances, with visits from German officers stiff as ramrods who could not understand that in the British Navy men off duty did not behave to each other in the wardroom as they did on the quarterdeck. For the official functions, *Clarendon*'s officers had almost to live in full dress, a costume not designed for modern life, especially in summer, and while the talk was all the time of peace, always in the background there was the knowledge that war might be near.

The whole of German society seemed to be in Kiel in a kaleidoscope of ships and yachts, and eventually the Kaiser himself appeared through the canal, the bows of his yacht, *Hohenzollern*, breaking the silk ribbons across the entrance to the new locks.

'Well,' Fanshawe said thoughtfully as they watched, 'with the new locks and the bends in the canal widened, their largest dreadnoughts can now pass directly into the North Sea. If that doesn't make the Kaiser more cocky than he is now, nothing will.'

As the assembled ships' companies cheered mechanically, the Kaiser stood at the salute in admiral's uniform on a stage built over the yacht's upper bridge, his withered arm carefully hidden. Fanshawe's nose wrinkled.

'Bloody poseur,' he commented.

The imperial yacht was followed by every kind of craft possible, from racing-eights to pleasure steamers, and one boat was swamped and a few loyal Germans drowned before *Hohenzollern* came to anchor, to be surrounded immediately by police boats to keep the enthusiasm at bay.

'We do it much better at Spithead,' Fanshawe said with lofty disapproval.

There were night clubs ashore and willing girls of Russian and Austrian nationality who caused Kelly's loyalty to Charley to slip a little and the increasingly fragile memory of the girl in New York to disappear like a puff of smoke. Sports were also held for the sailors and it was noticeable that the British were defeated at almost everything, much to the disgust of the lower deck.

'The bastards had preliminary contests before we arrived,' the master-at-arms told Kelly. 'Their teams are the pick of thirty thousand men.'

German orchestras played for them and they learned German patriotic songs like '*Was Blasen die Trompeten?*' and '*Die Wacht am Rhein*' and were told that there couldn't possibly be any war between their nations, because ethnically they were almost brothers and it was only the dirty French who were the troublemakers. To seal the friendship, the German submarine depot gave a dance, a very private dance, it was explained, where everyone would be in mess undress, and the Kaiser's severe displeasure was being risked because they were going to dance ragtime and be allowed to sit out, without chaperones, in the rose garden of a cafe chantant which had been taken over for the evening.

By this time, with a dinner and a ball ashore almost every evening, Kelly's eyes were hanging out on his cheeks and he had been looking forward to sleep. But this seemed to be a chance worth taking and those German girls who wore French-cut clothes were very attractive. Among them was a willowy countess from Mainz who went by the nickname of the Ice Maiden, because of her striking beauty, pale skin, blue eyes and white-blonde hair. She had a reputation for frigidness, it seemed, and with the experience of New York behind him and a few sparkling Moselles inside to work up a mood of over-confidence, Kelly set out to destroy it. The result startled him. Within an hour, he had left the cafe chantant and was alone with her at a night club where they consumed enormous quantities of caviar and champagne cup called bola, Kelly nagged all the time by a guilty feeling that he wasn't playing fair with Charley.

That the Ice Maiden wasn't as frigid as her reputation was proved beyond doubt when he found himself outside her apart-ment as dawn was breaking. Without a word, she pulled him inside, and was throwing her clothes across the room and reaching with her lips for his mouth and with long cool fingers for his shirt even before he'd managed to slam the door behind them. All his life, Kelly had worked on the principle that you could touch anything anywhere on a girl that was not covered with clothing but that the rest was verboten; but since New York all the rules had gone by the board, and shedding clothes right and left, he grabbed her hand and ran for the bedroom.

Two hours later, shakily aware how little he knew about sex, he was anxiously wondering what the next erotic item in the programme would be, when she started up with a yelp, clutching the sheet to her ample bosom.

'My husband,' she shrieked. 'He returns this morning from Brussels!'

Kelly had just made his escape to the end of the street when he saw a cab appear at the other end and draw up at the apartment block, and he returned thankfully to the ship ready to foreswear all official functions for the rest of the visit.

'Good time?' Fanshawe asked blandly as they sipped coffee in the mess.

'Too good.'

'Wonder what it is about you.' Fanshawe eyed Kelly curiously. 'Only got to blink those long red lashes of yours and they fall in droves at your feet. What's the technique?'

'No technique,' Kelly said. 'Just enthusiasm. Seafaring's no profession for a man who believes in personal chastity.'

Fanshawe pulled a face. 'Well, it's true one's away from women so long at times one feels like a wolf howling at the moon. But be careful, young Maguire. Seamen are notoriously sentimental. Every ship has its quota of three-badge men and elderly officers who ought to know better, who've been caught by some cheap little tart for no other reason than that they've been too long nourishing sentimental dreams at sea in the long nights and fallen for the first woman who crossed their bows.'

Feigning a stomach disorder, Kelly remained on board for the next twenty-four hours, but when a note appeared for him from the Ice Maiden to say that her husband had gone on to Berlin and that she planned to appear at a tea dance the following afternoon, he threw caution to the winds, and set off full of excitement, wondering what the evening might hold.

As it happened, it held nothing. He had barely got his arms round her when a German dressed in some sort of official uniform appeared and a moment later the manager climbed on to the rostrum, stopped the band and made an announcement in German. His face was grave and immediately the Germans started whispering among themselves.

'What's he say?'

Fanshawe translated. 'The Archduke Franz Ferdinand's been assassinated in Sarajevo,' he announced.

'Who's the Archduke Franz Ferdinand when he's at home? Where the hell's Sarajevo?'

'The Archduke was the heir to the Austrian throne and Sarajevo's in Serbia.'

'What does that mean?'

Fanshawe shrugged. 'It means war, old boy. I was talking to the navigator of *Hohenzollern* last night – chap called Erich

42

Raeder – and he said the Germans were scared stiff of an unexpected incident like this setting off a war between us. This time it's not like Agadir.'

Kelly frowned. At the time of Agadir, he'd been concerned only with keeping his nose clean to avoid the attentions of the sub-lieutenant of the gunroom, but even so he'd been well aware of the intensity of the crisis. The Germans had sent a gunboat to protect their interests in French North Africa and all the alarm bells in Europe had started to quiver. The crisis had been defused in the end but it had been a clear pointer to German attitudes and the deep and violent passions of resentment coursing beneath the glittering uniforms that thronged the Kaiser's palaces.

The dancing had stopped and people were reaching for their coats.

'You will have to return to your ship,' the Ice Maiden said, and he saw that her face looked bleak and worried.

'Surely there isn't that much hurry?'

She sighed. 'I think you will find there is,' she said. 'This is a black day for Germany. The Archduke represented German influence in the Austro-Hungarian empire, and the Emperor had even promised him recognition for his morganatic wife. All the work of fifteen years is gone.'

Four

That evening, soon after they were aboard, a despatch boat came into the anchorage and shot past the ship's stern. She had been to fetch the Kaiser from where he'd been taking part in a sailing race. He was seated aft, his appearance quite the opposite of when they'd seen him going to sea in the morning. He'd left on the yacht, *Meteor*, with a large party and, as the ship had passed close astern of *Clarendon* he had seemed to be in excellent spirits. Now he was alone, his staff grouped behind him at a distance, while he sat staring silently ahead, his chin supported by one hand. That evening they heard he'd left for Berlin.

The news had clearly brought the review week to an abrupt end, and as the British ships sailed for home through the Kiel Canal, they noticed they were being energetically photographed from all angles from the suspension bridges, while Zeppelins hovered above them in the sky like huge cigars, taking more pictures.

The swan song of the old navy came in a last review at Spithead for which *Clarendon* received a new commanding officer, Captain the Lord Charles Everley, a small gloomy man with sad eyes and the pendulous jowls of a bloodhound.

'Looks as if he's been struck by lightning,' Kelly said. 'Who is he? And where did he come from?'

'China Station.' Fanshawe always knew the details. 'Asked for a posting home. First wife died four years ago. Got a daughter twenty years old who's a bit of a problem. Got married again before he went out and hasn't seen his new wife much since. Perhaps he needs to.'

Even now, Home Rule for Ireland seemed of far greater importance than the possibility of war and Kelly stared at the assembled ships, feeling old and cynical and doubtful. The navy hadn't had a real war for over a hundred years, and men who had entered as cadets had retired as admirals without ever hearing a shot fired in anger, and he wondered how many senior officers there still were like his father.

With the possibility of war in the offing there had been an unexpected spate of letters from home but none of them had seemed to Kelly to contain much hope for the navy. Admiral Maguire had always set great store by ceremony and even now he seemed to be considering the ritual of being at war rather than the hard facts of death or defeat. 'The navy,' he had written, 'will see the thing through if it comes to a conflict. We have always known how to behave and have always been the envy of the rest of the world.'

Remembering what he'd seen of the Germans at Kiel, Kelly had an uneasy feeling that it was that very envy which had brought the present crisis to its climax, and that behaviour – high-nosed, haughty and self-satisfied – which might well bring the sort of result no one was expecting.

Suddenly the world seemed on the verge of a catastrophe just when it appeared to be at its most brilliant. Two mighty European systems, hostile to each other, faced each other in glittering and clanking panoply so that every word, every whisper, counted in the mounting crisis. There was a strange temper in the air that even Kelly was aware of. Every great nation had made its preparations and knew whom its enemy would be, and, rather than have fleet manoeuvres in the North Sea, Churchill had decided instead to have a practice mobilisation, calling out the whole of the fleet reserve. Twenty thousand men had reported and all the Third Fleet ships had coaled and raised steam for the review. As they left Spithead and dispersed for a two-day series of exercises, it took more than six hours for the enormous armada to pass before the royal yacht; though the exercises, Kelly noticed, bore little resemblance to war and still seemed more concerned with a sort of ceremonial dance arranged for ships. When they vanished to ports around Britain to give summer leave and demobilise the reservists, *Clarendon* went to Portland.

The news that greeted them was grave. The Ice Maiden had been right. Instead of blowing away, the crisis seemed to have gathered strength and there was a rumour that Austria was not satisfied with the Serbian acceptance of the ultimatum she'd presented and was demanding satisfaction for the assassination of the heir to the throne.

'If it does come to war and the French are in,' Kelly said, 'then *we'll* be in. With the whole of the French Fleet in the Mediterranean, they've only a few cruisers left to guard the Atlantic coast and we'd never allow the Germans to come down the Channel and bombard their ports within gunshot of our ships.'

On the Sunday, he went ashore with Fanshawe for a lobster tea and a discussion about their forthcoming leave. They were well aware of the sidelong glances they attracted. Naval men always possessed a mystique which did not emerge from the military. There *was* something about a sailor, and they possessed skills and knowledge that were never wholly understood by landsmen. To them the sea wasn't the terrifying thing it was to shorebound people, so that they carried out their duties with an air of confidence and superiority that was the stamp of a centuries-old tradition, and the style they acquired in the performing of them was present in every man in the fleet, from the youngest cadet to the oldest and saltiest admiral.

They spent a pleasant afternoon, aware of the admiration they evoked, but as they walked back to the landing stage, they saw two battleships, *Lord Nelson* and *Agamemnon*, steaming into the bay.

'That's odd,' Kelly said. 'They sailed this morning for Portsmouth to give leave.'

Buying a local paper at the landing stage, they read stories of increasing trouble in the Balkans, and next day the demobilisation of reservists was stopped. The newspaper headlines were larger than the previous day and orders arrived to coal as quickly as possible. A thousand tons of coal were tossed down on to the upper deck by automatic chutes and they were left to get it into the bunkers as well as they could.

The winches rattled away half the night, the whole ship enveloped in a fog of dust which encrusted on perspiring skins, and the next morning, as they received orders to be prepared to sail the following day, officers and men were recalled from shore by patrols and notices thrown on the screens of cinemas. The following morning they weighed anchor with the rest of the fleet.

'Scapa Flow for orders,' Fanshawe said.

The ships turned, squadron by squadron, gigantic steel castles moving across a misty sea, eighteen miles of warships running at high speed, the early morning light picking up the colours of the flag hoists fluttering at the yardarm and catching the curves of the ship's upperworks and turrets and the great rifled barrels of the guns. Kelly sniffed the air, conscious of the smell of salt on the wind and the subtle quality of the light on the water, an awareness he put down to his perception being heightened by the crisis and the possibility of death not far away in the future.

For the first hour they steamed in a westerly direction then, out of sight of land, altered course sixteen points and stood up-channel towards Dover. Soon afterwards, a signal was received indicating that strained relations existed between Britain and Germany, and all hands prepared the ship for war, fusing lyddite shell and placing warheads on the torpedoes. There was a strange feeling of finality as the work proceeded, and Kelly recognised that he was about to enter a new phase in his life when people like his father and Mrs Upfold weren't going to matter any more.

During the morning, they painted out the white recognition bands round the funnels and the commander took Kelly round the quarterdeck with a knife, with which they solemnly stripped down the canvas pipe-clayed coverings that had been made so immaculate for Kiel. As the crude iron of the berthing rail stanchions appeared, the face of the petty officer who accompanied them grew grave. 'We never went as far as this before,' he observed gloomily. 'Not even over Agadir.'

During the afternoon, a large French battleship dashed past at twenty knots, cleared for action and heading for Brest, and at dusk they went to night defence stations as the fleet ran at high speed and in absolute blackness through the Narrow Seas.

Shortly afterwards, *Clarendon* altered course away from the rest of the fleet, heading towards Dover. A merchant ship loomed up out of the darkness and an angry voice yelled 'Where's your bloody glims?' then, almost immediately, Dover's searchlights picked them up. The signalling light clattered and, as an answering flash came from the shore, the anchor splashed down.

–

The night was strangely tense. Everybody in the ship knew what was in the wind but none of them knew what war could mean. Nobody had been in a sea battle and only a few of the older men had seen action ashore during the Boer War. Unable to sleep, Kelly tossed restlessly in his bunk and fell asleep just before dawn, only to be wakened by Fanshawe's hand on his shoulder.

'Come and look at this, Maguire! You might not get the opportunity again for a long time at this range.'

Stumbling on deck, Kelly screwed his eyes up against the light. Not far away a three-funnelled cruiser that he identified at once as German was scuttling past for the broad waters of the northern horizon.

'Caught with his trousers down west of Land's End,' Fanshawe said. 'He's taking a bit of a chance trying to nip through the Channel with war in the offing.'

The German disappeared at high speed and coaling started again, all ships topping up their bunkers. That evening censorship came into force.

The next days were spent stripping ships of panelling and furniture to reduce the amount of woodwork on board. The seamen slung chairs and tables and even pianos over the side into the lighters with great glee, clearly thoroughly enjoying smashing up the officers' property. The frenzy finally reached masochistic proportions with the removal of cutters, whalers and skiffs to the shore, but, since Kelly's position, in the event of abandoning ship, was with fifteen others in a whaler that would take no more than ten in a flat calm, getting rid of the boats didn't seem to make much difference.

Later in the morning, there was a rush to get private belongings on the quay, and Kelly was ordered off the ship, staggering under a collection of diaries, last wills and testaments, family documents, silver and other valuables, all to be despatched home.

'My box goes to my house,' the captain told him. 'Together with my tin case and the silver cup I got for shooting. Better take a taxi.'

The address was in the best part of the town and the door was opened by a girl in a pink peignoir. Her feet were in bedroom slippers and she looked as though she hadn't been up long.

'Those Captain Everley's things?' she asked.

'They are indeed. The very same.'

She gave Kelly a broad grin. 'Wheel 'em in,' she said.

She was pretty and forthright, even if too heavily made up, and Kelly decided she was Everley's daughter – and by the look of her a handful.

'Better have a drink while you're at it,' she suggested. 'Can't send the navy away without a reward, can we? What'll it be? Whisky?'

Despite his protests, she poured enormous drinks for them both and sat alongside him on the settee, smoking a cigarette. 'Which one are you?' she asked.

'Which one what?'

'Which officer?'

'I'm Maguire. Kelly Maguire.'

She smiled, 'You've got a bit of a reputation, I hear.'

'Have I? What sort?'

'With the ladies.' She leaned closer. 'Why did you decide to go to sea? It's not much of a life for a man when he gets married, is it?'

'I suppose not.'

'Come to that, it's not much of a life for a woman. I used to like to touch a sailor's collar for luck, but I've come to the conclusion that luck's what a woman needs a lot of when she fancies a sailor.'

For a naval captain's daughter, she seemed a very odd number indeed, and Kelly began to wonder if instead she were just the housekeeper or a maid, or perhaps some poor relation who looked after the place when the family were abroad.

'No need to move away,' she said.

'I'm not doing.'

She smiled. 'I'm glad. I've always found the navy lives up to its reputation.'

'What reputation's that?'

'For being quick on the uptake.' She was pressing against him now and seemed to be inviting him to put down his glass and grab her. Carefully he placed it on the table beside him. After all, he decided, captain's daughters – or relations, or whatever they happened to be – were only human. So, for that matter, were naval lieutenants who couldn't get home.

The girl was eyeing him speculatively. 'You married?' she asked.

'No.'

'Girlfriend?'

'Not so's you'd notice.' Kelly mentally begged Charley's forgiveness. Temptation was sometimes too much for a man.

'Have another drink?'

'I've had two.'

'You know what they say: "There's cider down the eider-down." You can kiss me if you like.'

Kelly eyed her cautiously. 'Do you always kiss naval officers when they arrive with the captain's goods and chattels?' he asked.

She chuckled. 'I try,' she said. 'It's surprising how well they respond.'

With the peignoir open at the front and a couple of whiskies inside him, Kelly could see why.

'How about the captain? What does he have to say?'

She smiled archly. 'He doesn't know.' She settled against him and lifted her face. 'No need to hurry off,' she said.

A small voice sounded a warning. 'What about Mrs Captain?' Kelly asked cautiously.

She smiled and grabbed for him. 'No need to worry about her,' she said. '*I'm* Mrs Captain.'

–

Outside on the pavement two minutes later, Kelly drew a deep relieved breath. Captain's daughters were fair game but captain's wives were dynamite, and Captain Everley seemed to have one of the most explosive kind. No wonder he looked as he did. The poor bugger was one of Fanshawe's frustrated three-badge men and elderly officers who'd been caught by a tart.

The harbour was full of ships' boats by the time he returned, and more were being added. The evening paper seemed to be more full of cricket than war, because Hobbs had made the highest score of his career, but the last Germans were still heading for the quays, trying to get back home across the Channel before it was too late, their womenfolk sniffling, the children crying as though they sensed disaster, and the last reservists were beginning to come into the depots. They arrived on bicycles and on foot, some of them men who'd clearly prospered, others only too eager to be back where they could get three square meals a day.

Occasionally, a taut-faced woman with a child appeared, and occasionally a Territorial, in ill-fitting khaki and none too sober, going off to join his unit, his friends urging him to give the Germans hell or keep his head well down, or both. Standing on the jetty, Kelly was aware that the air was thick with rumours. Spies were said to have been shot already, and butchers behind the town to have killed off so many animals for rations they'd sunk down exhausted in the sea of blood they had themselves created.

A sub-lieutenant in a sporting check suit and a brown bowler hat appeared.

'On my way to join *Lion*,' he announced. 'I've come straight from Goodwood and I haven't the faintest idea where my uniform is.'

Kelly returned on board, certain by now that war was just over the horizon. Fanshawe met him. 'The Germans have demanded free passage for their troops through Belgium,' he said. 'And the Belgians have refused, and appealed to us to uphold their neutrality. I gather we've presented an ultimatum to the Kaiser. That means we're in, because they won't draw back now.'

On the quarterdeck, Captain Everley was complaining to the commander about the officer of the watch. In the panic, he had recalled the liberty boat too soon because of a signal that all ships' boats had to be out of the water by eight p.m., and had left the captain's steward on the quay.

'There are twelve hundred lieutenants on the navy List,' Everley was saying in his gloomy voice. 'That makes 'em two a penny. But in the course of God knows how long at sea, I've only met one good steward – mine – and he's been left ashore.'

The captain's secretary refused to give anything away, despite the fact that they all knew war was probably only hours away, and the next day everything that remained of a combustible nature which could be done without followed the boats and the woodwork ashore.

'Are we to strip the cabins, sir?' Kelly asked. 'I've heard that *Raleigh*'s removing the corticene from the mess deck.'

'*Raleigh*'s a blood-and-iron ship,' the first lieutenant said. 'We'll leave the corticene.' He gave a sudden smile. 'We might even get a few comfortable armchairs back on board, in fact, so that later we don't have to have a whip round to purchase some more.'

More ships turned up and the long summer afternoon of August 4th, 1914, was spent waiting for the British ultimatum to expire. A signal had already been received, stating that it was due to terminate at midnight, and in the early evening another signal arrived: 'Admiralty to all ships. The war telegram will be issued at midnight authorising you to commence hostilities against Germany.'

With its receipt the panic stopped. There was a strange calm everywhere now. All the decisions had been taken and now they could only wait.

'Ours not to reason why,' Fanshawe said. 'Ours but to do and die.'

'Forty-eight hours from now,' Kelly pointed out, 'we'll probably be dying like billy-o.'

He was keeping the first watch, from eight to midnight. It was hot and all the scuttles were wide open. But everybody seemed restless and the ship was humming with life.

The auxiliary machinery was whining and the ventilating fans provided background noise to the sound of a train squealing in the dock station and the marine sentry rattling his rifle butt on the concrete by the gangway. Cooking smells from the officers' galley added flavour to the smell of oil, steam and that curious extra acrid odour that was peculiar to marine machinery. From ashore he could hear the sound of the crowds coming on the still air. The streets were full, as though everyone was uneasy and waiting like the fleet, and faintly he heard the low tones of 'God Save the King' as some group in an access of patriotic emotion began to sing. Then he heard the chimes of a church clock coming over the water and turned to Fanshawe, who had relieved him.

'That's it, then! We're in!'

When he came on watch again at four a.m., Fanshawe said in matter-of-fact tones, 'We had a signal at 1.27 a.m., ordering us to commence hostile acts against Germany.'

'And did we?'

'Any moment now.'

As Fanshawe disappeared, Kelly found himself staring at the increasing light on the eastern horizon, suddenly confused by doubt. Was he as brave as he thought he was? Naval warfare was no longer a question of two ships lying alongside each other so that their crews could indulge in hand-to-hand fighting. These days, it was a matter of hurling huge quantities of high explosive across miles of sea, to wrench and tear at steel plating as if it were cardboard. A shell striking armour plate disintegrated in a flash into hundreds of red-hot, jagged splinters of steel that could tear a man in half.

Was he courageous enough to face the sights he'd undoubtedly have to face? Naval officers were trained to be a body of brave, self-sacrificing and intensely loyal officers, he'd often been told. But there was a great deal of difference between the word, which came from a book of rules, and the deed, which came from a man's guts, his heart and his breeding. He wasn't sure that he fitted all the requirements that were demanded of him and time alone would tell him if he were. What was worse, he'd noticed often that these same officers he was supposed to emulate, despite their undoubted courage and incontestable loyalty, had never had their critical faculties encouraged, so that none of them appeared to question anything, except within the rigid framework of that guide to the wise and law for the foolish, *King's Regulations and Admiralty Instructions*. He could only hope that not only would he be brave but that he would also behave with intelligence.

As he went off watch, the ship was alive with men, their faces grave, working for the first time as if they knew that life itself now depended on how well their jobs were done. He pushed through them towards his cabin and, almost instinctively, took out the picture of Charley that she'd given him on his last leave, and stuck it in the corner of the mirror. He had no idea why he did it. She was still only a child from the point of view of experience and knowledge but somehow the gesture indicated the curious loyalty that had always existed between them, and in his mind's eye he had a glimpse of her praying for him. Without thinking, he knelt by his bunk.

'Let me conduct myself well, Lord,' he asked.

He rose to his feet, faintly shamefaced, because he hadn't got down on his knees outside church since he'd been a small boy. But the gesture had been instinctive and he sensed that it was right.

Let me conduct myself well, he thought again. That was all he could ask.

Within hours the war had started for him.

Five

While they were at breakfast, a signal arrived detaching *Clarendon* to Commodore Reginald Tyrwhitt's command at Harwich, and the wardroom cleared at once.

'Pipe hands to prepare for sea!'

Pipes twittered and the master-at-arms and ship's corporals went through the messes which immediately became a seething mass of running men. The sky was dark grey like the side of a battleship, with a lighter sword-stroke of pearl low on the horizon in the east. Beyond the muzzles of the forward turret Kelly could see the bustling activity of the cable party and an officer silhouetted against the guard rail. A bell jangled.

'Engine room standing by!'

There was already excitement in the air. The war had only just begun and they still had no idea what to expect.

'Pipe all hands for leaving harbour!' The first lieutenant glanced at his watch. 'My respects to the captain. Tell him it's ten minutes to slipping.'

The deck began to quiver and smoke began to curl down from the funnel in a dark plume like an ostrich feather in a woman's hat. Everley appeared and placed himself in the centre of the bridge.

'Special sea duty men closed up, sir. Ship ready for sea.'

'Very well. Sound off.'

A bugle shrilled and there was the spatter of running feet.

'Signal from ashore, sir! Proceed!'

Everley gave a small frown and Kelly wondered what he was thinking about. Why hadn't he gone ashore himself to see his wife? Or did he, perhaps, prefer not to? God forbid, he thought, that I should end up like him, pretending, lying to myself. Thinking of Charley, he felt he never would.

Everley had moved to the front of the bridge now and was staring towards the bows. Suddenly his hangdog face seemed alive. Perhaps the poor devil preferred to be at sea. Perhaps at sea he felt safe. Perhaps at sea he didn't have to look at his wife and realise what a mistake he'd made. As Fanshawe had said, the navy was full of sad people like Everley, swept away by their emotions after serving too long in some torrid Far East port. The China Station where he'd come from was notorious as the graveyard of reputations, and men were always being sent home ruined by drink, speculative gambling, or women. Perhaps Everley was one.

One eye to port, Everley leaned on the bridge rail. At least, whatever else he'd lost, he'd not lost his touch. He made no gestures, just words spoken against a background hum from the ship's generators, the occasional clatter of feet in the distance and low murmurs from the men on the deck waiting for him to give his orders.

'Slow ahead together,' he said quietly.

Bells jangled and the quivering that ran through the deck increased.

'Slip!'

A harsh flurry of orders came from the forecastle with the rasping clatter of the wire. 'All gone forrard, sir!'

Everley peered over the bridge coaming. 'Watch her head, quartermaster. Half ahead port.' There was a pause. 'Slow ahead together.'

The white cliffs behind them began to swing and the oil-black water alongside slipped astern, littered with sagging armchairs, abandoned possessions, and the peacetime straw hats they'd worn ashore.

'Forecastle secured for sea, sir!'

'Very good. Fall out the hands and stand by to exercise action stations. I want every one checked.' Everley permitted himself a small frosty smile. 'After all, it *is* the first day of the war.'

As they turned west, heading towards the Outer Gabbard Light in the approaches to the Thames, the W/T office began to pick up signals from other ships and there was a stream of messages to the bridge.

'I think the war's started,' Everley said with an unexpected cheerfulness, as if all his life he'd been waiting for this moment.

Fanshawe leaned across to Kelly. 'Tyrwhitt's out, and itching to draw the first blood of the war,' he whispered. 'Third Destroyer Flotilla's making a sweep towards Holland.'

The sea was calm and the seamen moved about their duties quietly and efficiently. During the morning, the ship increased speed and the word was passed round that the destroyers were already being led into action by the light cruiser, *Amphion*. Immediately the air became electric.

'That was quick,' Kelly said. 'What is it? High Seas Fleet come out?'

'Nothing quite so important,' Fanshawe said, 'We've picked up a signal that a suspicious-looking steamer's been seen throwing things overboard in the mouth of the Thames. The destroyers are searching for her and now, it seems, so are we, because they might be mines.'

At 10.30, they sighted *Amphion* through the haze, accompanied by the sleek shapes of several destroyers, one of which immediately swung round to challenge them. Recognising *Clarendon*, she took up a position alongside.

'Steamer identified as *Königin Luise* seen laying mines,' she flashed across the grey water. 'Position west of longitude three east.'

Shortly afterwards, they came up on a converging course with other destroyers, and in the distance saw a small grey steamer heading eastwards at full speed, smoke pouring from her funnels. With *Clarendon* close behind and hauling up fast, the destroyers began to fire. Then *Clarendon*'s guns barked; the crash as the forward battery opened up seemed to be the signal for the start of their new life, and they caught their first whiff of cordite fumes in wartime.

'By God, we've hit her!' The first lieutenant sounded amazed. 'I do believe we've done our first war damage!'

The destroyers' shells were driving home on the steamer now. Two more ships had arrived and, in the distance, still more were in sight, steering to the sound of the guns across the grey horizon.

Königin Luise was sinking as they came up with her, her decks and upperworks smashed, and Kelly was aware of the first shock of war. He'd never seen a ship sink before.

'They're abandoning,' Everley said, and they saw men jumping overboard.

The German ship's engines had not been stopped and she was still moving slowly ahead until, turning on to her side, she settled down and finally rolled over and disappeared beneath the waves. Everybody had come on deck to watch, and they were all chattering and pointing, half-clad stokers mixed with the deck crew and Marines. There was a cheer as *Königin Luise* vanished but no jeers or laughter and not much excitement, just a general quiet awe. Like Kelly, most of them had never seen a ship sink before and the thought that next time it might be their own was enough to silence the wags.

Watched by *Amphion* and *Clarendon*, the destroyers were lowering boats now and they could see men being dragged aboard, some of them obviously hurt. There was clearly nothing for *Clarendon* to do and she was obviously in the way.

'Have the hands return to their stations,' Everley said. 'I think we're somewhat de trop here and the destroyers'll think we're trying to steal their thunder.'

Bells clanged and the deck quivered as they resumed course. Nobody had anything much to say. It was as if they were all deep in thought, aware of the implications of what they'd seen. As the day advanced, however, spirits picked up and the sinking of the single little ship became a major victory so that there were laughter and shouts from the lower deck that lasted all the way to Harwich. They had barely arrived, however, when Fanshawe, ashore to pick up signals, brought news that stopped the excitement dead in its tracks.

'*Amphion*'s gone,' he said in a flat voice. 'Struck one of *Königin Luise*'s mines on her way home. Practically everybody in the fore part of the ship was killed instantly.'

'Tit for tat.' Kelly looked at his watch. 'If it's going to be like this all the time, it's going to be a bloody busy war.'

Fanshawe smiled. 'Particularly for you, Maguire' he said. 'Orders have come through for you. You're due for a torpedo specialist's course at the end of the year, it seems. Something to do with joining submarines.'

'Good God! I applied for that years ago. I'd forgotten all about it.'

'When you sup with the navy, you need a long spoon. Until the course comes up you're posted to *Cressy*, Seventh Cruiser Squadron.'

'*Cressy!*' Kelly glared. 'For God's sake, *Cressy*'s a Third Fleet ship, a rotten old four-piper, and she's supposed to be full of bloody reservists, isn't she?'

Fanshawe's smile widened. 'There *are* a lot of elderly gentlemen aboard, I do believe,' he agreed. 'In fact, there are so many, they felt they had to lighten the mixture a bit with a few lively youngsters, and when the Old Man was asked to give up one of his watchkeepers, since you were going anyway, with the usual naval ingratitude, he decided it might as well be you. You go as soon as your relief arrives.'

-

It took Kelly's relief a fortnight to appear and as he waited it seemed as if the whole world he'd ever believed in had begun to fall in on him.

The British Expeditionary Force had gone to France in a holiday spirit, cheering and singing and in high good humour despite the fact that they were crossing the Channel in the discomfort which had always characterised the seaborne transport of the British army. Since they'd already heard of the German general who was leading the advance through Belgium, they had devised a brand-new comic song that delighted everybody – 'We don't give a fuck for Old Von Kluck' – and it could be heard on every dock and station platform. Despite their noise and their riotous behaviour, however, they were not all young men. There were the bald heads, greying moustaches and heavy paunches of reservists here and there, and their breasts sometimes bore the ribbons of the Sudan, South Africa and the North-West Frontier, because many of them were tattooed veterans with long service and many bad conduct marks, full of tall stories of Boers, Burmese, Chinese and Pathans.

Their age and experience had seemed to suggest confidence and skill but, unexpectedly, almost before they had arrived on the Continent, it seemed, from Belgium and northern France unexpected news of disaster arrived via an obscure little town called Mons that nobody had ever heard of. Those old soldiers, their backs still chafed by the rub of unaccustomed packs, were digging holes in the ground to avoid the shelling, and defeated British companies were actually straggling towards the rear. Beaten units that were the remains of famous regiments were trudging through the flood of refugees whose household goods were packed into carts and traps and barrows and perambulators, stumbling behind army wagons pulled by worn animals still galled by their brand-new harness. Limping into ugly little red-brick Belgian towns, khaki-clad men were falling asleep wherever they happened to stop, and the churches were full of wounded; while officers of the Guards, sons of titled families, gazed with dead eyes at the brassy sky from the fields where they lay sprawled.

When Kelly's relief appeared, it was possible to slip up to London before joining *Cressy* and the difference in the place became obvious at once.

The brooding face of Lord Kitchener, the new Minister of War, stared over his pointing finger from every wall and hoarding, exhorting all unmarried men to rally round the flag and enlist in the army, and there was a strange sort of excitement in the air that was driving young men to church to get themselves married before rushing off to answer his appeal.

After the initial anxiety, however, London had taken the news of defeat calmly and Charley fell into Kelly's arms as soon as he appeared at the door of Number 17, Bessborough Terrace.

'Kelly!' she yelled. Her young face went pink with pleasure and she hugged him delightedly, a little startled nevertheless that he looked so adult, so different from the boy she had known all her life, so stern, so responsible, yet somehow so vulnerable. In that moment she felt admiration, pride and a strange desire to mother him all at the same time.

'I heard your ship had gone to the north of Scotland some-where,' she said and Kelly's face darkened with indignation.

'She's not my ship any more,' he growled. 'They've posted me to a set of rotten old ships of the Reserve Fleet operating from Sheerness. They're donkey's years old, work up to about fifteen knots flat out and are full of fat old men from the reserve.'

She gave him a delighted grin. 'Well, I'm glad you've turned up anyway. You'll have heard your father's back in the navy, of course?'

Kelly's eyebrows shot up. That would please his mother, he thought. He'd long since guessed that she preferred her life with his father away from home, following his own fancies in London, indulging his little dishonesties and pretences of importance, so that she could follow her own interests. For years, he suspected, she'd drawn far more pleasure from her horses and dogs than she had from her husband.

'No, I hadn't,' he said. 'Where is he?'

'I don't know where. And my father's gone to France. He was given a brigade in the Second Division under General Smith-Dorrien. Your brother Gerald's regiment's somewhere near him.'

'Good old Gerald!' The words came out automatically because Kelly hardly knew his older brother. There were six years between them and Gerald had already left his prep school when Kelly had started there, so that they had seemed to bump into each other only at the end of term.

Charley was still chattering away, dancing excitedly round him like a cat on a hot pavement. 'Mabel's dragoon's gone, too, and I hear your Uncle Paddy's back in uniform and sitting with his fingers crossed outside the War Office, hoping they'll give him one of the new Kitchener battalions.'

Kelly whistled. 'Phew! What a change there is!'

'Not half. Mabel's dragoon was even sufficiently stirred by the war to propose to her before he left. Isn't it ripping?'

'Did she accept?'

'No. I think she was pretty rotten. He turned out to be rather a duck in the end and she might have let him go off thinking she was itching to get spliced.'

'Perhaps it's best,' Kelly said. 'Being a bundleman's not a good thing in wartime, and a girl ain't going to be any better off if she suddenly finds herself widowed, is she? What else?'

'Your mother's in England.'

'Doing what?'

'Looking for a house near London. She felt she needed somewhere handier than Ireland for when you all came home on leave. She's staying at Claridges until she can find somewhere. She and Mother got their heads together, because we're staying here for the duration, too, and they thought it might be nice for them to be neighbours again.'

Kelly's mother was drinking tea in the lounge of the hotel when he found her. She looked lost without her dogs, and her clothes, unfashionable and cut for the country, seemed quite out of place.

'Everything's changed so!' she said. 'Even your Uncle Paddy's gone now! Though God knows why, because everybody says the war's going to be over by Christmas!'

Kelly interrupted before she became too deeply involved in her complaints about the war. 'I hear you're looking for a house, Mother.'

She stopped dead. 'Of course I am. What can a woman do in London? The only place you can ride is Rotten Row and there ain't a fence in the whole length of it.' She gave her son a delighted grin. 'Got me eye on a place at Thakeham near Esher. It'll cripple us financially but now your father's been recalled there'll be a bit more money to spare. It's got eight bedrooms, so you'll be able to bring your friends home, and there are rooms over the stables for the grooms, if you want to bring your sailor servants.'

'Mother, isn't it a bit on the big side?'

'We can't live like peasants, boy. I'll be getting a couple of horses if you want to ride.'

'If you remember, Mother, I don't ride. I fall off.'

She shook her head. 'Never could understand that. Always seemed so silly. We have no servants, of course. Can't afford 'em. Only Bridget. She's too young to want much money.'

Kelly smiled as he remembered the giggling little Irish housemaid with black hair and startlingly blue eyes who had appeared to do everything at Balmero House. 'You made a mistake bringing Bridget, Mother,' he said. 'She's too pretty by a long way. Some enterprising Londoner'll snatch her up in no time, especially when they find she can cook.'

His mother shrugged. 'Oh, well, we all have to make sacrifices for the war, don't we? Especially with your father itching to get to sea and your brother Gerald complaining that his people haven't been in action yet. What about you? Where's your ship?'

'I don't know, Mother. I've left her, ain't I?'

'You don't mean you've—?'

Kelly laughed. 'Deserted her? Good Lor', no, Mother! I've been sent to another. *Cressy*. A rotten old tub. *Bacchante* class.'

'Weren't you pleased with *Clarendon*?'

'They didn't ask me.'

'You haven't been doing anything you shouldn't, have you?'

'Why should you think that?'

'Because I know you. Gerald, no, never. You, I'm not so sure about.'

–

It was raining at Sheerness when Kelly arrived and the station platform glistened greyly. He could see the greasy waters of the Medway and wondered why it always seemed to be raining when he joined a ship. Naval bases were never the most cheerful of places and they seemed to have their own particular set of clouds hanging over them ready to soak any wandering sailors trying to join their ships, always wetter than anywhere else, and wetter still on the quayside or the station where there was no shelter and the wind was at its fiercest.

A few men, peevish, frail-looking and red-eyed from booze, waited alongside a corrugated iron shed, their blue serge soaking up the rain like blotting paper. They were reservists and none too happy at being recalled when they'd been settling down comfortably into Civvie Street. Recruitment to the navy had never presented a problem in the past, but now, with the war waking up, the vast mass of fleet reservists were less a help than a hindrance, because there were so many of them. They couldn't be ignored, however, and it was for them that the *Bacchantes* had been brought out of retirement.

'At least,' Kelly heard one man say, 'the bastards float, and it's better than being sunk in the Merchant Service.'

Many of them were thickening round the middle and heavy with beer, and some of them were even elderly, stout and wheezing, reluctantly dragging behind them old kit bags stiff with deep sea salt.

None of them was in a particularly good temper because, to everyone's surprise, instead of wiping the Germans from the face of the earth, Britain was being hard pressed even to fend them off, and both services had set off on the wrong foot. While the army reeled back in confusion in France, the navy was smarting from a defeat of its own in the Mediterranean where a German eleven-inch battle cruiser, *Goeben*, with her escort, the four-inch *Breslau*, had been caught in the dockyard at Pola by the outbreak of war and had been allowed by some fatuous idiot with gold on his hat to escape through the Dardanelles, to be handed over to Turkey who were expected at any moment to enter the war on Germany's side. It had jarred the confidence of the country in the navy because, apart from a meeting between two armed merchant cruisers off the South American coast, there had been little to show and none of the great fleet actions for which everyone had been waiting. The German High Seas Fleet had not come out as expected to meet the Grand Fleet, which was anchored in Scapa Flow, diligently practising gunnery for the day when they did, and frightening itself to death with thoughts of torpedoes.

The officer who took Kelly's papers was a middle-aged man with campaign medals on his chest that Kelly couldn't even recognise. 'Maguire, eh?' he said. 'Ah, now, wait a minute!' He fished a paper from the shambles on his desk. 'The admiral wants to see you.'

'Which admiral?' Kelly had visions of some of his past catching up with him.

'He's just along the corridor. He's expecting you. I think you'd better go straight in.'

Halting outside a door that bore no name, rank, or official title, Kelly knocked with some trepidation and entered. Inside, he stopped dead as the man at the desk lifted his head.

'Father!'

'Kelly, my boy! How are you? Have you seen your mother?'

'I've just left her!'

The admiral smiled, a big man, taller than his son but lacking his alertness. 'Did she tell you she's got her eye on a house near Esher?'

'Yes, sir, she did.'

'Handy for the duration. Be a hell of a job getting to Ireland every leave, after all. She'll have to look after the horses herself, of course, because everybody's volunteered for the army.'

Admiral Maguire looked well content, and the gloom that had filled him ever since his retirement had dropped away completely. 'They had to call me back, boy, in the end,' he was saying. 'Like your Uncle Paddy. So you're going to *Cressy*, eh? Fine ship. Bit old nowadays, of course, but she looks well. Know Johnson, the captain? Younger than me, of course. Got a cool head, though. Just the man to look after a lot of reservists.'

'Father, are they *all* reservists?'

'Most of 'em. Plus a few cadets from Dartmouth and boys from *Ganges*, with a few chaps off the regular list like yourself to take care of things. They had to go somewhere, after all. Some have even gone into a naval brigade to serve with the army in France and I gather they don't like it very much. These chaps are lucky. At least they're serving in their own element, and you've got heavy calibre guns.'

'I hear they terrify their own gunners when they fire.'

The admiral smiled. 'Well, they won't need to fire much, will they? Size alone will frighten the enemy and submarines won't dare come within a mile of 'em. It's true, of course, that the *Bacchantes* need complements a bit out of proportion to their potential but no one's trying to believe these Third Fleet ships are tip-top, because we all know they're not. After all, they're only for trade protection.'

'Father, they're no good to *me*! They'll never see any action!'

The admiral gestured complacently. 'Good place for a youngster to make his mark and learn his drill, all the same,' he said. 'None of this nonsense about small ship routine that's running through the fleet. That's just slovenliness.' He rose to indicate that he was busy and that even as a father he had to bring interviews with junior officers to a brisk conclusion. 'By the way, you've been promoted acting full lieutenant. It'll be in the next list. And now I think you'd better cut along and report. *Cressy*'s coaling on her buoy in Kethole Reach and she's due for sea this afternoon, so you'll need time to find your way about her.'

–

Kethole Reach was no place to join a ship, because there was nothing on that stretch of the Medway but mudflats, and the thick black smoke belching from the funnel of the harbour launch covered Kelly with soot. Every now and then the stoker put his head through the boiler room hatch to look round, as though he were wondering where it was all coming from, and as he tipped ashes over the leeside into the flat oily current, the gulls swooped down, thinking it was garbage, before sheering off, screaming their disgust.

Kelly was still seething at what he considered his father's obtuseness. How many more men were there, he wondered, who could not see that an entirely new era in naval warfare had arrived? He had been the guest of the German submarine service in Kiel and it had been very clear to him that this new weapon had come of age so that the size of a battleship was no longer important. Far from frightening away a good submarine captain, size was an actual invitation, and a vast battleship like *Cressy* would be regarded, not as a danger, but as a prize. It seemed to be a fact that not the simplest ship's boy or saltiest admiral in the corridors of power could afford to overlook.

Conscious of his own silence, Kelly looked up. Perched on the canopy of the launch was a pale-faced boy who, up to that point, he'd barely noticed. He was small and with his cap flat-a-back, a cadet from Dartmouth who'd been in the sick bay with measles and was joining the ship after his term mates. Kelly thought he looked wretched. It was bad enough joining a ship like *Cressy* at any time; it was infinitely worse when you did it alone.

Realising that in his concentration he had probably presented a terrifying spectacle of age and experience, he tried to put things right by cheering the boy up.

'What's your name, youngster?' he asked.

The boy swallowed, his eyes round and scared. 'Boyle, sir,' he said.

'Worried?'

'A bit, sir.'

'I shouldn't be if I were you. But I'd square off my cap and hoist up my tie two blocks, all the same. Your collar stud's showing and I hear the captain of *Cressy*'s a stickler for smartness.'

At last, round a bend in the river, as a fat paddle-wheeled tug clawed her convoy of coal tenders past, *Cressy* hove into sight. Of 12,000 tons displacement, she was over 400 feet long with four tall funnels and a colossally wide beam reminiscent of the brass-and-white-paint ships of the previous century. She had been laid down in 1899 and looked every day of her age, out of date, slow and useless, and far worse after *Clarendon* than Kelly had expected.

It was clear she'd been made ready for sea in a hurry, with traces of rust hidden by red lead. The black-grey paint of wartime had been daubed across her, but there had been no time to chip and scrape because, even as ammunition had been hoisted aboard, her crew had filed up the gangway. Since she was not expected to steam far out of sight of land she was considered safe.

Captain Johnson was a strong-featured man with absorbed serious eyes. Like so many senior officers who had grown up in the starchy era of Victoria, he looked faintly old-fashioned with his winged collar and the narrower cap he affected, but he radiated confidence and, stripped of his uniform and badges of rank, Kelly realised, he would still have been picked out as a man of consequence.

'I understand you wish to serve in submarines,' he said as Kelly stood before him in his day cabin.

69

'Yes, sir. That's correct.'

'Think you're wise?'

'Yes, sir. They get more pay for a start.'

The captain permitted himself a half smile. 'You'll have to get a first-class certificate in the torpedo examination.'

'I have one, sir. From *Clarendon*.'

'I'm glad to hear it. Well, you'll be placed at the bottom of the ladder, of course, but I hear they're expanding the service, so you might be lucky. You'll go to HMS *Dolphin* where you'll be medically examined and after that you'll spend three months learning the trade. Think you can manage it?'

'Yes, sir.'

'Well, you might do well as a submariner. Since you're not likely to be with us for long, however, I expect you to do just that little bit extra. Is that understood?'

It was easy to promise a little extra, but with the crew still awkward and only a few key officers and ratings from the active list to handle them, it was harder to provide it. The Marine detachment were half Royal Marine Light Infantry – Red Marines – and half Royal Marine Artillery – Blue Marines – and the reservists contained men from every civilian trade, with many ex-members of the Fire Brigade, which they'd joined after their sea time because many of them had seen service in sail and had a head for heights. The leading signalman was a tall man with a drooping moustache – which, as a reservist, he was allowed to keep – who'd been a policeman in London and had a scarred thumb which he claimed had been bitten by Sylvia Pankhurst when he was trying to arrest her during one of the Suffragette riots.

For the most part, they didn't like *Cressy*. They were mostly from Chatham and therefore largely Londoners, townies – Cockneys to Devonport and Portsmouth crews – cheerful, quick-witted, fearless cock-sparrows, but limited by their gregariousness and their ability to be influenced by the bad characters that were always among them, and it occurred to

Kelly that, ever since before Nelson, the inexplicable thing about the navy was that its greatness had been built up by ill-used sailors in ill-found ships.

They were all crowded and the boys from Dartmouth had their gunroom separated from the CPOs' mess only by a screen of canvas and wooden battens, which caused a certain amount of dissatisfaction from the older men.

'It's not the language we complain of, sir,' one of them told Kelly indignantly. 'It's the bloody shindy they kicks up all the time.'

To cut down the risk of fire in action, they tried to strip off all the paint on the upper deck, especially where it was thick with the layers of years but, though the officers joined in, it was an impossible task and they had to let it go. With most of the officers older than himself, Kelly struck up a friendship with the navigator, a youngster like himself from the active list called Poade, a black-haired, enthusiastic, romantically-inclined young man with an occasional unexpected turn of cynicism.

'We're allocated to the southern force and we patrol the Broad Fourteens,' he said. 'In case you don't know, that's the term we use to designate the area of the Dutch Coast.'

'I've done my navigation,' Kelly said.

Poade grinned. 'It's supposed to be safe because they say the North Sea's nothing but an English pond.'

'It seems to me to be just as much a German pond.'

Poade smiled his enthusiastic smile. 'Their Lordships of the Admiralty appear to have overlooked that fact,' he agreed. 'A point to you, Maguire. With a twenty-eight-foot draught and ageing engines, we struggle along at not much more than half our top speed, but it's felt our bulk ought to deter the Germans from trying anything on around the mouth of the Thames, particularly with torpedo craft and minelayers; and we can bar the southern approaches to the North Sea and the eastern entrance to the Channel. We've maintained the patrol without incident since the war started.' Poade smiled again. 'It can't go on, of course. We're nothing but an invitation to the enemy to have a go at us – in fact, a few people have started calling us "the live bait squadron", and I gather Winston at the Admiralty's got himself into a fluff because he doesn't like ships like us being risked.'

–

The hot weather of the summer ended abruptly in the uneasy area of the north Channel which drew its temperature as often as not from the arctic icepack, and by late September the shallow waters with their extensive areas of shoal were cut across by white-capped waves, running all the way from the Norfolk coast past the Dogger Bank to Scandinavia and Holland.

Because they could withstand weather that held the destroyer forces inshore, the *Bacchantes* seemed to spend all their time at sea in a dull routine of patrols. The crews were still lubberly after their long lay-off and, in the grey waters east of the Sunk Light the weary but heavyweight section of the Nore Command exercised its duties with an uneasy awareness that it was more than normally vulnerable.

With the waves frothing over the shoals and the wind coming up-Channel in a series of squally showers, to Kelly life seemed nothing but a long procession of cheerless days surrounded by the whirr of fans and the creak of the ship's 12,000 tons of steel and machinery, with only short intervals alongside which always brought the dreary inevitability of coaling. Even visits ashore produced little in the way of fun because the Medway towns, despite the fact that they watched the old ships come and go with a personal pride and lumpy throats, were never very decorative or blessed with much in the way of entertainment beyond the sailors' level of utilitarian pubs.

To break the monotony, experiments were tried to increase the speed of coaling ship, paint was chipped again – with the same lack of success – and Kelly made his first hesitant steps as a camouflage expert. Camouflage was intended to make it harder for the Germans to take ranges, but his efforts, even if they pleased him, apparently didn't please the admiral.

'The object of camouflage,' his signal read, 'is not, as it would seem, to turn a ship into an imitation of a West African parrot but to give the impression that the head is where the stern really is.'

Then, unexpectedly, towards the end of the month the routine disagreeableness of beating into the iron-grey seas off the Hook of Holland came to an abrupt end, and the war came as abruptly to the Seventh Cruiser Squadron as it had to *Clarendon* and *Amphion* and the destroyers of Tyrwhitt's Channel bailiwick on the first day of hostilities. As the alarm bells went and the clatter of feet on the deck filled the ship, Kelly fell from his bunk and rushed to the bridge, to be met by the grinning Poade.

'The Germans are out!' he announced. 'We're to head north. Tyrwhitt's ships have left Harwich to meet 'em and Jellicoe's ordered the battle cruisers south from Scotland in support.' He smiled. 'We're at last about to offer our lives for our country!'

Kelly snorted. 'I'd rather make the Germans offer *theirs*,' he said.

There was an immediate air of tension about the old ship as they blundered north, cramming on every possible ounce of steam to get into the fight. Privately Kelly wasn't sure that they'd be able to do much even if they got there in time, except perhaps put in a few heavyweight punches, but he found himself praying under his breath all the same.

Oh, Lord, look after us, he kept repeating to himself. A chance meeting with a German battle cruiser could mean the end of *Cressy*, of all the *Bacchantes* come to that, even of life itself, and he still wasn't sure how he'd react to danger, because the undignified scuffle with *Königin Luise* could hardly be called a battle.

The day was calm, with a mist over the grey water. The old ships, punching into the sea and filling the sky with smoke that drifted low alongside in the squally weather to obscure their view towards the enemy coast, seemed as harmless as brontesauri.

'Fog ought to help us a bit,' Poade said. 'It'll add to the confusion of the Germans, and the Heligoland batteries won't be able to see us.'

'Perhaps we won't be able to see the Germans either,' Kelly said dryly. 'Or even the ship in line ahead. Where *are* the Germans, anyway?'

'Just to the north. They've been working a night patrol off Heligoland Bight and when the submarines spotted them it was decided to cut 'em off.'

As he spoke, the chief yeoman appeared with a signal for the captain. 'Destroyers are in action, sir!' His voice was brisk and excited. 'There's a signal, "Hostile cruisers latitude fifty-four N., longitude four E." Heligoland Bight area, sir.'

'Tyrwhitt's found 'em,' Poade whispered behind Johnson's back. 'Wait till *we* arrive.'

'At this speed,' Kelly said, 'that'll be when it's all over.'

The mist grew thicker and the old ships wallowed through a heavy, oily sea, ponderous mastodons of steel heading north-east. At eleven a.m., the chief yeoman popped up again.

'Harwich forces heavily engaged, sir, with light cruisers. They need assistance.'

Johnson turned to the voice pipe. 'Engine room, can you give us more revolutions?'

'No,' Kelly whispered to Poade in reply. And 'No' it was, so that the old ships, in line ahead, stumbled hopelessly through the thickening weather, helpless to give assistance.

The sky seemed to descend during the early afternoon, pressing down on the horizon, grey and threatening. The sea was flat and greasy-looking, and though they drove the old engines to their limit, the ship creaking and groaning, the whole structure shuddering at the effort so that plates and glasses and knives and forks did a quivering fandango along the wardroom tables, Kelly was right and they saw none of the action. In the afternoon, they heard the distant thudding of heavy guns and through the mist saw the smoke of a burning German ship, and they all stared eagerly towards the horizon.

'Beatty's turned up with the heavy boys,' Poade announced and, as bugles cleared the mess decks, men crouched behind the gun shields waiting tensely.

When they arrived two hours later, the battle was over and Kelly could feel the tension slipping away in a feeling of anti-climax. There was a little grumbling and a considerable amount of frustrated bad temper but there was nothing for the *Bacchantes* to do but for *Hogue* to take the damaged *Arethusa* in tow and for the rest of them to embark casualties from the destroyers. The little ships looked badly knocked about. The forecastle gun of one of them had received a direct hit and the bodies of its crew lay under a canvas screen, leaking blood which had run in rivulets down the ship's side, while in another the second funnel leaned at an angle where a shell had knocked it off-balance, and the ship's plates were scarred where splinters had clattered against her side.

The wounded, aware that three German light cruisers had been sunk, were in high spirits and didn't seem to have a very high opinion of the German ships' fighting qualities. 'They haven't inherited anything from the German Army,' a bandaged lieutenant-commander observed languidly as he was offered a cigarette. 'Trouble is, of course, German sailors are made in Kiel harbour and that's like the Serpentine. You can't train sailors on the Serpentine.'

The surgeon was working in the wardroom and sick berth attendants were stacking amputated limbs near the captain's cabin. With the wounded all aboard, they lowered boats to pick up German survivors. There were two or three hundred of them, wearing lifebelts and lifting their hands, shouting for help and trying to sing '*Deutschland über Alles*' from their rafts. Their thin cries came over the lifting sea through the mist in a curious ullulating sound like the calling of seals as *Cressy* searched the wreckage-strewn water. Picking them up made Kelly feel vaguely as he once had when out shooting in Ireland when he'd brought down a couple of startled thrushes with a left and right in his excitement. The German survivors and the bodies floating in the water gave him the same feeling that some dreadful mistake had been made.

There were so many of them and so little room, some of their wounded had to be put in the gunroom under the Dartmouth cadets' hammocks and, during the night, Boyle, the boy who'd joined ship at the same time as Kelly, appeared pale-faced outside his cabin to say one of them was calling out in pain. He was a young German officer, a military observer, who'd lost a hand. The pad over the stump had slipped but the sick berth attendant Kelly summoned rearranged it, and the young German nodded his gratitude to Kelly. He was a good-looking youngster with a little spiked moustache like the Kaiser's still standing up despite his soaking. His eyes were defiant and proud, though, and Kelly offered him a cigarette, aware that another emotion had gone by the board. He reminded Kelly of his brother Gerald and it was quite impossible to hate him.

As they turned and lumbered back to Sheerness, Poade stared at the grey sea. 'Always a bridesmaid, never a blushing bride,' he said.

'With the speed of this squadron,' Kelly growled, 'we couldn't catch a ship's boat pulled by a snotty-nosed boy. If we're going to wage war with ships like these, it'll be God help us.'

Six

The popular press went overboard about the battle. 'We've been to Heligoland and back,' the *Daily Express* crowed with glee. 'Please God we'll go again.'

'No great feat really, of course,' Poade allowed casually. 'But it was carried out under the Germans' noses and *that* establishes our ascendancy. Once we can get their High Seas Fleet into the North Sea, they'll be wiped off the face of the earth.'

Within forty-eight hours they were back on their patrol, the Dartmouth boys still queasy from the smell of blood left behind by the wounded Germans, and, almost immediately, Poade's enthusiasm was diminished by the news that a U-boat had shocked the Grand Fleet by penetrating the Firth of Forth as far as the railway bridge.

'At this moment, I suspect,' Kelly grinned, 'there'll be battle-ships and battle cruisers dashing in every direction for the safety of Scapa Flow.'

Four days later they heard that another U-boat had torpedoed the flotilla leader, *Pathfinder*, in the Channel, and Poade's gloom increased.

'These submarines are becoming a bit of a bloody nuisance,' he decided heavily.

Only Kelly seemed to lack surprise. He knew his father and had met many of his contemporaries, and he suspected that the setbacks they'd suffered so far could well be laid at their door.

The Broad Fourteens patrol continued in increasingly bad weather. It was a curiously remote kind of life. Apart from the days in harbour, they were entirely out of touch with the world, keeping lonely company in the southern North Sea. The blazing excitement of action that they'd all anticipated, which had been encouraged by the sinking of *Königin Luise* in the first hours of war, had simply not materialised and the war had begun not with the almighty smash they'd all been expecting but with a mere shift of scenery. They'd expected to thunder into battle with smoke pouring from the funnels and the guns blazing in some dramatic action filled with the roar of high explosive and the smell of burnt cordite, but, instead, all they'd done was sink a few German trawlers in the Channel which, unaware that the war had even started, had cheered them as they'd approached. As they'd taken the crews on board, the only difference had seemed to be that they'd had fresh fish to eat for a change, and now all they'd got were humdrum patrols without anything positive to show for them. It was hard even to feel useful.

Towards the middle of the month the equinoctial weather became bad enough to lash the 120-mile stretch of water from Dover to the Hook of Holland to a fury and stir its grey waves to a cauldron of stinging spray and opaque spindrift.

'In for a spell of bad weather,' Poade observed. 'Admiralty's radioed that the Dogger Bank patrol needn't be continued and that the seas are too bad for the destroyers, so that we've got to watch the Broad Fourteens on our own.'

'Oh, bloody marvellous!' Kelly glared out at the grey murk, uneasy, uncertain and angry. It was obvious to anyone with eyes to see that the submarine had advanced long since from infancy to pugnacious adulthood and to leave the old cruisers unescorted seemed to be a mistake of the highest order. 'That leaves us without any protection at all and, on this beat, with the Dutch coast on one side and a minefield on the other, there's no room for any variations of course. The Germans must know exactly where we are at any time.'

Spray lashed across the deck and his eyes narrowed as he peered into the mist. *Cressy* was lurching through the waves, massive, ponderous and threatening, but they'd all heard the nickname they'd been given and he guessed that their threat was an empty one. The squadron was even under strength because *Euryalus* was in dock, and the flagship was running out of fuel and would soon have to turn for shore.

'What happened to Winston's idea that the Broad Fourteens could be abandoned?' he said to Poade. 'Are they using us to entice the Germans out so that Tyrwhitt can get at 'em, or are we here just because we've *always* had ships here?'

Poade shrugged. 'I expect our elders and betters know more than we do,' he said. 'Though I've been told that Roger Keyes was heard on the telephone saying "For God's sake, take these bloody *Bacchantes* away." We'll be all right,' he ended. 'In these waters, submarines'll be at a disadvantage and, if the weather moderates, one of Tyrwhitt's flotillas will join us tomorrow morning.'

The following morning, however, the weather was still bad and the message they received announced that Tyrwhitt's flotilla had had to turn back to Harwich. 'The flagship's returning to base as well,' Poade said. 'For coaling. Drummond in *Aboukir*'s in command.'

The wind was coming in fierce short gusts now, plucking the funnel smoke downwards across the bridge to make them cough and dab at streaming eyes, and the sky was high without a scrap of warmth to it, its empty greyness turning the water into an angry pewter that seemed to reflect the tall dark sides of the old cruisers. Square, ungainly, their high freeboard blunt and blank as cliffs, they dug into the short steep seas like angry bulls butting at a gate. There was a hard chill in the air and Kelly was in no mood to be forgiving.

'Why doesn't *Aboukir* signal increased revolutions?' he demanded. 'At this speed we're a sitting target.'

'Conserving coal,' Poade said. 'Admiralty order.'

'It's asking for trouble. Pity we can't just zigzag a bit. I always found it a damn sight harder to hit a rabbit when it jinked.'

Staring at the chart, Kelly wasn't as convinced as Poade that the situation was a safe one. As the three old ships steamed in line ahead, the eastern horizon was still dark with the gale blowing into their faces. The chief yeoman appeared and, as he handed a signal form to Johnson, Kelly noticed that his fingers were stained blue by the duplicator he used to issue the captain's orders.

'Germans are out again,' Johnson announced bluntly. 'Light cruisers, destroyers and submarines.'

Under the narrow, old-fashioned cap, his face was keen, but there was an element of strain and worry, too, behind his eyes which indicated that he was as aware of danger as Kelly was.

'They've been seen from Esbjerg, South Denmark, heading north. Jellicoe's coming out, too, heading south past Flamborough Head towards the Horn Reef. It doesn't involve us.'

'It still leaves us isolated, sir,' Kelly pointed out.

'I doubt if we need to worry in this weather.'

Late in the evening, another signal was received, saying that Tyrwhitt had started off again for the Broad Fourteens with his flotilla of destroyers and should arrive the next day. At first light the following morning, the *Bacchantes* were still heading northwards, anxious eyes on the western horizon for the first sign of the destroyers' grey shapes to appear through the mist. As the middle watch ended, Kelly was staring round him, frowning. The waves looked black, racing in towards the ship like dark mountains of water, and he felt a tingle in his guts as he watched the sullen crests rolling past, exhilarated by the angry sea yet at the same time depressed by the absence of colour and the deep sense of foreboding in his mind.

Poade was also clearly uneasy. 'Seas are dropping,' he said. 'And that's no help. It's to be hoped Tyrwhitt arrives before the submarines start getting awkward.' He glanced at the chart. 'I'd have thought we'd be safer to head towards the destroyers instead of continuing on this course.'

Kelly peered through the mist across the broken seas towards *Aboukir*. The old ships one behind the other reminded him for all the world of three elderly circus elephants performing a routine march.

'What's the course, Pilot?' Johnson demanded.

'Oh-four-five, sir,' Poade said.

'Speed?'

'Ten knots.'

'How far are we from the Hook of Holland?'

'Twenty miles on the beam, sir.'

'We'll have to change soon or we'll run aground at Ijmuiden.'

The sky was the colour of old lead, darkening in the north to the colour of wet Cornish slate. Every time the ship pitched, the screws raced out of the water and there was a shuddering groan as the whole vast structure creaked and gave to the strain. There was a curiously depressing feel in the damp, salty air, and oddly there seemed no sensation of surprise as Kelly saw a fountain of water rise from the port side of *Aboukir* leading the line. It seemed somehow to fit in with the prevailing mood of the day.

He had just turned away to glance at the chart when, through the murk, he saw the column of water and spray lift in a sudden mushrooming shape, a grey-white tower soaring high above the decks, almost as high as the funnel, thick, sullen and ominous; then he saw smoke coiling upwards, and with surprise, saw the cruiser appear to lift into the air with it. There seemed to be no flame and no explosion and it was a moment or two before he realised that *Aboukir* had been hit by something. Then *Cressy* shuddered as a vast shock wave punched at her massive hull and, immediately, men crowded the decks to stare across the dark uneasy water.

'*Aboukir*'s struck a mine, sir!'

The roar of the explosion came across the misty sea as he spoke and, as the smoke cleared, through the murk they noticed *Aboukir* had stopped and Kelly was surprised to see she was already heeling so far over to port her starboard plates were visible, glistening wet and red in the increasing morning light. The iron-grey water alongside her, churned to foam by the explosion, was dotted with black heads, and more men were appearing from below until her decks were teaming with running sailors.

'I think they're abandoning, sir!'

Johnson snatched at his telescope. 'Already?'

Some of *Aboukir*'s boats, smashed by the explosion, swung in shattered wreckage from the davits. One of them had been lowered and stopped halfway down, and it hung lopsided and awkward-looking. A light began to flicker from the stricken ship's bridge.

'She's signalling, sir. It *is* a mine and they want us to come closer to pick up survivors.'

'She's going, by God!' Johnson said in surprise. 'Stop engines! Get the boats away! Maguire, go with them! You've got a sound head on your shoulders! It's got to be done quickly. Paymaster, we'll need blankets, soup and hot coffee, and warn the surgeons to be ready! And double the lookouts! *Aboukir* might be wrong. It might have been a torpedo.'

As the way went off *Cressy* a bugle blared. The alarm gongs were sounding through the ship and she came alive with men running along the broad decks to the boats. Bosuns' mates urged the men along, their pipes twittering as they ran.

'Away first and second whalers!'

The boats swung clear over the black water and the oarsmen and coxswains fell into the narrow wooden hulls. The second whaler was already dropping down the ship's side, the falls screaming as if they were alive. Kelly clambered into the pinnace. 'Lower away!' he shouted.

The waves shot up towards them, the wind snatching at their crests.

''Vast lowering! Out pins! Let go!'

The boat dropped with a lurch on to the crest of a wave and, as it began to veer away from the black bulk of *Cressy*'s beam, Kelly saw that *Aboukir* was now down by the bow, the watery sun shining on the white figures of naked sailors walking inch by inch down her sides as she heeled over, some of them standing, others sitting down and sliding into the water which was already thickly dotted with the heads of swimming men and the sprawled white shapes of the already dead.

Every one of *Cressy*'s boats had been lowered and mess tables, stools, spit kids, chests of drawers and chairs were being hurled overboard for *Aboukir*'s survivors to cling to. The main derricks, prepared in record time, were hoisting out boom boats and Kelly was just heading away from the ship's side when there was another terrific crash. *Hogue*, cautiously approaching like *Cressy* to pick up the swimming men, also seemed to lift out of the water, and the shock jarred Kelly even through the timbers of the pinnace. A second or two later there was another crash, deeper sounding and heavier, and a great column of water and a cloud of smoke lifted from *Hogue*'s side. The third of her four huge funnels collapsed at once like a pack of cards and, as she began to heel over, she appeared to have been cut almost in two.

'We're in a minefield!' the coxswain of the pinnace shouted.

'Minefield be damned!' Kelly snorted. 'I'll bet it's a submarine and *Cressy*'s a sitting target.' He turned to stare back at his ship, expecting her to get under way and move off, but she lay still, wallowing in the grey choppy water.

'For God's sake,' he burst out, as though issuing orders himself. 'Get going!'

Above the crash of the water, he could hear a sound from *Hogue* of breaking and splintering, as though every fragment of crockery, every chair and table, anything that wasn't riveted to the bulkheads was being fragmented. She was already well over to starboard.

'There must be half a dozen of the bastards,' one of the seamen yelled, then guns started to fire over their heads from *Cressy* and they could see the shell splashes in the sea.

'They got her,' someone shouted.

'Don't talk rubbish,' Kelly yelled. 'Pay attention to what you're doing!'

Aboukir was low in the water now, the sea lapping the bridge, and they could see men jumping from it into the waves.

'She's going!'

Slowly, with ponderous majesty, *Aboukir* began to turn turtle. The dark water heaved and great gouts of it shot upwards from open scuttles, then there was a rending sound as her boilers tore loose, and she fell over on her side and settled upside down, rocking gently, lifting to the surface again so that men started to climb back on to her slimy red keel. Not many succeeded because it was too steep and too slippery and those who did were cut by barnacles, begrimed and exhausted, and choking from the sea water and oil they'd swallowed. Then, slowly, she slipped beneath the waves, taking with her most of the wild-eyed survivors who clung to her keel.

Hogue, also by this time heeling to port, was firing at shadows and from below, as the pinnace pushed through the wreckage and began to haul gasping men aboard, Kelly could see dead-lights being closed and more mess stools, tables, timber and anything else which would float being thrown over the side. Boats were swung out on their davits and yelling petty officers were shouting a mixture of orders. Hammocks splashed into the sea and men began to jump.

At first it seemed that *Hogue* was not going to sink, but then they saw that the quarterdeck was awash and she, too, began to roll dizzily to starboard, flinging men across the broad decks to break arms and shoulders as they fetched up against bulkheads and stanchions. An explosion deep below water lifted her port side up and she lay almost on her beam ends, and as her gunners ceased their pointless firing they could hear shouts above them of 'Abandon ship'.

Putting the pinnace astern to clear the great leaning bulk, Kelly stared upwards. *Hogue* made him think of some vast block of buildings slowly tilting sideways towards him, then, as they drew away, he saw the captain walk over the side of the bridge and on to the bilge keel, where one of *Cressy*'s cutters took him off almost dry-shod. Falling heavily on to her side, *Hogue* set up a great swell that swept towards them, lifting them on its crest as it rolled past. For a moment, the water lashed at the sides of the pinnace then, as the huge keel showed, wet and red and barnacle-covered, swinging slightly as the ship settled, Kelly drove in among the swimming men again.

Awakening at last to the danger, Johnson had begun to take *Cressy* away at full speed in a zigzag past the area of wreckage and swimming men where her consorts had sunk. Her guns were still firing wildly and shells were dropping near her own boats.

'Give her all she's got,' Kelly yelled to the pinnace's engineer and they moved among the swimming men, dragging them aboard and distributing them among the cutters as they filled up.

One of *Hogue*'s Dartmouth boys, wearing only a singlet, was shivering with cold and Kelly shook him to life.

'Grab an oar, boy!' he shouted at him. 'Double bank! It'll warm you up!' and he saw the boy climb into a cutter and reach out to start heaving alongside a bearded, ear-ringed sailor.

Cressy was firing over their heads now and he saw the splashes grow nearer. He turned to wave a hand in warning but at that moment the pinnace's bows seemed to lift from a vast concussion below the sea and he saw seamen and planks and a brass ventilator hurled through the air. As the bows dipped again, he saw the timbers were shattered, then he was swept out of the boat by the rush of water that flooded along it, and was swimming for his life, the one thought in his mind the unfairness of it all – he seemed to be seeing more bloody war than was his share and to be sunk by his own side was just too much.

He came to the surface, spluttering furiously. *Cressy* was hurtling past, a vast black steel bulk towering above them, pushing men and wreckage aside with her bow wave. He could see her rivets picking up the light, and her ungainly turrets trained to port, the guns moving slowly like the antennae of a great steel beast, stupefied and worried, but without the intelligence to discover the whereabouts of her undersea tormentor. On the bridge officers were staring down at him over the steel coaming, and barefooted sailors were running along the decks with ropes. Then, as she moved past, he saw an explosion lift her stern and the shock came through the water like a blow from a fist. Once more, in a sickening repetition of the other two torpedoings, a great column of smoke, as thick and black as ink, shot skywards as high as the towering funnels, and, working up to her best speed, the great ship came to a halt like a charging rhinoceros hit by a high velocity bullet. As her bows went down, an angry wave of water foamed over the forecastle head and she stopped dead, steam roaring from the funnels in a shrieking din. Then she heeled, righted herself momentarily, and finally, like *Aboukir* and *Hogue* never designed to withstand torpedoes, began the same dismal, taunting sequence of keeling over to starboard.

Spitting water, almost weeping with rage, Kelly saw her start to dip below the waves like an oil drum split open at target practice, and men on her decks tossing over rolled hammocks to cling to as she began to sink. Slowly, she leaned over, checked, then went still further, the men at the guns still firing at an invisible foe. The Dartmouth boys, still in their pyjamas and looking like children, began to run for the side, and Captain Johnson, tall, wing-collared and old-fashioned-looking, appeared to be calming them as he walked among, or instructing, directing, as though nothing had happened.

Then, as her boilers tore loose in a devastating explosion, she turned turtle in the same sickening manner as her sisters, leaning over like a ponderous pendulum to splash down on her side in the water and continue turning until she was upside down. As she floated keel-up, a few desperate men, gasping and shouting for help, tried to scramble aboard but, still rocking after her wild swing, huge fountains of water driven upwards through her scuttles by the compressed air inside her, she slipped quietly below the sea.

As she disappeared, Kelly heard a rush of water like surf breaking on a beach and realised it was suction. He hardly had time to fill his lungs with air before it was upon him. His chest seemed to be bursting, and he had almost given up fighting when something told him to keep on trying and he started struggling afresh.

As he shot to the surface, something bumped against him in the icy water and he found it was a hammock. He looked round for something more substantial and as a coir fender bobbed up he grabbed it and pushed himself on it to a piece of floating timber which seemed to be the centre of one of the ship's targets and managed to flop across it.

–

Clinging to the baulk of timber, he was consumed with angry bitterness. What bloody luck, he thought, to become a casualty after only six weeks of war!

He was cold and numb and quite certain that all the feeling was going from his limbs, and he had almost resigned himself to drowning when he came to life with a jerk. This was a damn silly way to behave, he decided – giving up the ghost before he was properly gone. Once, as a boy, he'd fallen out of a tree and knocked himself unconscious, and had come round staring at the sky, convinced he was already dead. Then his brother Gerald, worried at his stillness, had given a nervous little kick at his behind. He had heard his voice – 'Come on, young 'un, you're not hurt' – and had literally forced himself back to consciousness.

Looking at his watch, he realised it had stopped exactly an hour after *Aboukir* had been hit. Only *Cressy* had launched her boats and the other two ships had gone down with nothing more in the water than a cutter or two. All round him were struggling men and he began to move among them, calming them, telling them not to try too hard, but to grab something that would float, and kick with their legs.

'It'll help keep you warm,' he panted, 'and it's too bloody far to swim to England from here.'

A few weak grins answered him and some undefeated spirit yelled 'Fuck the Kaiser!' Treading water, he stared around him, unable to believe that three great armoured cruisers had disappeared so quickly. Gasping, shouting men were fighting their way through the wreckage to grab at anything substantial enough to float, trying as they swam to divest themselves of seaboots and the heavy wool clothing that was dragging them down into the darkness, and there were screams as huge spars, freed below water, shot to the surface to break limbs and backs.

Exposure was already taking its toll and the stokers, who had rushed on deck from the overheated confines of the boiler room, were the first to succumb, lying back in the water as if going to sleep. A headless body drifted past, and Kelly saw two Dartmouth boys, neither more than fifteen, swimming desperately towards a raft, terror in their eyes as they breasted the corpses in their path. One of them was Boyle and, heading for them, he grabbed him and towed him to a lattice-work target that had floated free as the ship sank. A crowd of sailors clung to it and he pushed them aside and handed the boy over to a bearded petty officer before setting off back for the other. By the time he arrived at the spot where he'd seen him, however, there was no sign of him.

The water seemed to be crowded with men clinging to withy fenders and Kelly passed the ship's surgeon clutching the top of a small table and the chaplain hanging on to a lifebuoy. Beside him was the engineer commander, gasping in agony from two broken legs. Some of the swimmers seemed to have given up the ghost already and he called to them as he pushed among them, 'Come on, you chaps, who's for a dip?' and a few of them managed a cheer and struck out for floating wreckage.

Moving away, struggling to remove his clothing so he could swim, he found a life raft and climbed aboard. As other men arrived, he tried to organise it so that wounded and injured could be laid flat on it while the unwounded clung to the sides. As more appeared, it was clear the raft couldn't hold them all and he went over the side again to organise groups of men to cling to floating planks and spars.

How long he was in the water he didn't know but eventually someone shouted that he could see a mast and Kelly saw a Dutch fishing smack to windward. Immediately, the men grouped round the raft started singing – that compelling hymn all sailors demanded, sometimes in cynical enjoyment when securely shorebound, but always somehow with the feeling at the back of their minds that its words were their appeal to the Almighty not to forget them.

> *'Eternal Father, strong to save,*
> *Whose arm hath bound the restless wave…'*

The tune welled up stronger and, driven by its plea, Kelly set off swimming towards the lifting mast. As it drew nearer, he became aware that he was surrounded by dead bodies that carpeted the surface of the sea in grisly groups. They were bent over the spars and fragments of splintered wreckage to which they clung or had lashed themselves for safety, some of them stokers who had died blinded or sobbing with pain after being enveloped in a scalding miasma of steam. Shouting and swimming alternately, he pushed through the crowding bodies until he caught the attention of the crew of the smack at last and a small boat was launched to drag him aboard.

Soon afterwards, two small Dutch steamers and an English trawler arrived and began to haul the dead and dying on deck. They were all practically naked and some were so exhausted that, with the rolling, it was impossible to lift them aboard and a tackle had to be hoisted out. The Dartmouth boy, Boyle, was among those huddled on deck and as Kelly handed him his own mug of tea, he gave him a grateful look and drank, only to be promptly sick into the scuppers. Unaware that all he wore was his underwear and his uniform cap, Kelly nagged the smack skipper to put him aboard the British trawler, where *Cressy*'s engineer commander lay on the deck, his broken legs at an odd angle, the ship's chaplain alongside him.

He looked up as he saw Kelly. 'Hello, my boy,' he said. 'I was watching you there with that raft. That was splendid work you did.'

The trawler was crowded now but no one seemed to be angry except Kelly. Poade appeared, covered with oil but still enthusiastic and, like so many others, apparently regarding the sinking as a good sporting event.

'Bloody hard luck,' he said. 'And jolly well played, the Hun!'

Kelly turned on him furiously. 'Hard luck be damned,' he snorted. 'And bugger this "Jolly well played" nonsense! We got what we asked for! It was too damn silly for words waiting there like that to be torpedoed!'

'You couldn't leave all those men to drown!'

'By not leaving 'em, we added another seven hundred to the score!'

It was mid-morning when *Lowestoft*, flying Tyrwhitt's broad pendant, arrived, and the survivors on the trawler were pushed aboard the destroyer, *Malice*. Someone handed Kelly a cup of cocoa and he found himself staring into a familiar face.

'Kimister!'

'Ginger Maguire! Were you in one of *them*? The last I heard of you, you were in *Clarendon*.'

'I've had rather a varied career since then,' Kelly growled.

Kimister's expression was one of mingled thankfulness and envy. He was never sure quite how he wished to be treated by the war, whether he wanted to be kept safely out of danger or be flung into the middle of the fray so he could find out about himself. Since he was very doubtful about how he'd behave if he were called on to prove himself, he was grateful that so far he'd not been involved in anything very risky. His ship had just arrived from the West Indies and he was still suffering from a certain amount of anxiety because Tyrwhitt, alone among the British admirals, seemed to be showing any eagerness to get at the Germans.

He waved a hand. 'Look, come to my cabin. I can fit you up with my spare uniform.'

'You don't have to.'

Kimister smiled. 'You stopped Verschoyle bullying me lots of times,' he said. 'If it hadn't been for you, I'd have packed the whole thing in. I often thought in those days I wasn't cut out for the navy.'

'What happened to Verschoyle anyway?'

Kimister's expression changed. He had always been terrified of Verschoyle as a boy and now as a man he still was. Once it had been Verschoyle's fists, now quite simply it was his tongue.

'He's at Gib, lucky devil,' he said.

Kelly was unimpressed by Verschoyle's luck. 'I bet he's crawling round the admiral,' he said.

By the time they disembarked at Harwich, Kelly was looking reasonably respectable again in Kimister's second-best uniform, but most of the men around him were shoeless, and still in shirts, pyjamas and underwear, clutching blankets or sacks to them. A few wore white canvas trousers and navy issue sweaters and a lot of the officers had saved their thick llama watch coats, but many wore nothing underneath.

The Great Eastern Hotel had been commandeered as a hospital and all those who could stand up and walk lined up for steaming baths. Already the news had got around the town, and outside the building and in the lobby women waited, weeping or frozen-faced, to hear what had happened to their men. Other women were handing out mugs of tea and cocoa laced with rum.

As Kelly shared his mug with a shivering grey-faced Dartmouth cadet, his father appeared. 'Thank God you're all right, my boy!' he said. 'What happened?'

Kelly turned an angry face towards him. 'Some damned fool at the Admiralty left us out there like sitting ducks,' he said. 'They picked us off one by one.'

'Cruisers?'

'Cruisers be damned, Father! Submarines.'

'Rubbish, boy.' Admiral Maguire frowned. 'Submarines can't have done all that damage!'

Kelly stared at him. Up to adolescence, to George Kelly Maguire, God had been represented on earth by his father, a vague, gold-encrusted minor deity smelling of leather and tobacco and fine soap. When he was at home he had administered the law somewhere not far below Heaven, hearing everything, seeing everything, missing nothing; while the rest of the family, the dogs and the servants had hovered in the depths with nothing to lose but their chains. Now he could only regard him as a middle-aged, not very bright naval officer who had been indulged by his profession for far too long.

'Submarines, Father,' he insisted. 'And I dare bet, just one.'

Some idea of the size of the disaster was filtering through now. Nearly 1500 men had died within an hour and the war had come shatteringly home to the navy. Weaned on the exploits of Drake and Nelson, the disaster seemed to have stunned everybody.

A few cheerful spirits still managed to smile. 'One thing,' Kelly heard a half-naked gunner say. 'We'll get survivors' leave,' and he immediately realised that the leave he'd been owed since before the outbreak of war might at last be possible.

He was just wondering where his father had gone so he could tap him for a loan, when someone touched his shoulder. It was a captain with black side whiskers who was carrying a large sheaf of papers.

'You're young Maguire, aren't you?'

Kelly hadn't the slightest idea how he knew but he admitted that he was.

'Good. Come with me. I've got a little job for you. I didn't know you were in *Malice*.'

'Sir, I'm not—'

But the captain had turned away, striding on long legs down the stairs. It was clear he had assumed from his dry clothing that Kelly was not a survivor but part of the crew of the destroyer which had brought him ashore. He was talking to himself as he walked.

'What a bloody way to conduct a war,' he was growling. 'Germans sinking every bloody ship we've got and Winston over in Antwerp playing at bloody soldiers with the army!' He half-turned. 'They'll need to send in the Naval Brigade there, boy, did you know? Half of 'em still without equipment, too, with their bayonets down their gaiters and their ammunition stuffed into their pockets. Someone's got to stop the Hun getting the place. It anchors our left and guards the Channel.'

Kelly hadn't the slightest idea what the whiskered captain was talking about and he had to keep breaking into a run to keep up with him as he stalked along, throwing words over his shoulder.

'There's going to be a hell of an uproar in the press about sending all those kids from Dartmouth and *Ganges* to sea,' he was saying. 'No bloody landlubber'll ever believe a boy can learn more in ten minutes about his profession at sea in wartime than he can learn in fifty years in a classroom.'

There'd be a few parents, all the same, Kelly thought, who might have preferred that their sons had had the chance to learn something about life first. His mind went back to the Dartmouth boys running across the deck of *Cressy* and Boyle's terrified eyes as he'd towed him through the water towards the raft.

The captain was still arguing with himself. 'They'll all be writing to the papers,' he was saying with the fine arrogance of a man allowed to live a life that was entirely separate in thinking, behaviour and standards from the rest of the country. 'I wonder what those boys would have said if their parents had taken them out of the ships. They'd never have been able to face their friends again.'

He stopped dead abruptly and pointed. '*Audacity*'s down there,' he said. 'She's got a whole slop room full of blankets and uniforms. I want 'em. Now! Tell 'em I sent you. They know who I am because I've just put the bloody things aboard.'

'But, sir—'

'Go on, boy! Don't argue.'

Audacity was an old destroyer, and she was lying alongside the quay with a look of alertness about her, her springs taken in and held to the shore only by her bow and stern ropes. As Kelly searched for the lieutenant in charge of stores, he could hear the throbbing of her engines, smell the odour of hot oil and steam, and catch the hum of engine room fans. Whether the whiskered captain was known aboard or not, the lieutenant, who was a reservist, clearly had no intention of giving up his newly-acquired stores in a hurry.

'We need 'em,' he said. 'We're due for sea. We've been warned to stand by with steam up. Get 'em from your own ship.'

'I haven't got a ship. I'm from *Cressy*.'

Despite the urgency, the lieutenant was still not inclined to move quickly, and, unfamiliar with new procedures, was keen to keep his nose clean.

Kelly was almost hopping with rage at his casualness and pettiness. He'd obviously been brought up in the same school as his father, concerned with the ritual rather than the spirit, and he could well see why he'd been placed on the reserve.

As they talked, a motor car drew up alongside the ship, its brakes squealing, and Kelly heard shouted orders. Immediately, bumps and clangs above his head began to alarm him, then the quivering that had been running through the ship ever since he'd stepped on board increased.

'What's happening?' he demanded.

The lieutenant looked up. 'I told you. We've been warned to come to immediate notice for sea.'

Kelly's head jerked round. 'Then, look, please, for God's sake, can we hurry?' He endeavoured to bring home the urgency of his request. 'There are eight hundred men standing round in their birthday suits at the Great Eastern in need of clothing. They're cold. They don't have a thing—'

The clanging above his head interrupted him. As it increased he heard running feet – a lot of running feet. It sounded only too familiar.

'That's the gangway!' he bleated, and bolted for the deck.

He was just too late. The ship was already a yard from the quay. There was still time to jump but, as he cocked one leg over the rail, someone grabbed him by the neck. 'What the hell do you think you're doing, you bloody fool?'

He crashed to the deck with another officer on top of him. Struggling free, he sat up at last and pushed aside the other man, a lieutenant like himself.

'You benighted stupid idiot,' he shrieked. 'Now look what you've done!'

'I've saved your bloody life,' the other officer snorted. 'You ought to be grateful!'

'Well, I'm not.' Kelly yelled. 'This isn't my blasted ship! *My* ship's at the bottom of the North Sea with two others when she ought not to be, if anyone had had any bloody sense!'

Almost weeping with fury, he stared at the quayside, now twenty feet away and receding rapidly. 'I think the navy's full of bloody fools!' he stormed. 'Do you know what you've done? You've ruined my survivor's leave! I was swimming around in the bloody North Sea only a few hours ago and the only thing that kept me warm was the thought that I'd be able to go home and have everybody dance attendance on me. I've even got a girl to hold my hand and now I'm off to sea again because you're a silly fathead with his brains in his backside. If this bloody ship gets sunk, I'll *never* get my leave.' His fury died abruptly. 'Where are we going anyway?' he asked.

'Gibraltar.'

'Gibraltar! For God's sake, why?'

'Well, after all, old man, there *is* a war on.'

'Do you think I haven't noticed? What the hell are we going to Gibraltar for?'

'Take some bigwig, I understand. I'm damn sorry, of course, old fruit, but how was I to know you were a survivor? You don't look like one.'

Kelly stared back at the receding port, cursing Kimister's generosity. The ship was passing the seaplane base at Felixstowe now, her stern down in a welter of white water, her bows up as she headed for the Sunk Lightship.

'Gibraltar,' he said, faintly awed at the way the war was managing to sweep him along with it. 'My God!'

Seven

Worms of fury writhing in his brain all the way to the Mediterranean, Kelly learned that there was no bigwig on board after all and that *Audacity* was merely heading south to replace a newer ship on the Mediterranean station which was needed for the big fleet battle that was confidently expected before long to take place in the North Sea. As soon as the wires were ashore in the shadow of the Rock he stormed on to the quay to see the admiral and within twelve hours was heading for the destroyer, *Norseman*, which was due to move north to join the Grand Fleet.

He seemed to have saved the situation entirely, but as he stepped aboard and was met by the officer of the watch, he recognised him at once as Verschoyle, by now like himself a full lieutenant.

The thin, hard face broke into a broad smile. 'Ginger Maguire,' Verschoyle said. 'By all that's wonderful! I heard we were taking a passenger but I thought it must at least be an admiral, not a bloody little pipsqueak like you. Ah, well, it's all the same! We're due for a refit so I expect there'll be leave, and it's all one whether it's an admiral or you. Are you enjoying the war, Lieutenant Maguire?'

'So far,' Kelly admitted, 'no. Are you?'

'I intend to. That's why I'm glad we're going home, because we're due eventually for Scapa or Rosyth and that's where the commander-in-chief is. And where the commander-in-chief is James Caspar Verschoyle should be.'

'I hope you're lucky.'

'It won't be luck, old fruit,' Verschoyle said cheerfully. 'It'll be good solid planning. More planning than Their Lordships at the Admiralty appear to have indulged in since Nelson.'

Kelly made no attempt to be friendly and Verschoyle was aware of something very different about him. This, he decided, was not the young Maguire he'd known and happily bullied in the past. There was a thin edge of tension about him now, as though he would no longer accept being pushed around by Verschoyle simply because Verschoyle was a few months older, cleverer, more poised, more sarcastic and more cruel. This young man – and Verschoyle was the first to acknowledge he was no longer a boy – looked as though he could be dangerous if driven too far, and Verschoyle found himself treading surprisingly warily.

'How's that little flower of yours, Charlotte Upfold?' he asked.

'She's all right.'

'She has a pretty elder sister. I met her at a coming-out dance just before the war and now, happily for me, her family have taken a house near Esher, only nine miles from where yours truly lives. Don't you think that's lucky.'

Kelly glared. The idea that James Caspar Verschoyle was getting into his social life was almost more than he could stand.

'No, I don't,' he snapped. 'Because it means you'll be only nine miles from where I live now, and that's something I wouldn't wish on my worst enemy.'

Verschoyle found himself swallowing the insult. 'We are becoming vitriolic, aren't we?' he said. 'However, for your information, Sister Mabel's been writing to me, so perhaps next time you call on your own little flower, you'll find me in attendance on her elder sister.'

Kelly scowled. 'That'll be no bloody pleasure, I can assure you,' he said. 'In any case, I think you're a liar, because she's almost engaged to a chap in the dragoons.'

'Almost,' Verschoyle said blandly. 'But not quite, and in love, as in gunnery, a miss is as good as a mile. In any case, our friend is in France fighting for his life while I'm here in Gibraltar and due to go back to England where Mabel's waiting with her tongue hanging out for a little male company. I shall make a point of seeing her. I have her address and one might as well take advantage, what?'

Kelly scowled. 'I always thought you were a bit of a dirty dog, Verschoyle,' he said. 'Now I'm certain.'

Verschoyle smiled, but his eyes were hard. 'Don't you call me a dirty dog, young Maguire,' he said gently. 'I'll have you know I'm the best man there is with his fists in the fleet. I won the cruiser-weight championship of the command three months ago. I beat a stoker who looked like the Hunchback of Notre Dame, so if you call me names I shall be obliged to suggest we meet in the gym somewhere. There's nothing would have pleased me more from the first day you stopped me showing that little weed, Kimister, how to behave. How is he, by the way? Have you heard of him?'

'I'm wearing his clothes.'

'In God's name, why?'

'Because I lost mine in *Cressy*.'

For the first time, Verschoyle realised what it was that was so different about this old enemy of his. His eyes were full of knowledge and experience and the subtle difference about him came from having faced the brutal facts of war. Verschoyle had enjoyed the balmy weather of the Mediterranean ever since hostilities had started – had even managed to dodge a posting to the Far East – and he had imagined himself lucky to be out of the war because he was not called upon to endure harsh duties and harsher realities. Now, somehow, looking at Kelly, he had an uncomfortable suspicion that he was the loser.

'Were you in *that* little bunfight?' He put on a pretence of contempt. 'Well, I suppose one of those old cows was where you really belonged. You'd better go now. We're due to cast off any minute. If I get a chance while we're on passage, I'll trip you up. You might even fall in the sea.'

Norseman left Gibraltar on the third day of October. After an uneventful passage they reached the Sunk Light off the mouth of the Orwell, and Kelly was just looking forward to stepping ashore at Harwich when he realised that the ship had turned east and south and showed no signs of stopping.

Verschoyle gave him a beaming smile as he demanded an explanation. 'I'm afraid your travels aren't over yet, young Maguire,' he said. 'We're not going to Harwich after all. We're going to Antwerp.'

'Antwerp!'

'It seems Winston's got the Naval Brigade into a bit of a mess there. He offered to hold the place for the army and now they're stuck and we've been told to contact them. They're trying to get to Ostend, but some of 'em seem to have been cut off and we've got to find 'em.'

Off the Hook they saw the dead from *Aboukir*, *Hogue* and *Cressy*, still doing their ghostly patrol with the tide, six hours one way and six the other. The Scheldt was flat and greasy-looking as they turned into it and headed upstream and, as they approached Antwerp in the early hours of the morning, they could see the sky was full of smoke. As they lay off, the great Hoboren oil refineries lining the river were aflame from end to end, the oil running into the water to cause a blazing mass to flow into midstream. Deserted steamers lay at their berths against the wharves, licked by the flames in an eerie scene accentuated by the blackness of the night and the flash of heavy shells beyond the buildings. Kelly was told to report to the bridge.

'Ah, Maguire,' the captain said. 'I've got a job for you.'

'Not too dangerous, I hope, sir.'

The captain smiled. 'Shouldn't think so. But we can use that French lingo of yours.'

'Which French lingo, sir?'

'You've got French blood, haven't you?'

'If I have, sir, I'm not aware of it.'

'One of my officers said you had. Your mother's name's de la Trouve, isn't it?'

'Well, it's one of them, sir, but she doesn't speak French and no more do I.'

The captain smiled. 'My chap said you'd be modest about it. But he said you were good and I want someone who'll be able to find their way about in that shambles ashore. Since you're supernumerary and speak the lingo, it looks like you've got a job. Any objections?'

'No, sir. So long as it's understood that I'm not an expert.'

'I expect you'll do. We've been told to pick up stragglers, but it seems to me that we're no bloody good to anybody if they don't know we're here. So I want you to take the pinnace and a dozen of my jolly jacks armed to the teeth and establish contact with the troops ashore.'

Kelly doubted his ability to establish contact even with a public lavatory because his French was largely of the schoolboy variety, but the captain of *Norseman* seemed to have accepted already that he spoke the language like a native and he decided that he ought to be able to find an English-speaking Frenchman who could be bribed to help.

'When you've got 'em all together,' the captain was saying, 'send the pinnace back and we'll come alongside. I can't risk being shelled until I know where to go.'

As they crowded into the pinnace, the faces of the midshipman in command and the sailors packed in the stern, armed with rifles and strapped up like Christmas trees in their webbing, were lit by the flames ashore.

Verschoyle saw them off, bland and smiling as usual. 'If you don't make it,' he told Kelly, 'I'll offer my condolences to that virtuous little damozel of yours when I go to pay my respects to her elder sister.'

His smile grew hard as he spoke. Beneath his suave and self-satisfied surface, there was growing in him a thin core of envy for Kelly, even for the devotion he seemed to inspire in Charley Upfold. It was something Verschoyle, in his own shallow, indifferent, cynical circle, had never met before and he suspected that it sprang from some thread of loyalty and trust that neither he nor any of his girlfriends possessed. He gestured, unable to resist a small triumph.

'They wanted yours truly to go on this little caper,' he said. 'But I wasn't having any of that. I suggested you. It's known as watching one's stern. It's the Grand Fleet I'm going to, not Antwerp.'

As the pinnace headed upriver, with Kelly still glaring back at Verschoyle, the light of the flames became brighter and the sailors crowded to the side to stare at the shore. One of them touched Kelly's arm.

'Excuse me, sir. Are you Lieutenant Maguire?'

Weighed down by revolver and ammunition, Kelly turned. There was something familiar in the sailor's face. 'Yes,' he said. 'I am. And I know you, too, don't I?'

'Yes, sir, you do.'

'Then where—?' Kelly grinned. 'I've got it: You're the chap I pulled out of the sea after the Coronation Review.'

'That's it, sir. Albert Rumbelo. I'm an able seaman, now.'

Rumbelo had broadened out into a thickset sturdy man whose size seemed to dwarf Kelly.

'Been doing any more high-diving?'

Rumbelo grinned. 'No, sir. But I 'ave learned to swim.'

The lights in Antwerp were still on and shining on the black water. Along the lighter skyline they could see a fleet of dark little clouds, each one the smoke from a different burning part of the town. The air was full of scraps of charred paper and soot and in the distance they could see the flash of gunfire and hear the rumble of artillery. As the pinnace slipped alongside, Kelly jumped ashore with *Norseman*'s seamen.

'Wait here,' he called down to the midshipman. 'Lay off in the shadows so you can make a quick getaway if necessary. I'll flash with a torch when I come back.'

Heading into the town, almost the first thing they saw was a London Transport bus, heavily scarred by shell splinters but complete with red sides and even a sign to Cricklewood.

'I heard they sent a few over to take the lads up to the front, sir,' Rumbelo said.

The bus was empty and several of its windows were smashed and there was blood on the seats inside. Around it were wrecked houses and uprooted paving blocks, and here and there dead horses among the broken buildings, some of them still in the shafts of ruined service wagons. There was no sign of life, though a few of the houses bore tricolours and even an occasional union jack or a notice welcoming the Marines of the Naval brigade as the saviours of Belgium.

Across the road was a barricade of carts, felled trees and beds, and, nearby in a church, what seemed thousands of civilians in rows round the walls, crouching on piles of straw. Some of them, in an attempt at privacy, had heaped barriers of it between themselves and their neighbours, but for the most part they seemed indifferent to each other, respectable bourgeoisie sitting next to women who'd obviously been harlots from back-street slums. Old men waited on guard, sitting on chairs, their hands in their laps, a child whimpered and was rocked to sleep, and two young marrieds lay together, the boy holding the hand of a girl who looked as frighteningly young as Charley.

'*C'est bien triste.*'

The voice made Kelly turn. It was a priest and Kelly nodded, thinking that 'triste' was hardly the word. The scene transcended all sorrow.

In his halting French he asked about the Marines and was informed that most of them had already got away.

'*Et les autres?*'

'*Prisonniers, Monsieur.*'

It didn't sound very promising but they could hardly go back without trying a little harder.

A Belgian battery rattled past as they emerged into the street, swerving in the rough sandy track that fringed the pewter-coloured cobbles. The men's faces contained not terror but sullen disgust, and as they stopped alongside a group of tall buildings, the artillery men jumped down and stared up into the sky where a German monoplane seemed to hover, the first glimmerings of light catching the underside of its curved wings.

As they pushed past, they began to meet refugees, all heading out of the city towards the west, leading horses and carts hung with lanterns, and pushing wheelbarrows and perambulators full of what was left of their belongings. The carts seemed to be packed with children, as if the entire infant population of the neighbouring villages was in them, all dirty, grey-faced and nodding with fatigue. They passed at a walking pace, the drivers hunched over the reins. At first they came singly, but soon there were other small vehicles until they became a steady stream. Some of the carts were open so that they could see the loads they carried – a mangle, a blackboard, a tin trunk oozing clothing, a three-coloured madonna with a sad grin leaning against a cooking stove. Behind them was a woman leading a goat hung about with saucepans and a lame girl with a wooden crutch who was bent beneath a feather bed, her face stained with tears. Scattered among them were Belgian soldiers, some of them wounded, the stragglers from the Belgian Army which had withdrawn some days before to reform at Dunkirk and Ostend, smut-soiled men, scarecrow warriors too weary to brush away the phlegm from their moustaches or the dribbles of nicotine from their chins. Their narrow, hungry faces were hollow-eyed and passive with weariness.

Kelly tried his French on them uncertainly. '*Fusiliers marins anglais?*' he asked. '*Vous avez vu?*'

They seemed too tired to understand and merely shook their heads and begged cigarettes before stumbling on into the darkness.

'That was a lot of bloody help,' Kelly observed.

As they searched, shells started dropping beyond the buildings they'd just passed and they could hear the crack and see the flash over the roofs as they exploded.

'In the river, sir,' Rumbelo said. 'They'll probably 'ave to move *Norseman*.'

Finding a square surrounded by tall flat-fronted buildings with empty windows like eyeless sockets, Kelly split his party up and told them to explore the neighbouring streets and buildings and bring any British stragglers they found back to the square, then set off himself with three men under Rumbelo.

'Might as well have you handy,' he observed. 'You never know, you might get a chance to do what you promised in 1911 and save my life. Antwerp seems just the place for it.'

After a while, they came upon an armoured car with the letters 'RN' painted on its stern. There were the bodies of two men in it, a naval officer and a seaman who had been caught by shell splinters. While they were still inspecting it, a shadowy group of figures emerged from among the buildings, and advanced towards them, rifles at the ready. Kelly thought he saw Belgian képis and addressed them in French.

'*Qui est là?*'

Immediately a volley of rifle shots rang out and he and his party dived into an alley for shelter as the bullets dug plaster from the buildings around them and whined off into the shadows. There was a clatter of boots and a harsh yell – 'Get the buggers before they fetch their pals!'

Kelly stared at Rumbelo. 'They're British,' he said, and putting his shoulders back against the wall, he began to shout. 'Ahoy there! Avast shooting! This is the navy!' Immediately the firing died down and when it seemed safe to stick his head out, Kelly emerged into the square. The group of men were standing bunched together, looking warily at him.

''Oo the 'ell are you?'

'*Norseman* – come to evacuate you.'

There was a dead silence then a burst of ragged cheering as the men crowded round Kelly and his party. They were a mixture of Marines and sailors of the Naval Brigade. A few of them wore items of Belgian uniform and they looked exhausted, unshaven and dirty, but one of them still defiantly clutched a union jack and a banner with a skull and crossbones painted on it.

'Where are you from?'

'Well—' it was a burly Marine sergeant who spoke '—we were at Willryck, sir. Most of us are bandsmen acting as stretcher bearers. We gave our clothes to the wounded and had to borrow from the Belgies. We landed on the sixth and went straight up to the trenches. Not that anything much happened except that we got shelled. We never saw no Germans. Nothing but nine-inchers and four-twos. Krupp shells lobbing over us into Antwerp. Then we was pulled out for the second line. There was woods in front and a clear field of fire but still no Germans. By this time they were shelling the city and we lost some men from shrapnel. It never stopped all night. Is the war lost, sir?'

'Good God, not yet! We're here to take you off.'

'Where's the ship, sir?'

Kelly pointed and the sergeant shook his head. 'They started shelling round there, sir. Not half an hour ago. Some of 'em dropped in the basin.'

'Where are all the other men?' Kelly asked.

'There aren't any others, sir. Us lot – *Hawke* battalion and Marines – was supposed to cover the withdrawal but we never saw the others again. I heard they was ambushed on a train at Moedecke and only a few got away. The rest surrendered or crossed over into Holland and was interned.'

'There must be more, for God's sake!'

'Well, there might be, sir. But they'll take some finding, because they'll be hiding. Jerry's expected any minute.'

Kelly made his decision quickly. He could see Rumbelo and the other sailors watching him and he knew exactly what they were thinking: Marines were ham-fisted, club-footed lumps who cluttered up any ship they served in. Despite a splendid record stretching back over the centuries, they were always an isolated entity whose legs were being perpetually pulled by the seamen for their clumsiness aboard ship. This was just another case of them getting themselves and everybody else into trouble and having to call in the seamen to drag them clear.

'You'd better go and find them,' he said. 'Be back in an hour's time. Bring everybody you can. I'll wait here.'

The men disappeared none too willingly but, as Kelly waited in the square, small groups of men in the peakless caps of the Marines began to appear. Among them were wounded, and several were without their rifles.

One man had marched all the way back from Moedecke. 'They landed us still dressed in blue, sir,' he said aggrievedly, 'and re-equipped us on the dockside. Every man jack of us in an hour or so. It was a bit difficult with the boy buglers. They was so small. We went up to the front but you couldn't see a bloody thing for the dust from the lorries bringing the wounded back. The shells was smashing the woods and villages and someone rigged up a live electric wire and we dug deep holes against cavalry, and a line of stakes in case there was a charge.'

'Where are all the rest?'

'Christ knows, sir! Zeppelins was above us all the time, directing the fire and dropping incendiaries, and the Belgian Army was scooting down the Lierre road behind with most of their officers dead or wounded. We saw nothing but a few of our aeroplanes spotting for the guns.' The Marine hitched at his pack with the resigned air of a dumb animal. 'We marched through the city and crossed the river. Some of the chaps was so fagged they fell in and sank like stones. There wasn't no food so we pulled turnips out of the fields to eat. We got a train at Stekens, with the Uhlans just behind us, and squeezed in where we could. It stopped at Moedecke. Some bastard had switched us into a siding and the Germans was waiting.'

The solder's face was blank and exhausted as he continued. 'There was an embankment and buildings full of three-pounders and machine guns,' he went on. 'All the women and kids started yelling, and it was a right old massacre for a bit. We tried to answer but because of the din you couldn't hear orders. There was a zeppelin with a bright light just above us. We tried to get the train going but the driver and fireman had bolted and one of the stokers said the engine had been sabotaged. I shot a German when he tried to climb aboard but then the word was passed to surrender to stop the butchery of the women and kids. A few got away to Salzaete but some of us was cut off.'

The story was one of confusion and exhaustion and the Marine denied indignantly that he'd ever surrendered. 'I didn't feel like surrendering,' he said. 'I came back here because I thought the navy would fetch us off.'

'Well, they're going to.' Kelly said.

By now, he had collected around him eighty-odd Marines and sailors and the Marine sergeant was beginning to look more enthusiastic.

'There's a lot more along the road, sir,' he pointed out hope-fully. 'Hiding in a barn full of hay at St Nicholas.'

'Are they, by God? How far?'

'About nine miles, sir.'

'Christ, that's a hell of a way!' Kelly glanced at Rumbelo. 'Can you drive, Rumbelo?'

'No, sir.'

'Well, I can. Just. I've had a few goes. Let's get that armoured car we saw and see if we can start it.'

Watched by the exhausted, stupefied men who trailed after them like hopeful dogs, they dragged the two bodies from the armoured car and climbed in. It was little more than a tin box on wheels and full of dried blood, with a machine gun mounted on the stern. The Marine from Moedecke climbed in with them to handle the gun and show them the way.

'Keep these chaps together,' Kelly told the sergeant. 'We'll be back. If they get scattered, they'll not get taken off. Under-stood?'

'Understood, sir.'

With a lot of grinding of gears and a series of ugly jerks, the armoured car began to move.

'Easy when you know how,' Kelly said cheerfully.

After a while, they found themselves on the edge of the city, heading down a long road on which the cobbles set everything in the armoured car rattling as if it were alive. There seemed to be no sign of fighting except for an occasional figure crossing the fields and odd groups of Belgian soldiers. In the distance they could see shells bursting and burning houses sending up huge columns of grey smoke into the sky.

'Round the next bend, sir!'

A clump of trees hid the barn and, as the armoured car slid to a stop beneath them, faces appeared from among ruined farm buildings.

'The navy's here!' Kelly yelled.

There was a ragged cheer and exhausted, dirty men began to appear in ones and twos from the barn.

'How many of you?' Kelly asked.

A grimy unshaven corporal with a moustache like a walrus answered him. 'About forty-odd, sir.'

'Any more up ahead?'

'Up ahead of us, sir, there's only Germans. And not so bloody far up ahead neither.'

'Right, form up. We're marching off.'

The corporal looked worried. 'Sir, we've got men here who couldn't march another step. Their feet have gone. We've been marching ever since we landed and we ain't had nothing to eat for two days.'

There was an old farm cart by the barn, covered with rusting machinery. Kelly made up his mind quickly.

'Let's have that thing on the road,' he said.

'There's no horse, sir. It's dead in the field. Shell splinter got it.'

'Who said we needed a horse?' Kelly slapped the bonnet of the armoured car with a clang. 'I've got plenty under here. Get it unloaded, Rumbelo, and unhitch the shafts.'

There was new hope in the corporal's face as he turned away. A dozen men managed to manhandle the old machinery off the cart and push it on to the road where Rumbelo was already busy under the back of the armoured car with a drag chain he'd found in a harness store.

'Will it do it, sir?' he asked.

'Ought to.' Kelly stared down the long straight road. 'There are no hills and no bends. It might need a bit of shoving on to course here and there, but we ought to cover a lot of the distance. If we can reach the outskirts of the city they can be carried the rest of the way.'

They placed straw on the cart and hitched it by the chain to the back of the armoured car which Kelly, after a great deal of swearing and fumbling with the gears, managed to reverse. Exhausted and wounded men were lifted aboard and the rest formed up into a tattered little group behind.

'Right,' Kelly said. 'Let's go.'

The first two or three tries to start were failures but, after a while, with the engine screaming, he managed to jerk the cart into movement. There was a ragged cheer as they rattled slowly off along the road.

It was all of a mile before the road showed any sign of turning and, with the aid of crowbars and timbers that Rumbelo, with the thoughtfulness of a seafaring man with an eye to the future, had placed aboard, they managed to edge the cart on to its new course. Before long they were in the outskirts of the town where they had to cry quits because it was impossible to get the cart round the narrow corners. Lifting as many of the exhausted and injured men into the armoured car as they could, they drove them to where they'd left the first batch they'd found under the sergeant, to be greeted with wide grins and cheers.

Unloading them, they set off back to the cart, only to bump into the fitter men of the second group carrying their exhausted friends. Loading more into the armoured car, they set off back once more, to come to a jerking halt a quarter of a mile short.

'Now what's happened to the bloody thing?' Kelly demanded. 'Know anything about the clockwork in these things, Rumbelo?'

Rumbelo had lifted the bonnet and was poking into the tank with a stick. He held it up. 'Petrol, sir. Dry as a bloody bone.'

They were near enough now, however, for the remaining men to be carried without difficulty and by noon, they found they had collected 151 Marines and sailors. There were only a stumbling exhausted group, however, useless as fighting men. Many of them were vomiting for want of food and most lay on the hard cobbles of the square fast asleep.

Kicking them to wakefulness, Kelly led them back to where he'd left the pinnace. But the buildings along the quayside were blazing now and there was no sign of the boat beyond, a piece of wood floating in the scummy water with the ship's name on it, and the body of the midshipman, terribly burned, bumping gently in its lifebelt against the steps. After a while, the pinnace's stoker appeared. He was wet through and had a bandage round his head. He said the pinnace had been blown to pieces. He'd been flung overboard and had swum for the wharf-side only to see *Norseman* disappearing downriver amid a flurry of shells.

''Ow the 'ell do we get back now, sir?' he asked.

'God knows,' Kelly said. 'But we'll think of something. In the meantime, let's look for something to eat.'

Down a side street they found a deserted bakery full of bread and not far away an empty épicerie which supplied them with other food. Then the Marine sergeant discovered a small abandoned restaurant whose owners had disappeared, and three steaks lying on a table in the kitchen covered by flies.

'I don't like to be mean with food, sir,' he announced quietly. 'But I intend to have one of them meself, and since you've come to take us home, I reckon you and your coxswain ought to have the others.'

He cooked the steaks on a paraffin stove he found but, when they sat down at the kitchen table to eat them, to Kelly's astonishment, the sergeant emptied a pot of jam over his plate and began to eat with gusto.

'Felt like something sweet, sir, that's all,' he explained, faintly shamefaced.

A few of the Marines were a little drunk on wine they'd found, and it seemed to be time to move them on. But most of them could barely crawl. They'd force marched a matter of eighty miles and their feet were so swollen they couldn't get their boots off, and they had to be half-carried.

'We've got to find somewhere to hide 'em, Rumbelo,' Kelly decided. 'Until we can rustle up some sort of boat to get us downriver.'

'And when we've found somewhere, we've got to get 'em there, sir,' Rumbelo pointed out. 'I reckon it's going to be a case of forty blokes carrying eighty blokes. It can't be done.'

Kelly stared round him. The population of Antwerp seemed to have sunk into the ground. Everywhere, every street, every building, every shop, seemed to be deserted, so that they felt like intruders in a town filled only with ghosts. Suddenly he remembered.

'The bus, Rumbelo,' he said.

'The bus, sir?'

'Yes, Rumbelo. The London red we saw. It's built to carry around eighty-odd people. Why shouldn't it carry eighty-odd tired Marines and jolly jack tars?'

Eight

The bus was still where they'd last seen it, an odd anachronistic sight on the cobbled streets, its top deck brushed by the leaves of an acacia tree.

'You ever driven one of these things, sir?' Rumbelo asked.

'No. But I managed the armoured car and I reckon I can manage this.'

Kelly strode forward, suddenly full of confidence. For a change he was out of the reach of senior officers and was doing the leading himself. It seemed to suit him and his self-assurance grew by the second, so that he even began to enjoy himself, sure of his knowledge and ability and the certainty that a 151 men, exclusive of his own party, were relying on him to get them home. It was a formidable challenge for a young man without resources cut off in a defeated city, but he found himself responding to it with enthusiasm and even a certain amount of gaiety. This, he felt, was being alive.

'Get the sick, the halt and the lame aboard,' he said briskly. Then, climbing into the driver's seat, he pressed the brass switch that engaged the battery.

'Give her a swing, Rumbelo.'

To their surprise, the engine started clattering almost at the first heave at the starting handle, and with Rumbelo perched on the mudguard alongside him, Kelly cautiously depressed the clutch and pushed the gear lever forward. As they began to move, Rumbelo grinned.

'Getting better at it, sir,' he said. He turned and yelled into the cabin. 'Pass down the car, please. No waiting on the platform!'

'Dry up, Rumbelo,' Kelly ordered. 'I can't hear myself think.'

Jolting in a way that jerked the wounds of the injured men they'd packed aboard, they rolled forward, the solid rubber tyres rumbling on the cobbles. Nobody complained, however, and there were even cheers and yells of laughter from the fitter men marching behind.

Eventually, they found a tall four-storey warehouse near the river and lifted the injured men from the bus inside, where they immediately fell asleep on the floor. Then Kelly and Rumbelo drove the bus to the water's edge, put it into gear and jumped clear. With great satisfaction they saw it run down the slope towards the river with increasing speed and splash into the water, settle lazily on its side and finally disappear, leaving only the stern with the sign for Cricklewood above the water.

'There'll be a lot of people waiting in vain in the Edgware Road tonight, sir,' Rumbelo grinned.

When they returned to the warehouse, everybody but the Marine sergeant seemed to be asleep.

'Get 'em awake,' Kelly said. 'I'm going to find a ship.'

'Not a chance, sir,' the sergeant said. 'They're dead beat. They'll not move much before morning.'

Kelly stared irritatedly at the crowded bodies at his feet. 'Charming,' he said. 'That's a great help!'

Setting a guard of men from the *Norseman*, he instructed them to make sure the others were quiet, then he and Rumbelo climbed to the top of the building to see what they could discover. Projecting beyond the roof, there was a clock tower where the machinery was still clacking away merrily. Through the window they could see right over the city. In the distance heavy shells were bursting in salvoes in clouds of dense black smoke, as every prominent building in the surrounding countryside was fired on – every château, church and windmill. The long straight road by which they'd brought in the survivors from the barn at St Nicholas had shrapnel shells sparkling above it now, and a wood they'd passed was speckled with white puffs of smoke. The Marine sergeant, surprisingly recovered after his meal, joined them.

'The Germans wasn't all that bloody good, sir,' he said encouragingly. 'There wasn't many of 'em and they wasn't very well, trained anyway. They didn't bother with infantry attacks. They just drenched everything with shells then the infantry wormed their way forward into the gaps. It was all artillery and it wasn't possible to dig a trench because there was water a foot down, and we had to crouch behind bushes and trees.'

The German salvoes began to drop on the outer fringes of the city and the sergeant pointed.

'Them's the forts, sir,' he said. 'Five or six of them shells is enough to smash 'em. Casements and all. The Belgians threw in the towel. The water supply was cut and they had no materials or anything. Mind, there was one of our officers who got hold of a Belgian sapper officer and four privates and a Belgian boy scout, and between 'em they pushed charges into the machinery of around forty ships in the river. I heard 'em going off. *They'll* not be leaving.'

Local shelling started again, and they could see the missiles landing in a nearby square with vicious cracks and flashes of brilliant light to hurl jagged splinters against the buildings and gouge out great gashes in the brickwork. A chimney collapsed and a roof slid down in a shower of tiles and a cloud of dust. Immediately the sergeant disappeared to warn his men to lie low.

Staring over the roofs, Kelly could see leafy enclosed country and a ring of observation balloons round the city. 'That's why they're shooting so bloody well,' he said.

From the other side of the tower they had a view over the river and the wharves. A ship was burning but there was no sign of *Norseman*.

'They've obviously decided the Germans have nabbed us, sir,' Rumbelo said.

'They're not going to nab me if I can help it,' Kelly said, and Rumbelo grinned.

'Nice to know, sir. Because then there's a chance they won't nab me neither.'

—

The sun was well up above the roofs now and a few people had started to appear in the streets, heading west. At first there were only ones and twos and small groups but eventually they congealed into a mob that seemed to be totally dressed in grey. Then they saw that their black clothes were covered with dust, and they filed endlessly by, like a crowd from a race meeting, but in complete tragic silence. Every single individual wore an expression of personal sorrow, with a set staring face, every one of them carrying a heavy bundle in a mood of despair. Two young girls, hardly able to drag themselves along, were helping each other, their feet bloody from blisters, and a sick woman, already clearly dying, was being pushed past in a wheelbarrow by a sturdy daughter. Two old people struggled along arm-in-arm, clinging to each other as they'd probably clung to each other all their lives, and a small boy tried to encourage his mother, who was sinking under the weight of two babies.

'Jesus Christ!' Rumbelo sounded uneasy. 'Oughtn't we to be joining 'em, sir?'

'With those lot below?' Kelly said. 'They couldn't march another yard.'

As he spoke, he became aware of his own weariness. He seemed to have been on his feet for days now and the cobblestones had become painful to the soles of his feet. In the distance he could see a dock station, but it appeared to be deserted with a line of trucks, closely tarpaulined, waiting in a siding. Near it, tables stood outside a poplar-shaded cafe, but there was no one sitting at them and one of them lay on its side with two white chairs.

Soon afterwards, more German shells began to fall in the square and the streets about it, bursting with vicious cracks to blow in windows and slam shutters and send the cobbles flying like missiles. A cart pulled by a scrofulous grey horse had appeared, shifty-looking as though it were a criminal, but as the first shell exploded, the horse broke into a furious gallop, clattering off out of sight, dragging the remains of the cart away from the hole in the road where the driver sprawled and a wheel spun lazily before falling.

Several terrified rats began to bound across the square, like symbols of doom, and as the second shell kicked up the centre of the square in flying earth and stones, they were flung through the air by the blast like scraps of torn rag. The explosion came like the flash of a crimson flag, and yellow smoke curled as if it were the flirt of a dancer's skirt. Somewhere out of sight a woman began to scream in a harsh monotonous howl, then there was another bang and the clatter of flying tiles and the screaming stopped abruptly. This third explosion was so close they could feel the force of it against the walls of the warehouse. A fountain of smoke and rubble rose from the corner of the square, and a shower of stones and dirt came down along the wall. A house fell outwards, leaning over the street, unbroken, and seemed to stay like that for the whole of a second before it crumpled and dropped in the road in a confusion of tiles and broken bricks. From the centre, a cloud of dust rose, spreading like a curtain, and the window frames rattled. Unexpectedly, because they had believed the little houses around them were all empty, a door opened and a woman with a child began to run across the square.

Kelly began to shout. 'Come back! Come back!'

But a fourth shell landed a few yards from the third and, though it didn't do much good, the shrapnel whipping across the square accounted immediately for the running figures.

When they reached them, there appeared to be no bodily harm that they could see but the two lay silent, so close together, face to face, their fingers were touching.

As they carried the two bodies into one of the houses and laid them neatly on a bed alongside each other, the need to do something about the exhausted men under their charge became urgent.

'We've got to dig up some sort of boat and bring it round here,' Kelly said. 'Then we might get 'em to struggle into it. Let's see what we can find.'

There was a building on fire beyond the other corner of the square and, as they watched, the smoke grew thicker, dirty flecks of carbon drifting in the air beyond a ruby glow of flame. A little scorched breeze came, puffing up dust into the quivering air. A cardboard notice in the window of a house that said, ironically, 'Welcome to the British, our saviours,' flapped, then drooped again in the heat. From a long way off, to the east, a rumble came, less like artillery than the constant fall of heavy cases.

A few more Belgian stragglers appeared and they said that the German Army was already in the city in large numbers. Kelly could still see Belgian tricolours about, however, and was inclined to disbelieve them. Then suddenly they heard the clatter of hooves and they slipped hurriedly into an empty house alongside and slammed the door behind them. Through a dusty window, they saw horsemen with lances and strange flat-topped headgear passing the end of the street into the next square.

'Uhlans!'

The German cavalry, about fifty strong, clattered past, the pennants on their lances fluttering. Behind them came a squadron of hussars, strangely old-fashioned-looking in their frogged tunics and wide furred busbies. Behind the hussars was a long column of Belgian prisoners, many of them wounded, followed by German wagons and two or three field guns. As the column clattered across the cobbles, a Belgian who, judging by the scarf of office he wore, was an official of some sort, appeared and one of the Germans dismounted and handed him a sheet of paper which seemed to be a proclamation. Almost at once a drooping Belgian flag was hauled down and the German black eagle hoisted in its place. Companies of infantry began to file into the square, a monotony of field grey except for the red regimental numbers painted on the front of their helmet covers. They were so close they could hear their new leather boots and the harness of the officers' horses creaking.

Then a car with trunks strapped on behind honked its way through, carrying two monocled staff officers, and orderlies holding drawn pistols. More Germans followed, in good order and at an odd slow pace, marching up the street, staring at the closed shutters and the wreckage their own guns had caused.

They were singing – '*Lieb Vaterland magst ruhig sein, Fest steht und teu die Wacht am Rhein*—' and the voices came steadily to the beat of their feet in the hoarse confident words that Kelly had last heard in Kiel. By this time the square was becoming choked with vehicles and soldiers. As fast as it emptied on one side it was refilled from the other, and an orderly stood by a statue, holding four horses, his mouth open, bored and apathetic, and it occurred to Kelly that only a man sure of victory could look like that. A group of cyclists were erecting telephone wires across the end of the road and more men were tossing sandbags from the windows of a hotel, where they'd been jammed in the hope of a last stand. They were plumping into the street in clouds of dust, and nearby a soldier was setting up tables outside a cafe and German officers were already taking seats and calling for someone to bring them coffee.

'I suspect it's time we weren't here,' Kelly muttered, and they moved through the shabby little house, looking for a way out.

Forcing open a back door into a small yard containing a mangle and a tin bath, they climbed the wall into a set of allotments, and, reaching the road, began to run. Back at the warehouse, they found the sound of the Germans arriving had wakened sleeping men who were sitting up in ones and twos and reaching for rifles. Kelly gestured to them to remain where they were and the Marine sergeant went round them, pressing the over-eager back to the floor.

All night they remained hidden in the warehouse. From time to time groups of refugees struggled across the square, all heading west, and the rumble of artillery went on all next day. Occasionally it grew louder in a deep drub-drub of guns, an incessant wavering tumult of steel and explosive, on the outskirts of the city. Occasionally, they saw Germans, one group of whom halted at the far side of the square, pulling up with a whine of limber joints and axles and the shudder of wheels on the road. As the jostling of the trucks ceased, it left a curious silence, in which the distant rumble seemed louder than the men and the stamping horses and the creak and jingle of harness. Field kitchens arrived to cook a meal, the smell drifting into the warehouse to set the hungry Britons licking their lips.

'I could eat a mangy pup,' Rumbelo said wistfully.

As dusk came once more, Rumbelo and Kelly set off again to the waterside. A last sword-cut of yellow light silhouetted the buildings and the columns of smoke climbing up over the stricken city. There was no sign of resistance now but also no sign of the Germans in great strength. It was clear time was running short, however, because eventually German naval forces would arrive to take over the port. Together they climbed on to several deserted ships, but it was all too obvious that the naval officer the Marine sergeant had told them about had been aboard, with his engineers and his Boy Scout, and their cylinders hung in split and shining wreckage.

'Can't we rig a sail or something, sir?' Rumbelo asked. 'Or pinch a ship's boat?'

'As a last resort. But I'm responsible for about a hundred and fifty men now and I want something bigger than that.'

They decided to separate and meet back at the warehouse. The streets were dark when Kelly returned and, as the eyes all swung to him as he slipped through the door, he shook his head silently.

Rumbelo hadn't returned and Kelly waited impatiently, wondering what had happened to him. Nobody had any cigarettes left now and they were all hungry, dirty and tired. By the time Rumbelo had been gone for an hour, Kelly began to wonder if he'd lost his way, and when another hour passed he began to worry that he'd been caught by a splinter from one of the shells the Germans were dropping into the city and was lying wounded in a doorway somewhere. He was just about to set off to find him when Rumbelo appeared, his eyes excited.

'Sir, I've found a fishing boat! One of them wooden jobs! Like a Lowestoft trawler, only much bigger with an engine. She was full of soldiers but they've gone into the town. There's only a couple of sailors and perhaps a couple of soldiers left with her. We ought to be able to take her over. She's only a few streets away.'

Kelly nodded. 'Right, Rumbelo Let's see what we can do. Let's have that stoker off the pinnace.' He turned to the Marine sergeant. 'I want half a dozen men you can rely on. And, for God's sake, see that everybody's kept awake so that as soon as you hear from us you can get 'em moving. Quick!'

'Right, sir. Think we're going to make it home?'

'We're going to have a bloody good try,' Kelly said. 'Being taken prisoner's a rotten way to start a war.'

Followed by Rumbelo with his half-dozen men armed with rifles, they crept out close to the walls. The streets were silent with the silence of death, though they could still hear the cracking of shells in the distance.

Occasionally, they came across the bodies of Belgian soldiers lying in the road covered with greatcoats, capes or ground-sheets, their limbs decently composed, their great boots sticking up in ungainly fashion, and once two men sitting by a wall, killed by blast, a startled look on their darkening faces.

Rumbelo pointed, 'Down the next alley, sir.'

At the end of the alley, there was a wharf made of sleepers and alongside it a wooden trawler. It carried German markings and had obviously been sailed round from the Ems. There were two German soldiers in spiked helmets covered with canvas on the quayside, their backs to the town.

'I can get one, sir,' Rumbelo said, 'if you can get the other.' He unshipped the bayonet on the rifle he carried and signed to Kelly to do the same. 'One 'and over his mouth, sir, and in with it. Think you can do it?'

'Yes.'

'I hope to God you can, sir.'

Kelly didn't understand what he meant but, as Rumbelo gave the word and they ran out quietly, he clapped a hand over the German's mouth and lifted the bayonet – only to find he couldn't use it.

'In with it, sir!' Rumbelo hissed and Kelly saw that Rumbelo's victim was already stretched on the floor, writhing.

Swallowing, he thrust the bayonet home between the German's ribs and felt the resistance as it penetrated flesh, then the German stopped struggling and slid through his hands to the ground. In the light of the flames, Kelly saw he was only a boy, no more than eighteen or so, with staring blue eyes and a mouth that opened and shut like a goldfish out of water.

Sickened, he turned aside to vomit, and Rumbelo's hand came down on his shoulder like a swinging girder. 'Better him than you, sir,' he said.

As Kelly pulled himself together, Rumbelo watched with approval. He'd been brought up in a much harder school than Dartmouth but he could recognise courage when he saw it. In his time, he'd met plenty of officers and the best of them were invariably those with the tradition of service in their blood. They were often bastards, but they knew where their duty lay.

'Better get a move on, sir,' he murmured.

'Yes.' With streaming eyes, his stomach still heaving, Kelly waved to the other men and indicated the trawler. 'Spread out.

No shooting. We don't want to raise an alarm. And let's have the stoker closed up.'

Jumping aboard, almost at once they came face to face with a German sailor who appeared abruptly through a hatch. He was grinning, as though someone had been talking to him, and the smile was wiped off his face at once as he saw the British sailors. Then Kelly's rifle came round and, as the butt cracked against his head, he slid back down the ladder.

'After him, quick,' Kelly snapped, jumping through the hatch. At the bottom of the ladder, he saw another German sailor snatching something from a bunk and, as he saw a gleaming knife, he decided that it was his turn to feel what cold steel was like. But Rumbelo's rifle roared through the hatch and the German fell back, his chest covered with blood.

'Sorry about that, sir,' Rumbelo apologised. 'Didn't have time for nothing else. Nobody would probably hear it in here, though.'

'That's all right, Rumbelo,' Kelly said. 'I think you've just saved my life.'

'Makes us all square, sir.'

A third German was found in the galley and, with the unconscious man Kelly had hit with his rifle, he was pushed into the hold, and three British sailors crammed the German caps with their fluttering ribbons on to their heads.

'Send a man to those chaps on the quay,' Kelly said. 'Cut off their shoulder tags and collar numerals and search 'em for papers. They'll probably help Intelligence. And let's have someone off to the sergeant to bring down his men.'

Watching in the tension, listening to the stoker below deck cursing the unfamiliar engines and the crack of shells dropping two or three streets away, Kelly tried hard to remain calm. Rumbelo appeared, carrying a spiked *pickelhaube*, a fistful of shoulder tags and papers, and two German tunics, He was wearing another spiked helmet on his bullet head.

'Looks like a tit on a mountain,' Kelly said.

Rumbelo handed him the second helmet. 'Better put that on, sir,' he suggested. 'As we're going out, we might meet some more coming in.'

A few minutes later, the straggling column of exhausted men appeared round the corner, moving in little limping rushes, the man with the union jack at their head. Then the stoker appeared from the shadows. 'She's got a head of steam up, sir,' he reported. 'I'll be waiting for the telegraphs.'

They crammed the exhausted soldiers and sailors aboard. They didn't want to go below, preferring to meet danger with their heads above the deck, but Kelly insisted and they got them all into the hold in the end, except for a few whom he made lie down on the deck. 'If anybody sticks his head up until I tell him,' he said, 'I'll hit him with a marlin spike.'

Going to the tiny wheelhouse, he set one of *Norseman's* seamen on the wheel and leaned from the window.

'Let go aft.'

'All gone aft, sir.'

'Right. Slow ahead.'

As the little wooden trawler began to move forward, they saw half a dozen more small vessels of the same type heading towards them. Kelly saw the helmsman's face grow taut.

'Here come their pals, Rumbelo,' he said. 'Keep well away from 'em, helmsman. Make those helmets and caps conspicuous, Rumbelo.'

But Rumbelo had already seen the trawlers and was struggling into a German tunic dragged off one of the dead men. A moment later he handed the second through the wheelhouse window to Kelly.

'If anybody lifts his head, don't hesitate.'

'God 'elp 'em if they try, sir.'

As the approaching trawlers drew nearer, a man on the first one shouted across the water.

'*Hoch der Kaiser!*' Kelly yelled back, the only German he had ever picked up in Kiel. '*Guten abend, meine fräulein. Auf Wiedersehen.*'

Rumbelo shouted a few '*hochs*' and the Germans in the two trawlers waved as they passed, heading for the wharf.

'Right, Rumbelo,' Kelly said. 'Here we go! Full speed ahead! Slip down and see if everything's all right with the engine room.'

Rumbelo came back a little later, grinning. 'Everything's fine aft, sir,' he said. 'We've also found some food and fags. I think these chaps were bringing rations for their advanced elements. I've got some of the lads opening tins of sausages. When can they come up on deck?'

'When we've cleared Antwerp and not before. And pass the word for that union jack. Let's have it at the masthead in case one of our own ships decides to try a pot shot at us.'

Two hours later they were at the mouth of the Scheldt. The compass didn't seem to be working and Kelly eyed the sun and set a course west. He ought to strike England somewhere, he decided.

Almost immediately they went aground on a sandbank.

Despite all their efforts, they remained wedged on the mud for all of six hours. They were lifted off by the tide in the early hours of the next morning and, starting the engine, chugged off into the North Sea.

'God help us if there's a minefield around here, sir,' Rumbelo said. He eyed the horizon. 'We did all right, I think, sir. How about getting me in your next ship?'

'Not a chance, Rumbelo. I'm for submarines.'

Rumbelo grinned. 'I'm due for submarines myself, sir.'

As they chugged on, they could see the glow of the flames of Antwerp growing dimmer, and by late afternoon they were off the English coast in a thinning mist.

A lightship they saw turned out to be the Sunk so that they realised they were off the Orwell and turned the bows south, chugging towards the river mouth, the exhausted men below still sleeping. As they entered the river, a cruiser carrying a commodore's pennant crossed their bows heading for Harwich.

'*Arethusa*, sir. Tyrwhitt's flagship.'

'Acknowledge them, Rumbelo.'

As the flag Rumbelo had borrowed from the Marines dipped at the masthead, they saw officers on the cruiser's bridge studying them intently, through glasses. There was a flurry of movement as one of them moved to the after end of the bridge, then below him another man ran along the upper deck, and finally the cruiser's flag was dipped in response as she disappeared ahead of them.

Eventually they saw destroyers lying in trots, sleek black shapes in the growing dusk.

'We'll go alongside the outside chap,' Kelly said.

As they approached the outer destroyer, the officer of the watch appeared and waved them away.

'Ignore him, helmsman,' Kelly said. 'A spot of Nelson's blind eye never did the navy any harm. Starboard side to. Have the fenders ready, Rumbelo. Let's do the job in style.'

The trawler passed the destroyer, turned and came back up-tide. Again the officer of the watch waved them away furiously but Kelly continued to ignore him. The destroyer's deck was filling up now with men and everybody's eyes were fixed on the fishing vessel with its German markings. From a buoy further upstream, the cruiser which had passed them was just swinging with the tide and he could see officers on the bridge still watching them with glasses.

Ropes flew through the air. 'Who the blazes are you?' the officer of the watch snarled.

'Lieutenant Maguire sir,' Kelly yelled. 'Late of *Norseman* and before that *Cressy*. Together with *Norseman*'s pinnace party from Antwerp, survivors of the Tenth Royal Marine Light Infantry and the *Hawke* battalion of the Naval Brigade, and two prisoners.'

The officer's jaw hung. 'The devil you are,' he said. 'You'd better come aboard.'

As Kelly stepped on to the destroyer's deck, a midshipman appeared. 'Sir. Message from *Arethusa*. You're to report on board at once. We've called away the cutter.'

Kelly turned to Rumbelo. 'Hold your hat on, Rumbelo,' he said. 'Tonight I'll be setting down "reasons in writing". Let's have those shoulder tags and one of the *pickelhaubes*.'

As he stepped from the cutter to the cruiser's deck, a lieutenant commander was waiting to lead him to the commodore's cabin. Tyrwhitt was a sharp-featured man with a keen bronzed face, strong nose, determined chin and bright eyes shielded by huge eyebrows. There was no sign of ostentation or self-importance about him and his manner was brisk as he stared at Kelly under his shaggy brows.

'That's the first time my flag's ever been acknowledged by a vessel as scruffy as yours,' he said. 'Who are you?'

'Maguire, sir. Lieutenant Maguire. I thought you might like this as a souvenir.' As Kelly produced the German helmet he'd brought, Tyrwhitt's mouth widened in a smile.

'Where the hell did you get that, you young puppy?'

'Antwerp, sir. I took it off a German. I don't think he had any further need of it. We have two prisoners as well.'

Tyrwhitt gestured at a chair. 'Well, rest your legs, dammit, and tell me all about it, and let's have a drink while we're at it. What about Antwerp?'

'It's gone, sir. We saw the Germans arrive.'

'Well, that's that. Winston hoped to hold it because the Germans couldn't have advanced along the coast without it. However—' Tyrwhitt smiled and Kelly was aware of charm and kindliness beneath the rugged exterior '—that's not for you to worry about. I expect you'll be wanting to get some sleep and then back to your ship.'

Kelly swallowed. 'Sir. I haven't got a ship,' he said. 'I was in *Cressy*, and I'm a bit overdue for survivor's leave.'

Part Two

One

A thin drizzle was wetting the pavements as Kelly's taxi headed for the station. He was feeling on top of the world, certain by this time that he couldn't ever be killed and with a bit of luck not even wounded.

Despite his tiredness, he felt ready for anything, even a bit of a rakehell. This time, he decided, he might try to get Charley in a corner at the back of the house. Then he drew a deep breath, almost a steadying breath. Charley still wasn't that old and he'd have to watch his step or he'd be making a fool of himself and trouble for them both.

He sat up straighter in his seat. Through the rain that was smearing the windscreen, he saw a sailor trudging towards the station. He recognised him by his bulk as Rumbelo and stopped the taxi.

'Fancy a lift, Rumbelo?'

Rumbelo grinned and spat the rain from his lips. His blue serge was saturated.

'No overcoat?'

'Haven't got one, sir. It's in *Norseman*.'

'Did you get leave? I suggested under the circumstances that you ought to.'

'Yes, sir. They gave me leaf.' Rumbelo settled himself in the taxi, smelling of wet wool, and they spoke as old friends and shipmates separated only by rank.

'Where are you going?' Kelly asked.

'London.'

'Family?'

'Lor' bless you, no, sir. I ain't got any family. I'm an orphanage entrant.'

'Oh! What will you do then?'

'Hang about the pubs, sir.'

It seemed a desperately sad way for Rumbelo to spend his leave.

'Haven't you any brothers or sisters?'

Rumbelo smiled. 'Had a brother, sir. But my old man was a sailor, too, so there might be one or two others about as well.'

He seemed remarkably cheerful and his very cheerfulness depressed Kelly.

'You'll be seeing friends, I suppose.'

'Ain't got none, sir. Least, not ashore. My friends are in the ship I'm in. The ship's me home, see.'

'No girlfriend?'

'One in every port. Nothing regular, though.'

'Pity.' An idea struck Kelly. 'You any good with horses, Rumbelo?'

Rumbelo smiled, unperturbed, the typical seaman. 'Used to be a stable boy, sir. After I left the orphanage. Two years at it, and six months as a hotel porter before I joined the navy.'

'We've got horses, Rumbelo. At least, my mother has. I always fall off 'em myself.'

Rumbelo turned, his eyes shrewd. 'You don't have to be sympathetic, sir,' he said. 'I'll manage. I've managed before.'

'It's not that. It seems so rotten a chap like you having nowhere to go. After all, you did save my life there in Antwerp.'

'Just wiping off a debt, sir. You saved mine at Spithead a few years back, I seem to remember.'

'My mother might be glad of someone who's good with horses. She's potty about them. How about coming home with me? There are stables and I know there's a room for the groom.'

Rumbelo eyed him with a gentle expression. 'That's kind of you, sir,' he said, 'but I don't know.'

'I'm not offering charity, Rumbelo. It just seems rotten that a seaman under my command should have nowhere to go for his leave. Or perhaps you don't like being in the country?'

'I like the country, sir. But where can a sailor doss down in the country? London's different. Plenty of soldiers' and sailors' clubs. The Salvation Army looks after you, sir.'

'I think you'd better come home with me, Rumbelo,' Kelly said quietly. 'My mother will probably fall on your neck, especially if you can handle a pony and trap.'

Rumbelo seemed to be having difficulty speaking. 'Look, sir—'

'Forget it, Rumbelo. It's decided. After all, if we're going to serve in submarines together—'

'Are we, sir?'

'I thought you'd decided we were.'

Rumbelo grinned. 'I didn't know *you* 'ad, sir.'

There was a strange silence about the house when they arrived. Bridget, the little maid from Ireland, opened the door but instead of the wide, pink-faced grin with which she usually greeted Kelly, there was only a sniffle and a flash of red-rimmed eyes.

'Bridget, what's wrong?'

'You better see your mother, Master Kelly. She'll tell you.'

Alarmed, Kelly looked at Rumbelo, who was waiting quietly behind him. 'Just hang on, Rumbelo,' he said. 'Something's up. Bridget, this is Able Seaman Rumbelo. Take him to the kitchen and see he gets something to eat. I'll collect him later.'

His mother was sitting silently in the drawing room with the curtains drawn. She looked up as he entered but said nothing.

'Mother, what's happened? Is it Father?' With his own recent experience in *Cressy*, the first thing that occurred to Kelly was that his father had been sent to sea at last and torpedoed.

She said nothing but handed him a telegram. 'The War Office regrets to inform you—'

'Gerald!'

His mother nodded.

'Oh, Lord, no!' The news came as a shock. Kelly had already seen many men die, but he had never from the first day of the war been able to imagine himself dying; and it had somehow always been an even stronger conviction that it could never happen to Gerald. Gerald was like his father, stolid, unhurried, correct, never providing surprises but certainly never in trouble.

Kelly frowned, guiltily aware that, despite the initial shock, he felt remarkably little pain. Somehow, he felt, he ought to have a greater sense of loss than he did, a greater consciousness of hurt. But there was surprisingly little because, since his first day at Dartmouth, Gerald's leaves from the army had never seemed to coincide with his own and they'd grown up almost as strangers.

Troubled that his emotions weren't deeper than they were, he tried to find out more without causing his mother extra anguish.

'Where, Mother?'

'Somewhere called the Aisne. Where's that, Kelly? Your Uncle Paddy's there as well. At his age, too!'

'It's a river in France, Mother.'

His mother sighed. 'Somehow,' she said slowly, 'I always thought it would be you.' She drew a deep breath and Kelly watched her, living every moment of misery with her but bitterly recognising that he was unable to feel the same.

'The Upfolds sent a message,' she went on. 'The general's dead, too.'

'Brigadier Upfold?'

'They made him a major-general. To take the place of someone who became ill. They thought it was a nice safe job but it seems a shell hit his headquarters and there were quite a lot of them killed.'

Up to that moment Kelly's war had been almost too swiftly-moving for him to be able properly to absorb the tragedy of it. There had been no time to dwell on anything as he had been snatched from *Clarendon* to *Cressy*, from *Cressy* to *Malice*, and *Malice* to *Norseman*, and then on to Antwerp. He'd barely had time to assimilate the fact that he'd been in danger, and, so far, there'd even been a strong farcical element about it all.

He looked at his mother, his heart filled with compassion for her. Since he'd grown to manhood, he'd realised just what she'd had to endure in the manner of lies and disinterest from his father. Yet she'd never made any comment on her situation, trying to show loyalty and interest in her husband's career, sympathy in his retirement and encouragement in his re-employment. It was only now that Kelly realised just how much of it was based on pretence and how much of it was done for her children.

His mother spoke. 'Mabel's friend, that young man in the dragoons, was killed, too. Somewhere near this place, Mons, everybody's talking about.'

Her hand waved vaguely at the newspaper and Kelly could see the casualty lists, solid columns of type running the whole length of the sheet. They seemed almost too long to be believable.

'The Upfolds have rented a place about two miles away,' she went on. 'They thought it would be nice for your father and the general to be close. Now – well—' her voice died away.

'How is Father?'

She looked at him wearily. Her life had not been a satisfying one. Indeed, she had never really been able to understand how she had come to be married to Admiral Maguire, and had put all her future in the hands of her sons. Now, with one of them dead and the other a stranger after several years at sea so that he'd grown up differently from the rest of the family, tough-minded, self-reliant and touched with that element of variety all born sailors – in which category she did not include her husband – possessed, she knew that their positions had changed and that she was no longer the dominant one of the two.

'There's a letter on my desk,' she said. 'I gather he might go to the Middle East in some shore job for the Mediterranean Fleet. He's due home on leave. It's such a funny war, isn't it?'

–

Walking in the fields at the back of the house, Kelly pondered the strangeness of life.

With Gerald dead, he was now heir to his father's title. From now on he'd have to try hard not to get killed, because otherwise there'd be no one to take it over. Sir Kelly Maguire. He tried it round his tongue for size and was ashamed to realise he liked it. It would make Verschoyle green with envy if nothing else, but it was a poor way to come to it, having to have Gerald lying buried somewhere beneath the soil of France.

Rumbelo was sitting on the fence at the edge of the paddock, smoking a pipe bound with twine. Kelly could smell the navy twist fifty yards away.

'Hello, Rumbelo,' he said. 'You all right?'

'Yes, sir. Bridget – that is, the girl – showed me where I could sleep.'

'Is it all right?'

'It's fine, sir.'

'Bit spartan, I expect.'

'Better than a dosshouse or the Salvation Army.'

'Yes, I suppose so. I've just heard that my brother's been killed, Rumbelo.'

'Yes, sir. I'm sorry. Bridget told me. My brother was killed with the West Kents.' Rumbelo spoke matter-of-factly. 'Orphanage entrant, like me, but *he* decided for the army. They sent me a telegram to Gib. I hadn't seen him for years.'

'I'm sorry, Rumbelo.'

Kelly tried to change the subject. He had a suspicion that the war was going to go on a long time – at least, Kitchener seemed to think so and from the way it was shaping it looked as though he was going to be right – and they would have to get used to tragedy and personal loss. It seemed to be something it would be unwise to brood on.

Rumbelo seemed to sense his unease. 'If there's anything I can do, sir? Help about the place, for instance. I mean – I shouldn't think your Mum'll be doing much riding while you're home.'

'No, but she'll be using the dog cart. Can you handle one?'

'Done it often, sir.'

Kelly managed a twisted smile. 'Where have you been all this time, Rumbelo? I think we're going to enjoy having you around.'

'I think I'm going to enjoy being around, sir.'

'Yes – well – look, Rumbelo, I ought to go and see our next-door neighbours. Name of Upfold. How about giving it a try? This evening, say? I expect Bridget will be able to tell you where they live.'

'I'll make enquiries, sir.'

'Christ, Rumbelo, you sound like the family butler.'

Rumbelo smiled. 'Don't think that'd suit me much, sir.'

As dusk was falling, the dog cart with Rumbelo at the reins, clad in a pair of Admiral Maguire's flannel trousers and a jacket and an old shirt belonging to Kelly, clattered down the gravel drive and on to the main road.

'Know the way, Rumbelo?'

'I walked it to have a look.'

'My God, Rumbelo, you're efficient.'

'Thought I might just as well be on the safe side, sir. Sorry to hear about your young lady losing her father, sir.'

Kelly's head turned. 'How did you know about my young lady?'

Rumbelo's eyes were on the road. 'Bridget likes to talk, sir.'

'Yes, I suppose she does. I never thought he'd be killed, though. He seemed too old for that sort of thing. Her sister also lost her young man.'

'So I heard, sir.'

'It's a bloody funny war, Rumbelo.'

'I think it's going to get funnier, sir.'

'I think it is. I think we're going to need all the courage we've got before we've finished.'

'A sense of humour helps, I've found, sir. A bit of a laugh goes a long way.'

Charley saw them coming down the drive and was out on the front steps to meet them. She'd had her hair cut short and instead of the woollen stockings Kelly had always seen her in she was wearing silk ones. She smiled, suddenly shy with him, but fresh and clean and calm.

'Hello, Charley. This is Able Seaman Rumbelo. We've just come from Antwerp. He saved my life. I'm going to try to get him into the same ship as me. He hadn't anywhere to go to spend his leave so I brought him home. Everybody has to have somewhere to go.'

Charley smiled at Rumbelo. 'I think if you'd like to tie the pony up,' she said, 'they might be able to find you some beer in the kitchen.'

She was brisk, informative and no-nonsense, but she looked desperately pale, too, and there was a look of shock and a youthful lack of comprehension in her eyes.

'I'm sorry about your father, Charley,' Kelly blurted out.

'Yes. Mother's gone up to town about his estate.' Her eyes moistened and he kicked himself, wondering if he'd been unnecessarily cruel. Then she made a sad little gesture with her shoulders like a shrug, as though trying to ignore it. 'We've got over it a bit now,' she went on with a hard matter-of-factness that he knew was all put on to help her steel herself against what had suddenly become a very brutal and relentless stream of events.

'I'm sorry about Gerald,' she said.

'Yes. Poor Mabel, too!'

Charley sighed, then she seemed to take hold of her emotions, forcing herself to face the fact that their world – that place of warmth, security and stability they'd known as children – had started to fall apart the day the first shot of the war was fired and was vanishing now in a welter of adult unreason and misery. Young as she was, she'd reached the conclusion that all the tears that could ever be shed would never make it the same again.

'Mabel's going to be all right,' she said sharply. 'She's too good-looking and too stupid to be alone for long. He wasn't important to her, anyway. It's sad, isn't it, because he probably went away thinking he was, and probably even died thinking he was helping to prevent the Germans coming here to bully her.'

She sounded remarkably grown-up. 'In any case,' she ended, 'there's another one here already.'

'There is?'

'Yes. He came in a Morris runabout. He's naval. One of your lot this time. In fact, he told me a horrible story about you. He knows you. He said you were last seen in Antwerp rushing to the Dutch frontier to get yourself interned.'

'Verschoyle!'

'That's right! James Verschoyle. Do you know him?'

'I've always known him. What's he doing here?'

'He lives here. He always did.'

Kelly's face flushed with rage. 'Charley, I didn't go rushing to get myself interned in Holland! The pinnace I took ashore was blown up. Rumbelo and I and a few more brought back a hundred and fifty men.'

She didn't seem surprised. 'I know.'

'You knew?'

'I knew you wouldn't run away.'

'You did? How?'

'I don't know. I just did.'

'Go on. I'm no hero.'

'Well, you're different from James Verschoyle, that's true. He's the sort who does things in style. You're the sort who'll just keep on keeping on and I think before it's finished that's probably what we'll need. We'll all be in it eventually. I'm going to get a job working a typewriting machine.'

'But you're only a kid!'

'I shan't be much longer.'

Kelly looked round. Rumbelo had disappeared with the dog cart round the back of the house and he leaned over and kissed her gently on the cheek. She drew back from him, startled but obviously pleased, her cheeks growing pink.

'Now let's go and see this bastard who's with Mabel,' he said.

–

Verschoyle was startled to see Kelly, to say the least. Mabel Upfold was sitting at the piano and he was standing alongside her, languid and elegant as ever, turning the sheets of music over.

'Hello, young Maguire,' he said, recovering his poise quickly and moving forward. 'I thought you'd got yourself captured in Antwerp.'

Conscious of Mabel watching them from across the room, Kelly managed a death's head grin to her as he pretended friendship. 'I expect you did,' he said loudly. Then he lowered his voice to a whisper. 'And thanks for suggesting I bolted for Holland to get myself interned,' he added. 'I think you're a shit, Verschoyle.'

Charley had joined Mabel by the piano and they were waiting for the muttering by the door to come to an end. Verschoyle glanced at them, duplicating Kelly's fixed smile. Then he turned back to Kelly. The suspicions he'd had in *Norseman* that he'd grown harder and more dangerous had been amply confirmed, but his attitude to Kelly had been fixed over the years and he was unable to apologise or retreat. 'A few more words like that, young Maguire,' he murmured 'and I shall be obliged to punch your nose.'

'Any time you like.'

Verschoyle frowned. He had no real wish to indulge in fisticuffs. Standing in shorts and vest and gloves in the ring before the admiral and the rest of the fleet at a boxing tournament was one thing; brawling was another. He enjoyed the applause he got as a boxer but what lay in front of him now, he suspected, lay in an entirely different category. He had no fear of losing but he had an uneasy feeling that with this dour, dogged, hot-eyed youngster it was going to be a much more bloody affair.

'Not here,' he said quietly. 'Wouldn't be manners.' He turned to direct another beaming smile at the two girls then swung back to Kelly. 'Afterwards. There's a moon.'

'There's also a shrubbery at the end of the drive. I'll be waiting for you.'

Verschoyle smiled at the girls again. 'I picked up a nickname at Gib,' he pointed out. 'For boxing.'

'I heard it. "Cruiser." I'm going to bloody well sink you.'

'Tut, such language.' Verschoyle's smile was growing a little fixed. 'Very well, then. When we leave.' He turned to the two girls, his voice loud and cheerful again. 'How about playing that thing, "Fall In and Follow Me," Charlotte, so we can try a foxtrot or two?'

Charley shook her head, her face stiff and loyal to Kelly. 'If any dancing's being done,' she said. 'I'm dancing myself – with Kelly.'

'Ah!' Verschoyle was quite unperturbed. 'Oh, well, perhaps we can use the gramophone instead.'

The evening passed tensely, with Kelly glaring across the room, Charley, aware of his dislike and troubled alongside him, watching him carefully. Unaware of the boiling hatred, Mabel stayed by the piano. They were both making a great effort to be brave and Kelly held on to his temper for their sake. Feeling that circumstances precluded anything lighter than classics, Mabel stuck to Chopin and it was Charley, heavy-handed and indifferent as a pianist, who went determinedly for ragtime.

'Somebody's got to behave as though nothing's happened,' she said. 'The world's got to go on, in spite of Father.'

Kelly stared at her determined young face with admiration and she managed a quick smile.

'I play like the field coming up to the first fence at a point-to-point,' she said.

But at least she played with verve and the evening proved just bearable. As Kelly left, Verschoyle was still saying goodbye to Mabel. Charley saw Kelly to the door.

'What are you up to?' she demanded.

'Nothing.'

'Yes, you are. I've seen it all night. You're seething.'

'Well, wouldn't you be seething after what Verschoyle said? I didn't run away.'

'Of course you didn't. I know that. But setting about Verschoyle won't prove a thing.'

'Who says I'm setting about him?'

'Nobody, but I know you're going to.'

'How, for God's sake?'

'I just know you, that's all.' Charley looked at him sadly. 'Why do boys always want to fight?' she said. 'Isn't there enough pain in the world?'

Kelly stared at her unhappily. 'It's got to be done, Charley,' he said doggedly. 'If only to stop him spreading the story around. I've got a reputation and a career to think of. I'm sorry it's got to be done now, but leaving it and doing it later would be damn silly. If I could I'd sue the swine, but I can't afford that and wouldn't know how to, anyway, and besides he's got more money than I have and he'd get some rotten expensive lawyer to prove he was right, and then I'd be right back where I started – only worse.'

'What are you going to do?'

'I don't know. I'm still thinking.'

He kissed her good night with the gentleness of an excited prizefighter about to begin a sparring match, and left her to look for Rumbelo.

140

Rumbelo studied him shrewdly. 'Something up, sir?'

'Yes, Rumbelo. I've arranged to fight Lieutenant Verschoyle.'

Rumbelo stared at him for a moment. 'You've picked the wrong bloody man this time, sir, if you'll excuse me saying so.'

'No, I haven't, Rumbelo!'

'That one's a boxer, sir. And he's tall. He'll make mincemeat of you.'

'No, he won't! I've wanted to punch him on his bloody handsome nose ever since I first met him at Dartmouth, and even if he knocks me out, I'm going to put my mark on him.'

Rumbelo was silent for a moment. 'I saw him finish off Stoker Harben at Gibraltar, sir. And Stoker Harben—'

'—looks like the Hunchback of Notre Dame.'

Rumbelo's eyebrows rose. 'Does he, sir? I wouldn't know. I've never met him.'

'What am I going to do, Rumbelo? I've got to do something.'

Rumbelo considered for a moment. 'Well, sir, I told you I was an orphanage entrant and when I was a little nipper I was very small—'

Kelly gave an impulsive grin. 'I don't believe you. I bet you were born six feet six and built like a brewer's dray.'

Rumbelo grinned back. 'No, sir, it's true. And one of the first things I learned was that "Thrice blessed be he what gets his blow in fust".'

'Might not work with Mr Verschoyle.'

'It might, sir,' Rumbelo said, unperturbed. 'Mind you, this is none of my affair. Officers aren't supposed to have words in front of the lower deck, let alone using their dukes.'

'Something's got to be done, Rumbelo, ain't it?'

'All right, sir, how about this? I've seen Mr Verschoyle in action. He'll box. So don't let him.'

'How do I stop him?'

'Well, I've been in one or two rough-houses. Dockside pubs and that. I learned a thing or two. Get your blow in first. Tap his claret. Never mind this straight left to the jaw tripe. A set of fives on his hooter's much better. It'll bleed and spoil his shirt. It'll also stop him breathing and, if you hit him hard enough, he'll think it's broke and he's the sort to start worrying about his looks. Above all, it'll make his eyes run and then he won't be able to see you.'

Kelly grinned. 'Go on, Rumbelo. I don't think all this comes under *King's Regulations and Admiralty Instructions* but we'll forget that for the moment. Just now, you're the family groom giving advice to the young master.'

Rumbelo grinned back. 'Right, sir. So get in a couple of good ones on his conk and you've won. If you can manage to butt him on it accidentally on purpose so much the better. And once you've got him on the run, don't let him get his breath back. Just keep on hitting him.'

'You mean when he's down?'

'Up, down, anywhere,' Rumbelo paused. 'Well, if it's a pub rough-house you do, but it'd mebbe get round the Fleet, so perhaps you'd better fight fair. Or fairly fair, anyway. Just keep hitting him instead. Just don't give him a chance to come back at you. Keep him back-pedalling all the time. I reckon you're as strong as he is. Just a bit shorter in the arm.'

'A bit weaker in the head, too, I think. All right, Rumbelo. I'll do as you suggest. And thanks for the tip. And Rumbelo, you'd better buzz off. If you're seen, it'll be bad.'

'Aye aye, sir.'

'And not a word either.'

'Not a peep, sir.'

–

There was no sign of Rumbelo when Verschoyle's runabout came clattering down the drive. Kelly stepped in front of it and it slid to a halt with locked wheels, scoring the gravel.

Verschoyle beamed. 'You're determined to make an ass of yourself, aren't you, young Maguire?'

'Yes. And don't call me "young Maguire". You're a liar and a swine and probably too yellow to get out of the car and fight.'

Verschoyle sighed. 'Well, that's one way of making me,' he said. 'One isn't called a liar and a rotter and a coward often in the same sentence.' He switched off the engine and lifted a long leg over the door. 'Where do you fancy?'

'Among the trees here.'

'I hope you know what you're doing.'

'I know all right.'

'How about that groom of yours? I saw one round the kitchen when I was saying goodbye. I don't want him jumping on me and holding my hands behind me so you can hit me.'

The suggestion made Kelly see red and he forced himself to be calm. Rumbelo's words were still in his ears: 'Don't let him get your rag out, sir. He'll try. He'll try to make you mad so you'll do something daft. Don't let him.'

Icily, he said, 'He's been sent on. There's only me and you.'

Rumbelo, he guessed, was hiding in the bushes somewhere for a grandstand view.

Verschoyle began to unbutton his jacket. 'Oh, very well then.' He sounded thoroughly bored. 'But let's get this straight.' His smile had vanished and his eyes were hard in the moonlight. 'When people call me a liar and a coward, they must expect what's coming to them.'

'I'm ready.'

'I hope you are.'

Verschoyle dropped his jacket to the grass. Kelly struggled out of his own jacket, fighting to contain his boiling temper. Verschoyle's very calmness was acting as a goad.

'Right?'

'Right.'

Verschoyle straightened up, left foot and left arm forward, fight arm well back; right hand below his chin.

'You can always back out,' he said.

'Not bloody likely.'

143

'Very well, here goes.'

Verschoyle's left jerked out and Kelly was immediately aware of tears in his eyes and a very painful mouth. Vaguely he heard a voice that sounded like Rumbelo's murmur 'Oh, Christ!' somewhere in the shadows, then he forced himself to gather his senses and hold his temper in check. He knew exactly what he intended. He hadn't a cat in hell's chance of standing up to Verschoyle in a proper contest. His only hope was to make one of Rumbelo's rough-houses of it.

He backed off, while Verschoyle stood watching, a smile on his lips. He was still smiling when Kelly rushed at him.

Verschoyle hadn't been expecting such sudden or such early aggression. His reputation usually went before him and most people he met in the ring sparred carefully round him a few times to see what he was going to do. This time, however, the whole weight of Kelly's body hit him in the chest and sent him staggering backwards, his arms flailing as he struggled to keep his balance. While he was still wondering what had happened, he was aware of a sharp pain between the eyes and found himself lying on his back, staring at the sky. He put a hand up cautiously and realised his nose was bleeding.

'I think it's broken,' Kelly said cheerfully.

'Oh, Christ, no! Not that, you little bastard!'

As Verschoyle scrambled to his feet and pushed out his left arm again, he was bowled over once more by another violent rush and another heavy blow on his nose. His shirt was spattered with blood, and for a change this time, it was Verschoyle who lost his temper.

Rushing forward in a fury, he swung wildly, missed and tripped over Kelly's leg as he ducked aside. As he scrambled to his feet again, a clout at the side of the head sent him reeling, then another closed his left eye.

'You little bastard,' he snarled. 'That was cheating!'

'Well, it ain't the Marquess of Queensberry rules,' Kelly panted. 'But you've never known the meaning of fair play, anyway.'

Another clout sent Verschoyle reeling and, as he staggered back, a bunch of knuckles caught him in the mouth, splitting his lip and loosening a tooth. While he was still dizzy, a whole flurry of blows caught him about the head and he fell on one knee, aware suddenly that this was one fight he wasn't going to win. As he straightened up again, the madman opposite rushed at him and he went down once more.

Again he struggled to his feet but Kelly was showing no mercy. Rumbelo had stressed very firmly that he hadn't to let Verschoyle get his breath and as soon as he was on his feet and upright again, he flung himself at him, fists whirling. The fight had lasted no more than three minutes when Verschoyle found himself sprawled on the grass, his head in a bush, feebly waving a hand.

'All right,' he panted. 'All right. Pax, you rotten little swine! You didn't give me a chance.'

Kelly stared down at him, startled by the swiftness and completeness of his victory and knowing that Verschoyle's bullying was finished for ever. 'I'll never give you a chance, Verschoyle,' he grated. 'Remember that. Never. Just keep clear of me or I'll do it again. Somehow. Understood?'

Versehoyle's hand waved gently and, picking up his jacket, Kelly flung it at him, then, snatching up his own, he marched out of the gate and set off for home.

Two

When Admiral Maguire arrived home the next day, his wife's father was with him. Kelly hadn't seen his grandfather since the beginning of the war and the old man had aged. But the Irish fire was still there and he'd arrived in England to demand a job from the War Office.

'You're far too old, Father,' the admiral was telling him.

'Stuff!' The old man snorted. 'And nonsense! If they'll take a fool like you, surely to God they'll take me.'

As the door slammed behind him, the admiral looked at Kelly, uncertain whether to be irritated by the behaviour of his father-in-law, grieved by the death of his elder son or cheered by the growing reputation of his younger. 'Tyrwhitt called on me,' he said. 'Told me he's putting you in for a DSC. Good God, boy, you'll soon have more ribbons up than I have. By the way, what happened to your lip?'

'Walked into a wardrobe door, Father,' Kelly said.

'And who's the chap with the dog cart who met me at the station? He has the cut of a jolly jack.'

'He *is* a jolly jack, sir. Able Seaman Rumbelo. He saved my life in Antwerp. I'm going to see he gets something. He was splendid. He had nowhere to go for his leave and he understands horses, so I said he could come here. He's sleeping in the room over the stables. He helps Biddy with the ironing. Sailors make wonderful wives and mothers, I'm told.'

The admiral frowned. 'Damned rotten about Gerald,' he said.

'Yes, Father, it is.'

'Doing so damned well, too. Pushed up to captain. So many officers knocked out. Never thought Gerald would be. Such a quiet efficient chap. Never in trouble. Not like you.'

The admiral poured himself a stiff gin and downed it almost without thinking and without suggesting Kelly should join him. 'It's knocked your mother over, boy,' he went on. 'Especially with me heading for the Middle East. One thing I'll do, though, before I go, and that's see you get a good appointment – Scapa or Rosyth, in one of the battleships.'

Kelly shook his head. 'I don't think I want to go into a battleship, Father,' he said.

The admiral's eyebrows rose. 'Don't want a battleship? Good God, boy, that's where the excitement'll be.'

'I've seen quite a bit of that already, Father.'

'I mean when the Germans come out. We're still waiting for the fleet action.'

'Perhaps there won't be a fleet action, Father. Perhaps Fisher was wrong to plan for a big gun duel. Perhaps there'll be nothing except squadron skirmishes like Heligoland and, anyway, I'm due for submarines.'

The admiral gestured irritably. 'Nobody ever reached flag rank from submarines, boy.'

'We haven't had 'em very long, Father. One day somebody will.'

'I could get you into *Iron Duke*. Jellicoe himself would have an eye on you.'

Kelly's voice became dogged. 'It's not for me, Father.'

'For God's sake, boy!' The admiral's plump hand flapped peevishly. 'You're just wasting your time in those tin-fish things!'

Kelly found he was losing his temper. 'Tin fish be blowed, sir,' he snorted. 'One could sink *Iron Duke* without blinking an eyelid. Just pop up every now and then to get a sighting and let go while Jellicoe's flag captain was seeing defaulters on the quarterdeck.'

'Submarines are defensive weapons!'

'Father!' Kelly's voice broke in his earnest rage. 'Not very long ago I saw three twelve-thousand-ton armoured cruisers torpedoed and sunk in less than an hour with the loss of nearly two thousand men! Anything that can do that is damned o-ffensive!'

–

When Rumbelo drove Kelly over to the Upfolds that evening, he was very thoughtful. The war had already proved that there'd been a lot of wrong thinking in the past few decades and that great battle between the rival fleets for which the whole country had been waiting ever since August – what the lower deck called 'The Big Smash' – might never occur. Faced with the Grand Fleet at Scapa, it seemed obvious that the policy of the Germans would be one of hit and run, catching isolated units whenever possible but avoiding any great action as if it were the plague.

As they rolled up the drive Charley was waiting, wearing an old-fashioned look.

'Isn't it awful, Kelly?' she said. 'James Verschoyle's had an accident.'

Kelly's face was equally blank. 'Never!'

'Yes. In that car of his. He was due to take Mabel out for a spin but he sent a message round to say he couldn't make it. He skidded and was flung out, he said. He has a black eye and a broken nose.'

'Poor chap,' Kelly said.

She looked hard at him. 'What did you hit him with, Kelly? An iron bar?'

Kelly's face gave nothing away. 'I didn't hit him,' he said.

'Oh, yes, you did! I found the place where you did it, too. That shrubbery near the gate. The grass was all trampled and there was some blood. Mabel said he was a bit of a boxer. Champion of the navy or something.'

Kelly grinned. 'Well, he isn't any longer.'

She smiled back at him. 'Your mother telephoned my mother. She said you're going to get another medal.'

'So Father says.'

'For being at Antwerp?'

'For running in terror to Holland to get myself interned.'

'Don't be a goose! What's next on the agenda?'

'Submarines.'

'Aren't they dangerous?'

'I'm told disasters are of common occurrence.' Kelly was suitably nonchalant. 'But the pioneering stage's finished now. Submariners aren't experimenting any more now.'

'What are they like?'

'A sobersided lot. But sobersides aren't the only ones who'll enter the Kingdom of Heaven, and perhaps I can shake 'em up a bit.'

She blushed and shyly took something in a screwed-up piece of paper from a drawer. 'Kelly, would you wear this? For me?'

'What is it?'

'It's a St Christopher medal. Everybody's giving them to soldiers and sailors. I bought it with my own money.'

She laid the little trinket in his hand, and he was surprisingly touched by the gesture.

'It'll keep you safe.'

'I'm not worried about that.'

'I am. The things you get up to, I think you need it.'

'I'll have a word with Rumbelo. He'll keep an eye on me. I'm going to get him posted to the same boat if I can.'

'That's a good idea,' she said seriously. 'When do you have to go, Kelly?'

'Plenty of time, yet.'

'Phyllis Menzies is giving a dance at the week-end. Will you come?'

'I can't dance for toffee.'

'It doesn't matter. Neither can I.' She looked at him eagerly. 'Will you? Phyllis Menzies will be green with envy. She's potty over a cousin of hers and he's only just joined the army and hasn't got any medals at all. Will you be wearing both yours?'

'I haven't got the second one yet.'

'You couldn't wear one just for the night, could you?'

'Shouldn't think so. That sort of thing gives rise to what in the navy they generally call tooth-sucking.'

'Well, never mind. I'll *tell* her you're going to get it.' She looked at him gloomily, suddenly worried by his appearance of self-confidence and experience. 'I bet medals are good for getting girls.'

'Not half,' Kelly said cheerfully. 'Fall over themselves. Especially you.'

–

That night Kimister turned up on week-end leave from Harwich. There was talk in London of zeppelin raids and bombs, and his parents had left for a house they owned in North Wales so that he had nowhere to go. Somehow it seemed typical of them and Kelly began to see why Kimister was as he was. He was expecting a posting to a battleship.

'Destroyers aren't my cup of tea,' he said in his self-effacing way.

Come to that, he thought, neither were battleships or cruisers. He'd often wondered, in fact, what he was doing in the navy at all. His parents, unambitious, retiring people themselves, had wanted to be proud of their only son and, in a day and age when the navy represented the top of the social ladder, they had pushed him towards it, never forcefully but nevertheless inevitably.

Kelly was smiling. 'Well,' he said, 'I certainly heard that anyone who can survive a tour in them without going off his rocker or dying of seasickness can take anything.'

Kimister shrugged, wishing he had Kelly's self-assurance. 'Verschoyle got a posting, too,' he said. 'He's gone to *Inflexible*.

I must say Scapa would have been a pleasanter place without him near.'

Verschoyle had been his bête noire since the first day he'd picked on him for blubbing on arrival at Dartmouth and the thought of having him near depressed him.

Kelly tried to cheer him up. 'You'd better come to the dance,' he said. 'I expect they'll be glad of another male, with everything in trousers in the army.'

'Will Charlotte Upfold be there?'

Kimister cheered up at once and Kelly looked quickly at him. 'Why?' he demanded. 'You got a crush on her or something?'

–

The dance was a lively affair of bright-eyed girls and young men in brand-new uniforms. Kelly was still wearing Kimister's second-best and it didn't fit him very well, but at least it made him look like an old campaigner and, with a ribbon on his chest, he wasn't at all averse to the glances of envy that were directed at him.

Kimister's eyes, dark, gentle and sad, were always on Charley and, when the music started, he came to life with a jerk and was quick to grab her and whip her on to the floor. Since she'd taken great care that the story of Kelly's new medal had already gone the rounds, he found himself in great demand among the older people, who had acquired from the newspapers an idea that war at sea was a bit like Henley regatta, except that people occasionally got hurt, and that sailors were a type of merry assassin who enjoyed blowing other men to pieces for sport with their great guns. He finally broke free from them to snatch Charley from Kimister and stumble round the floor with her.

'Told you I was a rotten dancer,' he said.

'No, that's my fault.'

151

In fact, Charley was good enough to feel weightless in his arms and he even felt skilful enough to try a few extra steps that inevitably ended in disaster.

'You have to concentrate,' she said in a fierce whisper as he sorted out his feet.

'Well, stop taking my mind off it. How do you find Kimister? I think he's got a crush on you.'

'He always has had. Ever since I met him at Dartmouth. Poor Kimister.'

'*Poor* Kimister?'

'He's so nice. But there's nothing there, Kelly.'

The words seemed to damn Kimister completely but they were true. There was nothing to Kimister, no backbone, no determination, not even any personality. In a strange way, Kelly realised he was closer in spirit to Verschoyle, in spite of everything. At least Verschoyle had the moral courage to be something – even if it was only a cad.

After the dance, he drove them all to Esher in the dog cart to put Kimister on the last train for London. He was stumblingly shy with Charley as they stood on the platform waiting for the train and, to the forthright Kelly, embarrassingly unassertive as he said goodbye to her.

'Poor old Kimister,' Kelly said as the train drew away.

'Now *you're* at it,' Charley pointed out.

Kelly shrugged. 'Well, the poor cuss is so lacking in go.'

'He needs a girl.'

'Maybe he does,' Kelly agreed. 'But he's not having mine.'

Halfway back to Thakeham, he slipped his free arm round her, and she wilted against him, sighing happily. Nothing in the world could have stopped her being in love with him.

'Won't it seem funny when we're married after knowing each other all these years,' she murmured.

What crossed Kelly's mind was something quite divorced from the romantic notions that were filling Charley's. 'With you army and me navy, we'd have a family of Marines.' She gave him a startled look as she suddenly grasped that the implications of the statement overshadowed her own naive romanticism, then she seemed to accept it quite capably and nodded.

'I expect it'll be all right,' she said.

'It won't be yet, of course,' Kelly said. 'They don't regard you with much favour if you marry before you're thirty.'

'Thirty!' She sat up abruptly. 'But that's lifetimes away!'

'I couldn't afford it before anyway,' Kelly pointed out.

The pony had ambled to a halt and was cropping the grass. Charley chewed over what Kelly had said then she accepted that, too, confident she could handle it. 'Doesn't it seem strange to be talking like this,' she said. 'It's not all that long since you were teaching me how to work ferrets and not long before that hitting me over the head with my own dolls.'

Kelly was suddenly sober. 'Things happen quicker in wartime,' he said.

She nodded agreeably and turned to him in a way that was quite natural and unaffected and reminded him of birthday parties he'd been to before the war when girls in frilly pink frocks had lifted up their faces to him behind the door as they played Postman's Knock. She seemed so young and untouched, he felt almost middle-aged as he kissed her.

She sighed. 'I wondered when you were going to get round to it,' she said.

Three

Without a ship to go to, Kelly had expected his leave to last at least until the New Year but, at the end of October, Jacky Fisher returned unexpectedly to the Admiralty and immediately, it seemed, he noticed that George Kelly Maguire was still kicking his heels in London. With Rumbelo long since departed for HMS *Dolphin*, the submarine school in Portsmouth, a telegram arrived instructing him to report as torpedo instructor to HMS *Defiance*, the torpedo school at Devonport.

Even as he arrived, news broke of another naval disaster off the coast of South America, and a total stranger with a face as long as a fiddle greeted him with the information as he stepped aboard.

'Von Spee caught the South American Squadron off Coronel,' he said. 'Cradock's gone, and we lost *Good Hope* and *Monmouth*. They were Third Fleet ships full of reservists and didn't stand a chance.'

The story was implemented as soon as he reached the wardroom. Caught in thick weather and silhouetted against the evening glow, it seemed that Cradock had remembered the scandal that had followed the escape of *Goeben* and *Breslau* and the still-pending court-martial of the admiral concerned, and had decided that, despite his undergunned, obsolete ships, no one was going to accuse him of hesitancy and had preferred to risk annihilation rather than hazard his reputation. The blame clearly lay with the Admiralty where, despite the time available to send reinforcements, he had been allowed to face a much superior German squadron with old and inadequate ships.

'Seems to me,' Kelly said grimly, 'that the naval staff in London exists chiefly to cut out and arrange foreign newspaper stories in scrap books.'

Added to the escape of *Goeben* and *Breslau* and the disaster on the Broad Fourteens, this new defeat could only shake even further the confidence in the navy. Somewhere, somehow, something was still radically wrong and the newspapers were not backward in their criticisms.

The effect of the battle in Plymouth was pall-like. Utter strangers were stopping each other on the Hoe to ask 'Have you heard?' Coming after the loss of *Aboukir, Hogue* and *Cressy*, this latest disaster was almost too much to bear, and there was a great deal of argument about the value of the Grand Fleet sitting up in Scapa.

The answer came with the arrival of the battle cruisers, *Invincible* and *Inflexible*, from Cromarty. They had been detached from Jellicoe's command and were already in dry dock having their bottoms scraped and painted, while stores for six months' sailing were being trundled aboard before they left to seek out the victorious German squadron and bring them to book.

'Thank God for Jacky Fisher,' Kelly said. 'At least he has the initiative to go after the Germans' guts.'

His view was supported by Verschoyle, whom he met in the bar of the Duke of Cornwall. Despite the fact that the crews of the two great ships were staggering like flies with weariness from the breakneck speed with which they were preparing for sea, Verschoyle seemed entirely untouched and even able to take time off to enjoy himself.

He smiled at Kelly, superior as ever, and after a few preliminary condescending insults, outlined what was happening, aware in his gossipy, cool way of everything that was going on.

'Sturdee's due to take over command,' he said. 'He's been at the Admiralty as chief of war staff concerned with tactical measures and he's been told in no gentle manner by Fisher that, since he made all the plans, he'd better go himself and carry them out.'

'Told you so himself, I suppose,' Kelly said.

Verschoyle gave him a pitying look. 'I never expected to have to put up with you, Maguire.' There was resentment in his tones. Their positions were changing and he was no longer the dominant figure. For years he had bullied Kelly but the world in that direction was no longer his oyster and from now on his movements would have to be more wary and he would have to keep a tighter hold of his tongue. 'At least not so soon after getting rid of you in Antwerp.'

'Or at Thakeham,' Kelly grinned, aware for the first time in his dealings with Verschoyle of self-confidence.

Verschoyle sniffed. He had lost none of his contempt but, Kelly noticed, he was careful not to call him 'Young Maguire'. The tension and the dislike were still there but Verschoyle was sufficient of a naval officer not to let it show too much in public.

'I have a cousin who's engaged to one of the war room staff,' he said coldly. 'Sturdee's been told to sail on November eleventh – and that doesn't mean November twelfth – and that if the ships aren't ready for sea, he's to take the dockyard workers with him. There's quite a bit of alarm and despondency in case he drops 'em off in small boats à la Captain Bligh. For the first time in my experience, somebody's got their skates on. We were sent down here so fast the recall wasn't even sounded round the Cromarty and Inverness pubs and half the crew had to join by rail.'

The following afternoon, black clouds of smoke boiling from their funnels, the two great ships were hauled into the fairway by tugs and began to butt south-westward into the wintry South Atlantic to find Von Spee.

Plymouth was still holding its breath when a signal arrived ordering Kelly to the submarine school for a shortened course, and he was just packing his bags when the electric news flashed through the ship that Von Spee's squadron had been caught and destroyed in its turn with the loss of two armoured and two light cruisers. The victory was celebrated in the wardroom of *Defiance* with a great deal of noise and a tendency to break chairs. Since the British casualties amounted to no more than twenty-five, Kelly assumed that Verschoyle had managed to profit from it.

More news was just beginning to filter through when he reported to *Dolphin*. Sturdee, it seemed, had imperturbably finished his breakfast of porridge and kippers before setting about the Germans in the best nonchalant British style, and Von Spee had gone down in a holocaust of shelling with his flag-ship, *Scharnhorst*, and more than 750 men, before *Invincible* and *Inflexible* had turned their great guns on *Gneisenau* and finally on *Nürnberg* and *Leipzig*. The newspapers were in raptures for days.

—

On a spit of land opposite Portsmouth Naval Harbour, *Dolphin* was a hive of activity and Kelly was given a cursory medical examination by an elderly fleet surgeon who looked like a vet.

'Any trouble with your lungs?' he demanded.

'No, sir.'

'What about when you were sunk in *Cressy*? Swallow any oil?'

'No, sir. None.'

The medical officer frowned, as if disappointed to have found nothing wrong. 'You're not very tall, are you?' he said.

Kelly's eyes glittered. 'I'm not joining the Brigade of Guards, sir.'

The surgeon gave him a sour look and grunted. 'Expect you'll do,' he growled. 'At least you've got plenty of bounce.'

There was still a great deal of euphoria in the air over the victory at the Falklands as the course began, but doubts about the Admiralty and senior officers began once more to creep in as rumour claimed there had been a great deal of luck in it and that Sturdee's well-publicised imperturbability had, in fact, been dilatoriness so that he had very nearly missed his chance. He was even, it was said, being asked why he had allowed just *one* of Von Spee's ships to escape. Jacky Fisher's known viciousness appeared to be in control again and it seemed to be no bad thing either.

The North Sea remained stagnant and still the lower deck's 'big smash' did not come. The German fleet remained beyond the mines in the Jade River, refusing to come out, though there were numerous alarms and excursions when they were reported on their way. Though the winter remained a quiet one, the war seemed to be spreading. Vast battles had been fought in Russia and, with Turkey now in, British and French warships were patrolling the Aegean in the hope of inducing *Goeben* to emerge through the Dardanelles. A few gun duels between warships and Turkish shore batteries found their way into the newspapers and there was a great deal of diplomatic activity to bring the Greeks in, but it was still the vast killing match in France that overwhelmed everyone. In a mere four-month period, the Allies had suffered a million casualties and it suddenly occurred to someone that they were neither advancing nor killing Germans at a greater rate than they were being killed themselves and that it might be a good idea, instead of trying to hammer down the front door, to try to sneak in through the back. A plan was evolved to force the Dardanelles and in March the attempt was made by the British and French Mediterranean Fleets. It produced no great success and three Allied ships were sunk at once and three seriously damaged. Somehow, the war didn't seem to be going too well.

By skilful concealment of his ignorance of some of the more elementary facts about electricity and the internal combustion engine, Kelly passed his examinations without much difficulty and promptly began to wonder if he'd done the right thing. It had been the extra few shillings a day that had first attracted him and then the thought that it might persuade their Lordships of the Admiralty that he didn't want to be posted to a big ship. Experience had already shown him that submarines were dark, cold, damp, oily and cramped, full of intricate machinery, and giving, in the long run, only a small chance of survival.

Then he realised he was letting his fears run away with him. Submarines had seemed much more fragile and rattly than he'd expected, very different from the sleek stream-lined craft he'd imagined. Acquiring knowledge of them had appeared for the most part to be an attempt to understand the confusion of pipes and wires and to keep out of everybody's way while they manoeuvred the training craft. In the end he had mastered most of it, but he recognised that most of what he would eventually know he would learn now that he'd finished his course.

Leaving *Dolphin*, he was ordered to pick up a draft of men from HMS *Vernon*, an old three-decker which lay on the mud at the upper end of Portsmouth harbour and was the home of torpedoes and electrics. As he stepped ashore, Portsmouth looked the same as ever. The top masts of *Victory* could be seen over the square dockyard buildings and the ferry to Gosport could be heard clanking on its chains across the harbour. A train at the nearby harbour station shrieked and there was such an element of normality about it all, it didn't surprise Kelly in the slightest to find Rumbelo grinning at him from the middle of the draft, the ribbon of the DSM on his chest, and when the rear rank started whistling 'Anybody Here Seen Kelly?' he had to grin back.

'Hello, Rumbelo,' he said, as he moved along the line of men. 'You made it then?'

His posting was as navigator to a newly-commissioned submarine, *E19*, which was lying in the submarine base at Parkeston Quay, Harwich. Since the quay formed part of the railway station, there wasn't far to carry their kit, and there was no need to put in a word for Rumbelo because the captain, a long-jawed, black-haired lieutenant-commander called Lyster, had already asked for him. An extraordinary figure in cricket sweater, knickerbockers, tartan socks and black-and-white beach shoes, Lyster introduced Kelly to the first lieutenant, a bearded cynic called Bennett, and stood watching, as though assessing his new officer.

'You given to worrying about superstition, Maguire?' he asked.

Wondering what was coming, Kelly shook his head. 'No, sir.'

Lyster nodded approvingly. 'Keep it that way,' he said. '*E19* was originally numbered *13* and on her trials she suddenly ran amuck and started porpoising all over Gare Loch. We couldn't hold her. Forty seconds to thirty feet and then she was banging her guts out on the bottom and the next minute trying to leap out of the water like a porpoise.'

Bennett grinned. 'Quite a time was had by all,' he said.

'I refused to sign for her,' Lyster went on, 'and she went back to the yard. In the end, it was decided it was her number that was wrong and it was changed to 19. Since then she seems to be all right. You'll find this is a good ship. Including you, we have a crew of forty-two, plus one terrier and two white mice, which the Admiralty allows on the ship's books to give warning of chlorine. Having less altitude, as the Flying Corps says, they die before we do, you see. Unfortunately, the family always seems to increase to six and that's not allowed in the regulations, and doubtless the clerks at the Admiralty are still working out what to do about it. It will be one of your jobs to winnow 'em out if they get beyond that figure.'

He changed the subject abruptly to Rumbelo. 'Noticed he had a DSM,' he said. 'Know anything about him?'

'Yes, sir. I put him in for it. He's an old friend.'

'So much the better,' Lyster said. 'Makes for family feeling. Had leave lately?'

'Before I did my course, sir.'

'Well, you're lucky. You'll be getting some more. We all will. We're due for the Middle East.'

'What's happening in the Middle East, sir?'

'The Dardanelles.'

'I thought that was over. The Turks sank half the Mediterranean Fleet with mines, didn't they?'

Lyster shrugged. 'The army's decided they know more about it than we do and they're going to take over and make a landing. We're being sent out with three other submarines to try to get through the minefields to stop Turkish reinforcements coming across the Sea of Marmara.'

'We'll never do it, sir.'

Lyster smiled. 'We already have,' he said. 'Norman Holbrook did it in *B11*.'

—

There was an odd sort of wariness about *E19*. Even the newcomers to the crew had heard of her strange antics on her trials and it seemed as if they were all waiting for the next example of wild behaviour. The interior of the boat was a mass of intricate machinery that restricted headroom, with a passageway through the middle scaled off, section by section, by bulkheads. There was no space to sling hammocks and the crew slept wherever they could, among the machinery or on the boards of the central passageway which covered the batteries, while the wardroom was nothing more than a curtained compartment smelling of damp and diesel oil, containing a table where the navigating was done – as often as not with one of the machinists working alongside – one bunk, and a single chair where the officer off watch passed what little leisure time he had. Above, so that it was almost impossible to stand upright, was an array of pipes, wheels and dials and the all-important glass face of the depth gauge. It was about as big as a henhouse and just about as comfortable, and at sea they had to live on the 'hot-bunk' principle of rolling into the bed just vacated by the man who'd relieved them. Under way it was impossible to speak without shouting because the rush of air down the shaft of the control tower, the whine of the steering gear and the roar of the engines drowned everything, and the stoker in the engine room even had to hit the steel plates of the deck with a spanner to attract the attention of his artificer.

They carried out working-up exercises in the north Channel but there was no sign of anything untoward until shortly before they were due for leave. Standing on the bridge with Kelly alongside him, Lyster was admiring his black-and-white beach shoes. He was not hard to get on with but was a great chaser of females, a sarcastic, sardonic man who seemed inordinately proud of his strange footwear.

'Bought 'em in Worthing,' he pointed out cheerfully. 'When I was spending a week-end with a girl.'

Through the hatch opening they could hear the heavy diesel engines and the roar of the air they demanded and, below, a voice that sounded like Rumbelo's was cheerfully singing a popular song which, with their destination known, had caught their particular fancy.

> 'Oh, the moon shines bright on Charlie Chaplin,
> His suit wants pressin',
> His shoes want blackin',
> And his little baggy trousers they want mendin'
> Before they send him
> To the Dardanelles...'

There was a lop on the sea and the sky was hidden by low dark-bellied clouds. In the distance the land had lost its tawny hue and was a dark blue-grey, like cooling iron fresh from the furnace. A slash of spray came over and Lyster spat the salt water from his lips and brushed the drops from his leather coat. 'We don't permit ourselves the luxury of ducking, Maguire,' he said severely as Kelly straightened up.

Occupied with thoughts of the Mediterranean, Kelly barely heard him. The war certainly seemed to move him about in great dramatic sweeps, but he was young enough nevertheless to enjoy the prospect. They were all well aware that the submarines were to be risked where the battleships had failed because they were cheap to build and more easily replaced, and if nothing else it would be different from tramping about the cobbled streets of Antwerp and from *Cressy*'s ponderous march across the Broad Fourteens.

The sky seemed to grow darker as the clouds crowded against each other. The water looked black and oily and lifted sluggishly in the wind, and the line of the shore seemed to grow more ominously, menacingly, dark. The song from below had stopped, almost as if the drab colours above the conning tower had penetrated below to the crowded little world of pipes, wheels, and levers and subdued the singer. For a while they progressed at slow speed down-channel testing equipment then, without warning, Lyster called out, 'Prepare for diving manoeuvre! Exercise alarm!'

As they went tumbling down the aluminium ladder to land heavily on the deck plates, the klaxon shrieked throughout the boat and the machinists grabbed the valve handles and swung from them.

'Take her down and steady her at fifty feet,' Lyster said, slamming the hatch, and with a roar, water rushed into the tanks. The submarine dipped so quickly Kelly had to grab for the ladder to stop himself falling.

The dive appeared to be unusually steep and he was watching the depth gauge over Bennett's head when a shout, loud and urgent, brought his head round.

'Outboard air induction valve doesn't close, sir!'

'That's torn it,' someone gasped and Lyster jerked upright.

'She's at it again,' he said and, as the bow sank, a face appeared in the opening of the engine room bulkhead.

'We can't stop the leak, sir! Head valve must be jammed!'

Lyster acted immediately. 'Blow all tanks! Both planes to rise! Surface!'

Within seconds the depth gauge needle had dropped to sixty feet, seventy, eighty, then the boat balanced briefly on an even keel and began to tilt towards the stern.

'God damn this bloody tub,' Lyster snorted. 'There's a jinx on her!'

As the stern dipped further, Kelly began to slide aft and had to grab an overhead pipe. The boat was still tumbling towards the bottom, this time stern-first, her descent so steep that everything not fastened down rolled dangerously down the centre aisle. The two men operating the hydroplanes slid from their seat into the valve station and Rumbelo, flung through the forward hatch, clung to it with frantic fingers. His eyes met Kelly's and Kelly was relieved to see they were steady. It made things seem better and he gave him a sickly grin.

As the boat settled, Lyster's head lifted slowly as if it were heavy. 'Stop blowing,' he ordered. 'The boat's out of control.'

As *E19* reached the ocean floor, a terrifying roar came from the engine room as water rushed through the leak, then the boat hit with a shuddering jolt and they sprawled on the deck, all of them tumbling and sliding helplessly about. The lights went out and for a few moments there was only terrifying darkness. Then, as the emergency lighting came on, they held their breath, blinking at each other in thankful relief.

Bennett was gazing intently at the depth gauge. The vibrating needle had stopped at a hundred feet, which was as far as it would go. Mingled with the heavy smell of diesel oil, there was now a new odour as fear opened pores and activated the sweat glands of the crouching men. With the rise in tension there was also a rise in temperature. Like animals feigning death, everyone had frozen into rigid positions and the control room was as quiet as the grave, the air hanging heavy like the still period before the beginning of a thunderstorm.

There seemed something ominous in the long gap in information from the engine room. The usual funny comments didn't come and men began to crowd in, their faces damp and drawn with strain. Still no one spoke. The silence had a glass-thin brittleness, and a heavy tension seemed to have settled over them. Beads of sweat showed on Lyster's face and the muscles of his jaw stood out. His shoulders were hunched, and the lines at the sides of his mouth seemed deeper than before, the hollows under his eyes like coal smudges. In the silent control room the creak and tick of strained plates sounded malevolent, and an enormous sense of claustrophobia gripped Kelly so that he wanted to scream.

They were all waiting tensely, Lyster bent down near the eyepiece of the periscope, ready to raise it the moment they regained control, and Kelly saw everybody watching him with wide eyes and grey perspiring faces. Still no one moved, all eyes firmly fixed on the commanding officer, waiting for the next order. The tension was agonising and the silence seemed to go on for hours.

Then Lyster came to life at last. 'Take the angle off, Number One,' he said quietly.

As Bennett struggled with the tanks, there was nothing the rest of them could do except wait. The seconds ticked by like slow ponderous steps, while they remained still, not speaking, not daring to speak, avoiding each other's eyes. Then the boat lurched again and somebody out of sight shouted 'Shut that bloody door!' Struggling against the tilting deck, Kelly could see water running down from forward.

Bennett was still working over the panel, desperately seeking an explanation for the boat's behaviour, and they were all acutely aware of the fatal danger of chlorine if the sea water should reach the batteries before they could surface. Kelly's brain seemed paralysed.

Lyster raised his head, frowning. 'Submarines,' he said sourly, 'are sensitive fish. I'm told it's possible to trim one so accurately that, by raising or lowering the periscope a few inches, the whole boat can be made to rise or sink in the water.' He stared round him bitterly. 'But not *this* one. Pilot, ask the engine room how long they'll be.'

Kelly was just struggling on hands and knees against the angle, bracing his feet against a pump, a valve, a convenient pipe, towards the engine room when a hollow voice announced, 'Air induction valve working and closed, sir.'

'Thank God for that,' Lyster said. 'Bring her up, Number One.'

There was no further sign of difficulty as *E19* rose safely to the surface. The tension dropped away like a discarded cloak and, though the smell of fear still filled the control room, they dabbed at their perspiring faces, trying to pretend they hadn't had a moment's anxiety. As the conning tower broke surface they all breathed a sigh of relief, staring at each other with awkward grins, every one of them hoping he'd shown no sign of doubt, almost as if they'd been involved in some joint misdemeanour against the navy, some group behaviour of which they could all be ashamed.

Lyster was staring at the depth gauge with a deep frown, his eyes glittering angrily.

'This bloody boat,' he said, 'needs looking at again. All the way through.'

Four

There was a blazing row on the casing of *E19* with the engineering manager of the yard and Lyster going at it hammer and tongs.

'Ten to one Lyster'll win,' Bennett offered as he watched with Kelly from the bridge. 'He has a very persuasive manner.'

'He looks to me as if he's about to shove the manager overboard,' Kelly said.

Lyster remained in a bad temper for the rest of the day and that evening the manager came back aboard with a group of workmen under a foreman. The whole lot of them looked chastened and faintly ill-at-ease and Lyster gave them no encouragement to cheer up.

'Why is it naval officers consider themselves among God's chosen few?' they heard the manager ask bitterly in an aside.

Kelly grinned. 'Perhaps it's because we *are* among God's chosen few,' he said.

Lyster swung round to Bennett. 'I'm sending the hands on leave at once,' he announced. 'If we wait for that bloody lot to finish we'll miss our sailing date. See to it, Number One.'

With the deck occupied by dubious-looking wires and boxes of tools, and overalled workmen cursing in every compartment, they sent off half the ship's complement who made in an excited group for the station, like all sailors ashore heading for women and drink, searching for that something all sailors expect to find when they strike land and never do. *E19* became a cold cheerless cylinder with Lyster, who seemed to prefer to forego his leave to sit on the workmen's necks to make sure they neglected nothing, in a foul temper whenever he appeared from the depot ship. Kelly was pleased to welcome Bennett back and vanish with the second batch.

He slept most of the way to London and in the train to Esher he was surprised to bump into Rumbelo.

'Hello, Rumbelo,' he said. 'Where are you going?'

Rumbelo coughed and looked faintly embarrassed. 'Just going down for the day to see Biddy, sir,' he said.

'Biddy? Not *our* Biddy?'

Rumbelo smiled. After a lifetime of grey orphanage rooms and grey orphanage helpers, after a service life full of the harsh interiors of ships and the sometimes harsher interiors of seamen's mission halls, the little Irish girl at Thakeham had brought some colour to his life. For the first time he had sat at a table and eaten off a tablecloth, and for the first time had slept in a bed with sheets and been regarded with an unexpected affection.

'Why not, sir?' he said. 'She's a very presentable young lady. Thought I might go and help her turn the mangle and do the ironing again.'

'Good God, Rumbelo, have you got a crush on her?'

Rumbelo was silent for a moment. There hadn't been a lot of love in his life and he was touched and flattered to be the recipient of admiration. He and Bridget had already exchanged laboriously-written ill-spelt letters which he kept in his ditty box and read and re-read when his shipmates weren't looking. Rumbelo had discovered that life was twice as meaningful when you had someone to share it with and at Thakeham it seemed he had a whole houseful of people from Bridget upwards.

'Well, I dunno yet, sir,' he admitted. 'But I never will have, will I, if I don't sort of investigate, as you might say?'

Kelly grinned. 'Good for you, Rumbelo. Where are you staying?'

'At the YMCA at Waterloo, sir.'

'Can't you find somewhere nearer?'

'There's nowhere in Esher, sir.'

'That room over the garage's still empty.'

Rumbelo grinned, 'Couldn't do that, sir. Got to do this sort of thing proper.'

'You mean you need a bloody chaperone?'

'Sort of, sir. Biddy don't think it ought to be done without, and no more do I.'

'Right. From now on I'm your chaperone. You can't court a girl in Esher while you're based in London.'

-

It was a strange sort of leave. Kelly had half-expected to spend it having a riotous time but, with spring just beginning, all he wished to do was walk with Charley. Perhaps the very unexpectedness of the leave gave the days a quality of brilliance against the darkening mood of the country, which had settled down to the humdrumness of wartime life after the blazing excitement of the first few weeks. Perhaps also it was that Rumbelo was conducting a serious courtship just round the corner, and when Kelly went to catch the train to London, he was busy down the platform talking in urgent whispers to Bridget.

The occasion was a solemn one, and the leave-taking was a curiously subdued affair. Charley's mother had given her permission to say goodbye at the station and she was taking it seriously, as though she felt she represented the whole of British womanhood. She'd grown up a lot in the eight months since the war had started, her face narrower but still filled with the same fierce strength and honesty, gentle but full of cheerful pugnacity, wry humour and kindness.

As the guard started pushing people aboard, Kelly kissed her gently. 'Well, here goes,' he said. 'Off for the chopper.'

Her eyes blazed and she was suddenly terribly afraid. 'Don't say that,' she said harshly. 'Don't ever say it! It makes it sound as though the whole thing's ordained!' Her small features were taut and strained behind her anger and it sobered Kelly at once.

He pulled a face. Everybody aboard ship said things that were more fatalistic than normal, because of the sure knowledge that some of them might not be alive in a year's time. But they didn't brood much over it. They were normal healthy young men far more concerned with enjoying the present than dwelling on the future.

She stared at him with worried eyes. 'I'll pray for you, Kelly,' she said, and the words seemed to knock the stuffing out of him.

–

Two days later, with the wind north-west and the barometer falling, the submarine depot ship, *Adamant*, led four of Britain's newest submarines, *E11*, *E14*, *E15* and *E19*, across the Bay of Biscay in line ahead. There was no other shipping in sight and the empty world of long green rollers was streaked with white under a heavy sky. *Adamant* looked like a steam yacht and rolled heavily enough to show the anti-fouling below her waterline. Because of the demands of fighting ships, she had no means of defence except for a dummy gun her engineers had made out of a stove pipe.

The submarines, all of them identical in design, pitched and rolled with a livelier movement, *E19* bringing up the rear, and every shower of spray that flew over them slopped water into the control room through the open hatch, to be mopped up by a waiting sailor with a rag and bucket. On the diminutive bridge Commander Lyster stood beside the helmsman and gave orders through the voice pipe to the engine room or to the first lieutenant in the control space below. Crammed along-side him, Kelly stared into the compass, swathed in a leather coat and sea boots, watching as the hissing crests of the seas, approaching from the starboard quarter, foamed round the base of the conning tower and receded to show the black bulging cylinder of the pressure hull beneath. The dockyard mateys who had replaced the air induction valve had announced that there was now nothing wrong with *E19*. Lyster had nevertheless insisted on a full series of exercises but there had been no further sign of the odd maverick behaviour beyond a little unsteadiness when they dived, and somewhat reluctantly, he had signed all the necessary documents that shifted the responsibility for her from them to him.

The wind eased as they passed Cape St Vincent and altered course for Gibraltar. The sea was dark blue now and the sky was lighter but clouds were massing in the east.

'We're off Cape Trafalgar now,' Lyster pointed out dryly to Kelly. 'Where Horace Nelson, patron saint of the Royal Navy, was martyred in 1805. I hope you're duly affected, Pilot.'

'I'm overcome with aggressive spirit, sir,' Kelly grinned. 'One almost expects to see wreckage floating about.'

A French cruiser passed them, heading into the Atlantic, crashing through the seas on some urgent mission, the spray lifting high over her masthead. Entering the straits, they kept to the African side to take advantage of the inflowing current and entered Gibraltar in the evening to make fast to the north mole. As they coiled the ropes and the deck party wiped their hands, Kelly found Rumbelo alongside him. 'Well, Rumbelo,' he said. 'Here we go again.'

'Yes, sir. Here we go again.'

'Come to any arrangement with Bridget?'

'Not exactly, sir. But, on the other 'and, not exactly not, neither. We thought we'd wait a bit. Wartime doesn't seem to be the time to hurry into marriage.'

Kelly shrugged. 'With people being killed right and left, Rumbelo, I'd have thought that it was *just* the time.'

The next morning was bright, with the mountains of Africa showing shadowed and purple across the straits, and there was a Mediterranean warmth in the air that was a pleasant change after the North Sea. That evening, they saw the lights of Algiers, but two mornings later the weather deteriorated again, and they were glad to reach the harbour of Malta and head towards the ramparts of St Angelo. With the crew lining the super-structure as the boatswain's pipe sounded the 'Still', a bugle replied from high up on the ramparts, and they threaded their way among the harbour service craft, pinnaces, shining Maltese gondolas, dghaisas, and feluccas that passed like white birds. In the largest dry dock they could see the towering superstructure of *Inflexible*.

'What's she doing here?' Bennett asked.

'Damaged, in the recent vulgar scuffle in the Dardanelles,' Lyster said shortly. 'Seems the bigger they are the harder they fall. Four battleships for the price of a few Turkish mines seems to me a damn good bargain.'

Staring at the high steel tower of the battle cruiser, Kelly wondered if Verschoyle were still aboard her. Not for one minute did he feel any relaxation of his dislike and distrust of him. Verschoyle was Verschoyle, bland, privileged, moneyed, with influential relations who would see that he received all the right steps up the naval ladder without undue delay. There was a faint tinge of envy as he thought of him. Somehow Verschoyle was always with him, always unreservedly untrustworthy, always dangerous, always unpleasant and coldly tricky, and probably clever enough to have wangled a transfer to a home-based ship.

They made fast alongside HMS *Egmont*, an old wooden man-o'-war converted into a depot ship, and were joined the following day by *AE2*, an Australian E-class boat, which had just had a hurried and tricky passage through the Suez Canal at a time when the Turks had been massing for an attempt to capture it.

They had all set their hearts on getting through the Dard-anelles. It was firmly believed that the Turkish fleet was intending to make a sortie through the straits backed by *Goeben* and *Breslau* which, now officially Turkish, were expected to support any movement of troops south caused by the landing of an Allied army. They all knew they were there for no other reason than to try to force a passage through the Narrows before the army's landing took place, and the hazards were clear to every man among them. Most submarine losses were due to mines, and the winding waters of the Dardanelles were known to be thick with them.

As they waited for orders, they discussed how they might tackle them. Bennett had the wardroom gramophone grinding out a crackling version of 'Put on Your Tata, Little Girlie,' but it didn't detract from the sobriety of the occasion.

'If we dive below them, of course,' Lyster said, 'we'll probably catch their mooring wires, but that ought not to explode them, unless we drag the damn things down on top of us.'

Kelly spread the chart on the table among the coffee cups. 'How about nets, sir?' he asked.

Lyster was sitting on the only chair, his feet up on the bunk, staring at his shoes. He forced himself to pay attention. 'We've got a jumping wire and a cutting edge on the bows,' he said. 'We ought to be able to go through them.'

'How about shore batteries?'

'We can dive.'

They couldn't answer back, however, because they had no gun, but they had to take a risk somewhere and the current would be the biggest problem. It ran at up to six knots and the distance they had to cover was thirty-five miles. They couldn't pass through the Narrows against it submerged all the way. Somewhere en route they would have to surface to recharge the batteries. The problem was how to do it without being spotted and shot at.

They had plenty of time to think about their difficulties because *E11* had been having trouble on passage with her starboard propeller shaft and, detailed to stand by her in Malta when the other boats left, *E19* followed with her and arrived off the island of Lemnos three days later.

Close to the entrance to the Dardanelles, the island had been yielded by Turkey to Greece at the end of the Balkan

Wars and its use had been granted to the Allies by the Greek Prime Minister, Venizelos. Mudros Harbour, a vast expanse of water with two or three miles of good holding ground, contained two small islands that divided the outer harbour from the inner harbour and formed narrow passages which made them safe against U-boats. Near the entrance and a mile or so inshore, four hills rose drably out of the shimmering landscape. All supplies came from Alexandria or Port Said and the one disadvantage of the place was that it was open to southerly gales which blew through the entrance to make boatwork impossible.

The shining sheet of dark water was overflowing with ships, and they counted a dozen battleships, with cruisers, destroyers, transports crowded with troops, hospital ships, supply ships and swarms of smaller craft and foreign vessels, among them Greek sailing ships and the Russian five-funnelled cruiser, *Askold*, which was immediately christened *The Packet of Woodbines*. The harbour was surrounded by a flat plain, bare of anything but low scrub, rising to the inland hills in arid contours. White dots of tents, ammunition dumps and military encampments were spread everywhere, and they could distinguish a column of marching men moving along the coast by the cloud of dust they trailed along behind them.

'I always thought the Aegean was a thing of beauty and a joy for ever,' Lyster said as he stood with Bennett and Kelly on the casing. 'Wine-dark seas and cool islands full of sloe-eyed houris and that sort of thing.'

'What are houris, sir?' Bennett asked.

Lyster gestured airily. 'Girls. Much the same as the model you get in Worthing and Brighton when they're stripped to the buff, I understand.'

'One thing,' the coxswain observed from behind them. 'It's a long way from my old woman.'

Stations were made out at once for the sacking of Constantinople.

'The captain, of course,' Lyster said cheerfully, 'will have to proceed immediately in search of rare and priceless gems. Only to add to the Allied coffers for the war effort, of course.'

'As second officer,' Bennett pointed out, 'I think my job will be to inspect the ladies of the harem. Yours, Pilot, had better be to engage the attention of the Chief Eunuch by occupying him with polite conversation.'

'Sorry, sir.' Kelly shook his head. 'Regret to say I show a great distaste for the duty allotted me. Better let the coxswain do it.'

The coxswain grinned. 'If the fall of Constantinople don't take place, sir,' he said, 'you'll have to put it down to a lack of patriotism on the part of the non-commissioned officers. I reckon the first lieutenant will need an assistant when he inspects the harem. You can put me down as a volunteer for that.'

Five

Ringed by bare hills, they seemed to be in the crater of an extinct volcano, and dead dogs and cats, even dead horses and mules, floated among the ships, their legs sticking up like the periscopes of adventurous submarines.

As soon as they made fast alongside *Adamant*, they realised something was wrong and they soon learned that *E15*, which had reached Mudros while they had been escorting *E11* from Malta, had started for the Sea of Marmara two days before but had run aground near Kephez and been shot up by shore batteries. Casualties were not yet known but a seaplane had seen the boat high and dry and attempts to destroy her before the Turks could salvage her and use her against the Allies had failed.

'They think she was caught in a flow of fresh water coming down from the Sea of Marmara,' Lyster informed them as he returned aboard. 'They lost control and were swept on the rocks. And she's not the first, it seems, because the French have also lost *Saphir*, one of their boats. There are other problems, too, I'm told – an old iron bridge dumped off Nagara Point, north of Chanak, for example.'

'Together, doubtless,' Bennett observed, 'with an assortment of rusty perambulators, bedsteads and old Turkish tramcars.'

'Wouldn't it be a good idea to make some attempt to find out where exactly this fresh water flows?' Kelly said. 'Somebody must have some information. If the differing densities are what caused *E15*'s troubles, we ought to find out where the currents run.'

'We can certainly try.' Lyster smiled. 'Look it up, Pilot. Roger Keyes is out here as chief of staff and he'll already have thought of it, if I know him. He might even have some information on the subject and he's the last chap in the world to deny anybody a bit of aggression against the Bashi Bazouks.' He studied his shoes and smiled. 'In fact, I heard a funny story aboard *Adamant* about the currents. It seems some member of the Sultan's household was once dropped in a weighted sack into the Marmara when he was no longer considered necessary to the smooth functioning of the household – probably been trying to take one of the ladies of the harem for a dirty weekend to Scutari or something – and ten days later, when they all imagined he was well on his way south to the Mediterranean, they heard a great deal of screaming from the ladies of the seraglio and there the old boy was, bursting out of his sack and bumping against the shore under the windows. See if you can find out why.'

It didn't take long to discover that there was a deep current setting strongly towards Kephez where *E15* had run aground and that the submarine *B6*, an old boat without bow planes, had behaved very oddly during her attempt to salvage her. On the other hand, Holbrook, in *B11*, had reported an entire absence of anti-submarine nets.

Lyster rubbed his nose as he listened. 'Seems to require a lot of thought,' he commented dryly. 'In the meantime, my shoes have finally fallen apart and I think I ought to go ashore and buy something to replace them. What language do they speak here, Number One?'

'God knows, sir.' Bennett shrugged. 'But I suppose you ought to be able to get across with French.'

'You speak French, Pilot, don't you?'

'Not for a minute, sir.'

'I thought you did.'

'Somebody's got it wrong, sir. It follows me around.'

'Ah, well.' Lyster shrugged. 'I expect you'll manage.'

Despite the spring flowers and the sweet-smelling air, Mudros town was nothing but a wretched collection of red-roofed houses dominated by a large white church, mostly inhabited by Levantines who scraped a living from petty commerce and offered goats, fish and olives to the fleet, any one ship of which could have bought up their whole wealth in a week.

There were no shoes for sale because the army had been there first and Lyster had to be satisfied with a pair of Levantine sandals. Instead they decided to try a bathe and hired a pair of miniature donkeys with made-up saddles. But the going was hard and there was a strong wind full of grit. As they left the town for the beach, they passed a funeral, and, as they pulled to one side, the wind blew back the pall. Beneath it was the body of a naked old woman and the guide they'd hired explained that as there were no trees on the island there was no wood for coffins either.

The sea was full of soldiers shaving in the salt water and trying to find relief from the heat, and they heard stories of rampant dysentery and disease in the Allied camps. The soldiers were in high spirits, however, looking forward to getting ashore on Turkish soil and heading for Constantinople, and officers were busy buying donkeys to carry their kit.

While they were in the water, to Lyster's disgust someone stole his new sandals. 'Always the trouble with these bloody Eastern Mediterranean countries,' he said bitterly. 'You pay one chap two bob to guard your belongings and along comes another chap who pays him half a crown to let him pinch 'em.'

The harbour seemed to be more crammed with shipping even than when they'd first arrived. Ship after ship steamed in until there were almost 200 anchored there. In addition to the zigzag-camouflaged warships, brightly painted Greek caïques, pleasure steamers, trawlers, ferryboats, colliers and liners had been pressed into service, to say nothing of *Askold*, and French warships with what looked like top hats on their funnels, among them the old battleship, *Henri IV*, which had scarcely a foot of freeboard and was so turreted she looked like a mediaeval castle. Swarms of cutters and motorboats moved about and every vessel flew its flag, while the smoke from hundreds of funnels rose into the air. It was always possible to hear bugles or military bands across the water and men could be seen on every transport, drilling on deck or practising climbing down rope ladders to boats.

Lyster returned from a conference on the flagship with the date and details of the plan for the landing. 'There's just one snag,' he said. 'The transports arrived with all the equipment and guns wrongly embarked and they've had to send 'em back to Alex for disembarking and re-embarking in the right order.'

'Andrew Cunningham of *Scorpion* told me that the destroyers patrolling the beaches say they can hear Johnny Turk digging trenches like billy-o,' Bennett said. 'They're shoving new gun positions up all over the shop, and they could even hear 'em driving in stakes and erecting barbed wire. They passed it on to the High Altar but nobody seems to be making preparations for landing troops under fire.'

Despite the rumours, there was an immense enthusiasm everywhere and nobody appeared to think of failure, and the troops lining the decks of the transports shouted and catcalled to one another, cheering every ship that departed or arrived. On April 24th, they heard that the Australian submarine, *AE2*, had been ordered to make the attempt to pierce the Narrows and reach the Sea of Marmara and she vanished eastwards just as the orders to start the military operation arrived.

The ships began to move out at once, steaming for their rendezvous off the Turkish beaches. All painted grey or black, they headed for the entrance to the harbour in line ahead, and in all the ships that were to remain behind, the men lined the rails to cheer.

Kelly watched them with a strange feeling of sadness. Despite the laughter, the air seemed supercharged with emotion. In

France, attacks such as the one these men were approaching had ended in windrows of dead. As the ships passed, the soldiers were singing in surprisingly sweet voices that left a bewildering sense of loneliness. Doubtless, out of sight, harassed officers were checking lists but the excitement aboard the transports reached out to every other vessel in the harbour, and Kelly, aware that he was looking at history, felt his heart thumping against the wall of his chest.

As they passed *E19*, Lyster ordered his men up on the superstructure and they yelled and waved as yellow dust blew from the shore in the brassy sunshine. They could feel the grit in their teeth as they paid their compliments to the passing army, but there seemed to be no sense of foreboding among the khaki-clad figures lining the rails of the troopships. On one vessel, an elderly merchant captain sailed past, holding his cap high in the air in answer. Not once did he lower the cap, merely changing it from one hand to the other as he passed the naval vessels.

During the day they thought they could hear the fleet's guns on the wind but no one could be sure and they waited impatiently for news of the landing. By evening a few ugly rumours arrived and it soon became clear from the snippets that reached them that the assault had not been the success that had been expected. In spite of victory in one or two places, for the most part only a toehold here and there had been achieved and the troops were already exhausted.

They were in deep gloom when a signal arrived to say that *AE2* had passed through the Narrows and had torpedoed a Turkish gunboat, and a cheer rang through *E19*. Further information, however, indicated that for *AE2*'s solitary success she had used up every torpedo she possessed. Failing her again and again, they had run too deeply or off course and her victims had escaped.

Since it seemed good sense to take a closer look at the entrance to the straits, Kelly had himself put aboard the destroyer, *Scorpion*, which was engaged in giving fire support to the troops ashore. Cunningham, her captain, was a smooth-faced, smiling man not a great deal older than Kelly but possessed of enormous self-confidence, one of the new young commanding officers thrown up by the war. He handled his ship well and there seemed to be an enormous feeling of solidarity between him and his crew.

Battleships and cruisers offshore were shelling the Turkish positions and Kelly could see the vast fountains of earth, dirt and smoke leaping into the sky. The sea was flat calm and shining like a looking glass, and destroyers crammed with men and towing boats carrying still more of them kept closing the beach, and they could occasionally see lines of small figures moving forward, crumbling, and moving forward again. The Turkish gunfire didn't appear very heavy and was slow and ill-directed but one gun firing out to sea was particularly troublesome and was already known to *Scorpion*'s crew as 'The Wrath of God.'

Some neat problems in naval bombardment were being taken in their stride, however. Discovering that the flat trajectory of the four-incher could not reach its target without hitting the top of a cliff occupied by Allied troops, Cunningham had solved the difficulty quite simply by ordering the charges cut in half with a knife. A signal to the flagship for a range table for half-charges brought a prompt response and the gun was used as a howitzer.

'Doubt if it would obtain the approval of the pundits at Whale Island,' Cunningham said with a grin.

While *E19* chafed, *E14* was sent off to follow *AE2* through the straits and, with *E11* under repairs, *E19* was ordered to make ready to follow at once. Twenty-four hours later *E14* signalled that she, too, was through the straits and *E19* was told to stand by. All day they waited their turn but then they heard that the French were determined to have some part in the affair and a share in any glory that was going and had insisted on their own submarine, *Joule*, having a shot. A few hours after her departure, however, *Adamant* picked up a Turkish signal announcing that she'd been sunk, and the same night a message in English from the German cruiser *Breslau* announced that *AE2* had also been destroyed.

Lyster's face was bleak. 'Thought the odds were beginning to turn rather in our favour,' he said. 'Instead, overnight, they seem to have tipped a little t'other way. Let's check this bloody boat again. We don't want that damned jinx taking over at the wrong moment.'

–

By this time the land battle was raging furiously, and it became important that another submarine should make the attempt to slow down the Turkish supplies. With Lyster nervously sitting on everybody's neck to make sure they did their inspections properly, Kelly was ordered aboard *Lord Nelson* to receive their orders from the chief of staff.

Keyes turned as he entered his cabin, an angular, ugly figure, 'Where's Commander Lyster?' he demanded.

'He's worried about the boat, sir. He preferred to check everything personally.'

'Doesn't he have a first lieutenant for that sort of thing?'

'*E19*'s rather a special case, sir. She has a lot of bad habits.'

Keyes seemed satisfied with the explanation. He was a tall, well-decorated man with a large mouth, large ears and long neck. Despite the broad ring of a commodore, however, his manner was brisk and friendly. 'I've heard of you, haven't I? When I was Commodore, Submarines. You're the chap who was decorated for bringing half the British Army out of Antwerp.'

'Yes, sir. It all sprang from the mistaken belief that I speak French. It seems to haunt me, sir. Even here.'

Keyes' mouth widened in a grin and he thrust forward a packet. 'Here are your orders. The Turkish battleships, *Turgut Reiss* and *Heireddin Barbarossa*, are to be considered priority targets because their forward gun turrets have been replaced by howitzers that can lob sixteen-inch shells over the hills on to our beaches. Any questions.'

'No, sir.'

'Putting a submarine successfully through the Dardanelles will have much the same effect as putting a ferret down a rabbit hole. Battleships will be operating in the entrance to the straits in support of the army, so we can expect mines to be launched in the Narrows. You're to endeavour to hamper the movements of minelayers and generally run amuck in the Marmara. Report by W/T as soon as you're through.'

–

It was after midnight as they made their way towards the entrance to the Dardanelles. It was a lovely night, clear and calm, with a moon and a myriad stars throwing a pale light on the sea, and the escorting destroyer, seamen's hammocks lashed round the bridge against splinters, was a silent black shape on the smooth water.

The air was warm and from the conning tower they could smell the land, a musky smell that was a compound of dust and smoke and cut grass and another sicklier scent that they knew came from unburied bodies exposed to the sun. Through the hatch floated a snatch of song – 'Oh, the moon shines bright on Charlie Chaplin' – and Kelly frowned, wondering how many of the men who'd sung it so often in Mudros Harbour were now contributing to that wretched scent that floated out to them from the land.

Lyster was wearing his knickerbockers and tartan stockings but, despite his strange gear, he was in a sober mood and had held prayers on the superstructure before they'd left. While still ten miles from the entrance to the straits they could see the beam of a searchlight on the Asiatic shore, probing towards them.

'Kum Kale,' Lyster said.

Above the hum of the engines, the rumble of distant guns came on the breeze and they could see the flashes of bursting shells flickering against the land. Beyond the pale beam of light that probed the entrance, there were other searchlights moving about on the northern shore.

There was a thin streak of unease in Kelly's mind, a feeling of foreboding and fear. It's just a touch of the hump, he kept telling himself, yet deep down the bitter, old and wrinkled truth was that he didn't trust *E19*. Would she behave as she had in the Channel before they'd left England? She had never run wild since, but there was no guarantee that she wouldn't.

He had written two letters before he'd left, one to his mother, in which he informed her that he hoped he'd always be able to bring her credit whatever happened to him – a straightforward duty letter to someone he supposed he loved but wasn't sure about because he rarely saw her. The other was to Charley and in it he admitted that he was scared stiff but that, since everybody else was being brave, he expected he would be, too. He tried hard to tell her he loved her but, doubtful of the truth of the statement and even uncertain of its meaning, he drew back at the last moment and the rest of the letter remained merely chit-chat.

He forced his attention to the job on hand. More searchlights seemed to be coming on and against the spill of their light he could see the contours of the land.

'Cape Helles, oh-three-four degrees, sir,' he called out. 'Kum Kale one-two-nine.'

There was land, black against the sky, on both sides of them now and heavy shells occasionally whooshed over their heads with an unstable hissing noise towards the British lines.

'And his little baggy trousers they want mendin'…'

The song came again and Lyster barked an order through the hatch. 'Shut up, that man,' he said and the song came to a sudden stop. 'Keep silence down there, Number One. There must be no mistakes.'

They had planned to enter the straits after the moon had set, and proceed on the surface as long as possible to conserve the batteries, but so slowly the wash would not attract attention from the shore. At first light in the morning, they would dive. As they arrived at the entrance, the moon was still just above the water, picking up the white cliffs of the shore, and they waited by the side of the black and sinister-looking destroyer for the moment to go. The perfect stillness of the night accentuated the tension, then, as the moon slipped away, swallowed by its own silver path along the sea, they crept away from the destroyer's side and headed at seven knots for the centre of the straits, only the popple of the engines and the slap of the water against the hull to break the silence.

Lyster seemed tense and agitated. 'Those bloody diesels sound louder than I've ever heard 'em,' he grumbled. 'Somebody ashore's bound to pick 'em up.'

Everything was ready for instant diving, only Kelly on the bridge with Lyster, all the others below waiting for the alarm. The black outline of the hills was sharp against the sky but there was no sign that they'd been spotted.

'Perhaps the gunfire drowns the noise,' Lyster commented.

As he spoke, two enemy searchlights lit up the southern shore, one at Kephez Point, the second one a little lower, and began to sweep the waters with their long beams, touching the outline of the conning tower with silver. A more powerful light at Chanak threw a beam of a yellower hue as it searched the higher reaches. As they drew nearer, it seemed about to pick them up when the Kephez light went out abruptly, and they were able to proceed further on the surface than they'd hoped. Then the clear ray from Kephez sprang on again and Lyster called out 'Diving stations.' As they scrambled below, he slammed the hatch shut above them, and dead slow, at twenty feet, they continued within a mile of the European shore until the periscope showed the faint contours of the hills on the northern side.

'We're abeam of Achi Baba,' Lyster said. 'Start the motors. Flood main ballast.'

Metal clanged on metal as orders echoed back and forth.

'Open One and Two Kingstons and One and Two Main Vents.'

'Number One full. Number Two full.'

'Flood Three.'

Water thundered into the tanks and *E19* settled deeper into the water. For a long time no one spoke, then Lyster ordered the boat up to thirty feet.

'Periscope up!'

Putting his face to the rubber eyepiece, he glanced round, then slapped the periscope handles up.

'Down periscope,' he said. 'Take her down to eighty feet.'

Apart from the diving hands, the crew had fallen out and were crouched over steaming mugs of cocoa when there was a metallic clang forward. Heads came up at once and they listened in dead silence as the sound moved along the outside of the hull.

'Stop port!' Lyster snapped.

The telegraph rang and the port propeller stopped. The ominous sound grew and filled the control room. It was as if an enormous door was slowly being dragged open on rust-stiffened hinges. They had picked up a mine wire and somewhere at the end of it there was a mine, its horns ready to break off at the slightest touch and allow sea water to get in to spark off its firing circuit.

The helmsman turned his wheel to stop the head swinging and Kelly found himself putting his cup down on the chart table very gently, as though the slightest additional touch might explode the mine above them. The wire appeared to be caught on one of the propeller guards, rasping and scraping along the steel, then the submarine lurched as it dragged clear.

There was a moment's total silence before Lyster spoke.

'Ahead port,' he said quietly. 'Plot the position.'

More wires scraped along the hull, the sound a harsh grating noise so that it was like being inside a kettle drum. Every time,

186

Lyster stopped one of the propellers and there was dead silence as they listened, except for the hum of the electric motors, the buzz of the hydroplanes and the rattle of the steering gear. Every unoccupied eye was on the deckhead as they tried to work out exactly where the obstruction lay.

Then, for ten minutes there were no scrapings and clangings along the hull and Lyster's head lifted so that he was staring at the confusion of pipes above him as if he were trying to see beyond them to the dark waters of the Narrows. The control room was silent except for the occasional scrape of a shoe. Kelly tried hard to analyse his feelings. In his heart of hearts he knew he was afraid but it never occurred to him to worry that he would let his fear take control. He'd been trained to hold it in check and, with every man who entered submarines aware of the danger of their trade, there was no place for a man who couldn't handle the knowledge.

Lyster's voice broke in on his thoughts. 'Take her up to periscope depth, Number One.' he said. 'We have to accept the risk of a mine. We've only an hour of darkness left and we can't afford to find ourselves high and dry on a sandbank. Up periscope.'

As the shining column hissed out of its well, he bent and stared into the eyepiece, then he turned, his face puzzled. 'We're abeam of Kephez,' he said. 'What's the time?'

Kelly told him. 'And that's damned funny, sir;' he said. 'We're not due there for another forty-five minutes.'

'What's our speed?'

'We've only been making four and a half knots through the water and there's a two to four knot current against us.' Lyster stared at the chart and jabbed with a finger. 'We're here,' he said. Then he shrugged. 'But, what the hell? Why complain? There are some very odd currents in these waters and we've struck one that's helping us. We'll steer for Kilid Bahr on the west side to avoid the set towards Kephez. Shove the periscope up again.'

Even as it ran up and Lyster put his eye to it, his voice cracked in a shout. 'Down periscope!' A second later they heard a clang against the hull as a shell burst in the sea nearby, and a clatter like hailstones on a window as shrapnel flung through the water rattled against the conning tower.

'They've spotted us,' Lyster said. 'I saw the damn thing shoot. It seemed to fire right into my eye.'

There was a tense wait and for another ten minutes they headed north in silence. They all knew now that they'd been seen and, however successful they were at passing through the straits, there'd be a reception committee of trawlers and gunboats waiting for them at the other end. By the plotting table, Kelly saw Rumbelo watching him and it suddenly seemed important that, come what may, he should be returned to Biddy.

After another five minutes, Lyster ran the periscope up again. He turned from the eyepiece, grinning. 'We've made it,' he said. 'We're past Nagara Point. There's marshy land there that keeps us hidden. Take her down to seventy feet, Number One.'

Relaxed, they pushed steadily on, rising to periscope depth every few miles to check their position.

'We're opposite Gallipoli,' Lyster announced eventually. 'Looks like a pile of white bricks surrounded by fishing boats.'

The off-duty men sat quietly, drinking tea that tasted of diesel and unwashed bodies as they dived under the last mine-field, moving as little as possible to conserve the oxygen. Clothes were soaked with sweat and, despite the fans, the smell from the unemptied sanitary buckets behind the engines pene-trated the whole ship. The air grew thicker until the interior of the boat looked as if it were full of grey smoke as, with the last of the batteries' power, they headed for the European shore; then, still moving forward at dead slow speed, they lurched heavily and came to a stop.

'What's the depth, Number One?'

'Fourteen fathoms, sir.'

Lyster turned. 'Fall out diving stations,' he said. 'We're in the Sea of Marmara close to the Gallipoli shore. So close in fact, we've just run into it.'

Six

They lay on the bottom in twenty fathoms all day. By the time diving stations were ordered again, the atmosphere inside *E19* was thick enough to look like a London fog and they were all grey-faced and breathing heavily.

'Take her up to thirty feet,' Lyster said at last. 'And do the thing slowly, Number One. We don't want anyone having a heart attack.'

Lethargically, hands reached for valves and wheels, and air rumbled into the tanks. Lyster crouched near the periscope handles.

'Up periscope!'

As the submarine surfaced and the hatch was cautiously lifted, the stale air whistled noisily through the opening and in return came the welcome smell of a dying day. Kelly joined Lyster on the bridge, gulping at the fresh breeze. The night was still and bright with stars, and over the monstrous rush of air the engines snatched through the hatch he could hear the barking of a dog somewhere ashore. It sounded familiar and rural and reminded him strongly of home.

'Start the charge, Number One,' Lyster called down. 'But be ready to break off and go to diving stations.'

As the diesel motors sucked the icy draught into the boat, the atmosphere cleared at once. From the stuffy fug of an enclosed over-used hutch it changed at once to the damp sharp air of evening.

'Let's have the W/T signal away,' Lyster said as the radio operator climbed to the conning tower to rig the wireless mast and aerial.

They waited tensely for the first cheep from the receiver that would give them a sign that an outside world existed, and there was the silence of disappointment as the operator failed to raise the British ship waiting on the other side of the spit of land that separated them from the Mediterranean.

'What's wrong?' Lyster snapped.

'Don't know, sir.' The radioman was tense and nervous at the responsibility, and ham-fisted in his efforts to succeed. 'Might be anything – batteries, connection, valves. I'll have to check.'

Lyster called down the hatch. 'Pigeons,' he said. 'Quick sharp!'

But the seaman in charge of the homing birds had been too fond of animals and had fed them so well they were loathe to leave their happy surroundings in the forepeak. They were still struggling to get them into the air when the radioman announced he'd found the fault. 'Defect in the aerial, sir. Oil cup where it comes through the deck had leaked. I've repaired it.'

Contact was made and purple-blue sparks began to leap from the damp aerial wire as the longs and shorts of the Morse sign were flashed.

'That ought to cheer Keyes up,' Lyster said. 'I bet he was biting his nails a bit.'

They spent the rest of the night on the surface, charging batteries, only sinking to the bottom as daylight came, to wait until the next night for a further move. The hours passed slowly as they slept and wrote letters and played the gramophone. One of the torpedomen produced an accordion for an impromptu concert and, as the daylight began to fade above them on the surface of the sea, they took stations again and Lyster brought the boat to the surface.

'Up periscope!'

As he put his face to the eyepiece, they saw him smile. 'There's a small warship of some sort out there,' he said quietly. 'Gunboat perhaps. Bring her head round.'

As they manoeuvred, he took another look. 'There's a light cruiser just beyond her,' he announced. 'Just the sort to be fitted out as a minelayer. I think we'll have a go at that first. Flood the tubes.'

The rush of air indicated that the forward tubes were flooding and the report came briskly and eagerly from the torpedo compartment. 'Tubes full, sir!'

'Charge firing tanks!'

'Both bow tubes ready, sir!'

Lyster called for increased revolutions and as the speed was stepped up, they heard the thud-thud-thud of a ship's propellers overhead.

'Seem to be suspicious,' Lyster observed. 'But I don't think they've seen us and the water's got a bit of a lop on, so we might escape unnoticed. Bring her up to twenty feet, Number One. And see she doesn't break surface.'

Standing by the navigating table, Kelly watched the men at the other side of the control room with a thudding heart. This was the moment about which he'd talked so often with his father, the unhurried creep forward, raising the periscope only to get their bearings. Lyster's voice came, sharp and authoritative, a small edge of excitement beneath the calmness, and Kelly began mentally to retract all the clever, boastful things he'd said about submariners. Lyster was an old hand at the game and even he was touched by the tension about them.

'Steady! Stand by starboard tube!'

The silence seemed endless, then, as Lyster called 'Fire!', they heard the clatter and thud as the torpedo left the boat, followed by the violent hissing of rushing water. *E19* lurched and the planesmen spun their wheels to keep the bow from rising. The seconds ticked by in silence.

Lyster pulled a face. 'I'm afraid we've missed,' he said. 'But I'm blowed if I can see how. The torpedo must have gone underneath. What was she set to run at?'

'Ten feet, sir.'

'Sure?'

'I checked it, sir.'

After the tension, the disappointment lay heavily over them all. Lyster was frowning deeply and biting at his lower lip. A submarine was only as good as the only man who could see, and it clearly worried him that they might think him inefficient.

He made an attempt to lighten the mood. 'Oh, well, we've got more where that one came from,' he said briskly. 'Have the tubes recharged.'

All that day they waited for the return of their victims but the sea seemed suddenly to have emptied. Lyster was nervous and irritable, and more on edge than usual because the flat calm sea made the feather of foam from the tip of the periscope visible from the shore.

'They've all gone home for supper,' he said sourly.

During the following afternoon, they sighted two dhows, small wooden vessels which weren't worth wasting a torpedo on, and *E19* rose to the surface in front of them. Immediately there was a panic aboard the nearest vessel and two or three men jumped overboard, only to regret their hasty decision immediately and swim back to their ship to be picked up again. Turks in fezzes stood on the foredeck, their arms in the air, and they could hear their wailing pleas for mercy.

'Put 'em in a boat, Pilot,' Lyster ordered. 'See what they have on board.'

Armed to the teeth and feeling unnecessarily dramatic, Kelly had himself rowed across to the dhows. They were filled with fruit and tins of meat for the troops down the peninsula, and in the hold he found cases of shells. When he reported his find to Lyster, he grinned.

'Blow 'em up,' he said. 'Make a good job of it.'

They put the Turks into their boats, helped themselves to tinned meat and fresh fruit, and planted a charge. The explosion was a highly satisfying affair, with planks and masts hurtling hundreds of feet in the air as the shells in the holds were detonated. Handing tins of meat, fruit and water to the wailing Turks, they pointed the way to land less than ten miles away and *E19* slipped beneath the water again.

Almost immediately, Lyster spotted smoke on the horizon and increased speed to investigate. It drew away from them, however, and disappeared.

'Must have been a bank holiday yesterday,' Lyster said. 'They seem to have wakened up again.'

After tea, they sighted another steamer, this time a much bigger one, and Lyster studied it carefully through the periscope.

'All we have to do is stay here,' he said. 'She's heading right across our bows. Charge firing tanks. Life seems to have returned to the Sea of Marmara. This time it ought to be easy.'

But it wasn't, and he watched their torpedoes run straight and true under the ship and vanish on the other side.

'For God's sake,' Lyster cursed. 'What the devil's wrong with them? Bring her up, Number One. I'm going to frighten her to death instead.'

As the submarine surfaced, Lyster scrambled on to the bridge and yelled through a megaphone.

'Abandon ship, or I shall fire a torpedo!'

The Turks clearly understood. The captain left the bridge with the ship still moving, and a lifeboat was lowered which capsized as it struck the water. As the ship finally stopped, more boats were lowered to pick up the swimming men. The ship was carrying munitions and the same procedure they had followed with the dhows was gone through. The ship's papers were snatched up, the men in the boats were sent on their way with water and food and a chart, and Kelly went aboard with Rumbelo carrying a demolition charge of gun cotton. Placing it in the after hold, well stacked around with six- and fifteen-inch cartridge cases, they set the fuse and hurried back to *E19*.

Going astern, they had hardly stopped engines when there was a loud report, and a column of smoke and flame shot up, and the ship's decks seemed to lift bodily upwards. Shells and cartridge cases were flung in all directions, then the ship lay slowly on her side, lifted her stern in the air and vanished in a matter of seconds.

'Well, we've accomplished something at last,' Lyster said. 'Very pretty, Pilot. I think you're earning your keep.'

They had now been in the Sea of Marmara for four days and, despite the disappointments over the torpedoes, they had done enough damage to warrant their being there. The following day, they sighted several ships but they were all too far away and going too fast for them to attack, and towards the end of the afternoon, with nothing in sight, they surfaced to charge batteries, passing half-submerged by a small coastal village where a host of fishing vessels cut the sky into strips with their masts. Lyster tensed.

'Diving stations,' he called.

As they tumbled below, he reached for the periscope. 'Take her down to fifty feet, Number One. There's a battleship beyond those fishing boats. *Barbarossa* or *Turgut Reiss*. Let's have a go. Hard a starboard, coxswain. Flood bow tubes. Charge firing tanks.'

'Both tubes ready, sir.'

'Let's hope they work this time. We've got *AE2*'s disease and we're running short.'

They held their breath as Lyster moved slowly round the periscope in the crowded control room. Every minute seemed an hour as he gave his orders. Unable to see what was happening, they could only use their imagination and construct the scene from Lyster's orders.

'Stand by!'

The tension in the control room could have been cut with a knife.

'Fire both tubes!'

The clatter of the torpedoes leaving broke the tension at once. Lyster slapped up the handles of the periscope and stood by it, waiting. There was a long silence, then Lyster frowned and bent to the eyepiece.

'Up periscope!' He straightened as the periscope rose. 'Damnation!' he said savagely. 'The bloody things have just risen to the surface and stopped. I can see the compressed air puffing out of the stern. Take her down, Number One. There's a torpedo gunboat out there – *Berki-Satoet* class – and a couple of trawlers trailing a wire rope that looks as though it supports a net.'

They lay on the bottom for an hour while propellers passed overhead. Standing by the chart table, Kelly unashamedly confessed to himself a feeling of quivering funk. If the sweep caught them it would be only a short time before they were destroyed. But no one else showed any sign of anxiety and no one looked at him, so he could only assume his fear didn't show and that they, too, were feeling the same as he did. When Lyster put the periscope up, all the searching ships had disappeared and the sea was empty.

As the conning tower broke surface, Lyster climbed through the hatch to the little bridge, Kelly close behind him.

'See 'em?'

'See what, sir?'

'The torpedoes, man! We need 'em and this looks like a good opportunity to make a search for 'em. I want to sink something before we return.'

They moved slowly on the surface in a large circle, looking for the torpedoes, and Lyster brought up Rumbelo and another man who was reputed to have the best eyes in the ship.

'I see one of 'em,' Rumbelo said and then they all saw the long shape bobbing up and down some distance away.

'Stop motors,' Lyster ordered. 'We've got to do this quickly before it's too dark. We'll hold the boat here. Then if the damn thing goes up it won't harm us.'

As he began to drag at his sweater, Kelly pushed forward. 'Not you, sir. You're needed on board in case anything turns up. I'm a good swimmer and, with respect, it's my job.'

Lyster studied him for a moment then he nodded. 'Very well,' he said.

Tying a spanner round his neck with a length of line, Kelly stripped off his clothes and dived in. The torpedo's head was undamaged and it had clearly run beneath the target but the safe period of the first part of its run had passed and the propeller blades in the nose had charged it so that the firing pin was barely a sixteenth of an inch from the detonator. The slightest jar could set off the fulminate of mercury and blow him to bloody fragments. As he realised the danger, he edged away instinctively then, realising that having accepted the task, he could hardly back away from it and hand it to someone else, unwillingly he moved closer and, swimming round the torpedo, he eyed it warily. Beyond it he could see *E19*, with Lyster waiting anxiously on the bridge with Bennett. There were several other men on the superstructure, among them the burly figure of Rumbelo, his face concerned.

Taking the spanner from his neck and twisting the line round his wrist so that he couldn't drop it, he started with infinite care to unscrew the firing pistol. Slowly, treading water, he drew it from the nose of the torpedo and set it to safe. Then, moving along the side of the missile, he pushed the starting lever forward in case there was enough compressed air still inside to start the propeller again.

'Rig the derrick,' he heard Lyster call as he swam back to the submarine to take the end of a line. 'And look slippy. The light's going.'

After a lot of careful manoeuvring, the seventeen-foot torpedo lay alongside *E19*, harmless now, and a sling was passed under it at the point of balance and a shackle attached, with a tail line to stop it swinging.

'Keep a sharp look out, Number One,' Lyster said. 'And let's have extra men up with glasses. Keep the hands to diving stations just in case.'

As the torpedo was hoisted inboard and lowered to the deck, the warhead was removed, then Lyster, after a careful study of the horizon, ordered the forward hatch to be opened.

'And make it quick,' he snapped.

There was intense activity on the foredeck, because with the hatch open they were helpless to dive, but the torpedo was hoisted up and lowered into the submarine just as the light finally disappeared.

'Right,' Lyster said. 'Get the hatch on and the derrick unshipped. At least we're no longer shy of weapons and we might have better luck next time.'

–

Throughout the whole of the next day, still nothing was seen of the cloud of Turkish transports they had expected, and it wasn't until almost evening that Lyster ordered diving stations.

'Ships off the port beam,' he said as he tumbled below. 'And one's a troopship by the look of her. Take a peep, Number One.'

One after the other they put their faces to the rubber eyepiece of the periscope. Crossing their bows was a big ship crammed with soldiers and equipment that were clearly being rushed as reinforcements for the fighting on the peninsula.

Lyster bent again to the eyepiece. 'They're not even keeping a lookout,' he said. 'There are two elderly gentlemen on the bridge, both stout and wearing fezzes, smoking and leaning on the compass. I think we'll stir 'em up a bit. Hard a starboard. Forty feet. Slow ahead port.'

As they increased speed, the familiar thud of propellers came down on them.

'Up periscope!'

'We have to be careful here, sir,' Kelly warned, one eye on the chart. 'We need to give Nagara a wide berth. There's a treacherous shoal and a strong set across it and probably fresh water currents.'

'We'll be all right.' Lyster seemed indifferent. 'Bring her up, Number One.'

As the air rumbled into the tanks, the boat tilted, and then steadied.

'Hold her there! Stand by starboard tube.' Lyster suddenly grinned. 'Hello,' he said, 'the old gentlemen have seen us. One of 'em's jumped about three feet in the air. He knocked the other chap's fez off when he swung his arm round to point. There are what you might call hurryings and scurryings and wavings of arms going on. Chaps rushing in all directions and the two stout gents looking as if they'll fall off the bridge at any minute. All vastly entertaining. Pity we have to spoil it all. I think they're going to try and ram us. Hold her there. Stand by starboard tube. We've plenty of time before she turns.'

There was a long silence and Kelly realised he was holding his breath. Bennett was breathing through his nose and it was making a faint snoring sound in the silence.

'Fire!'

The familiar lurch came as the torpedo clattered from the tube, and the diving hands spun their wheels to stop the boat rising. The seconds ticked by, then there was a heavy thud and Lyster's face broke into a grin. He reached for the periscope.

'We've got her!' His voice was high with excitement. 'Come and take a look at this!'

The troopship had stopped. There was a fierce fire burning, and the deck had filled with a heaving mass of figures which seemed to cover the whole ship, running from the flames and scurrying across the hatch covers. They were on every ladder, fighting to pass each other, and the whole ship seemed to be one pulsating mass of humanity. The panic was obvious and in the confusion some of the men were jumping into the sea, making small splashes round the ship's side as they hit the water.

'She's going, sir!' Kelly could see the ship keeling to starboard and he was reminded vividly of *Hogue* as she had leaned over him in the pinnace. Then he saw another shape beyond the trooper, hidden by its bulk. It was coming up fast, a white bone of foam at its bow.

'Sir, there's a gunboat! They're on to us!'

Lyster shouldered him aside and grabbed for the eyepiece.

'Hard a starboard! Take her down, Number One! Let's get away from here!'

But as Bennett flooded the tanks, the submarine lurched violently and, as he tried to correct, the bow dipped.

Lyster's voice came sharply. 'Hold her, Number One!'

But the tilt grew steeper and they had to grab for handholds as they began to slide forward. The parallel rules fell off the chart table with a clatter and Kelly stumbled as he stooped to pick them up.

'Blow One and Two!'

Staring across the control room past the gleaming column of the periscope to the port bulkhead where the dial of the depth gauge gaped into the compartment like the eye of a sea monster, Kelly held his breath. The men at the diving and blowing panel were watching their spirit levels intently, their hands on the complex of levers and wheels. From aft the hum from the motors sank to a lower pitch and he caught a strong smell of hot diesel, oil, sweat, unwashed bodies and fear. At the helm, the coxswain was wearing a nagged look, and Bennett's eyes were narrow in a taut face. The cramped atmosphere of the control room seemed to enfold them. They hadn't shaved or washed for days and, as he studied the tense hairy faces, Kelly felt his chest muscles tighten.

Heads turned uneasily. Bennett's eyes were wide now, uncertain and angry. Trying to relax and force himself to breathe more slowly, Kelly was only aware of the tinny clicking sound of the gyro compass, loud in the silence, that seemed to beat like a metronome in his brain. Then suddenly, unexpectedly, the dormant lunacy that had always controlled *E19* started to work its evil again.

'She's rising, sir!'

'Hold her!'

'Eighty feet! Seventy feet! Sixty! Fifty!'

'What's wrong with this bloody boat?' Lyster snapped. 'Hold her, Number One, for God's sake!'

His voice cracked with tension. 'Bring her down, Number One! Bring her down! The conning tower's out of the water! Hard a starboard, helmsman! Flood One, Two and Three!' Immediately every mind had gone back to the tense half-hour when *E19* had run away with them in the Channel before they'd left England. This was infinitely worse because above on the surface now there were enemy craft intent not on saving them but on destroying them.

As Bennett struggled, there were two enormous clangs like hammer blows on the pressure hull so that they knew shells were exploding in the water alongside. As he flooded the tanks, the bow dipped once more and for a moment *E19* steadied, then started to plunge terrifyingly downwards again. At ninety feet, Lyster called out.

'Half ahead port engine! Perhaps that'll help.'

The boat steadied once more but they had only just drawn deep relieved breaths when she lurched and began to dive again, bucking like a wild horse as she settled towards the bottom.

'She's heavy, sir,' the man at the hydroplanes yelled.

'How's the bubble?'

'Horizontal now, sir.'

'Start the pump on the auxiliary! What's causing the negative buoyancy, Number One?'

'Can't find a thing, sir, unless we've sprung a leak.'

'Must be fresh water here with a different density,' Kelly said. 'It's affecting the trim.'

Even as he spoke, *E19* began to rise again and Lyster cursed. 'One of those bloody shells must have damaged the forward planes,' he decided. 'If we can make it round Nagara Point, we'll be all right. Those damn destroyers spot us every time the periscope breaks surface. The water's like a millpond.'

By the light in the eyepiece of the periscope, Kelly saw they had broken surface again and Lyster tried a quick glance round. Immediately, he slammed the handles up. The 'clack' was loud in the silence of the control room. 'Down periscope!'

He swung round as the periscope hissed into its well, his voice breaking the tension. 'For God's sake, Number One, get us down! There's a torpedo boat heading straight for us! Crack the outboard vent.'

As the planesmen leaned on their wheels, the bow went down once more and they heard the thud-thud-thud of propellers as the destroyer roared over them, then suddenly *E19* took a steep inclination by the bows and started to rise yet again. All efforts at regaining control were useless and the diving planes made not the slightest effect.

'Down, man,' Lyster yelled. 'Flood One, Two and Three! Flood Four! Flood Auxiliary!'

Again the submarine dipped under and, closing off the forward tank and stopping the movement of water ballast from aft to forward, Bennett endeavoured to catch her at fifty feet, but now the planes seemed unable to hold her at all and she went on down – eighty feet, ninety, one hundred. This was the limit of their guages and what happened after that God alone knew.

The strained plates creaked and a light bulb suddenly popped, and the man on the forward diving plane started to mutter a prayer, his words loud in the silence.

'Full astern!' Lyster snapped. 'Blow the auxiliary!'

'She's coming up, sir!'

The needle jerked itself reluctantly from the hundred feet mark and began to rise rapidly. The submarine leapt to the surface with increasing speed. While Bennett struggled with the trim, Lyster kept his eyes glued to the periscope.

'That bloody torpedo boat's circling us and there's another coming up from the south!'

As Bennett poured in the ballast again, his face haggard with the strain, the bows went down once more and immediately he had to start to expel it again in a desperate attempt to regain control. But down and down *E19* went, faster even than before, the inclination becoming more pronounced until the boat seemed to be trying to stand on its nose. Eggs, bread, food of all sorts, knives, forks, plates, came showering forward from the petty officers' mess, and everything that could fall over fell over. The men, slipping and struggling, grasped hold of valves, gauges, rods, anything to hold them at their posts.

When they were just wondering why the sides of the submarine didn't cave in under the pressure, the needle jumped back from its stop and the submarine began to rush stern-first to the surface.

'That bloody gunboat!' Lyster yelled, then they all felt the submarine lurch and there was a crash as the shell struck them astern.

'Close watertight doors!'

There were two more bangs in quick succession and one of the stokers appeared from the engine room in a waft of hot oil and a cloud of blue smoke; beyond him Kelly could see balls of incandescent copper flying off the switches and wicked blue-green electric flames leaping and dancing.

'We're taking in water astern, sir,' the stoker reported.

'Much?'

'A lot, sir.'

One of the shells had hit them on or near the conning tower and cascades of icy green sea were coming in from overhead, drenching the wardroom curtains. It was obvious, with the weight of water increasing all the time, that they would now never be able to hold *E19* on the surface but, holed as she was, they also dared not dive.

Lyster straightened up. He looked old and weary. They were finished. They all knew it.

For some reason the shells had stopped *E19*'s mad behaviour and she lay wallowing on the surface quite placidly.

'All right,' Lyster said wearily. He was in control of himself again, the old, imperturbable, odd-looking figure in knicker-bockers and cricket sweater. 'I'm going to scuttle. Stay with me, Number One, to attend to it. All hands on deck. Prepare to abandon ship. Where's the Chief ERA?'

'They're bringing him forward, sir,' one of the stokers said. 'He's been hurt.'

The sea continued to pour in on them with a terrible and relentless drenching noise, and the water round their feet crept higher every second. Electrical contacts spat venomously with little lightning flashes and Kelly wondered if he were about to be electrocuted.

The forward watertight door had been shut and one of the seaman was sobbing. 'My pal's in there, sir! My pal's in there!'

Shivering with fear, Kelly was aware of men beginning to assemble in the control room, clutching a few personal possessions, even pictures of wives and girlfriends. Their faces indicated that they were near to panic but they were still behaving calmly with solid naval discipline.

Two of the stokers appeared with the ERA. There was blood on his face and he was vomiting badly. There was dead silence and all they could hear was the monotonous, pitiless sound of water pouring in on them.

Lyster gave a heavy sigh. 'Very well,' he said. 'Abandon. You go first, Pilot, and warn me when the water gets too high.'

As Kelly reached for the ladder, Bennett turned to Lyster.

'Sorry, sir. There was nothing I could do.'

'Not your fault, Number One. This bloody boat's behaved like a fairground horse all its life. I always knew it'd finally do its stuff at the wrong moment. Let's get on with it.'

As Kelly scrambled through the hatch, Rumbelo joined him and moved to the stern with another man. The water was already lapping against the conning tower.

'Sir,' Kelly yelled. 'She's going!'

Lyster's voice came up. 'I've just time to get my brief case. Get going, Number One!'

Food, clothing, flotsam and jetsam of all kinds were floating out of the submarine which now lay, bow down, and beginning to heel over to starboard, men pushing through the hatch one after another. The Turkish torpedo boat was still bearing down on them and one of the men on the stern of the submarine raised his hands. The water was lapping higher against the conning tower.

'Hurry, sir, she's going down!'

As Kelly yelled, the submarine lurched and the man on the stern with his hands in the air staggered, off-balance, and fell into the water. Rumbelo immediately went after him in a neat racing dive that impressed Kelly as he remembered how he'd last seen him enter the sea.

'Sir, hurry, for God's sake!'

No more than a few men had escaped and, as Kelly turned, he saw Bennett's face appear at the top of the ladder. Kneeling down, he reached through the hatch to yank him to the surface, but as he did so the submarine lurched again and seemed to stand on its nose. In his mind's eye he saw all the men still below hurled down the length of the centre passage, flung forward as if thrown down a lift shaft, followed by everything that was not fastened down. Momentarily, she steadied again, the stern going down, so that the boat straightened, then, as he clung to the binnacle for support, without a sound or a sigh, without even an eddy or a ripple on the surface of the water, the submarine slid away from under him.

For a second he had a glimpse of Bennett's horrified eyes as he tried to fight his way through the water gushing through the open hatch to reach Kelly's straining hand, then *E19* simply vanished from beneath his feet. There was a huge fountain of spray and a roaring sound like a gigantic whale blowing, then he found himself swimming with no sign of the submarine and only a few heads around him in the water to indicate what had happened to the crew.

Seven

Dripping and miserable, Kelly was dragged over the side of the torpedo boat's dinghy, the water pouring from his seaboots and thick clothing.

The officer in command spoke English. 'I regret we have not been able to save any more than these men you have with you, sir,' he said.

Kelly nodded wretchedly. *E19* hadn't run very much amuck, and their wartime career had been short and not very sweet.

A gentle drizzle of rain began to fall as they headed shorewards and as it touched the surface of the sea, it seemed to Kelly like a benediction that was unbelievably sad and sweet. Thinking of Lyster and Bennett and the others who were dead, life seemed so beautiful he couldn't imagine himself ever being dissatisfied with it again.

Then the reaction came as he remembered he was a prisoner – a useless appendage to the war because the Turks didn't want him and he was no good to the Allies. The realisation that he was facing jail like a common criminal came as a shock and he suddenly wondered how long it would be for.

Nobody was under any delusion any more that the war was going to be a short one. It hadn't ended by Christmas, 1914, as they'd been promised, and there was little likelihood that it would end by Christmas 1915. For a moment, as he saw captivity and humiliation stretching away for years into the future, he felt like weeping. For God's sake, he thought wildly, he'd be an old man when they let him free again!

All of them quiet and brooding on their ill-luck, they were taken to Scutari on the opposite side of the Bosphorus from Constantinople, and the next morning a military guard brought dry clothes consisting of the overcoat and trousers of an ordinary Turkish soldier's uniform, a pair of slippers without socks, and a fez. What was left of their own uniforms was taken away, then, amidst a large crowd of spectators, they were fallen in on the wharf and, surrounded by guards with fixed bayonets, were marched through the town. People gathered on the sidewalk to watch them. Shopkeepers and their assistants crowded to their doors, trams and cabs stopped, and here and there from behind heavily-curtained windows they could see a female shape watching.

'Even the bloody 'arem's taking an interest,' Rumbelo growled.

In perfect silence they marched along, the little gutter boys making faces at them and occasionally drawing their fingers across their throats. At the office of the town major they were marched in front of a tall good-looking man smoking a cigarette through a holder about a foot long.

'You must not look on yourselves as prisoners,' he said cheerfully. 'But more as honoured guests of Turkey.'

They were escorted up several flights of stone stairs and pushed into a large empty room containing little else but portraits of Enver Pasha and Talaat Bey, the leaders of the Young Turks Party. It was dirty and stuffy but as they opened windows to let in air, the guards appeared and closed them all again.

'It's fifty feet down,' Rumbelo announced indignantly. 'I'm not going to jump out of *that*!'

Straw palliasses were brought but within an hour of lying down on them they discovered they were crawling with bedbugs and, by the dim light of a broken gas mantle, they started to do battle with them.

'Makes you wonder whether it's best to kill 'em when they're young,' Rumbelo said, 'or leave 'em till they're grandparents and likely to die of old age.'

The next day half a dozen Turks were pushed in with them and spent the morning spitting and emptying their bronchial tubes on the floor until Rumbelo, brought up in an orphanage and with the navy's entrenched ideas of tidiness and hygiene well drilled into him, threatened to knock their heads together and throw them out of the window. For the rest of the day they seemed to be gagging on their own phlegm, but they didn't spit any more.

The next morning they were informed that they were to be moved to Afion Kara Hissar, in the centre of Asia Minor, and a week later they stared up from the station at the ruin of a fortress situated on the summit of a sheer and precipitous rock.

'Looks tough,' Kelly observed.

'More'n you can say for the town,' Rumbelo said. 'That only smells strong.'

The old fort, which also contained a few French and Russians, was cold enough for the sentries to snuggle into their boxes out of the wind that came out of the desert of mountain and rock, and food seemed to consist of little else but a wholewheat mush called porridge for breakfast with a lunch of wheat 'pillao' and duff. The rooms were comfortless and, to depress them further, there was the uncertainty of their future, because the Young Turk government was unreliable and erratic and might just as easily murder them as treat them with kindness.

Beginning that night, for their entertainment a band consisting of a big drum, a piccolo and three brass instruments serenaded them every evening in the square outside their quarters. It was purgatory because they were far from expert and after a fortnight of it, since the repertoire consisted of only five tunes, they always knew when the brass would be short of wind, the piccolo would play false notes and the big drum would come in late.

Driven almost to distraction, Kelly decided to retaliate. The Russian prisoners could sing magnificently and, led by an officer of the reserve who was said to be the tenor of the Moscow Opera, their haunting songs could always be guaranteed to silence everyone. Pitting themselves against the band, with everyone else joining in to lend weight, the soloist sang the lament then, gathering speed, the tune broke into a gallop, faster and faster until the Russians seemed to be flinging their tortured souls into a furnace where joy, sorrow and despair could be utterly consumed until, after a final frenzied chorus, they became silent. The band had crept away. They never returned.

At the end of the week they were taken to the bath-house in the company of a lot of Turkish soldiers but on return to their quarters, they realised the few belongings they'd collected had been searched and when Kelly objected they were simply moved to another room. They were bundled out, protesting, and razors, insect powder, toothbrushes and private letters were removed. Then the commandant appeared, wearing a uniform surtout of pearl grey and a hat that was a caricature of the one worn by Enver Pasha. His moustache hid a weak, cruel mouth and his expressionless face was pale because, like many wealthy Turks, he never took exercise. A pair of deep-set lustrous eyes brooded on them.

'Your men are to be put into the dungeons,' he announced. 'Turkish officers in Egypt are being ill-treated and I have been ordered by my government to make retaliation.'

'That's damn silly,' Kelly snorted.

'I have no alternative.'

'All right,' Kelly said impulsively. 'I'll go in their place.'

Rumbelo tried to protest but Kelly shut him up.

'You're better outside,' he said. 'I need someone to keep an eye on things.'

The dungeon seemed completely dark but then he saw there was a bed and a small table, and high up in the wall a tiny hole as a window, through which he could feel the cold air. The floor was swimming in water. The day was drawing on and when

Rumbelo brought his food it consisted of bread, water and three small potatoes soaked in oil. Hunger overcoming disgust, he started to eat, but the oil was stale and sour and the water was brackish.

'This is a bloody fine kettle of fish, Rumbelo,' he observed, trying to smile.

Rumbelo scowled. 'The lads is narked, sir.'

'Tell 'em not to do anything to jeopardise their own comfort. They haven't got so bloody much.'

The mattress was so full of bedbugs Kelly had to sleep with the ends of his trousers tucked inside his socks as they swarmed all over him.

'I've killed as many as I can,' he told Rumbelo as he brought his food next morning, 'but they're remarkably quick movers. I've taken to sleeping on the floor.'

'It's wet, sir.'

'Yes, but there aren't any bedbugs there.'

The following evening a lamp was provided but was soon taken away and not returned and the floor remained wet. For twenty-four hours a day the wind blew through the single small window, making the place like an ice box so that at night he had to shiver in his greatcoat and blanket. He had started on the self-imposed torment with an attitude of nobility and high-minded duty, thinking it a sacrifice he could endure for a little while. It was the sort of thing he felt officers did for their men – at least they did in the *Boys' Own Papers* of his youth – and he'd decided it would do him no harm. A fortnight later, with his clothes permanently damp and the diet consisting almost entirely of bread and water and half-cooked potatoes and grain in a tepid broth, he was so bored he'd have welcomed a book of multiplication tables as light reading matter and he was no longer sure that he hadn't been a damn fool.

The commandant was suitably apologetic. 'It is nothing personal, you understand. You should consider it in the light of an honour that you are suffering for the sins of your government.'

'St Kelly Maguire,' Kelly announced to Rumbelo when he appeared. 'Martyr for Mr Asquith.' He felt a little lightheaded and faintly hysterical and he put it down to the strain of solitary confinement. 'How are the chaps?'

'They're fine, sir. Thanks to you. But they're still narked.'

'Tell 'em not to worry. It can't last much longer.'

But the next night, he felt awful and went to sleep with dreams of Mr Asquith and Sir Edward Grey weeping over his fate, but proud of the honour he was doing them by representing them in Turkey. Then the dream changed to Enver Pasha and Talaat Bey laughing at him and he woke shivering in a cold sweat.

'You're ill,' Rumbelo said accusingly when he appeared with his food next morning.

'No. Nothing at all.'

But the following night was a nightmare and when his food came he didn't even bother to get up.

'There was a rat in here last night,' he said, 'I heard it eating my bread.'

That night, he thought he was dying and the next morning, Rumbelo didn't argue but picked him up in his strong arms and elbowed his way past the startled sentry and into the corridor.

Leaning against Rumbelo's big chest, Kelly smiled. 'I didn't know you cared, Rumbelo,' he said.

Dimly he became conscious of Rumbelo arguing at the top of his voice with an officer and then being carried along another corridor to a lighter room where there was glass in the window. There was a bed and sheets and even a doctor in white. Ignoring the Turkish attendants, Rumbelo stripped off his clothes and put him into the bed and dragged the blankets up to his neck.

'Thanks, Mum,' Kelly whispered.

There was a blank of several days before he was aware of Rumbelo again, ludicrous in his scraps of Turkish clothing, sitting stern-faced and at attention alongside the bed.

'What happened, Rumbelo?' he demanded.

'You was took ill, sir.'

'What was it? Typhus?'

''You 'ad pneumonia.'

'Did I, by God?'

'Your mum would never 'ave forgive me if I'd let the bastards get away with it, sir. Nor no more would Biddy. You was always her favourite. I'd never have been able to face her. The doc says you're all right now, though.'

Rumbelo looked at Kelly. He had never known his parents and could barely remember his brother, and somehow Kelly's family, linked to him by Biddy, had taken their places in his processes of thought, while Kelly had supplied the need he felt for someone to admire. He was under no delusions that he would get special treatment if he let him down but it didn't alter the fact that he had a very special place in Rumbelo's heart.

'I made bloody sure you were all right,' he went on. 'I slept here and dared 'em to chuck me out. They didn't try.'

'Good old Nanny! You probably saved my life.'

With good food and warmth, Kelly soon recovered. Within a week he was sitting up and within another week was back in his old quarters. He was never sent back to the cell.

The Turks continued to be a strange mixture of chivalry and brutality, one moment treating them with kindness and consideration, the next buffeting them with the butts of their rifles. They were an odd confection of the ancient East and the modern West, one of the officers, a young man called Bakhash Bey, who seemed to be part of the old Turkish nobility, stopping occasionally to discuss music or the latest shows in London with Kelly, while his servant, a wrinkled Anatolian peasant, went in for the dubious habit of rubbing curds and whey into his hair when he had a headache.

After a while, a few more prisoners arrived – some of them Australians captured at the Dardanelles. They were soured by their ill-fortune, disliked the British and were inclined to take orders from no one. Rumbelo, who had organised a trading concession with a large splay-footed sentry he called Cinderella, brought in news of the treatment they were suffering at the hands of the guards.

'The buggers kicked one of 'em to death,' he said. 'They had swords and knobkerries and were boasting how they smashed our chaps in the trenches.'

Soon afterwards a few Arabs, who'd been caught helping the British, were brought in and, since their room was immediately underneath, once a week, on an evening they came to dread, they could hear the screams of men being tortured.

'If I ever get out of here,' Rumbelo growled. 'I'll kill one of these bastards. I swear I will.'

The days went by slowly then unexpectedly they were moved away, leaving in carts by road through fields of tall corn and poppies and stopping at a caravanserai en route for the night.

The serai was built round a courtyard and they were all crammed into one dilapidated room. But, as soon as the Turkish sentry had locked the door and vanished, Kelly discovered that the window could be taken out, lock, stock and barrel, and they all climbed through and dived among the drovers making their evening obeisances to Allah, hiding their faces and praying Mussulman-fashion, their heads to the floor.

A boot crunched in the gravel by Kelly's ear. '*Çhok fena*, Monsieur Maguire,' an officer's voice said. 'When a Mussulman prays, he has his head towards Mecca. You and some of your friends have yours towards Piccadilly Circus.'

They climbed to their feet disgustedly and were marched back to their quarters. The following morning, the carts reappeared and they continued their journey.

Shakan, where they finally stopped, was as comfortless as Afion Kara Hissar, but instead of being in the mountains it was on the plains south of Smyrna. It lay on the edge of myrtle-scented gullies and was permanently swept by cold winds that brought clouds of gritty dust.

'I'm going to get out of this bloody place somehow, Rumbelo,' Kelly said. Rotting for the rest of the war under Turkish sentries who would make a goat faint from their smell, and trying to wangle a little comfort from cafe-jees with faces like mouldy hams didn't seem to present much of a future.

Rumbelo was more cautious. 'Wait your chance, sir,' he advised. 'Don't do nothing rash. It'll come.'

Autumn arrived and then winter and they celebrated Christmas in comfortless fashion with a little illegal alcohol brought in by Rumbelo's latest trading partner, a fat Jewish interpreter who seemed to be followed permanently by a squad of camp guards on the lookout for attempts to escape. Rumbelo called them Snow-White and the Seven Dwarfs and somehow managed to bribe them into supplying a few extras.

That night patriotism was at fever heat. A French voice began to sing the *Marsellaise* and, on the instant, every man present took up the song, so that the sound spread like a flame, echoing and re-echoing through every corner of the dusty building. Afterwards three Russians sang *Bozhe Tsarya Khrani* then the few British sailors, clad in scraps of Turkish uniform, sang their own national anthem, faintly ashamed that they knew only the chorus.

Early in January, the Jewish interpreter arrived to announce that the Dardanelles campaign had ended in failure and that the British had evacuated the peninsula, and soon afterwards, to add to their gloom, they learned that the Allied war effort had suffered yet another setback with a British–Indian army besieged at Kut on the Euphrates, after making a lunatic attempt to reach Baghdad.

'Who wants Dad's Bags, anyway?' Rumbelo growled. 'It's full of bloody Turks.'

They had begun to suspect that they were going to sit out the war in their dusty, gritty camp when the British contingent was sent for by the camp commandant. With the Australians the party had now risen to thirty-five.

'We have to clear the camp,' the commandant announced. 'Kut is expected to surrender very soon and then this place will be needed for the enormous number of men who will fall into our hands. You are to be sent to Syria.'

They were all making searches in their minds to decide just where Syria was placed for escape when the commandant spoke again.

'There are Arab insurgents in Syria,' he said. 'And they have acquired explosives and persist in wrecking the line between Damascus and the Suez Canal. You will therefore be split up and placed in the first carriages of trains and the information passed on to the Arabs.'

Kelly protested forcefully, using every argument about Geneva Conventions and the International Red Cross he could think of, but the commandant shook his head. 'I have my orders,' he insisted.

'It's against all the usages of war!'

The commandant smiled. 'But it is also a very good idea, is it not?' he said.

Three days later Kelly's party were marched into a cold, gritty halt in the middle of the plain and pushed into a carriage. It was French-built with a corridor running down the centre. The guards, led by a young Turk called Mazhar Osman Effendi, were looking very uneasy and didn't appear to relish the job they'd been given. There was a great deal of confusion as the sailors climbed in one side of the carriage and out of the other for sheer devilment, and then, pushed back, crossed over and descended once more where they'd climbed in. The Turks began to shout and Kelly stared coldly at the Turkish officer.

As the Turk deposited his luggage on the seat next to Kelly, Rumbelo leaned over. 'Just in case you're interested, sir,' he pointed out, 'he carries his pistol inside his jacket over his left 'ip.'

How long they were in the train they didn't know because they lost all count of time. They slept sitting up on the hard seats or stretched in the alleyway between. At every stop they were surrounded by the Turkish soldiers while Osman Effendi disappeared for a meal. Stewed fat mutton and coffee appeared twice a day and once they were allowed to take a bath under the tank which was used for filling the engine.

They reached Aleppo through the mountains of Central Anatolia and at Damascus were joined by another small group of prisoners as hungry and dirty as they were themselves. As the train drew up, they were shoved inside and once more Osman took his seat alongside Kelly, clearly considering himself a martyr to Turkey's war effort.

The journey was an agonising nightmare of dust, heat and boredom. There was a complete lack of comfort and nothing to see but dead brown hills with occasional clumps of palms shading the low black tents of nomad Arabs. Deraa, Amman and Ma'an passed, ugly stations crowded with Turkish troops, veiled women and Turkish civilians in fezzes and strange old-fashioned Western suits. The stops in between were mere halts round huddles of buildings where the wind swept through like a scorching blast. At Shahm, they were taken off the train and pushed into an empty stone building with a sand floor where cattle had been housed.

The building was loud with the sound of flies, and later they made out the scratching of rats. All night they could hear the clatter and roar of steam from nearby trains and as they boarded the northbound train next day, Kelly could see a desperate look in the eyes of the ragged men.

A few Turkish women who climbed into the rear end of their carriage displayed great interest in them, peering round the curtain which screened their end of the compartment. They had all noticed that, while the older Turkish women skulked behind thick veils that completely hid their faces, the younger and prettier women wore thin ones through which their features could be seen and that they were always finding excuses to pull them aside. Apart from the kohl they persisted in putting round their eyes, many of them looked surprisingly delectable after being locked away from female company for so long.

The night was as bad as all the others, hot, dusty and uncomfortable. A hamman-jee offered baths in a van down the train to everyone but the prisoners. Someone passed round a chattee full of water and a few biscuits for breakfast and they were just gnawing at the great doorstops as the train, its whistle screaming, rocked round a bend, throwing out clouds of smoke from its wood fuel.

Rumbelo was staring out of the window, his eyes narrow and calculating. 'If we could jump out here,' he pointed out, 'we could be among them rocks before you could say Jack Robinson. How about it, sir?'

But before Kelly could reply, there was a terrific roar behind them and a spouting column of black dust and smoke a hundred feet high. Out of it came shattering crashes and loud, metallic, clanking noises as steel was torn up, and lumps of iron and plate fell off the train into the scrub alongside the track. They saw the wheel of a wagon thud down into the dust out of the sky and bowl alongside the track like a hoop, then the carriage lurched to a stop and they were all thrown from their seats. Finding himself on top of Osman, Kelly immediately punched him in the throat. The Turk's eyes widened and his mouth opened to make a gagging sound. Hitting him again in the face, Kelly fished under his jacket for his pistol. As he dragged it free, he saw one of the Turkish soldiers further down the compartment struggling to his feet with his rifle, and promptly shot him in the chest.

'Good on yer, mate!' An enormous Australian leapt over him and snatched at the dead soldier's rifle and, as the other Turkish soldiers scrambled to their feet, he shot one, and reversing the weapon, clumped another at the side of the head to send him head-over-heels into the arms of his friends. Rumbelo was right behind him, yelling with rage, and as the Turks were smashed down their rifles were snatched from their hands.

The women behind the curtains were screaming and the Australian grinned. 'Them judies needn't worry for me,' he said. 'What now?'

Kelly stuck his head out of the window. Rifle fire was coming from the rocks on the right hand side of the track and the Turkish soldiers were jumping out of the doors on the left and crawling under the halted carriages to fire back. Others who had been riding on the roof were being knocked off by the rifle fire and were landing in the dust alongside the rails. Then, as they watched, a wild line of robed horsemen came tearing from among the rocks heading for the train.

'For God's sake, Rumbelo,' Kelly said. 'For seafaring men we seem to be seeing an awful lot of the war on land!'

The Turkish rifles rattled, and several of the ragged figures fell and several horses went down.

'Let's get out of here,' Kelly yelled. 'This way!'

'The buggers'll shoot us,' the Australian yelled.

'The other way, the bloody Turks will.'

Jumping from the carriage, Kelly began to run for the rocks followed by the rest of the prisoners in a ragged cloud. The Turkish riflemen ignored them and, clearly regarding the Arabs as much more dangerous, were concentrating on them. Armed with rifles and swords, the horsemen swept past the running men and began to climb into the train. Above the rattle of the rifles and the yells and the roar of escaping steam, Kelly heard screaming and, turning back, saw the Turkish women being dragged from the train.

He flung himself down among the rocks, and the Australian fell on top of him.

'You little beaut',' he crowed. 'We did it!'

Looking round for Rumbelo, Kelly saw that out of the whole party, only he had failed to make it. He was lying out on the dusty slope, hit in the thigh, and as he saw him trying to struggle to his feet, without thinking, he shoved the pistol into his belt and began to run.

A few bullets kicked up dust and stones near him, but the Turks were more concerned with shooting at the maddened Arabs and he slithered untouched to a stop alongside Rumbelo. The Australian appeared behind him and, together, they lifted Rumbelo and struggled back up the hill.

'You mad Pommy sod,' the Australian stormed as they flung themselves down behind the rocks again. 'Them Turks shoot fellers that do that!'

The Turkish soldiers were recovering quickly now that the first surprise was gone, but the Arabs seemed to have gone stark, raving mad and were rushing about at full speed, bareheaded and half-naked, screaming, shooting, slicing at anyone within reach with their great curved sabres. A Turkish soldier running along the side of the train was spotted by a horseman in a black cloak who went clattering after him, swinging his enormous sword. The Turk's head leapt off as if it had been lifted by a spring inside his neck, and the body, still running, went on for a few more steps before it rolled over in the dust. The Arab lifted his bloody weapon, yelling, then a rifle cracked and he disappeared in a whirl of arms and legs over the tail of his horse.

The Arabs had clearly heard of the Turkish practice of placing prisoners in the first carriage and had waited for it to pass before setting off their charge in the middle of the train. The explosion had smashed one of the carriages to splinters and the bodies of its occupants lay among the shredded wood and tangled steel. All the wagons in front had been dragged from the track and stood lopsided, and all the ones that followed were derailed and smashed.

The raiders were flinging things from the train now – carpets, mattresses, quilts, blankets, clothes for men and women, clocks, cooking utensils, food, ornaments. A group of hysterical women, their veils snatched away, were tearing at their clothes and hair, shrieking wildly, and the Arabs were grabbing at the best-looking of them and systematically stripping them to the skin. One of them, no more than fifteen and stark naked, was being heaved up the hill by a huge Arab in filthy rags, his face twisted in a great grin.

The Turks were beginning to organise themselves now but the Arabs had got away with a great many rifles and several of the carriages had been set on fire. Riding and running for the rocky hillside, more Arabs fell, but it was clearly never their intention to get too involved in a battle and they were retreating.

'Come on,' Kelly yelled. 'Keep up with 'em! If we stay here we haven't a chance!'

He started up the slope, with Rumbelo clinging on to him and the Australian. Just ahead of him several Turkish women were being pushed along by a group of Arabs, and the young girl, her naked body slender as a reed, was being dragged shrieking behind her huge captor.

Beginning to advance warily from the train, the Turks were firing as they approached. Struggling up the slope, Kelly's party carried Rumbelo over the crest of the little hill to find the Arabs gathering on the other side, yelling and laughing, quite indifferent to the fact that several of their number had been shot. The big man had hoisted the naked girl on to the saddle of his horse and was already clattering off through the dust. The other Turkish women were shrieking wildly and one of the horsemen grabbed at one of them and, throwing her down, fell on top of her. Kelly gave him a kick that sent him sprawling, and as he scrambled to his feet, his lips drawn back over brown teeth in a snarl, a grey horse slithered to a stop alongside them.

Catching a whiff of scent, Kelly looked round to see a slight figure dressed in white, its face covered with its head-cloth against the dust. The Arab released the Turkish woman at once and turned away; the figure on the horse gestured and several riderless animals were brought up.

'Get up!' The words were in English and the voice was light like a boy's.

They climbed on to the horses in ones and twos, Kelly holding Rumbelo in front of him. The figure in white was followed by a tall man in black robes and the two of them were rounding up their followers with urgent gestures. The Arabs were loading their horses with their loot and tying ropes to the wrists of the Turkish women. One of them resisted fiercely and the man who was struggling with her lost his temper, and began to beat her with his fist. The slight figure in white appeared again and a whip came down.

The Arab released the woman and she ran for the crest of the hill. As she reached the top, she was hit by the scattered firing from the other side and they saw her stop dead and turn slowly to face the sun, almost as if in obeisance, a red splodge across her chest, before falling backwards out of sight.

As the rider in white pointed and the Arabs began to move off, Kelly saw only a pair of fine dark eyes and straight heavy eyebrows. The rest of the face, pale in texture, unlike the other Arabs, was still covered with the tail of the head-dress. The heat increased as the sun rose higher and they rode in silence except for the sobbing of the women clutched on the saddles in front of their captors, and the clatter of hooves against the grits and stones and the flat shaley surface of the rock. Behind them a train of ragged prisoners and dismounted Arabs followed. The Arabs had all drawn their head-cloths across their faces against the dust that the wind was whipping up, and pulled the browfolds forward like visors so that they only had a narrow, loose-flapping slit of vision.

Kelly squinted into the sun. Rumbelo was sweating profusely and the heat of his body made Kelly sweat, too. The glare was tremendous because the soil was a pale whitish-grey and the light struck up at them in a mad fashion. After a while, the big Arab left the side of the slim rider in white and moved through the other men collecting what appeared to be rags before eventually appearing alongside Kelly with his bundle. As they halted, he showed Kelly how to tie one of the rags round his head and pull it over his eyes. The other ex-prisoners did the same, then the little column went on again. The women had stopped sobbing now and seemed to have accepted their captivity.

'Well, sir,' Rumbelo panted as they jogged along, 'I dunno who the 'ell's got us now, but we don't seem to be prisoners no more.'

They plodded on all day, stopping only twice to drink water from goatskins. The Arabs chattered to themselves and tormented the women, who actually seemed to be recovering their spirits now and were answering back, all except the wretched girl whom the big Arab kept well apart from the others, fondling her breasts and legs and pawing her salaciously.

Towards the end of the afternoon, they came to a hill which gave a little shade against the lowering sun and they saw a scattering of black tents, low and shapeless against the blueness of the shadows. As they drew near, women and children and old men approached. A few words were exchanged and several of the women, whose men, it seemed, had been killed, burst into a frenzied wailing. As they dismounted, the white-clad leader handed over the grey horse to a ragged youngster and strode towards a striped tent set apart from the others. The big man approached and indicated another tent which was hastily being evacuated.

Rumbelo was lifted down and an old woman appeared, followed by a boy carrying a basket. As they held him down, she extracted the bullet and bound the leg up with cool mosses.

'Just the bloody stuff to give 'im gangrene,' the Australian said.

There was a lot of activity about the camp and fires were lit so that they could smell the smoke of wood and burning dung. After a while, a dish of rice, mutton and bread was brought and they went at it like wolves. Dark, brackish water arrived for them to drink, and they had just finished when the tall man in black robes appeared in the tent door. He pointed at Kelly and indicated that he should follow him.

'Off to meet His Nibs, sir,' Rumbelo said. 'The boss himself.'

The black-clad man led the way towards the striped tent. The interior was filled with carpets and there was a small folding table of filigree work with a brass tray on top of it bearing a coffee pot.

The Arab indicated one of the carpets and Kelly sat. As the Arab disappeared, the other end of the tent opened and the slim white-clad figure appeared under a draped fold. As Kelly rose to his feet, it straightened up and Kelly's jaw dropped. The figure, which he'd assumed under the Arab robes to be some young sheikh or the son of a sheikh, was most obviously and enjoyably a girl. She wore no head-dress, but a long kaftan was partly open at the front to reveal firm full breasts and long legs in cotton trousers.

'Good God!' Kelly said.

The girl eyed him gravely. 'You are surprised?'

'Who wouldn't be? Who the devil are you?'

'I am Ayesha, daughter of Jellal el Arar, of Medina. Who are you?'

Eight

Circumstances had changed rapidly enough to make Kelly catch his breath. From being a ragged, half-starved prisoner cut off from civilisation and the company of women, it seemed he was now a privileged guest, and the guest of an extremely attractive girl at that.

'My name's Maguire,' he said. 'Kelly Maguire. Lieutenant, RN. I'm from the British submarine *E19*. We were sunk eight months ago near Nagara. All but nine of us were drowned.'

The girl nodded. 'There were other submarines, too,' she said, 'I heard about them. I learned everything that went on at Gallipoli.'

'But who *are* you?'

She shrugged. 'I am an enemy of Turkey. That's sufficient. It's my intention to return you to your people. You will be sent to Egypt.'

Kelly's heart leapt, and he grinned. It provoked the sober little face in front of him to give a small smile.

'Why?' he asked.

'Because only through a victory by the British and their allies can we hope to obtain the freedom that we need.'

'Who?'

'The Arab nation.'

'The Arabs aren't a nation.'

'That's a mistake the Turks have made. Arab civilisations are of an abstract nature, of course. Moral and intellectual rather than applied and their lack of public spirit made their excellent qualities futile.'

The words were delivered with gravity but in perfect English and Kelly was curious. 'Where did you learn to speak English like that?'

The girl lifted her nose in the air. 'That is an arrogant question. After all, you cannot speak my language.'

'But you speak it so perfectly, and with such a high-class accent.'

'Naturally I learned it at Cheltenham Ladies' College. I think you had better sit down before you fall down.'

Kelly sat down and the girl handed him a cup of coffee, pouring it herself.

'I have no servants,' she said. 'Only one woman. I attend to most of my own needs.'

'But what the blazes is a product of Cheltenham Ladies' College doing here?'

The small nose lifted. 'The products of Cheltenham Ladies' College don't all grace the soirées of London. Cheltenham Ladies' College has always accepted girls from other parts of the world. In my year there were three from the Middle East, two from India, and one from West Africa. British public schools are full of the products of the British Empire.'

Kelly felt a little dazed. The girl sounded very much like Charley and even had the same stubborn, self-willed manner.

She tried to explain. 'My father is the Sheikh of Arar. But he isn't a wandering sheikh who lives in tents and breeds goats. He does business in Medina, before the war with the French and the British. He felt that the British Empire was the only hope for the Arabs and he sent his children to England to school. My two brothers went to Eton.'

Kelly was eyeing the girl with approval. Under the robes it was quite clear she was slim and shapely. Her neck was slender and carried a proud little head. Her nose was slightly curved and thin but her lips were well-formed. It was her eyes that attracted him most, however. Like so many Middle Eastern women she wore kohl on them, but they were large and expressive and surrounded by long dark lashes, and her hair was drawn back from her face over small ears and fastened with a jewelled slide behind her head.

She was still speaking. 'When the war broke out,' she said, 'my brothers were recruited at once into the Turkish Army. Many Arabs serve with them. They have to. They have always had to. Even my father holds an honorary military position. So far, they have been used only for garrison duties and it is their intention to disappear as soon as possible. I was the only one who was free, and my father permitted me to come here to do what I could. Jemil, who brought you here, is my body servant.'

Kelly gestured. 'Do all those – all those men out there – do they know who you are?'

'Of course. They are my father's servants. They do as they are told. Jemil sees that they do, and so long as they are told to kill Turks, they don't care who tells them.'

'I always thought that in the Arab world a woman was only a chattel.'

'My family are not wandering herdsmen. We are civilised people of education and wealth.'

'But don't you have to do what your menfolk tell you?'

She smiled proudly. 'That is just what I am doing. I am carrying out my father's orders. The Arab nation cannot afford to have men like him and my brothers put to death by the Turks for dissenting. But no one – least of all the Turks – questions what happens to a girl. I am here until the moment comes for the revolt, and then my father and my brothers will join us.'

'When will that be?'

'When the British and the French finally become aware that in the Arabs they have a potentially strong ally. And then, with our help, they will capture Damascus and Baghdad and threaten Constantinople. It is many generations since we passed under the yoke of the Turkish Empire and we have found it a slow death. Apart from a few clever ones like my father who learned to run with the hare and hunt with the hounds, our goods have been stripped from us and our spirits shrivelled by the Turkish military government.'

'And now?'

She smiled. 'There have always been rebellions – in Syria, Mesopotamia and Arabia – and we have always refused to give up our tongue for the Turkish. Instead, we have filled the Turkish language with our own Arabic words.' She moved restlessly. 'But we have lost our geographical sense and our racial and political memories, and Enver Pasha has forbidden Arab societies, scattered Arab deputies and proscribed Arab notables. He even suppressed Arab manifestations and the Arab language.'

She was silent for a while, and Kelly was conscious of the feeling that he was listening to a British intellectual. Only the awareness of her slight frame and the perfume she wore made him realise that she wasn't one.

Her face was stern as she continued. 'But a few stiffer spirits refused to be put down,' she said. 'Suppression filled them with an unhealthy violence and we became revolutionary. One day we shall ask the Allies to help us, to provide us with guns and aeroplanes and motor cars and some of their battalions. We need machine guns and explosives to disrupt the Turkish railways. Today's work was only a trivial affair. Our explosives were stolen from the Turks and they're hard to get. One day some man will arise who will understand us, some man the Arabs can follow, and then the Turkish Empire will fall, because it is rotten already and they will not be able to hold on to it. In Syria this feeling for freedom is already strong. They have our men in their army but they dare not trust them.'

Kelly felt bewildered. 'And do you think you'll win?' he asked.

'In the end.' The girl nodded, full of enthusiasm. 'There has already been trouble in the Hejaz, and the Sherif of Mecca refused to join the Holy War that the Turks declared in an attempt to strengthen their hold on us. Last year, weak leaders in Mesopotamia, Damascus and Syria opposed a mutiny against the Turks, but the oppressed of our nation are calling out to us. The Sherif sent his son to get a report. A second son went to Medina to raise troops from the villagers and a third was sent to sound out the British about their attitude. But public opinion isn't ready and too many think Germany will win the war.'

'Never!'

'The campaign in the Dardanelles has failed.'

'There'll be others.'

'Like Mesopotamia? There were fifteen thousand men shut up in Kut. Starvation and disease have reduced them now to ten thousand and eventually there will be still less.'

'They'll be relieved.'

'Not the way the British Army is setting about it.'

She spoke with complete confidence in her beliefs and military knowledge. 'How would you do it?' Kelly asked.

'With promises of guns and help, the Arabs could harass the Turks enough for the British to break through.'

'Is that what the Arabs want?'

She smiled. 'We are quite indifferent as to whether General Townshend is relieved or not, but we are eager to harass the Turks for you. Kut means nothing but Baghdad and Damascus do. With our help, the British could capture Akaba, Gaza, Jerusalem and Damascus, even as far north as Alexandretta. The Turks would then have to withdraw from the Narrows, and the Black Sea would be open to Allied ships.'

It sounded logical. The idea of using the Arab tribes to harass Turkish communications was a sound one. No one could live as they could in the desert or move faster across its arid wastes.

'But time is running short,' the girl went on. 'With the Arab peasantry in the grip of Turkish military service and Syria prostrate, our assets are disappearing. We must strike now, however feebly, and keep on striking. That is why I am here. As soon as it can be arranged, you will go to Tripoli and from there a boat will take you to Egypt. You must tell your people there of our aims and our hopes and our needs. You must do something for us.'

'You're very brave,' Kelly said.

Two large kohl-rimmed eyes met his. 'I'm often frightened. Perhaps we have moved too soon. But on the other hand, perhaps a few lives must be paid for the sake of our pride.'

She seemed so intelligent, so unbiased, he felt he had to make a protest. 'Those women who were captured: can you accept that? As a woman?'

She shrugged. 'Arab tribes have raided other Arab tribes since the beginning of time. They've always taken their women this way, and in any case, many of these women in Turkish families were originally Arabs. They are not dismayed.'

'But you?'

'I'm supposed to be emancipated. I'm supposed to be able to handle a rifle and shoot a man without turning a hair. I was educated in England where you have Suffragettes. Why should it be different here?'

'Doesn't it worry you?'

As she frowned in an effort to explain, she looked remarkably like Charley trying to explain her own devotion to another, different ideal.

'Sometimes it bothers me a great deal,' she admitted. 'The worst is that I don't know what I am supposed to be. At Cheltenham I was taught to regard as savages people who held the beliefs my people held. But I am one of them. So what am I? What am I supposed to think? Am I a civilised woman behaving in an uncivilised fashion? Or am I merely a savage taking what she can get when and where and how she can get it?'

There were unexpected tears in her eyes and the stern, grave face had crumpled a little.

'I do not accept the Arab attitude that I am a mere chattel,' she went on. 'But I also cannot accept the Western attitude that I am an individual. Yet who among those out there can I regard as an equal? I'm lonely, I'm not an Englishwoman but I'm also not a savage.' Her voice was despairing. 'I don't know what I am!'

They stayed with the Arabs for six days. A messenger was sent off the following morning towards Tripoli and they were warned that within a week they would be on their way.

Rumbelo's wound began to improve and the fever he'd started began to subside. Arab clothing arrived in the tent and they all stared at each other, grinning.

'I look like a cross between Abdul the Damned and Ethelred the Unready,' Kelly said.

Because of the heat, for the most part they remained in the tent during the day, but every evening Jemil called for Kelly to lead him to the striped tent set apart from the others. At first Ayesha was grave and commanding, not giving an inch to the fact that Kelly was a man, but after two or three days he became aware of a difference, an unexpected shyness, and an attendance on his wishes and opinions. On the fifth night, the messenger returned from Tripoli and Jemil appeared at once. Ayesha was waiting for him.

'There is a boat arriving in Tripoli,' she said. 'You will move off in the morning. We shall see you safely there.'

'Isn't it dangerous for you?'

She avoided meeting his eyes. 'No more dangerous than anything else. I have promised that you shall go to Egypt. The British have an office there which deals with Arab affairs. Go to them. Tell them about us. Tell them we need their help.'

Greatly daring, he touched her hand. She didn't pull it away and he took hold of her fingers. Abruptly, she lifted her head and looked him in the eyes. She was so small she made him feel tall and strong.

'We shall come back,' he said.

She gave a small, twisted smile. 'I shall not be here to see the victory.' Her hands were still in his, her head back, her eyes on his face. 'But it will not matter. I am enough of a believer in Islam, despite Cheltenham, to accept that death is only a step to a better life. I shall not see the end of the war.'

Her fatalism was curiously frightening. 'Of course you will!'

She shook her head, clearly unperturbed. 'My father has two sons, both of far more importance than I. I shall never marry. I shall never know what love is.'

'Do you want all these things?'

She looked up at him. 'I want to be a woman. That is all.' There were tears in her eyes again and to Kelly they were a clear green light. As he pulled her closer she abruptly flung herself into his arms.

For a moment he thought of Charley but it seemed to be a decision that needed little consideration. Ayesha was literally begging for love and, for God's sake, he couldn't just push her away and go full astern after she'd saved them from years of imprisonment. Surely there were times when a man could push moral aspects aside.

'Ayesha—' Kelly's voice came out as a croak and he had to clear his throat.

She seemed to think he was about to reject her. 'It doesn't matter,' she said quietly. 'I understand how you feel. You are an honourable man.'

Not as honourable as all that, Kelly thought.

'Your English boys found me attractive when I was in England.' The small voice was plaintive, almost pleading. 'But they tried hard always to behave with honour.'

Not me, Kelly told himself, feeling his pulses race. By God, not me! Not after eight months locked away from women. 'I haven't a scrap of honour, Ayesha,' he said. 'Not in circumstances like this.'

Her face was grave as her hands unfastened the girdle that held the robe round his waist, then her fingers slid inside it, cool and soft against his flesh. As she moved closer to him again, her head against his chest, her eyes turned shyly downwards, he pushed the garment she wore down from her shoulders.

Nine

The following morning they were on the move again, heading towards Tripoli.

Ayesha, wearing the white robes once more, her head-cloth across her face, rode several horses' lengths in front. His face shadowed by the browfold of his headgear, Kelly watched her intently, ridiculous thoughts running through his head. There had been other girls before – the girl in New York and the Ice Maiden in Kiel – but they'd been older than he had and had made the running, enjoying teaching him the facts of life. This was different. He'd been the dominant partner and had known that this was what Ayesha had wanted.

He had awakened dazzled and humbled with her sleeping quietly alongside him, her head on his shoulder, her lips parted, her body soft and warm against him.

'I'm glad it happened,' she had announced gravely as her eyes had opened. 'It makes so much more sense of all the rest of life.'

She was trying hard to be strong-minded, frank and intelligent, as doubtless she'd been taught by her English teachers. Cheltenham Ladies' College would have been proud of her, and he wondered how much Jemil knew. The old man's face was expressionless and he had greeted Kelly unemotionally as he had brought the horses round.

They rode all day and camped at night alongside the road to the coast, Ayesha keeping herself well away from the, with Jemil between her and the rest of the party. During the following day, Kelly rode alongside her. She didn't look at him but held her head up, her eyes in front.

'I long for you,' she said quietly.

That night, Kelly lay apart from the rest of the group, listening, his heart thumping at every sound. But no one came near him and, unable to sleep, his mind filled with thoughts of Ayesha, he tossed restlessly in his blanket. Then, long after everyone was asleep, he heard a stone click and caught a whiff of perfume. A moment later she was alongside him, clinging to him. Taking his hand, she laid it on her breast inside her robe and her lips sought his fiercely.

'I could not stay away,' she breathed.

They made love like children, without regard for the others, and as she lay panting alongside him, he glanced up. Dark against the night sky, a tall figure was waiting and he caught his breath. Then he realised it was Jemil and that the old man was a party to the business.

She left his side before daylight, and as they mounted in the grey light of dawn, her face was covered again and she rode ahead of them as if she'd never noticed Kelly. Eventually, they saw the sea in the distance and began to descend to the coast. The water was shining in the sun over the flat roofs of the port. As they stared at it, Ayesha dropped back.

'Here we must be careful,' she said quietly, the keen military planner once more. 'Turkey might be dying of overstrain, but her military governors are men of agility and suppleness. Many of them are descendants of Greeks, Albanians, Circassians, Bulgars, Armenians and Jews, and though Turkey might be decaying, *they* are not.'

For a few minutes they rode together down the hill until they reached the first scattering of houses. Turkish troops moved about, their ear-flapped khaki caps over their eyes against the sun.

'I shall never forget you,' Ayesha murmured.

'Ayesha, what can I do?'

Her head went up. 'Only tell your people our needs,' she said.

He was just about to reply when she reined in, and he saw a Turkish outpost ahead of them.

'If anything happens,' she said, 'take the road to the right. It leads direct to the water's edge. You'll find plenty of friends.' Her hand touched his. 'We shall be able to hold them up if they are suspicious. Your duty will be not to hesitate.'

'I can't leave you.'

'You are used by your training to obey orders. You must not look back.'

As she kicked her horse into motion, the little column edged forward, and immediately the Turks began to emerge from a small red-tiled hut to fill the road. An officer wearing a sword appeared and the men parted for him.

Ayesha stopped. On their right was a narrow road winding between cypresses down the slope. 'That is your road,' she said quietly. 'Don't hesitate. It takes longer than this one but it will lead you into the city. You are a naval officer, so you should be able to find the sea, I think.'

As she moved forward, the little column lengthened, first Ayesha, then Jemil, then the others, with the British party waiting at the rear as they all passed, and as the leading riders stopped, the whole column came to a halt, strung out in small groups along the road like a broken bead necklace.

'The road on the right, Rumbelo,' Kelly said quietly. 'If there's shooting, that's where we go. Without hesitation. Pass the word.'

'What about His Nibs? If there's shooting, he's going to be the first to cop it.'

'Those are our instructions. We're expected to do as we're told.'

Rumbelo frowned. 'I don't like leaving people in the lurch, sir, when they're making sacrifices to help us.'

Kelly scowled, his own thoughts mixed and angry. 'What's the good of them making sacrifices if we don't take advantage of them? If there's trouble, we go at once. Pass it on to the others.'

They waited as a noisy argument full of shrill voices started. The day was cold and the wind blew a gritty dust in their faces. The horses fidgeted restlessly and Rumbelo shifted uncomfortably in the saddle. Up ahead the voices were growing louder and the Turkish officer was pointing to the rear of the column where they waited.

'We've been spotted,' Rumbelo whispered.

A shot rang out, the echo clattering across the valley. Immediately, as though they'd been instructed what to do, the Arabs in front of them flung themselves from their saddles and dived among the rocks, their rifles pointing towards the Turkish outpost. The Turkish officer was lying on his face in the road and the horses were curvetting and struggling as their heads were dragged round in an attempt to escape. More shots came and one of the horsemen fell off to hit the road in a puff of dust, and Kelly saw the slim white-clad figure in the middle of the skirmish sway, then there was a whole fusillade of shots and the Turks ran for the hut and the drainage ditch at the side of the road. Jemil was wrenching his horse's head round and, as they kicked their heels into their mounts and bolted down the road to the right, Kelly saw he was gripping the reins of the grey pony and that the white-clad figure was clinging to its neck.

The road dropped away so steeply Kelly was convinced they were about to come a cropper, but they clattered downwards, hidden almost at once by cypresses and lemon groves. Above them, on their left, they could hear the rattle of firing and, glancing back, Kelly saw Jemil's big mount thundering after them, followed by the grey.

As they halted among the houses, wondering which way to go, Jemil crashed through them, still leading the grey. Ayesha was clinging to the horse's mane, her head-cloth still in place across her features. Dragging their horses' heads round, they followed Jemil through the narrow streets, raising the dust and sending children and chickens flying. Eventually, in a small square, Jemil halted and dismounted. Speaking quickly to a group of Arab loafers, who appeared to be waiting for them, he gestured to Kelly and they followed him through a doorway with a pointed arch. The loafers snatched at the reins and the horses were spirited away. Within a minute the square was empty and the dust was settling.

As Kelly pushed into the dark house, he saw the big Arab had snatched Ayesha into his arms. Her head-cloth had fallen from her features and he saw a slim hand come up and lift it back into place, then their ears were filled with the sound of running feet as a Turkish patrol hurried past in search of them.

For a moment they held their breath, waiting for the thunder of rifle butts on the door, but nothing happened and eventually the owner of the house appeared, his face worried. Jemil barked at him and Kelly caught the name Jellal el Arar. The owner bobbed his head and gestured. As Jemil disappeared down a corridor, the rest of them were about to follow but Jemil reappeared and pushed them away, gesturing that they should wait. Then the owner of the house returned, calling softly, and two or three women arrived.

'What's happened?' Kelly demanded and Jemil shook his head, barking a few words at him that he didn't understand.

For a long time, they waited in the shadows, the whole lot of them crammed into a large room with a tiled porch, then the owner appeared and called Jemil. When Jemil returned he pointed at Kelly and led the way down the corridor.

Inside a shadowed room, Ayesha was stretched out on an Arab bed. She had been hit in the shoulder by a heavy lead bullet which had struck bone and spread, leaving a terrible wound the women were trying without much success to bandage. They had torn away her robes and he could see her small breasts, streaked with blood, as they fought to staunch the bleeding. Her black hair was spread across the pillow and in the pallor of her face her eyes looked enormous and tremendously, feverishly, bright.

'Can't we give her something to ease the pain?' Kelly whispered.

The owner of the house shrugged. 'Where do we get such drugs, effendi? We have none. What there were the Turks took.'

It was a torment to watch the agony in Ayesha's face. As Kelly went to her she looked up at him. 'You will be all right now,' she said in a voice that was only a half-whisper but was still commanding. 'These are friends of ours. They will find a guide for you as soon as it is dark.' She stiffened in a sudden spasm of pain and Kelly bent closer.

'We've got to get you away from here,' he said.

She managed a weak smile. 'That would be nice, but I would only be a burden. My friends will care for me. I hope you do not blame me for making your escape more risky.'

Lifting her good arm, she reached up and touched his cheek with the back of her hand. 'Perhaps one day you will come back here as a tourist and we shall meet again and drink coffee decorously as old friends.'

'We're more than friends.'

She didn't seem to hear. 'Or perhaps you'll arrive leading a victorious army on Damascus and Constantinople.' She smiled again. 'But, of course not. You could never do that. You are a sailor.'

Crowded uncomfortably, they waited all afternoon as the shadows grew longer and the muezzins started their evening chant. No one came near the house, though over the wailing from the towers they occasionally heard scattered shots coming across the town. In the dusk, a small figure appeared. He was a hunchback, grinning and deformed, and Jemil pointed to Kelly.

'I must say goodbye to her,' Kelly said.

Jemil looked angry but he disappeared into the other room. After a while he returned and nodded.

The change in Ayesha was horrifying. Her face had sunk and the muscles of her neck were drawn taut. She tried to speak and, unable to, he saw tears roll down her cheek. Her throat worked but nothing would come and her eyes, fever-bright in the deathly-white face, burned in their sockets.

As he moved forward, Jemil tried to hold him back. From Ayesha's frantic eyes, he knew she wanted him nearer and he pushed the old man aside with a violent shove and knelt by the bed.

'I'll come back,' he said. 'I'll find you again.'

He spoke cheerfully but he knew only too well that she could never recover from that ghastly wound which had torn away half her shoulder and back. Her breast was moving quickly up and down in little fluttering gasps and, feeling as if tears were falling on his heart one by one in small, icy drops, Kelly bent over and kissed her forehead. For a second the eyelids opened and a rational look came into the eyes through the pain, then the curtain of darkness came swiftly down once more. Jemil turned and roughly pushed Kelly from the room.

'How's His Nibs?' Rumbelo asked.

Kelly swallowed, unable to speak. At last the words came, stumbling and awkward, his voice dry and harsh and sticking in his throat. 'His Nibs,' he said, 'is dying.'

–

A week later they stepped ashore in Alexandria. They had been met outside the harbour by a destroyer and Kelly had stood in the bows of the felucca and shouted up to the spruce figure in white staring coldly down at the ragged figures on the scruffy vessel's decks.

'Lieutenant Maguire, of the submarine *E19*,' he yelled. 'With survivors and ex-prisoners of war.'

The officer leaning over the rail stared in surprise. 'Good God,' he said. 'You'd better come aboard.'

Three hours later, still in their rags, they were in the presence of the admiral. An army colonel was with him to claim the Australians.

'Well, what the devil do we do with you?' the admiral asked. 'There's no longer any fleet at Mudros. Do you want to stay in the Med?'

'Not particularly, sir,' Kelly said. The Middle East could start up too many memories.

'Well, it's always been the policy for escaped prisoners to be sent home. They don't like to chance them being captured again in case they suffer from it. There's a destroyer heading for Gibraltar at the end of the week. You'd better be aboard her.'

Kelly moved restlessly. 'There's one thing I must do first, sir,' he said. 'I believe there's an Arab Bureau in Egypt.'

'That's right,' the admiral agreed. 'Down in Cairo. Doesn't do much.'

'I have messages for them from the Arab leaders. They're anxious to start a national rebellion, and they think it would not only help them but also help us.'

'That's interesting.' The admiral looked at the Australian colonel. 'You'd better give your story to the Intelligence boys, and when I've heard from them we'll see if there's anything we can do about it. You'd better get out of those rags, though.

He looked up at Kelly. 'You any relation of Admiral Maguire?'

'He's my father, sir.'

'Is he, by God?' The admiral seemed surprised that anyone whom Admiral Maguire had sired could be so enterprising as to get himself not only captured by Turks but could also escape. 'Then you'd better see him while you're in Cairo. He's on the mission staff down there.'

Riding to Cairo in the train in the sweltering heat, Kelly's mind was a blur. Dressed in a civilian suit the admiral's flag lieutenant had lent him until the Egyptian tailor could fling together a white drill uniform, all he could see as the track followed the Nile were small haggard features and two feverishly bright eyes in a ghastly caricature of the face that had once looked at him with longing. It appeared in the clumps of palms

238

and the waves of shimmering heat and among the slow-moving dhows. Every group of women he saw stirred his memory and every light voice he heard made him turn his head.

Cairo was full of troops, all listless in the enervating lassitude that lay over the city. Rising out of its steamy soil, the heat intensified in a pall of dust and filth that lay over the streets. The dirt was everywhere. Cairo, corrupt, lackadaisical, easy-going and romantic at night when you couldn't see the dirt, was always a city of beggars and fabulously rich families. Troops marched in squads among the teeming thousands in their white jellabas, with military cars and dozens of army mules. There were British and Indians and Gurkhas and troops from West and East Africa, and no sign of the war anywhere.

Faintly disgusted with the scene, Kelly went into a bar where staff officers in immaculately pressed uniforms looked down their noses at his shabby figure in the rumpled linen suit. The man on the next table kept staring at him and eventually he realised there was a cold curiosity in the glance.

As he turned the man spoke. He was a middle-aged major, red-faced, balding, with cold eyes and a face like a meat axe.

'You British?' he asked.

'Yes,' Kelly said. 'I am.'

'Likely-looking young feller.'

'Thanks.'

'Pity you don't volunteer.'

'What for?'

'What for? The army, man! The army!'

The major had a loud voice and looked as though he'd arrived in uniform from some Middle East business venture. Several eyes turned in Kelly's direction, most of them also cold and disapproving.

Kelly stared back at the major, a hot flush of anger filling his cheeks. 'I don't see the need,' he said, and the major's face darkened.

'Don't see the need?' he snorted. 'Back home, boy, they're bringing in conscription!'

'Won't affect me.'

'Why not? Got something wrong with you?'

'No.'

The blustering voice rose. 'Then you could bloody well volunteer, couldn't you? Out here, we're in need of everybody we can get. Others have. Businessmen like me. Even the bloody archaeologists digging up the desert. There are any amount of wogs, of course, but *they* were never any bloody good to anybody and never will be.'

Black rage filled Kelly, and he finished his beer and rose. Everyone had stopped drinking and he was conscious that they were all hanging on to his words. He glared round at the immaculate khaki figures, deciding that he loathed the lot of them.

'They won't want me,' he said loudly, 'because I happen to be already in the navy. I'm a submariner, as a matter of fact, and I was sunk in the Dardanelles and I've just escaped after being a prisoner of the Turks.'

The hard red face sagged. 'Oh, my God,' its owner said. 'I didn't realise. Look here, boy, may I shake your hand and buy you a drink?'

'You can choke on your bloody drink!' Kelly snorted. 'And it might interest you to know that, but for a few of those men you dislike so much dying to save me, I'd *still* be a prisoner of the Turks!'

–

His father's office was in a block of flats, and the admiral, dressed in white, seemed to be very comfortably established with a woman secretary who looked as though she'd been chosen for her looks rather than for any ability she might have.

'My boy!' Admiral Maguire jumped to his feet as Kelly appeared. 'I got a signal from the C-in-C to say you'd turned up. My God, what a shock! Have you informed your mother?'

'I sent her a telegram,' Kelly said.

His father had grown fatter, as though the fleshpots of Cairo suited him, and Kelly wondered bitterly how often he, too, used the bar he'd just left.

Admiral Maguire sat down. 'I couldn't believe it. What a war you're having, eh? You won't have heard of your Uncle Paddy, of course?'

'No, Father. What about him?'

'Did rather a good job at Ypres and they gave him a battalion. He was killed at Neuve Chapelle.'

Kelly thought of the boozy middle-aged man who had seemed to be lolling about the house throughout his entire youth and found he could feel remarkably little emotion. Uncle Paddy seemed to have redeemed a lot of his former lack of effort, however, and perhaps he had made a better wartime soldier than a peacetime one.

'It's quite a place, this,' his father was saying. 'We have so much to do and find it damned hard to do it because the wogs don't help much.'

'Don't use that word, Father!'

The admiral's head jerked up as his son barked at him. 'What word?'

'"Wog." If it hadn't been for those men, I wouldn't be here now. They deserve a bit more dignity than a name like that.'

The admiral's eyes widened. 'But everybody calls them—' he stopped. 'If it weren't for the –I mean – oh, my God, boy, you can't stop calling them wogs just because—' he stopped again, at a loss. He didn't know another word and he didn't know what to say.

–

The Arab Bureau was in a vast shabby old palace that was full of jangling bells and bustle, and the smart men in neat uniforms irritated Kelly.

He was still seething from his father's lack of sensitivity. They had tried hard to behave warmly to each other but it had remained an uncomfortable interview with neither of them able to touch anything in the other's affections. The admiral was obviously enjoying his war and, with Kelly still bitter at his imprisonment and shocked by Ayesha's death, their conversation had limped to an uncomfortable halt and they had both been glad to say goodbye.

The hallway of the Arab Bureau was filled with military policemen in starched shirts and shorts, who clearly didn't approve of Kelly's ill-fitting suit. One of them stepped abruptly in front of him with the smack of boots on the floor.

'Whom do you wish to see, sir?'

Kelly explained his identity and his errand and they stared at each other, baffled. Obviously no one there had ever thought much about helping the Arabs to wage war.

'Better show him into *him*,' one of them said.

Following the military policeman down a long shadowed corridor, Kelly found himself in a dusty room full of maps and papers, where a fan revolving in the ceiling stirred up the stale air. A small, fair-haired staff captain with a long jaw was sitting behind the table and as Kelly appeared he got up and approached to shake hands.

'Well, a new factor's certainly needed here in the Middle East,' he admitted as he listened to Kelly. 'Gallipoli was a disaster, thanks to lack of interest at home, and the Indian Army's made a hopeless mess of Mesopotamia.' He gave a curiously effeminate shrug. 'We need something that will outweigh the Turks in numbers, output and mental activity.' Standing with his feet together, he rested his heavy jaw in his right hand and put his right elbow in the palm of his left hand as if he were hugging himself. Yet there was a curious tension about him and a strange burning quality of leadership.

'There's been no encouragement from history to think that those qualities can be supplied ready-made from Europe, however,' he went on cheerfully. 'The efforts of the European powers to keep a footing in the Levant have always been uniformly disastrous.'

He seemed clear-headed and incisive and Kelly broke in, driven more by emotion than anything else. 'You've got to do something for these people,' he said.

The staff captain shrugged. 'Well, the solution would have to be local, but fortunately the standard of efficiency need only be local, too, because the competition's Turkey and Turkey's rotten. Personally, I think you're quite right and that there's enough latent power among the Arabs to do the job. After all, they've served a term of five hundred years under the Turks and if *they* don't know them, no one does. What had you in mind?'

'I was told that the Sherif of Mecca's with us.'

'I've been told that, too. In fact we had his son, the Amir Abdulla, down here to sound us out.'

'And are you going to do anything?'

'Things have a habit of moving slowly in Cairo.'

Kelly could hear a proud voice pleading for understanding. 'There's a whole nation of allies here,' he said earnestly. 'Only wanting to help us by helping themselves. Can't you bloody idiots in Cairo give them guns and rifles?'

The staff captain laughed, a curiously shrill laugh, then his face became grave again. 'Well, military thinking's somewhat atrophied out here, I have to admit, but we do have a few clever chaps in Intelligence. We had hopes of Mesopotamia because the Arab independence movement had its beginnings there, but I think we can forget it now since Kut, and unfortunately the Indian government's none too keen on pledges to Arab nationalists which might limit their own ambitions.'

'Do bloody politics have to come into it?' Kelly snapped.

The staff captain pulled a face. 'Unhappily, yes. Nevertheless, conditions are suitable for an Arab movement. Perhaps we should get in touch with them.'

Kelly decided that the staff captain was laughing at him. He seemed too much of an intellectual to be involved in the war, and his own thoughts concerned only a dying girl and a set of promises he'd given.

'I'd like to know how it goes,' he said icily. 'My name's Maguire. Kelly Maguire. Lieutenant, RN. I've no idea what my ship is because I've had two sunk under me and God alone knows what will happen now. But you can get me through the Admiralty.'

The little staff captain twisted round, moving his hand in a delicate gesture as he reached for a pen. 'I'll not forget,' he promised. 'And so that you can be reassured of my good intentions, I'll give you my name, too.' He wrote quickly and passed the paper across. 'Lawrence,' he said. 'Thomas Edward Lawrence.'

Part Three

One

'You're different, Kelly.'

Charley's eyes rested on Kelly's face, puzzled and troubled by the grimness she saw there. 'You seem older.'

Kelly shrugged. 'Marines and pongos can be made up in boxes of a dozen,' he said. 'Sailors are always different. And I'm older because it's eight months since I saw you and a lot's happened in that time.'

They were alone in the house at Bessborough Terrace because Mrs Upfold had disappeared to see *Chu Chin Chow* with Mabel. With them were a highly-decorated young man from the Royal Flying Corps on leave from France, and the young man's mother. The young man's father, like General Upfold and Uncle Paddy, had disappeared to France in the early days of the war and, like them, had vanished in the first awful clash of gigantic armies. Half the country seemed to have been bereaved already by the ill-prepared offensives of 1915 and only the almost hysterical certainty of victory with a big new push said to be coming on the Somme enabled everybody to go on believing in the future.

At last, however, Mrs Upfold seemed to be regarding Kelly as a possible future husband for her younger daughter and he had noticed that, despite the young airman, even Mabel had eyed him with a renewed interest.

'I have to trust you, Mr Maguire,' Mrs Upfold had said archly as she had disappeared. 'Especially with my baby.'

'Your baby's safe with me, Mrs Upfold,' Kelly said coldly 'She always has been.'

'She thought you were dead at first,' Charley pointed out with a chuckle as the party disappeared. 'And I think it worried her a bit because she'd begun to think that someone who could get a medal as quickly as you got yours might possibly have a future, after all.' She stared at him. 'Everybody went into mourning,' she ended.

'Did *you*?'

'I didn't think you were dead.'

'Why not?'

'It didn't seem like you.'

'What? To be dead?'

'Yes. You're the most alive boy I know.'

'I'm not such a boy now, Charley. I'm twenty-three and a half. Time's running out for me.'

As they talked, they heard a low wailing in the distance and Charley put her hand to her mouth. 'Oh, dear,' she said. 'It's an air raid. The zeppelins are such a nuisance these days.' She gave a little giggle. 'At least it'll keep Mother out a bit longer. They'll have to go to a shelter. I don't think she'll ever get used to it.'

Certainly London was different. The streets were full of Australians, New Zealanders, Indians, Canadians, Montenegrins, Portuguese, Belgians in tall forage caps, and a few lost Russians in blue. At every alley-end shysters sold iron crosses and spiked helmets won in France by better men, and all the smart women seemed to be on the arm of a wounded officer. Despite the vitality of the young men, however, there was a lot of gloom such as Kelly had never noticed in the services, a great deal more military punctilio – especially from fat little men in officers' uniforms who were running remount parks, stores depots and maintenance units – and more prostitutes than he'd ever seen before.

He became aware of Charley studying him. 'You *have* changed, you know,' she said. 'You're harder, somehow, more commanding.'

Kelly gestured. 'Perhaps I am,' he agreed. 'Having a ship sunk under you makes a chap grow up, and I've had two.'

He had been well aware for some time that things which had once interested him no longer did, and on his first day at home he had cleared his room of the belongings that had been in it all his life, his books, the remains of his childhood toys, even the picture of 'When Did You Last See Your Father' which had graced the walls from the first day he'd been aware of things.

He was different. Suddenly, unexpectedly, he was a man. Until now, he'd still been a youth, an efficient naval officer but still only a youth. Now for the first time he was thinking as a man and was beginning seriously to consider his career. He'd had a tremendous start and he could well imagine Verschoyle with his forked tongue talking about influence. But there hadn't been an ounce of influence anywhere. His father had pulled no strings and on the only occasion when he'd offered to, Kelly had rejected his offer.

'They're recommending me for another gong,' he said sharply.

'Another one?'

'They always give one to you if you escape. Sort of consolation prize for being captured, I suppose.'

Charley's eyes glowed with pride. 'I say, how marvellous, Kelly. You will be a swell. But I know you deserve it. Bringing all those men back, too. Especially Rumbelo with his wound. He thinks you're God.'

'Just his half-brother.'

'He's hoping you'll ask for him again. He thinks you bring him luck.'

Kelly smiled. 'You can bet your last bob I shall,' he said. 'Rumbelo's a handy man to have alongside you and I think *he* brings *me* luck.'

The air raid sirens had stopped now but they could hear policemen cycling past in the street outside blowing whistles. There were a few screams from women hurrying for the shelters and a little shouting. Being bombed was still a new experience to people who so far hadn't even been touched by the war.

'Do you get the zeppelins over here much?' he asked.

Charley smiled. 'More than I enjoy. You can always tell when they're close. There's a battery of guns in the park down the road and when they start they almost lift the roof off.' She jerked the curtains tighter across the windows for safety and turned again to Kelly. 'Was it awful being sunk in a submarine?' she asked.

'I don't know,' Kelly said honestly. 'I was on the bridge.'

'Aren't you worried about going back in them?'

'I'm not going back in submarines. They've slung me out. That pneumonia I had in Afion Kara Hissar. They won't touch anybody who might have anything wrong with his lungs.'

She looked concerned. 'Is there anything wrong?'

'Not now. But it's the policy. They can't take a chance. Perhaps it's as well, anyway. There's not much of an opening in Heaven for submariners. Because they go down, I suspect they all go to the other place and it's the Flying Corps who'll have all their own way upwards. They're putting me in a destroyer.'

'As captain?'

'Good God, no! First lieutenant. As soon as I've done a short refresher navigation and gunnery officer's course. Without those I'll be about as much use as a blind bunting tosser. Or at least, that's what they think. *Mordant*'s about the oldest they've got in the North Sea, anyway. I expect they think if I get sunk again they won't have lost much.'

She looked worried. 'Don't you want to be captain?'

'Of course I do!' Kelly stared at her in amazement. 'Every naval officer wants to command his own ship.'

'I think they *should* make you a captain. After all, they're giving you another medal.'

'Doesn't cut much ice with the Admiralty. If I suggested that, they'd soon send me away with a naval flea in my ear.'

'Will you stay in this country?'

Kelly smiled. It was slowly becoming easier to smile. The pain was fading and the anger was dying. 'If you can call Scapa

Flow in this country,' he said. 'As far as I can make out, it's about as far into nowhere as you can get. James Verschoyle's up there.'

'He'll go green with envy when he sees you with yet another ribbon.'

Kelly smiled. 'I suspect Verschoyle will look after himself. I hear from Kimister that he did well at the Falklands with Sturdee. I expect he's let it be known in the right quarters.'

'Will there be a battle, Kelly?'

'In the North Sea? Perhaps. I don't know. The Germans seem to prefer to avoid one. With Tyrwhitt in the Channel and Jellicoe sitting off the north of Scotland, they know damn well that they can never get out. And after all this time, I wonder if *we're* all that keen to see 'em. After all, we're doing exactly what we wish to do without even putting to sea. Principle of the fleet in being.'

'What's that?'

'Exactly what it says. Simply existing there as a permanent threat. If the fleet were scattered the threat would disappear and the Germans could come out.'

'It seems an awfully negative way of fighting a war.'

'It's a good way of avoiding casualties. Besides—' Kelly leaned over and kissed her gently on the cheek '—sometimes, when I see people like my father, I tremble to think what might happen if they did meet.'

'We'd wipe the floor with them!'

Kelly wasn't so sure. 'There are still a lot of Victoria's heavy weather men afloat, Charley. The Germans have proved they're good and I often wonder if we're as good as we think we are.'

Charley looked shocked. Set on a path towards being a naval wife, she had tried hard to absorb naval thinking and the habit of naval self-confidence, and Kelly's ideas didn't seem to fit into them. 'But that's blasphemy, Kelly! The Germans are good only because they're new. They have no tradition!'

'Sometimes I wonder if we have too much. It's true you can build a ship in two years and it takes two hundred to build a tradition, but there are a lot of people who think that tradition's all that's necessary, and there's a lot that's out of date.'

Charley began to feel she'd got herself in deep waters. 'I don't understand, Kelly.'

Kelly wasn't sure he did himself. But since his return home, he'd been doing a lot of reading and asking a lot of questions and it seemed to him that, while Germany's nautical house had been put in more efficient shape since 1914 Britain's had gone rather the other way.

He pulled a face and smiled. 'I'm just wondering if we aren't placing too much reliance on the big gun,' he said.

Charley frowned, puzzled. With the war now two years old, she had begun to grow cynical herself at the pratings of the press and the older generation. With casualties running into hundreds of thousands, the exhortations to fight for God, King and Country were wearing as thin as the claims that Britain had the finest army in the world. Like many of her friends, she had taken to helping in the casualty wards of London hospitals and she had often come away with the thought that those people who talked glibly of a holy war and their pride in the army ought to see the mustard gas cases, while God, King and Country often seemed a dangerously voracious trio.

Nevertheless, Kelly was still different enough to frighten her a little. Was this the young man she'd promised herself, ever since she'd been able to understand, that she would one day marry? There was a tension about him she'd never seen before. Even after surviving the sinking of *Cressy* he'd not been quite so hard as he was now. Despite being heavily in touch with the emotions of her friends who'd been caught up in the war, she found his attitudes worried her because he was an extrovert character, self-confident enough to breast the miseries of the times without too much difficulty, and she had a feeling that he knew things she could barely imagine. She had no doubts about his courage, of course. She'd never doubted that, and he wore ribbons to prove it, but there seemed an awful lot of sacrilege in what he said. She changed the subject hurriedly.

'Was it awful being a prisoner, Kelly?'

'Bit smelly. The Turks stink like goats – *old* goats.'

'You were very brave to escape as you did.'

'It wasn't me. It was the Arabs who died.'

It was easier, he noticed, to think now of Ayesha dead without something sticking in his throat. There was a lot to be said for the resilience of youth. When he'd left Cairo, he'd promised himself he'd never forget her. Probably he never would but youth continued to find the world full of excitement, and it was hard to dwell too long on death. The best warriors were all young. Not only were their muscles elastic; so were their minds.

An anti-aircraft gun down the road banged and Charley put her hand on Kelly's arm.

'I think we'd better hide under the stairs,' she said.

'I'd rather go outside and have a look.'

She stared at him in alarm but, deciding that if it were good enough for Kelly, it was good enough for her, she agreed.

'I'm not sure it's safe,' she said. 'Everybody's picking on the government about the way they're allowed to come over. Everybody's very angry.'

'I expect it's wind-up among the hot-air merchants of the press.'

'Well, people have been killed.'

'Nothing like the number the government and the Press Lords have killed between them in France.'

She looked quickly at him, puzzled once more by his bitterness. The telephone went and she answered it, grave, sober and a little anxious. She looked at Kelly as she replaced the instrument. 'That's the local police station,' she said. 'Mother picked up the sergeant when he ran into a lamp post on his bike in the blackout and filled him full of brandy. Ever since, he keeps us up-to-date with what's happening. He says five zeppelins have crossed the coast and are headed for London. It looks like being a noisy night.'

252

They went on to the front steps. Several people were arguing round a gas lamp which was still alight, then a policeman wearing a placard saying 'Take cover' on his chest appeared and a man in ragged clothes shinned tip the post, opened the glass and smashed the mantle.

'Look! Kelly, look!'

Charley was pointing upwards. Searchlights had sprung up all over London and at the junction of half a dozen beams a long cigar-shaped object, yellow in the light, was lifting its nose lazily upwards. They saw puffs of smoke as though from exhausts as it moved, then, with gathering speed, it vanished from sight in the cloud. Guns began to fire from every direction and they could see the sparkle of shell bursts in the sky. A woman ran along the street in a panic. 'I can hear another one coming,' she was screaming.

Over the city, dark with the absence of lights, they saw the glow of flames and more little red flashes high in the sky over Woolwich, where the searchlights were groping into the darkness.

'They've gone,' Kelly said.

A searchlight only a few streets away came on, piercing the darkness and illuminating Charley's upturned face. Following the beam, they saw that the cigar-shaped aircraft had reappeared, above their heads this time, and immediately guns began to fire.

'Oh, Lor',' Charley said. 'They're right above us! I'm going under the stairs!'

Kelly grinned. 'Perhaps I'll come with you.'

The Upfolds had cleared the area under the staircase and laid mattresses in there in case of the need for shelter. On a shelf was a bottle of sherry and a bottle of brandy and they helped themselves as they sat on the mattresses.

'I'm told they never hit anything,' Kelly said self-importantly. 'At least nothing that they're hoping to hit.'

As he spoke there was a whistling noise and then a crash. Kelly looked at Charley in the light of the candle.

'Seems I was wrong,' he said.

She looked scared and, as another crash made them jump, she edged nearer. A third crash seemed to shake the house and the brandy bottle tottered and toppled over. Kelly caught it and, as he put it back, he realised Charley was clutching him.

'It's all right, old thing,' he said. 'Nothing to worry about.'

'To me, it is.'

There was another crash, this time apparently just outside the front door, and they heard glass tinkling. Charley flung herself at Kelly and buried her head in his uniform.

'It's all right!'

Tenderly, he lifted her chin and kissed her and, still clutching him, she kissed him back, fiercely, in a way she'd never done before. Immediately, he was aware of a new feeling in his loins. He'd always regarded her merely as the girl next door, the girl he was eventually going to marry, and always in an uncomplicated asexual way, but now, suddenly, with her young breasts pressing against his chest, her legs warm against his, he was aware that she was far more than just that.

'Steady on, old thing,' he said uncertainly.

'I don't want to steady on!' Her voice was shaking and she clearly had no intention of letting go.

There was another whistle and another tremendous crash and a roar of tiles sliding off a roof, and Kelly pushed Charley down and flung himself across her in case the stairs came down on them. As the din died away he found her staring up at him, her lips parted, her eyes bright and a little worried, but also suddenly full of a new fierce determination.

'Charley—'

'It's all right, Kelly.'

'Charley—'

'Oh, for Heaven's sake, Kelly,' she snapped. 'Stop pretending!'

'I'm not pretending.'

'Yes, you are. I'm nearly seventeen now and I'm frightened and I want you. And you know I want you. It's often occurred to me that if they drop a bomb on me and I go to my Maker without ever having you, I shall never have been fulfilled.'

She took his hand and placed it firmly on her breast and the softness of her flesh under his fingers stirred him.

'Charley—'

'Kelly, for Heaven's sake, stop saying "Charley!"'

Guiltily, Kelly still hesitated, but she clutched him more tightly.

'You're not frightened, are you?'

'Yes.'

'What of? Me?'

'No, your mother.'

By this time, however, he was ridden full pelt by his desire and he knew it would be difficult to draw back. Navigating carefully through the shoals of thought, he made a last feeble effort.

'Suppose they come back?'

'Suppose they do?' She sounded indifferent, and, reaching up, she gave him a kiss so experienced it made his blood run hot.

'Who taught you to kiss like that?' he asked.

'Nobody.'

'Then how did you know?'

'Love and how to set about it's the only thing girls ever talk about.'

His pulses quickened and their mouths searched for each other in the shadows.

'We ought to be under cover,' Kelly said insanely.

Charley giggled. 'I bet you mean "under covers."'

She grabbed for him clumsily and, choked with emotion, he began to fumble with her dress. Her lips sought his again, desperately, urgently.

'Oh, Kelly!'

There was something in her voice that was plaintive and imploring and young, something that begged him to be gentle, and, realising what was happening, he sat up abruptly.

'For God's sake, Charley,' he croaked. 'I nearly—'

She drew away from him, her face frustrated and sullen. 'And why not? I'm not a child!'

'Still too much of a child for that.'

She started to weep quietly with disappointment and misery. 'You might be killed,' she said. 'I might be hit by a bomb. Anything might happen. I might never see you again, and I've never had any — well — any experience. I don't know what to do and I expect you've been with lots of girls.'

'No, I haven't.' Well, he thought, not many. Just as many as any normal sailor came across in his life at sea.

'I bet.' She was still sullen. 'I know sailors.'

'You only know me.'

'That's what I mean.'

He put his arms around her, but this time he was careful not to let his emotions run away with him. 'Not now, Charley,' he urged. 'Not this time.'

'I can't see why not.'

'Because I promised. That's why not.'

'You're very honourable all of a sudden.'

He stiffened. 'I've always been honourable where you're concerned, Charley.'

'Yes,' she said. 'That's the trouble.'

Then she gave a little giggle, recovering quickly. 'It's all right, Kelly. Mother's bound to start sounding me out and it'll be nice to be honest.' She kissed him gently. 'And thank you. You *are* honourable where I'm concerned. I'm not sure it suits me always, but it's nice to know I rouse such emotions in you.'

Kelly frowned. 'I'm damned if you do,' he said frankly. 'In fact, you rouse the most dishonourable emotions.'

Two

Crammed into the compartment of a train heading north, Kelly began to wonder if he'd been a damned fool. After all, there *was* a war on and morals *had* gone by the board a little. All the same, he decided firmly, Charley *was* different. Charley was Charley and that was all there was to it.

They'd continued to see each other until his leave had ended. They'd gone to the cinema and the theatre and driven into Surrey for the day in a little runabout Kelly had bought out of back pay, returning almost hysterical with laughter because, unable to get up the Hog's Back in bottom gear, they had ground up it all the way in reverse, to the amazement of the drivers of motor cars and traps travelling in the opposite direction. Despite their happiness, however, they were both aware of a change that had taken place between them and now, suddenly, they were wary of each other, skirmishing almost, conscious overnight that their relationship was different. They were no longer children, no longer merely next-door neighbours. They were adult and Charley was frighteningly womanly.

Kelly shifted in his seat, wondering if Charley's devotion was not even sometimes too much of a good thing. With the uncertainty of a very young man, he even saw himself trapped by it. He'd never asked for it, indeed, had never worked to produce it. It had developed quite naturally from the normal friendship of two close friends.

He frowned. Sometimes, he thought, it took his breath away. She had it all cut and dried and what was he supposed to do if he met someone else? Charley had never had any doubts and that in itself served to worry him more. Marriage was something older men considered; young men didn't even bother to think about it. The world was full of girls, all interesting and as far as Kelly could make out, most of them itching to get close to a young man. Wasn't it a little unwise to tie himself down to one, to arrange his future before he'd even lived his present?

Then he remembered that he hadn't tied himself down. There had already been other girls and he knew that Charley knew there'd been other girls. It said something for her character, in fact, that she'd never shown the slightest sign of jealousy, as though, despite her youth, she'd accepted that he was a sailor and was going to meet other girls, and that she must not concern herself with them.

He sighed. There was a great deal more to this business of living than met the eye. In a ship, in the company of men, at sea as part of a unit that was based on comradeship and loyalty, life was twice as simple. Ashore it was full of complications.

He shifted his position again. His limbs were cramped by the crowding in the compartment and the corridor outside was packed with more men. A sailor was singing.

> 'Oh, I wonder, yes, I wonder,
> Did the jaunty make a blunder
> When he made this draft chit out for me?'

The voice sounded bored, but then they were all bored. It took twenty-four hours to reach the north of Scotland and the 'Jellicoes,' as the trains were called after the commander-in-chief, were crammed, cluttered, cold and interminable. For Kelly, Crewe, Carlisle and Carstairs would always be inextricably entwined with this long journey to war. There had been nothing to differentiate between any of them except at Carlisle where everyone had hung out of the window on the lookout for hot meat pies only to be greeted by an elderly optimist offering home-made ices.

'Got any 'ot 'uns, mate,' a disgusted matelot had demanded.

They were now on the last lap of the journey, on the High-land Line north of Perth, and everybody was waking up after an uncomfortable night's sleep and peering through the steamed-up windows, certain that they'd arrived at the end of nowhere. In the corridor, movement was almost impossible over the obstacle course of men, cases, kitbags, hammocks and rolling beer bottles. The air was dense with smoke and stale alcohol and smelt more like a ship's bilges than a train. A ribald request to the stationmaster at Invergordon to 'get a bloody move on' had brought only the dignified reply that 'the Hielan' Railway was no' designed to stand the strain o' a European war.'

> *'Oh, a million miles I've travelled*
> *And a thousand sights I've seen…'*

The voice in the corridor sounded weary now, and Kelly saw the sailor stop dead and light a cigarette. 'Shorter cruisers, longer boozes,' he said gloomily.

They reached Thurso at midnight and it was as black as the inside of a coal bag. The dawn came with a rough day and enormous waves crashing over the harbour.

'Oh, Jesus,' the sailor who'd been singing said. 'A calm day over Caithness's no bloody indication that the Firth's calm, and a wild day means it's bloody near impassable. I wish I'd been drafted to the Gosport Ferry.'

A bored voice took up the refrain. 'Blackpool Pier would suit me, mate.'

The Pentland Firth was one of the worst stretches of water in the world and this morning it was tempestuous and, as he peered through the jagged, slanting rain at the iron-clad heights of Dunnet Head, Kelly felt a ghostly pity for the haggard shades of the Spaniards, fleeing westwards through these terrible seas round the north of Scotland with their defeated Armada. The steamer, stinking of coal and oil and old paint, heaved its black sides through the crashing waves. The Firth didn't contain ordi-nary waves, but mountains and chasms of green sea, and soldiers and sailors alike wallowed in the scuppers in a swill of water and vomit.

When they reached Scapa, the storm had died a little and only a hard Orkney wind was jabbing out of the watery sky. The vast landlocked anchorage, fifteen miles long by eight miles wide, looked like a jagged hole punched in the southern half of the islands, and the grim shadows of the fleet could be seen against Hoxa and Switha Sounds and the empty undulating land among the grey farmhouses with their patchwork fields where seagulls were swarming round a plough. The colours ranged from pastel greys and greens and ochres to deep blues and astonishing turquoises.

As the light lengthened, they were able to pick out of the retreating murk the lean shapes of the ships to which they'd been assigned, which would serve as homes or sepulchres according to the luck of the draw. No one was looking forward to the exile, because exile was only tolerable in pleasant conditions, and in Scapa there was nothing to relieve the monotony.

HMS *Mordant* was a three-funnel ship of a thousand tons with a designed speed of around thirty knots, three four-inch guns and four twenty-one-inch torpedo tubes. She had little to recommend her except her battle-worn appearance – grey sides, streaked with dirt and rust and clawed by the talons of the sea – and Kelly decided that much the same comment could be applied to her captain.

Commander Henry Bellweather Talbot was a small man with a battered, exhausted, perpetually perspiring face, whose whole appearance was so changed when he took off his cap to reveal a totally bald head that in the wardroom he was known as the Wet Boiled Egg. He smoked a pipe so constantly it seemed to be part of his face and he was bored with Scapa Flow and didn't even seem to think much of his ship.

'She has such a low freeboard,' he said, introducing her to her new first lieutenant, 'that in any sort of seaway it's impossible for the men to remain on the upper deck, never mind fight the guns or man the torpedo tubes.' He gave a bored yawn and went on wearily. 'When she isn't rolling or pitching, she's doing both; and the boiler room intakes are so exposed the stokers go on watch in oilskins. Finally, she carries two boats on davits near the break of the forecastle but, since a head sea over the bows can shatter even the navigating bridge, naturally we lose them every time there's foul weather.'

'How about the German destroyers, sir?' Kelly asked.

'Much better designed. If we ever meet 'em, we can expect to be blown to bits in a matter of minutes. "M" boats are nothing but toy ships and they'd probably have been better never built, but on the other hand, Number One, you'll find they're a splendid school for seamen and anyone who can serve in them without going off his head can take anything.'

Kelly grinned. 'I think I'll manage, sir.'

'Glad to hear it.' Talbot sounded indifferent. 'Right spirit, after all. But then, it's difficult to go aboard any ship nowadays without finding the quarterdeck plastered all over with "England expects that every man will do his duty." In spirit, if not in paint. To me it always seems like telling a man to do what he intended to do all along. One other thing: *Mordant*, despite her appearance, has a reputation as a tiddly ship and it'll be your job to see she remains one. In the navy cleaning ship is a fetish. In this ship it's a disease. Make it so.'

Fortunately the other officers, Lieutenants Shakespeare and Heap, the watchkeepers, and Naylor, the sub, were easy to get on with – non-regulars who brought a breath of fresh air into the stuffy corridors of the navy to counter the heavy breathing of the captain. Lieutenant Wellbeloved, the engineer, an ex-ERA steeped in the traditions of the navy, Mr Hatchard, the gunner, and the surgeon, Chambers, were also pleasant enough men, though all thoroughly under the thumb of the captain and unlikely to cause problems.

Mordant was tiny and salt-encrusted with work. So far no one had discovered how to provide guns, torpedoes and speed in so small and slender a vessel and provide comfort at the same time for the crew at sea. For the lower deck, life was a wet, cold boredom, crawling down ladders from duty to a wet cold mess deck to eat wet cold biscuits and lie wet and cold in a wet, cold hammock. For them in bad weather, even speaking was hard work and thinking an effort as they watched the water, foul with vomit, hurl itself across their living quarters, carrying mess-traps and clothing that couldn't be retrieved. The officers' quarters were a little better, but not much. You could hear the propellers and the vibrating rattle of the steering gear, while, with the lack of ventilation when the upper deck was awash, the air was invariably blue with tobacco smoke, oil fumes and the all-pervading stink of an inefficient lavatory in the lobby.

Though the Flow was supposed to be a sheltered anchorage, often the weather was so rough the gulls were tossed about like limp sheets of paper and the big ships took it green over the bows even when motionless. In a gale it was a smother of white foam with the wind howling from the north-west with the violence of despair. Rain squalls and banks of fog succeeded each other like waves of attacking infantry and the long Atlantic rollers swept all the way from Newfoundland to hurl themselves in a cataract of foam on the rock-bound coast, so that it became impossible to get the mails on board from among the cargo of vomiting messmen; and liberty boats could not go ashore and they were isolated for days in their own little steel cases. Even when they could reach dry land, there was little to divert them, only a nine-hole golf course for the officers and a single canteen on Flotta for the men, where the beer was so awful the sailors complained it was impossible to get drunk on it. Even then they could go only in small groups for fear of swamping the meagre facilities and, since the Flow accommodated over a hundred ships, the shoregoing delights were not often enjoyed and every junior officer who had been at Scapa for more than six months seemed to have applied to join some other branch of the service. Both Shakespeare and Heap had asked for submarines and Naylor, the sub, was trying to get some influential relative he possessed to pull strings to get him down to Tyrwhitt's force at Harwich. Swinging round a buoy for months at a time didn't seem to be an aid to morale.

Nevertheless the fleet was a fine sight, with the big ships moored in menacing rows. *Revenge, Ramillies, Resolution, Royal Oak, Emperor of India, Benbow, Marlborough, Iron Duke, Hercules, Collingwood, Neptune, St Vincent, Colossus, Superb, Bellerophon*, and God knew how many more – Kelly knew he'd be able to recite their names on his death bed. Despite the loneliness and emptiness, the scene filled him with pride.

There was only one entirely unavoidable problem – time. There was just too much of it, and he could only thank God it wasn't winter when night arrived at three o'clock in the afternoon, but approaching midsummer when they could walk all night on the decks. Leisure was the difficulty and the lower deck grew sick of making mats, embroidery and knitting, even illegal crown and anchor, and, because they were so far from the run of events, there was no interest even in politics, and the opinions of the *Daily Mail* and *John Bull* got short shrift.

A faint murmur of excitement stirred the fleet when the Germans bombarded Lowestoft in April and everyone began again to hope for a confrontation. But to everyone's disgust, the fleet didn't move. It ought to have been obvious that the Germans couldn't hope to meet Jellicoe head-on but the months of waiting had made everyone desperate and hearts rather than heads were behind the hopes.

The reaction of the rest of the country was exactly the same. Though few lives had been lost at Lowestoft and there was little damage to military objectives, 200 houses had been wrecked and the spontaneous result was an uproar that made everyone at Scapa squirm with the guilty feeling of achieving nothing.

'What's the fleet doing?' It was in all the papers and in every letter from home. It was all right for the government to write heartening notes to the Mayor of Lowestoft assuring him that it would prove highly dangerous for the enemy to try this sort of thing again, but more than pencilled encouragement was needed. The Mayor, like many others, was calling for the extermination of the German High Seas Fleet. To the man in the street, the principle of the fleet in being as a deterrent seemed to be proving more and more a myth and the solitary naval hero was Tyrwhitt at Harwich, who seemed to be the only admiral to have come out of the war so far with any real credit.

Talbot seemed to sink deeper into his gloom. 'I've been up here since 1914,' he said bitterly. 'I missed the Heligoland Bight, Falklands and Dogger Bank actions and they didn't even send me out to try my luck in the Dardanelles. The only battle I've taken part in was the Battle of Scapa Flow.'

'I've never heard of that one, sir,' Kelly admitted.

'It didn't reach the popular press,' Talbot explained. '*Falmouth* reported firing at a submarine and every damn destroyer in the Flow raised steam at once and moved about the harbour at high speed, filling the sky with volumes of black smoke. Even the Admiral Commanding Orkneys and Shetlands hoisted his flag in one of 'em and joined in the fun and games. The excitement was added to by the discharges of four-inch guns from any battleship which imagined she'd seen a periscope, and by the fact that all the big ships got out their picket boats which cruised about vigorously under the command of midshipmen looking for periscopes. What they'd have done if they'd met one I can't imagine. Put a bag over it, I expect. Needless to say, there was no submarine and since then we've been overworked and overstrained, and it's only the thought of dying that keeps me alive. But for the hope that one day the Germans *might* come out, I'd apply for the Chiltern Hundreds and resign my commission to enlist in the army.'

On the rare occasions when it appeared, the sun looked remarkably like an underdone fried egg and its ability to generate heat lived up to its appearance. The mud was grey. The sky was grey. The islands were grey. The sea was grey. The ships at their moorings were grey. War, Kelly supposed, was a grey business.

Every morning the battleships, cruisers and destroyers followed each other up the Flow at regular intervals to carry out gun and torpedo practices, and at night the sea was lit by the gunflashes and searchlights of ships carrying out night firing, while at regular intervals a complete battle squadron disappeared to sea to carry out heavy practice in the western entrance of the Pentland Firth. The destroyers, hospital ships, colliers, oilers, ammunition ships and other fleet auxiliaries lived up Gutter Sound at Longhope, their crews idle, bored and mutinous. In the big ships it was a little better and they could even dance, one man clutching another to the ribald comments of his mates, could even manage cinemas or enjoy concert parties. In the destroyers there was no room for anything and not much time either, because they were always slipping out to sea on an exercise, to escort trawlers or minesweepers or bring some ship in.

Conscious that it was his job to keep the crew happy and well aware that he could expect little help from Talbot, Kelly organised walks on the islands, inspecting the antiquities, observing the bird and animal life, or merely taking exercise. Football was played as if it were the last thing they were to do on earth and there were matches on any flat piece of boggy ground. Boxing competitions, sports and pulling races were held, but all the time he was aware of how much more determination these activities would require when the winter came with its bitter winds and snow.

'This must be the last place God made,' he wrote to Charley. The influence of the lonely sea and the grey sky was having a sharp nostalgic effect on him that nudged him as it had nudged sailors from time immemorial, so that he felt sentimental, frustrated and randy, and was kicking himself for drawing back. It seemed so long since he'd seen a girl, he felt they'd have to fit him with a collar and chain the next time he went ashore. After all, he thought, as Charley had said, he *might* be killed. Though he couldn't imagine it. He couldn't imagine what it was like to be dead, except that it would be cold and dark and empty, like being trapped in a vast unlit room.

Charley wrote back regularly, but never about what had happened or might have happened between them. 'There were twenty-one bombs on Ashford in Kent,' she announced in matter-of-fact terms, 'and they dropped forty-one in the fields near the Admiralty gunpowder factory at Faversham.' It was almost too matter-of-fact for Kelly.

Perhaps it was harder for Charley, he decided. He found he still couldn't think of Ayesha without pain but whether it was the pain of love or the pain of guilt he wasn't sure. At least, however, he'd experienced love. Charley, he knew, never had.

Rumbelo appeared. A desperate letter had arrived for Kelly: '*I have to go back to surface ships, sir. They say that bullet over the knee will efect my climbing and that I might jam the ladder in an emergency. How about asking for me, sir? I'll not let you down.*' It wasn't hard to persuade Talbot that Leading Seaman Rumbelo was the best helmsman in the navy and that good helmsmen were useful in a destroyer; and a special request was sent to the drafting depot. The reply came remarkably quickly in the form of a curt reply that Rumbelo was a Portsmouth rating, that it was quite irregular for such a person to be sent to *Mordant*, which was a Chatham ship, and that he was due to go to *Partridge*, from his home port, instead.

'It's nothing but a piece of red tape,' Kelly snorted, and by the following day had persuaded Talbot to go ashore at Kirkwall and get in touch personally with someone he knew in the drafting depot, asking for Rumbelo's papers to be closed in *Partridge* and transferred to *Mordant*.

'You're bloody persuasive, Number One,' Talbot said. 'It's all highly unorthodox.'

But it put Rumbelo on one of the 'Jellicoes' heading north, all the same.

Occasionally they slipped out through the Hoxa Gate, always hoping against hope that they were going south after the German High Seas Fleet. But they never were and they were always back within forty-eight hours.

'These bloody big ships are nothing but a drag,' Talbot said bitterly, biting on the stem of his pipe. 'There hasn't been a major naval battle since Trafalgar and the way things are going there never will be. We scared the Germans so much at Heligoland and the Dogger Bank they're afraid to shove their noses out beyond the Jade.'

Then Verschoyle turned up. A new Verschoyle noticeably less arrogant towards Kelly since their last meeting, but now wearing the aiguillette of a flag lieutenant.

He studied Kelly warily, even with a certain amount of uncertainty. He was not unaware of Kelly's new medal or how he'd acquired it and he had a feeling that despite his own poise and cool cynicism, despite his cleverness, he was being left miles behind.

Kelly was staring at him with disconcerting, unyielding hostility.

'I thought you might still be in *Inflexible*,' he said bluntly. 'In fact, I'd almost hoped you'd slipped out through the hole the Turks made in her at the Dardanelles.'

Verschoyle smiled to indicate that he accepted the comment as a joke. 'Left her before then,' he said. 'When Sturdee transferred his flag to *Benbow* I went with him. Rather a good idea, I thought. Naval blue blood tends to congregate in the flagship. Kimister's up here, too, did you know? In *Collingwood*, and wet-henning about in his usual vigorous manner. How are you, young Maguire, anyway? Up to snuff? Heard you'd been getting yourself into trouble in the Middle East.'

'Nothing I couldn't handle,' Kelly said coolly. 'And don't call me "young Maguire."'

'What'll happen if I do? Another bloody nose?' Verschoyle's eyes hardened. 'You know, you *did* break my nose.'

'I'm not very sorry.'

'I had to have surgery.'

'Afraid it might spoil your looks?'

Verschoyle smiled. 'When a chap's good with the girls, it's a pity to have to put up with difficulties of that sort,' he said. 'How's Mabel Upfold?'

'Thinking of getting engaged.'

'Household Cavalry again?'

'No. Much more ordinary. Flying Corps.'

'Not much future in that. I'm told their life span's about three weeks in France. How about you and the Little 'Un? Misbehaved yourselves yet?'

Kelly's eyes narrowed. The fact that they very nearly had had nothing to do with Verschoyle.

'Funny, that,' Verschoyle went on placidly. 'Hard to understand. She's been in love with you as long as I can remember. Sticks out like the proverbial chapel hat peg. God help her when she finally gets you. With the energy you've got, she'll think she's nesting with a railway accident. You'll have her doubling round the bedroom like a Whale Island gunnery instructor, I'll be bound.'

He smiled, wondering again what quirks of character were essential to produce such devotion and why, despite money, poise and position, there was so little of it in his own home and so little to cherish in his loveless affairs with girls.

'Actually, Maguire,' he said, 'you ought to get moving. Kaiser Bill's bound to grow tired eventually of watching the High Seas Fleet rusting in Kiel and give it a shove out into the North Sea. Then the big smash'll come and, in a destroyer, your chances of survival will be pretty slender.'

Kelly was giving nothing away. 'I'll chance it,' he growled.

'Of course—' Verschoyle waved a hand '—Silent Jack Jellicoe's not really the man for the job. Too cautious. Too plodding. Too bloody small for that matter. He's a bit of a ditherer underneath, I reckon, and he'll probably miss his chance, anyway, unless David Beatty drags him into it. Haig told my father he thought he was a bit of an old woman and that he'd probably not know what to do with a battle if he had one tossed in his lap.'

Kelly had always assumed the commander-in-chief to be all-powerful and all-wise. He was one of Jacky Fisher's choices and, though it was obvious he lacked Fisher's drive, the idea that he was far from perfect had never occurred to him before.

'Why shouldn't he know what to do with it?' he asked.

'Lacking in the gift of insubordination.' Verschoyle shrugged. 'Something Nelson had in abundance. I know. I see a lot of him these days. Goes by the book. Has all the Nelsonic virtues but that one. Believes in blind obedience to orders and has an obsession about submarines.'

'Aren't you behind him?'

'I'm behind *my* admiral and my admiral ain't commander-in-chief. He doesn't go along with Jellicoe's belief that half his fleet might be disabled by torpedoes before action's joined.'

'He could lose the war in an afternoon.'

Verschoyle sneered. 'He could also win it in an afternoon, too,' he said. 'But he won't. He treats the fleet as if it were the Crown Jewels and Grand Fleet Battle Orders all subordinate the offensive spirit to defensive precautions, especially against the torpedo. Besides which, there's too much centralised command, and signalling every bloody movement from the flagship will only produce an acute form of tactical arthritis. Still—' Verschoyle gestured '—I doubt if some of our senior officers could act without them, anyway. They're not exactly Nelson's band of brothers. Burney's a solid piece of wood, Arbuthnot's an ass, Evan-Thomas is dull, Jerram lacks initiative, and Sturdee's so bloody conceited you have to drop on one knee every time you see him. Pakenham's a gentleman, of course, and Horace Hood's probably the best brain in the service, but they're only in subordinate commands so they can't do much.'

Even to Kelly, who was far from enchanted by his superior officers, it sounded like blasphemy, but Verschoyle had the bit between his teeth now, and Kelly unwillingly offered him a pink gin to keep him talking.

Thanking him with elaborate courtesy, Verschoyle went on. 'Suspect the thinking's all wrong,' he said. 'The battle plan surmises that the Germans'll *wish* to stand and fight. But suppose they prefer to run away?' He took a sip of his gin. 'If they do, there won't be any big gun duel and then all these plans – all these bloody great ships, too – will be useless, won't they?'

Despite their wary dislike for each other, they were both experienced officers now and able to talk rationally of service matters without hatred, and Kelly became aware once more of something that had never escaped him – Verschoyle had a sharp, incisive brain. Right or wrong, he'd clearly been thinking deeply.

'Is all this why you've turned up here?' he asked. 'To let us know what's wrong with the Grand Fleet?'

Verschoyle finished his gin. He would never have admitted it but he was beginning to wonder if his attitude of looking after himself and leaving his advancement in rank to his influential relatives was a sound one. There seemed about Kelly a hard-headed assurance, an awareness of himself and his capabilities that came entirely from experience. The Falklands had been too much of a walk-over for anyone, however well he'd done, to feel that he'd gained much from it.

Despite his thoughts, Verschoyle's face didn't slip. He couldn't ever have admitted his envy. 'No,' he agreed. 'I've brought orders. *Mordant*'s to move down to Rosyth to join the Thirteenth Destroyer Force. They're with Beatty so perhaps he'll manage to get you killed.'

Three

Rosyth was certainly an improvement on Scapa, and Edinburgh a vast change from the grey streets of Kirkwall, but the destroyers' berth was not a great deal more comfortable than Gutter Sound and getting out was never a pleasure trip. The light cruisers were off Charlestown, with the battle cruisers between them and the bridge, while the destroyers lay higher up at Bo'ness in a welter of colliers, provision ships and other fleet auxiliaries; and the shape of the harbour made it necessary for everybody at the western end of the anchorage to thread their way through the lines of battleships and battle cruisers – the 'Behemoths' and 'Sea Cows', as they were contemptuously called by the destroyermen – every time they moved.

For the battle cruiser people, it was possible to spend every afternoon in Edinburgh, but for the destroyers Edinburgh was always too far away and, ashore, all they could do was walk or visit Dunfermline by the Charlestown express, which the driver let them drive for a shilling tip. Once they managed to get up a game of hockey with the young ladies of the physical training college there, every one of whom seemed to be frustrated by the lack of men and panting to get them in dark corners, but it all came to a stop just when it was beginning to look promising, because the directors of the college took a jaundiced view of it, and they had to go to the cinema instead.

At Rosyth, also, the eagerness for battle was even worse. Admiral Beatty was a lot less patient than Admiral Jellicoe and it was obvious throughout the Battle Cruiser Squadron that it wouldn't require much to send them all to sea. But there was doubt even about Beatty. Square-jawed and broad-shouldered, he seemed the epitome of a fighting admiral but there was still more than a suspicion that while Jellicoe could do with some of Beatty's drive, Beatty could probably do with some of Jellicoe's technical knowledge.

'He's more of a swashbuckler than an admiral,' Lieutenant Shakespeare insisted in a wardroom argument. 'Like Drake. He's not the tactician Nelson was.'

'He's self-assured,' Heap countered. 'And he works hard. I hear that he and Jellicoe have concocted a scheme to bring the Germans out. Expose light units off the Danish, Dutch and German coasts as a bait.'

'Suppose the Germans are scheming along the same lines,' Kelly said dryly. 'And this bombarding of British towns is an attempt to lure *us* out.'

It was almost as if a fleet battle in the North Sea were a psychological necessity because nobody was enjoying themselves and more than likely neither were the Germans. With the war still rolling bloodily across northern France, there was a great feeling of guilt that they were lying in comparative idleness, and every man who returned from leave came back with dark stories of people asking 'But what the hell does the fleet do?' And while it was easier to get ashore than at Scapa, there wasn't very much joy in it. Complete strangers were in the habit of approaching officers in hotel lounges and sailors in pub bars demanding to know when they were going to fetch the Germans out, and an uneasy feeling was growing in Kelly that that affection with which the navy had been regarded before the war was beginning to give way to something not far removed from contempt.

Occasionally they justified their existence by putting to sea with the aircraft carrier, *Engadine*, to exercise her aeroplanes, *Mordant* a few cables astern like a faithful spaniel ready to retrieve anyone who fell in the drink. Mostly the weather was too bad to achieve much but once there was a grisly crash when an aircraft landed in front of the carrier and emerged horrifyingly mutilated by the ship's propellers and with the pilot mercifully stone dead. They fished him out quickly and a young sailor about to heave his heart up at the sight got a quick nudge from Rumbelo as Kelly appeared. He was always looked at somewhat askance for the medal ribbons that graced his chest and the knowledge of what he'd done to get them, and the young sailor managed with an effort to hang on to the contents of his stomach.

When they returned with the wreckage and the remains of the pilot, it was a pitch dark night and was raining persistently with a sullen quality only possible in Scotland. Four cruisers without lights were just aweigh when the destroyers arrived, under the impression they were a mile further down the anchorage, and they all had to go full astern and lie inert, in a galaxy of signalling, megaphoning, bad language and narrow shaves, with a picket boat caught in the middle hooting on its klaxon like a cock pheasant gone mad.

There was another day when they dashed across the North Sea to converge on the Dogger Bank in search of a collier that was adrift, a salt-caked, rust-streaked old tub wallowing in a heavy leaden sea.

'Nanny to a bleedin' collier,' a wag in the waist of the ship yelled. 'Eight soddin' knots! Come on, you ocean bloody greyhound, you, keep up!'

'With the rotten stuff they give us to burn—' the answering yell came thinly on the wind from a man on the collier's bridge wearing a green jersey and a bowler hat '—we couldn't even keep up with the bleedin' times!'

On other occasions they escorted the cruisers north for firing practice, and returned to Rosyth in a large detour to avoid minefields; and once, with one of the light cruiser squadrons, they went out to find a mythical minesweeper, and the buzz went round that this time they were really the bait to bring out the High Seas Fleet. It ended up with condenser trouble and a brush with a zeppelin, in which shots were exchanged for bombs, but entirely without damage to either side.

Finally they escorted Beatty himself to sea, seven huge ships led by *Lion*, the flagship, all silhouetted against the sky, each one of them with a plume of smoke rising like a dusky feather. As they zigzagged, the sunlight caught their sides so that they appeared to change colour as they altered course, on one tack bright and silvery, on the other black. A stab of white rising at their ram-bows and another at their stern contrasted with the deep blue of the sea as they moved in two solemnly portentous lines, at the head of each one and down the flanks the black smudges of the destroyers, all of them oil burners that threw off little smoke except when some careless stoker changed the width of the air inlet baffles on the boilers.

On the starboard beam, there was another group of ships and, five miles away, units of the Third Light Cruiser Squadron, pearl-grey shapes in the distance, with, just visible beyond them, the raking masts of the First Light Cruiser Squadron, their hulls below the horizon. At intervals a light winked on the flagship, to be repeated right and left, and as it grew dusk, the light cruisers closed in to become three lines, each ship following the pale blue stern light of the shadowy form ahead in their stately march across the darkening sea.

Coming back was different as they laboriously staggered homewards in the teeth of a south-westerly gale with the wind shrilling in the rigging and the sky a dull grey broken only by the never-ending procession of low clouds scooting along to the north-east. Monotonously, as the ship dipped her forecastle into a maelstrom of leaping seas, a mass of seething foam rushed aft and broke against the conning tower then, as she lifted up again, was caught by the wind and flung upwards to fall in sheets across the upper bridge.

Ducking behind the canvas dodger to avoid the weather, his bones crying out for mercy from the hammering of the sea, Kelly began to wonder what on earth had prompted him to ask for destroyers. Talbot's mouth, clenched on his pipe, was sour. 'The rocking horse motion of a ship whose waterline length seems to have been designed deliberately to make the worst of steep waves isn't in my opinion the best way of passing the time,' he complained. 'We live in conditions that would make a fakir's bed of nails seem comfortable.'

Blinking the salt out of his eyes, Kelly was aware that his feet felt like blocks of ice. He could only see about a mile in the spindrift and spume, and all this, he thought bitterly, was just to give the battle cruisers a blow because they hadn't been out for weeks.

'It's different for them,' Talbot said, fighting to apply a match to charred tobacco. 'A gale can't wreck their cabins and mess decks, and they think it's rough if they get a spot of spray on their waistcoats.'

As Kelly went below to eat, the water was running down his neck and a playful sea filled his boots. In his cabin all his personal effects were sloshing about the deck and all the drawers were full of water. A dirty trickle from a faulty pipe had soaked his bunk and Charley's photograph was floating in the wash basin in the splinters from a bottle of shampoo. He couldn't have cared less at that moment if *Mordant* had sunk.

'I often wonder why I didn't join the army,' he said to Chambers, the surgeon.

He had long since grown bored with Talbot, who seemed to enjoy subscribing to the legend that all destroyer captains were mad. He was sour, depressed and perpetually grumbling through his pipe, and for an incurable optimist like Kelly was hard to live with. When I'm captain, Kelly thought often, I'll not be like that. So far, he seemed to have gathered round him quite a list of naval captains he'd served under whom he preferred not to emulate – Acheson, Lord Charles Everley, Talbot. Perhaps it was a good thing, he decided. At least he'd be himself. And in any case, it would be a long time before he had command of a ship – even a small one like a destroyer.

Yawing wildly, they rounded the Old Man of Hoy in a gleam of wintry sunshine, *Mordant* snarling and straining in every plate, hinging her bows into the yeasty foam of rolling water from the north Atlantic, then sweeping drunkenly upwards again from the valleys of the ocean, streaming green-white pennants of water from her stem, before reeling corkscrew-wise into the seething turmoil of another trough. Lifelines rigged, deadlights screwed down over scuttles, the sweating hull ran with condensed breath, and there was a permanent slosh of sea water across the corticene where the plates leaked when the port side was the weather side. Metal and glass clinked inside the lockers, and all the hanging gear leaned drunkenly from the bulkhead as the ship sliced through the waves, the water lifting in green walls around the bows and sheets of spray shooting overhead like heavy rain. The other destroyers were often quite invisible beneath the water they displaced, and even the battle wagons rose and fell with the sound of thunder as they pressed majestically on, jettisoning great streams of ocean from around their cable chains and steaming round their hawseholes like a set of angry dragons.

A zeppelin raid on Edinburgh served to make them resentfully happy that other people were having to endure a measure of discomfort, too, but the war seemed no nearer ending. Fisher and Churchill had gone from the Admiralty after the Dardanelles disaster, and there was nothing but stalemate in France. Kut had held out longer than anyone had expected but half the Indian Army seemed to have gone into captivity with its fall. On the credit side, the Germans continued to put their foot in it. They'd already angered the Americans by shooting Nurse Cavell in Brussels and sinking the *Lusitania* off the Old Head of Kinsale. And, with their country beginning to chafe under the naval blockade, it was firmly believed that the Big Push that was to come on the Somme was going to end the war. Everybody talked about it openly in the pubs.

Only in the North Sea was there no news. The raid on Lowestoft remained unforgotten and there was still an angry murmuring going on that the navy was letting such 'insults' be inflicted with impunity. If they had a Grand Fleet – and some people were actively beginning to doubt it – then what was it doing swinging at anchor in the north instead of getting out and retaliating? There was a rash of bloody noses and split lips among the liberty men returning aboard, and Kelly came face to face with Rumbelo who was sporting a black eye.

'Hello, Rumbelo,' he said. 'I didn't think there was anybody big enough to give *you* a shiner.'

Rumbelo grinned. 'Probably there isn't, sir. I let him get away with it.'

'*Let* him get away with it?'

Rumbelo sighed. 'It's not easy having a pint these days, sir,' he said. 'There's always trouble with the dockies and the chaps back on leaf from France.'

'Is that what it was? A dockie?'

'No, sir. A Gordon Highlander. Just a little feller. But he'd been shot at in the mud round Ypres ever since 1914. He'd lost all his pals and was fed up. And he looked it. Coat plastered with dried mud and eyes like somebody had been peeing in snow. He wanted to know if the fleet needed any assistance from his mob.'

Kelly frowned. 'And you? What did you do?'

'Tried to talk him round, sir. Only he didn't fancy being talked round and he took a swing at me.'

'Hit him back?'

Rumbelo gave a wry gentle smile. 'No, sir. I thought he'd been through enough.'

Talbot was not unaware of what was going on. Only a deaf man could have been, because the criticism of Jellicoe could be heard everywhere. 'It's about time,' he said, 'that somebody organised a plan to bring out the High Seas Fleet.'

As it happened, he hadn't long to wait.

A royal command round of golf with his captain on the Queens-ferry links took Kelly ashore and they were just returning aboard when he noticed a flag hoist on the signal bridge of the flagship.

'"*Lion* to battle cruiser force and Fifth BS,"' he read. '"Raise steam for twenty-two knots and report when ready to proceed."'

Talbot applied a match to his pipe, unperturbed. 'Another false alarm, I expect,' he said.

But as they went aboard, the signal was also addressed to the destroyers and Talbot raised his eyebrows.

'Inform the engineer officer, Number One,' he said.

Shortly afterwards, Talbot was called aboard the flotilla leader, the cruiser, *Champion*. When he returned he looked more bored than ever.

'What's on, sir?'

'Gather we're supporting a minelaying expedition in the Bight. Our destination's a rendezvous near the Horns Reef. Another routine show. Tell the engine room to get a move on with raising steam.'

'We're *raising* steam,' Wellbeloved snarled in answer to the message.

'The owner requests "as fast as possible."'

'We're not just practising!'

The sky was full of blazing red and orange, striking out in rays from behind storm clouds. It looked foreboding and Kelly was reminded of what Fanshawe had said aboard *Clarendon* as they'd reached Kiel – all those years ago in 1914. There had been a vermilion sunset then and Fanshawe had said it looked like blood. He wondered what had happened to Fanshawe. He'd never heard a word from him since the beginning of the war and somehow it seemed to accentuate the briefness of naval friendships, perhaps even their existence.

The buzz had already gone round the lower deck – as though they could read the admiral's thoughts.

'Are they out?' Hatchard asked Kelly. 'Is it the big smash?'

'Captain says it's only routine,' Kelly insisted. 'But we'll run a check on the guns all the same.'

The afternoon was quiet and Kelly noticed that, despite Talbot's gloom, Hatchard called the gun captains to his cabin and demanded a check on every inch of the weapons systems. 'If the Germans *are* coming out,' he told Kelly, 'then I'll take back a lot of rude remarks I've made about them in the past. It's been bloody uphill work keeping the chaps up to scratch for nothing.'

Wellbeloved reported the engine room ready and the glare of the afternoon light was just changing to the muted shades of evening when a steam pinnace arrived from *Champion*. An officer climbed aboard – without a word to any of them – and they watched with interest as he disappeared to the captain's cabin. He left in exactly the same way, causing a great deal of speculation about his errand, and as they talked, Lieutenant Heap, his telescope to his eye, pointed out that the battle cruisers appeared to be preparing to slip their moorings.

'Heavy stuff for a minelaying expedition,' he observed drily.

Talbot appeared, his pipe between his teeth and dressed in his best uniform. He looked as though he were ready to dine with the admiral. 'Let's get under way,' he snapped. 'Send the town criers round.'

As the bosun's mates went through the ship, on the mess-decks everything became purposeful confusion. Stokers struggled to get below to the boiler rooms. Pulling on jumpers, seamen struggled to get up the hatch and fall in on deck. Guard rails were taken down and lifelines rove and the accommodation ladder hoisted inboard and stowed. Rumbling noises aft and the clanging of bells indicated that the engineers were trying the steering engine and telegraphs.

'They think the Germans might be coming out,' Talbot finally admitted. 'Torpedo boats and seaplanes sniffing round the North Sea have decided that there are more submarines about than usual. A whole lot sailed on the seventeenth and, ever since, they've been sighting wakes, periscopes and flocks of seagulls following things that aren't wholly visible. In addition, Admiralty direction finders have established from W/T traffic that the High Seas Fleet's moved one and a half degrees west, which takes them from Wilhelmshaven to the Jade Estuary. And *that* means something's afoot.'

–

The evening lights were shining palely along the Firth, and the teatime fires were glowing in the cottages and bothies along the water's edge as the battle cruisers, vast castles of steel, slipped their moorings and began to move under the humps of the Forth Bridge towards the sea, each following the stern light of the ship ahead.

Hatchard was already on the forecastle waiting the order to slip. Aft on the quarterdeck, Sub-lieutenant Naylor waited with a pair of red and green flags to indicate whether the propellers were in danger of fouling anything or not. On the bridge, Petty Officer Lipscomb, the yeoman of signals, handed Talbot a megaphone.

'"Proceed" bent on, sir,' he reported.

'Carry on.'

Flag hoists fluttered up to the yardarm and an answering flag went aloft from *Champion*.

'Approved, sir.'

Talbot turned his head, sending a shower of sparks from his pipe. 'All ready, Number One?'

'Ready on the forecastle, sir,' the gunner announced.

'All ready, sir,' Kelly said.

'Slip.'

As the tide swept *Mordant* clear of the buoy, Talbot spoke quietly. 'Half ahead together.'

The First Destroyer Force led the way down the harbour, followed by the Ninth and Tenth and then the Thirteenth. As they moved forward, *Mordant*, waiting with engines idling just sufficiently to beat the tide, edged into the stream to take up her position. Watching the destroyers, counting them – thirty of them – Kelly saw the flat-topped shape of a seaplane carrier in the dusk.

'*Engadine*'s moving, sir,' he called. 'We'll have eyes, anyway.'

The shore lights of Leith and the Fife coast slid past in a long procession as the wind snatched at the flag hoists and chilled the lookouts behind the bilge screens and the guns' crews huddled under the gunshields. May Island winked its last farewell as the bow slapped at the waves and the first spray came up to shower the forecastle. A bright phosphorescent wake started astern.

The three light cruiser squadrons were up to strength but the Third Battle Cruiser Squadron, under Admiral Hood, was still up at Scapa doing gunnery exercises. Then they saw the vast shapes of the dreadnoughts of Evan-Thomas' squadron and the speculation as to what was in the wind began again.

Talbot was stuffing his pipe with tobacco, working at it carefully, painstakingly, as though it had to last him through any emergencies that might arise in the next forty-eight hours. Slowly he struck a match and lit it, puffing deeply and sniffing the air. For the first time since Kelly had known him he seemed alert, like a hound smelling the scent, his eyes keen, his expression hard and interested.

'If the big boys are coming out,' he said, 'it *must* be the Germans.'

Four

They had been out all night.

As they had cruised east in leisurely fashion across a calm sea to form an inverted U ahead of the battle cruisers, the calling gulls, which had followed like crows after a plough, had been left behind one after the other, and now the North Sea seemed empty.

The visibility was good and they could see the battle cruisers in two lines, with Evan-Thomas' battleships to the north-west. Five miles ahead of *Lion* was the light cruiser screen, spread out on a line bearing roughly north-east to south-west. The squadrons were in two groups of ships, five miles apart with the First Light Cruisers on the northernmost end of the line, while the destroyers had come yelping up astern in the dark behind *Champion*. In a rush and rattle of spray-thrashed steel, their funnels glowing and the roar of the boiler room fans filling the air, they had taken up their positions with the seaplane carrier near the battle cruisers.

The midday sky was high but without colour or warmth between the cloud, and more than ever Kelly was aware of the smell of salt and the sting of the wind on his cheek. The ship seemed alive and eager, the runnels of spray on the paintwork edging downwards in the wind, the quiver and throb of the ship broken by the jar as she tossed her head and flung the swell away like a bridegroom throwing off the confetti on his wedding night. He seemed to be seeing things twice as clearly as normal – the light, the vibrance, the small waves picking up the colour of the sky – in a heightened sense of awareness, and he assumed that the possibility that he might be killed had made him more perceptive than usual.

As they continued to head east, they were sent below one after the other to snatch some food and Kelly looked up as Chambers, the surgeon, entered the wardroom.

'There's death in the air,' the surgeon said. He was a cheerful young man fresh from medical school and the words brought Kelly's head up with a jerk.

'Got the glumps, Doc?' he asked.

'No.' Chambers smiled. 'Actually, in spite of my profession, I haven't seen much of death yet. Haven't had time. Just aware that there's something about us today. Aren't you?'

Kelly grunted. It was no time to brood or indulge in self-pity. 'Don't understand death,' he said shortly.

'You've seen enough of it.'

'It's different in the navy. The sea swallows the debris.'

As they talked, Higgins, the wardroom steward, put his head round the door.

'Lieutenant Maguire, sir! You're wanted on the bridge. Signal's just come through.'

Cramming the rest of his food into his mouth, Kelly went to his cabin to put on as many clothes as possible, and stuff his pockets with notebooks, pencils, chocolate and anything else he might need for a prolonged stay at action stations. As he headed for the bridge, he bumped into Rumbelo who gave him a quick grin.

'This is it, sir,' he said. 'The big smash at last. We'll have something to tell 'em when we go home.'

'Let's hope so,' Kelly agreed. 'Let's hope it isn't someone else who has to go home and tell 'em what's happened to us.'

There was a sudden tension about the ship that was obvious in the alert manner of her seamen, and the keenness of the eyes that scanned the horizon. When Kelly reached the bridge another message had been intercepted and Talbot and Heap were staring towards the east with narrowed eyes.

'*Galatea*'s sighted two hostile cruisers,' Talbot informed Kelly. 'Bearing east-south-east, course unknown. The fun's about to begin, Number One. Go and tell the ship's company.'

The atmosphere was electric and exultant. They were sailing into history at thirty knots.

But what history? Defeat or victory? None of them believed it could be the first.

They had been on the bridge since sailing, their nerves stretched to the utmost so that they longed to relax; and, strained by reaction and tiredness, Kelly found confused emotions were chasing through his consciousness. Though he was acutely aware of the danger, he brushed it aside. Feelings were a bit of a luxury anyway, at a time like this, and there was something obscene about physical danger and death that was best not dwelt upon.

As he made his way through the ship, he saw men moving to their action stations. The wardroom was being taken over by the surgeon and packets of bandages were being stacked in odd corners. Hoses were laid out ready and tense faces peered at him.

'What's up, sir?'

'Germans are out. We'll probably find ourselves in action before long.'

The boiler room fans were roaring to force the draught and Wellbeloved's face was serious.

'I hope we can keep up,' he said.

'Think we might not?'

'It's a long time since we slipped for bottom cleaning.'

The engine room telegraphs clanged and Wellbeloved's eyes shot to Kelly's face. 'Increased revs,' he said. 'You'd better get back.'

When Kelly returned to the bridge, the destroyers were punching into the sea in a dogged manner to keep up with the bigger ships. Talbot handed him another signal form.

'From *Galatea*,' he said. '"Enemy in sight."'

Now that W/T silence was no longer an advantage, the whole of Beatty's fleet opened up with a garrulous interchange by wireless, flag and searchlight. The horizon seemed to be filled with the masts and upperworks of ships from which, in darts of light or fluttering flag hoists, messages were hurriedly passed. Fifteen minutes later another signal was intercepted from *Galatea*.

'Have sighted a large amount of smoke as though from a fleet... Seven vessels besides destroyers... They have turned north.'

The destroyers were pouring through the sea now like hounds after a fox. Despite the calm, it was a rough ride and the crash and clatter of the shuddering ship as she jolted between the waves was deafening. *Mordant*'s wake cut through the water with those of the other destroyers like white lines scraped across a dark scalp by a giant comb. Above their heads the flags snapped and chattered, the halyards thrumming from the quivering mast.

Talbot was staring forward, his eyes alight. He seemed to have come alive, standing tensed and ready, one hand on the binnacle, the other on the single rail that supported the painted canvas screens which were all they had in the way of a bridge. To port the great hulks of the battle cruisers – *Lion, Princess Royal, Queen Mary, Tiger* – seemed to thunder through the water, leaving Evan-Thomas' Fifth Battle Squadron wide and ten miles astern.

It was incredibly exhilarating and, for the first time since he'd joined the navy, Kelly realised that he wanted to live and die in destroyers. He wasn't a submariner by temperament – he hadn't the coldly precise nature of a submariner, any more than he had the calm stolidity of a big ship man. This was what he wanted – the rough and tumble of small ships. Comfort meant nothing when set against this excitement.

Lipscomb, the yeoman of signals, appeared, his face solemn. '*Galatea*'s under fire, sir.'

A seaplane buzzed low over them, heading on a northeasterly course towards *Galatea*'s position, and they watched it until it disappeared in the patchy clouds.

'Let's hope he doesn't run into a zeppelin,' Heap said.

As they increased speed, the wind was carrying the puther from the funnels of the bigger ships across their line and they could taste the grit in it.

'Finely divided particles of carbon,' Talbot drawled. 'Commonly known as smoke.'

Kelly's blood was tingling in his veins at the knowledge of what lay ahead. He'd already seen more action since the war began than most men had, but there was a new and incredible excitement in the thought that he was about to take part in the first great fleet action since hostilities began, the big smash they'd been awaiting for so long, when hundreds of steel ships and thousands of men would pit their strength against each other for command of the North Sea.

Bunting was fluttering on *Lion*'s signal bridge for the battleships trailing astern, then another hoist followed, topped by a blue and yellow destroyer flag. Lipscomb reached for the answering pendant as he read it aloud.

'"Destroyers take up position…"'

As he finished reading, the answering pendant rushed up to the yardarm.

'It's going to be a general engagement,' Talbot said. 'Two months after joining, Number One! You're going to be lucky! I've been waiting for two years and barely seen a sight of 'em. If we don't catch 'em this time, the fleet's going to demand blood for supper.'

Turning north-east to where the contact had been made had brought them to the starboard side of *Lion* and soon afterwards the flagship turned south-east and the battle cruisers formed line astern, a great phalanx of grey steel drawn out towards the horizon.

'Looks as though they mean business,' Heap observed. 'I think we must be trying to get between the Hun and his base.'

In the middle of the afternoon, they sighted smoke to the north-east and the flotilla increased revolutions, pressing on at full speed in showers of spray, while the First and Third Light Cruiser Squadrons took station astern of the battle cruisers. Then, as they turned into line, Kelly caught a flash on the horizon and realised he was looking at silvery hulls and battle cruiser upperworks. Beneath the smoke he could distinguish five shapes accompanied by torpedo craft. The outlines of masts were joined by funnels and the upper parts of hull.

'There, sir,' he said, pointing. 'The Germans! Fine off the starboard bow. I see two funnels. Looks like *Moltkev.*'

'Range fourteen miles!' The call came on the wind in a bored well-drilled voice, and he saw the men at the forward gun lift their heads and begin to stare ahead.

The turbines were howling at full power now and they had to cling on with both hands to stay on the shuddering bridge as the ship bucketed through the water. His glasses to his eyes, Kelly called over his shoulder.

'They're steering a converging course!'

'So much the better,' Talbot said. 'We'll reach 'em quicker.' It was an electrifying sight. After two years of waiting and expectancy, the two great fleets had finally met. Tension filled the ship, reaching from the bridge into every compartment and gun position. Glancing down, Kelly saw Rumbelo closed up on the forward gun, his bulky figure tense and alert.

Talbot was leaning forward over the bridge rail, his pipe trailing a thin stream of blue smoke. His boredom was gone with the weariness of two years of waiting, and he was as eager as anyone else in the ship, his manner so projecting itself that Kelly found his blood quickening at the thought of what lay ahead.

'They'll have to fight this one to the bitter end,' Heap pointed out cheerfully. 'No running away this time. And if Jellicoe's out and heading towards us, we've got them.'

The battle cruisers had turned east-south-east and were crashing towards the Germans between two lines of destroyers,

287

with Pakenham's *New Zealand* and *Indefatigable*, also surrounded by destroyers, five miles to the north-east. Not a man could be seen on their decks. Volumes of smoke poured from their funnels, and their turrets, trained expectantly to port, made them look eager for battle.

Kelly found himself holding his breath, waiting for the first crash of guns, the overture to the coming battle. His mind was occupied with responsibilities and his eyes were all over the ship. The clouds were clearing a little now, and the surface of the sea was picking up the light, though there was a faint mist covering the water and making the horizon hazy. The flotilla's speed had increased slightly and *Mordant* had slipped back a fraction. Talbot had stopped chattering now and *Mordant*'s bridge was silent so that the crash of steel against the water, the hiss of the waves, and the shuddering of the ship filled their ears. Over the roar of the blowers, they could hear a constant clatter and tinkle below, as if the whole vessel was full of loose objects all being thrown around.

'Flagship's signalling, sir!'

Flags fluttered up from *Lion* to be passed down the line of ships. '"Assume complete readiness for action in every respect"' the yeoman read out.

The battle ensign jerked to the yardarm. All over the ship men were testing communications and instruments, and fire parties were assembling at their stations. Gasmasks, goggles and life-saving mats were placed ready as the final preparations for action were made. Splinter mats, boxes of sand, stretchers, spars and spare electrical and engineering gear were laid out and secured. Galley fires were damped down, surgical instruments sterilised and anaesthetics prepared. There was a strange sort of cold-bloodedness about all the preparation for death and destruction that took the breath away, but the very intensity of the preparations drove away any thoughts of foreboding.

'"Form line of battle," sir,' Lipscomb sang out, his glasses to his eyes. '"Second Battle Cruisers astern of First, Thirteenth and Ninth Destroyer Flotillas."'

The battle cruisers were increasing speed now, with the Fifth Battle Squadron trailing well astern and fighting to catch up. The course changed to easterly and Talbot smiled.

'Getting out of the smoke,' he said. 'It's fouling their range.' He occupied himself with refilling his pipe. 'They like to have their battles nice and tidy. Four hundred revolutions, please.'

'Course alteration, sir?'

Talbot lit his pipe and nodded and *Mordant* heeled over so that they all took a staggering step to one side before they recovered their balance.

'Smoke's easier. Not in our eyes now.'

Realising he was holding his breath in excitement, Kelly drew in an explosive gulp of air. They were still waiting for the first crash of the guns, their eyes glued to the distant ships. As the two fleets closed each other, Evan-Thomas still trying desperately to catch up, the visibility remained good but the patches of thin mist over the water were increasing and varying in density, and were not being dispersed by the sun.

'At a disadvantage with the light,' Kelly pointed out. The British ships stood out sharply against a clear sky while the Germans were vague and dim in the mist.

The wait seemed interminable. They could see the Germans more clearly now as they lifted above the horizon, though their shapes were blurred by the mist. Still the two fleets held their fire.

'I think we're going to shake hands first,' Kelly said.

Then, as the battle cruisers came into line with *Champion* and her destroyers, the Germans opened fire. They were almost entirely merged into a long smoky cloud on the eastern horizon, and from the bridge of *Mordant* they saw a series of sparkling flashes run along their line, that ripple of fire the Germans always favoured.

'Here it comes!'

'For what we are about to receive may the Lord make us truly thankful.'

The roar as the British heavy units opened fire in return seemed to shake *Mordant* to her keel. A great rolling cloud of ginger smoke drifted away from the long rifled barrels, and the heavens seemed to fill with the din. As the smoke lifted higher to mingle with the clouds, the sky seemed to sink.

For a quarter of an hour the interchange was furious but it was all so much like the firing exercises they'd carried out it was hard to believe that a battle was taking place, that men were about to die. The two fleets were on more or less parallel courses now, each ship waiting for the range to close before letting fly, but it all seemed so cold-blooded and mechanical, there seemed no chance of anyone seeing red or going berserk – as if all that were needed were a cool scientific calculation and deliberate gunfire.

But the bloody realities of battle soon appeared and, even as he saw one of the German ships flare into a yellow sheet of flame, Kelly also saw flashes on both *Lion* and *Tiger*.

'They've got our range,' he said.

The battle cruisers were lying to port now, the long barrels over the port beam firing salvoes. Vast columns of water like a forest, higher than the mast, were being thrown up all round *Lion*, to cascade over the bridge and decks in mountainous walls of water. Then a flare of yellow through the forest of gingerish-looking splashes caught Kelly's eye, different from the red jabs of her guns, and he realised the flagship had been hit again.

'They've got *Lion*, sir.'

'Q Turret,' Talbot said, staring through his glasses. 'Top's peeled back like an old sardine tin.'

As he spoke, a huge flame shot up from *Lion* and for a moment Kelly thought the flagship had gone with everybody in her. But as the smoke cleared he saw the remaining turrets fire together and the men by the forward gun began to cheer.

'She's all right,' Heap said. 'They've switched to Pakenham's ships.'

It was still hard to accept the deadliness of what they were seeing, despite the flames they could see pouring out of *Lion* just abaft the second funnel, and the engagement remained an exhilarating affair; etched in a strange beauty in the cold northern light. Ahead, astern and on either side of the destroyers, the sea was a succession of water spouts, and the noise had increased to incredible proportions. Black smoke was still pouring from the flagship, but then they saw that *Princess Royal* was taking punishment, too, and had been hit forward. Now it was *Tiger*'s turn, and finally *Indefatigable*'s.

'We seem to be getting rather a pasting,' Talbot observed.

The British guns, Kelly noticed, flashed as they fired, while the Germans' seemed to emit a ball of flame and brown smoke which rolled out comparatively slowly from the barrel. Several 'overs' landed nearby and, as they steamed through the collapsing waterspouts, the decks were deluged by water that smelt of cordite.

'*Indefatigable*'s been hit again!' Heap said.

Round the huge ships, the sea was being churned to foam by the shell splashes, and the air seemed to be yellow with the fumes of lyddite. Almost swamped by the German salvoes, their view of the enemy was obscured by their own funnel smoke.

'*Indefatigable*'s not following the line, sir!'

Heap's voice rose in his excitement and, as they turned to watch, they saw that as the flagship turned to port she was being followed round by *Princess Royal*, *Queen Mary*, *Tiger* and *New Zealand*, while *Indefatigable* was continuing in a straight line, smoke pouring from her deck. Then another salvo hit her and they seemed to feel the agony even in *Mordant*.

The two shells fell on *Indefatigable*'s upper deck, one on the forecastle and one on the forward turret, and as the smoke increased she began to heel over.

'Good God!' Heap's voice cracked. 'I think she's sinking, sir!'

The great ship seemed to be sagging by the stern, moving like a crippled animal dragging its hindquarters, then she was suddenly enveloped in a sheet of flame that rolled along her deck from forward, a dull red ball of fire which flared up the masts in great tongues and spread fore and aft to unite in a black cloud of smoke and sparks.

'Good God!' Heap said.

'Poor bastards!' The voice came from below the bridge. 'They ain't drawn *their* money's worth.'

A vast pall of dense dark smoke had billowed out of *Indefatigable*, rolling low along the surface of the water, with great gouts of it shooting skywards in every direction, its centre lit by the red glow of flame. As it mounted in a solemn dignity to the sky, at the very top of it, 200 feet high, a fifty-foot steam pinnace, apparently intact but upside down, was poised in the air. The cloud of smoke and flame seemed to hang for minutes in the heavens then, through a hole in the dark, rolling pillar, Kelly saw the bows of the ship lying on their side. Then there was another streak of flame and a fresh cloud of smoke, and the bows disappeared.

As they stared, a large, fully-rigged ship with all sails set sailed between them and the Germans like a ghost vessel, something from another age lost in the vast holocaust of twentieth century destruction. They stared at it in wonderment, finding it hard to accept this anachronism in the middle of a great battle. Still staring at *Indefatigable*, Talbot hardly noticed it.

'That's put the cat among the bloody pigeons,' he said slowly. 'See any survivors, Number One?'

'No, sir. There can't be many. There wasn't time. But there's a destroyer moving across.'

The news spread through the ship like wildfire. Never had the grapevine worked so fast. '*Indefatigable*'s sunk!' It was possible to hear the shouts from station to station even on the bridge, as the men on the port side passed the word to those on the starboard side who couldn't see.

Any belief they'd had that the engagement was nothing more than a bloodless exercise had now wholly disappeared and the feeling seemed to have spread through the fleet, because the great ships were hammering away at each other now in what seemed a berserk rage, thick clouds of cordite smoke, brown and bitter-smelling, drifting over the water. The Fifth Battle Squadron was trying to engage the rear German ships at long range, and for a while the German fire seemed to diminish and they saw that the third of the German vessels was blazing.

'This bloody visibility doesn't help,' Talbot snarled.

'Fifth Battle Squadron's cut the corner again, sir,' Heap reported, his glasses to his eyes. 'I think they're in range. They seem to be making good practice, too.'

The din was incredible now, the air full of rolling thunder, overlaid with the higher-pitched crash of the sea and the rattle of the ship, and the thin human voices making their reports above the brazen roar of the guns. The fire of the battle cruisers seemed to have done little harm to the Germans but the battleships' bigger guns at last seemed to be doing damage and they could see hits all along the German line.

'Flagship's signalling by searchlight to *Princess Royal*,' Heap said. 'Wireless must be out of action and she's using *Princess Royal* as an intermediary. Battle cruisers turning towards now. They're shooting damn well, too. *Queen Mary*'s taking on two at once. But I think she's having a bad time herself.'

'It's reports I want,' Talbot said coldly. 'Not a running commentary.'

Turning to deliver the rebuke, he stopped dead as Heap's jaw fell.

'Oh, my God!' Heap said.

Swinging round, Talbot snatched for his glasses. The Germans were shooting superbly and *Queen Mary* was being engaged by two ships at once. Several salvoes struck her together and, as they watched, there was a tremendous explosion forward. A vivid red flame shot up and a huge pillar of smoke climbed to a thousand feet in height, swaying slightly at the base, the top expanding like a mushroom and rolling downward. Flames rose and fell in the stalk of the monstrous growth and, as the battleship staggered and took on a heavy list, there was another explosion amidships. A huge piece of debris soared upwards and they saw the masts collapse, and the stern sticking high in the air, the propellers still revolving and men crawling out of the top of the after turret. As they passed, it rolled over and blew up, throwing great masses of steel in the air in black wobbling arcs out of the cloud of smoke. The centre of the smoke seemed to be a glaring blood-red triangle emitting thick fumes like a vast blow lamp and pulsating like a setting sun, then a new, long, pale tongue of flame shot out of the smoke and they saw shells flung into the air and exploding. A turret turned over lazily and then a mast.

'The damn thing's blowing up like a Chinese cracker,' Talbot gasped. 'What the hell's wrong with our bloody ships?'

The air was full of fragments and flying pieces of metal as the great ship fell apart like a collapsing house, then they saw bows and a mast sliding out of the smoke that lay across the surface of the sea.

Talbot stared, puzzled. 'She's all right,' he said. 'She's still there.'

'No, sir,' Kelly pointed out bleakly. 'That's the next astern. It's *Tiger*. She's going right over the spot where *Queen Mary* was. She'll tear her bottom out on her.'

But *Tiger* continued without pausing and Talbot looked round. 'That was quick,' he said. 'There was nothing there. She went up like a powder cask.'

'So much for the theory that big guns and speed are preferable to armour plating,' Kelly commented. 'That's two to one to the Germans. Another hour of this and we shall have nothing left.'

Lipscomb's voice interrupted them, stolid, as though nothing had happened, as though a thousand men hadn't just died in a matter of seconds before his eyes. 'From flagship to destroyers, sir,' he said, blank and unperturbed with years of reporting signals, devoid of emotion or feeling and apparently indifferent to disaster. '"Opportunity appears favourable for attacking."'

Talbot looked at Kelly. His face was bleak and he seemed to have aged suddenly, as though the loss of two ships were the end of that confident dream they'd all dreamed for two years, of pulverising the German fleet when at last it ventured out. For a moment he looked shocked and unbelieving, then he hitched at his bridge coat and thrust his shoulders back.

'Here we go, Number One,' he said. 'Take your partners for the waltz.'

Five

All eyes had turned towards *Champion*. Lipscomb's voice came automatically, dry as dust.

'Signal from flotilla leader, sir. "Thirteenth Flotilla to attack the German line with torpedoes. Three-oh knots."'

Leaning against the front of the bridge, his pipe between his teeth, Talbot called for the extra revolutions, and *Mordant*'s bow rose as her stern went down in a froth of foam to the drag of her racing propellers. As the line swung, the deck heeled abruptly as the revolutions increased, and *Mordant* began to shake like an excited horse, the eager rumble of her engine room blowers giving her a living animal sound over the drenching hiss of the sea. The bow wave rose higher and the white foam at her stern spread wider as the engine room staff forced every ounce of power out of her, the din drowned the noise of gunfire, so that all they could hear was the crash of steel, water and wind, and the scream of the turbines and the roar of the boiler room fans.

'Starboard twenty!'

The speed increased further as they rushed forward in a long curve to the attack. German destroyers flying red pendants were already moving out at high speed from the enemy line to foil the attempt.

'*Nestor*, *Nomad* and *Nicator* are within range, sir,' Heap reported. 'They should open fire soon.'

'Shift from target to target as necessary.'

'*Nestor*'s opened fire, sir.'

Gunfire started ahead and increased, so that the wind was full of the peppery reek of cordite. The speed had reached thirty-two knots as they approached the head of the German line. Two of the enemy torpedo boats, hit by the leading destroyers, had already stopped, blowing off steam and leaking smoke as they wallowed in the water, one with a distinct list to starboard already. The firing of the rest became wild.

'Range eight thousand!'

The German cruisers were firing over their torpedo boats now in a vicious hail of heavy shell, and the splashes rose all round the British ships. A salvo of four-inch shells wailed like demons over *Mordant*'s masthead and crashed like stones into the sea beyond her, then, as splinters flew and a fresh mountain of water rose ahead, broke and cascaded across the deck, she steamed through it so that the men on her bridge found themselves wet through, blinded and coughing with the bitter smell of high explosive. Where shells had fallen, the sea was pockmarked in patches of scummy-looking discoloration, as if someone had been emptying huge buckets of ash into the water, and as the trigger-happy gunners joined in, Talbot's expression lifted into one of almost demoniacal glee.

'It's a regular Brock's Benefit,' he said gaily and Kelly found himself envying him his cheerful aplomb.

A peculiar moaning told them that another lump of steel filled with explosive had just gone by, and as he examined himself to see if he was frightened, Kelly came to the cheering conclusion that he wasn't and that rather he was only excited and anxious that he should do well.

The ships around them had opened fire with all their guns now but the gunlayers were confused by the number of targets that presented themselves and each gun was firing independently. But with the sea and the spray and the smoke, accurate shooting was impossible and no one seemed to be hit.

'*Nestor*'s getting her torpedoes away, sir!'

The explosive cartridges by which *Mordant*'s missiles were ejected had been inserted and the torpedo crews were crouched by the tube mountings, their figures tense and expectant.

'Stand by!' Talbot's eyes were on the torpedo director. 'Fire when your sights bear!'

The torpedoes went away at intervals of a second or two, each leaving the tube with the sharp crack of the cartridge and leaping out like a giant salmon to take the water with a tremendous splash before diving to its preset depth. The navyphone screeched.

'Bridge? All torpedoes fired and running correctly.'

Talbot glanced to starboard. The torpedoes' tracks were clearly visible.

'Hard a–port!'

As they turned away, shells bursting all round them, Heap sang out.

'*Nomad*'s hit, sir! She's flying "Not under control."'

Kelly's head jerked round. *Nomad* was wallowing in the water, smoke and steam pouring from her engine room, and as they raced past, someone waved from the bridge. The heavier German ships were less than a mile away now, firing with everything they had, then they were passing and re-passing each other like a flock of disturbed birds, shooting at point-blank range. The battle cruisers, both British and German, were turning from the attacks as the destroyer battle developed, and the sea suddenly seemed to be full of ships of all sizes, hurtling back and forth in the smoke and spray, every gun blazing, heeling into the turn, their masts at a steep angle to the water, their battle flags whipping in the wind, the staccato bark of the four–inch guns cracking over the general din.

'What a bloody scrum,' Talbot observed.

As the destroyers cleared the smoke, fresh white pillars of water leapt up among them like giant ninepins, to be knocked down and leap up yet again without ceasing as the guns of the bigger ships came into action.

'One of the Germans is hit, sir.'

'Our torpedo?'

'Impossible to say, sir.'

As they hauled out of the action, there was a clang and a crash aft. They heard the hum of fragments and caught a glimpse of polished steel flashing past the bridge, then the sub, Naylor, appeared. He looked shaken. 'Stern four-inch hit, sir. And one of the boats has gone up in splinters.'

Watching the Germans, Talbot didn't turn his head. 'Casualties?' he asked.

Naylor swallowed. 'Gun crew, sir. Lieutenant Shakespeare's dead. There's a bit of a fire but it's under control.'

'I think we'll be all right now,' Talbot said. 'We're through.'

'Sir!' Lipscomb's voice shoved itself through a chink in the din. 'Signal from *Southampton*. To Grand Fleet. "Have sighted enemy's battle fleet bearing south-east."'

'That's torn it,' Talbot observed mildly. 'The whole bloody lot are out. This is going to be the most unholy smash that ever was. Let's hope Jellicoe arrives before long or he'll be too late.'

Beatty's ships were still standing on towards the south-east but then Heap's voice came, flat and unemotional.

'Battle cruisers turning away to starboard, sir. In succession.'

'The last one's going to be damned close,' Kelly observed.

Heap continued to stare ahead. 'Fifth Battle Squadron's still standing on towards the enemy, sir.'

Evan-Thomas' ships, occupied with the German battle cruisers, were dourly heading towards the enemy battle line, taking the brunt of the attack while the British battle cruisers swung away.

Heap's voice rose. 'They're turning now, sir! In succession. To starboard.'

'It's going to be a damned hot corner by the time *Malaya* turns. They'll be in range of the whole German battle fleet.'

Shells were falling round *Barham* now, then they saw the splashes appear round *Valiant* and *Warspite*, both of which were seen to be hit. *Malaya*, the last ship in the line, had turned early and, despite their wounds, *Warspite* and *Malaya* were hitting back hard and they saw two salvoes strike one of the German ships and sheets of flame lift over her masthead as she glowed red fore and aft like a burning haystack.

The battle cruiser squadron was heading north-west now, leading the High Seas Fleet after them.

'Flotilla leader signalling, sir!'

As the recall came and they swung after the battle cruisers, they passed *Nomad* lying dead in the water, stopped and helpless. A line of battleships appeared on the port bow through a heavy bank of mist and funnel smoke that stretched across the horizon.

'We're all right now,' Heap said cheerfully. 'Here's the Fifth Battle Squadron!'

Talbot took his pipe from his mouth and spoke coldly. 'That, Heap,' he said, 'is the German Battle Fleet.'

Almost immediately, they were in the thick of a hair-raising bombardment delivered at a distance of a mere 3000 yards as they heeled over to try to make another torpedo attack.

'*Nestor*'s hit, sir.'

Nicator was swinging out of line to avoid the damaged ship; *Mordant*, just behind, had to do the same.

'Hard a-port,' Talbot snapped. 'Shove her over, coxswain, or we'll divide her neatly into two equal halves!'

The Germans were smothering *Nestor* and *Nomad* with shells as they passed. As *Mordant* bucketed by, on the blind side, trying to keep up with the battle cruisers, they saw *Nestor* dead in the water, too, the waves lapping her deck, steam billowing from her engine room. A German destroyer bearing down on her, thinking her easy prey, staggered as she was hit by salvoes from semi-automatic weapons and sheered off quickly, but *Nestor*'s crew were getting rid of confidential papers and putting rations into boats and rafts. Wrapped in a cloud of smoke and spray, in the centre of a shrieking whirlwind of shellfire, she was already down by the stern, then above the din they heard the defiant cheers of her crew as her bows lifted and she sank stern-first, to leave only a patch of oil and debris to mark her grave. Over the water as they drew away they could hear voices still thinly singing the National Anthem.

In the distance, *Nomad* was the target for what appeared to be a whole German battle squadron and was also sinking by the stern, burning furiously, her flag still flying, a mass of yellow flame and smoke as the lyddite charges detonated along her length. Her two after funnels seemed to have melted and collapsed, and red showed through the gaping wounds in her sides. Clouds of grey smoke poured from her and in places the hull seemed to glow with heat. But men were still running along her deck and it seemed amazing that they could still live in that hell.

A string of flags jerked up to *Lion*'s yardarm and Kelly dragged his eyes away.

'Flagship altering course, sir,' he said. 'Heading further west.'

'How many German ships do you make it now, Number One?'

'I count sixteen or seventeen. With four *König* class in the van. Older pre-dreadnoughts bringing up the rear.'

Seconds became minutes and every moment Kelly expected to see a sheet of flame ripple down the sides of the German vessels and a hail of shell fall round them.

'Perhaps we can get among them,' Talbot said.

'Range one three five double-O. Range one three two double-O.'

'*Nicator*'s altering course. We're getting out of it.'

As the ships changed direction, the Germans began to open fire and a salvo crashed down around them.

'Range obscured!'

About three or four miles to the north, the British battle cruisers were steaming away, making a great deal of smoke and firing over their sterns at ships on the starboard quarter. Two miles behind them the Fifth Battle Squadron trailed, followed by the Second Light Cruiser Squadron, still under persistent fire.

'Bit of a shock to the system seeing the whole German fleet sailing down our throats, what,' Talbot said cheerfully.

'Let's hope the Hun'll shortly enjoy the same sensation,' Kelly said.

'Amen to that.'

Vast masses of smoke were forming an impenetrable pall over the sea and the rapidly narrowing area of water was being flailed to foam by the passage of dozens of ships. The Fifth Battle Squadron was still involved in its turn to starboard and under heavy fire from the approaching German Battle Fleet, and they saw the shells splashing round them, almost obliterating them. It was an incredible sight they were seeing. Though part of the battle, they were also spectators and could watch the German ships switch to a leisurely target practice with the light cruisers as their victims.

A sheet of yellow flame enveloped one of the leading ships but then the flickering line of gun flashes started again and Kelly looked at his watch, counting the seconds.

'Twenty-one, twenty-two, twenty-three—' Heap was counting out loud and Talbot turned on him.

'Dry up, Heap,' he snapped.

There was a series of ear-splitting cracks and lugubrious moans as the salvo arrived. With the positions changed, the light had improved and now it was the Germans who were dazzled by the setting sun.

'What's the time, Number One?'

'Seventeen fifty-five, sir.'

'Less than three hours to darkness.'

Both fleets were under fire now and there was an immense fascination in watching the deadly and graceful splashes rising mysteriously from the smooth sea, the torrents of spray from them smashing down across the deck.

'I make that fifty to sixty shells within a hundred yards of us, and a few more further off,' Talbot said calmly. 'Keep us zigzagging, Number One. The Hun's working a ladder. We'll sheer in towards them as they approach and away again as they start coming back.'

It was already well into evening when Lipscomb's voice drew their attention to the flagship. 'Sir, *Lion*'s signalling to the Grand Fleet! Jellicoe's arrived.'

'I'll bet that'll make the Germans jump,' Talbot said. 'Thank God for the haze. Their damned zeppelins won't have spotted them.'

'There they are, sir.'

Mile on mile of ships began to appear through the smoke and haze of the late afternoon to the north-west. The tables had been turned completely. The Grand Fleet was steering south-west, the great vessels moving ponderously to deploy. The news that they'd been sighted had spread round *Mordant* at once, and there was a burst of cheering from aft. The air was already full of signals as the huge ships began to pick their targets in the fast-moving multitude of grey shapes.

'Open fire and engage the enemy.'

'Remember the Glorious First of June.'

'When is the Glorious First of June?' Talbot asked.

'Tomorrow, sir.'

Talbot glared into the smoke at a flickering light. 'What's that chap signalling, Lipscomb?'

Lipscomb coughed. '"It seems to be getting a bit thick this end," sir. "Where is the enemy?"'

Talbot stared about him into the murk. The German ships were clearly in sight to the destroyers and must have been quite visible to the battle cruisers.

'For God's sake,' he snorted, 'why doesn't Beatty tell 'em?'

Large masses of smoke from the hundreds of ships making at full speed for the scene of the battle lay between the lines to the north-east where they combined to form an impenetrable pall, pierced here and there by the flashes of salvoes, the detonation of shells and the flames from fires. Jellicoe's escorting vessels had turned towards the German ships; one of the light cruisers, under the fire of the whole German line, seemed to be blotted out by explosions and a destroyer caught fire and slowed to a stop, down by the bows at once.

'God Almighty,' Talbot said, his voice faintly awed. 'It's worse than Phil the Fluter's ball.'

As they watched, two of Arbuthnot's armoured ships of the First Cruiser Squadron turned between them and the German line and began to move into an appalling concentration of fire.

'What the devil are they up to?' Talbot demanded.

Arbuthnot's ships were being hit repeatedly and as the leading one heeled to a salvo just abaft the rear turret, a red sheet of flame leapt up. She recovered, righted herself and steamed on, only to be hit by yet another salvo, this time in front of the foremost funnel. At once she seemed to glow red all over, swell and burst into fragments in an enormous cloud of black smoke which rose to a height of several hundred feet then, dispersing, showed no sign of a ship at all. Below them on the deck the sailors began to cheer wildly and Kelly swung round.

'Shut those men up, Heap!' he snapped. 'That's not a Hun! I saw the white ensign. It was *Defence*. That's *Warrior* astern of her and *she's* being hard hit, too!'

As they watched, the German fire switched to another British ship which hauled out of line behind the battered and burning *Warrior*.

'It's *Warspite*. What the hell's she up to?'

The battleship was making a half turn, with the whole of the leading enemy division concentrating on her. Naylor, the sub, was just directing a camera at her when Talbot saw him.

'Put that damn thing away,' he roared. 'She's going to be destroyed!'

Warspite had reached a position about 8000 yards from the Germans when she slowly turned again, lashing out viciously with her fifteen-inch guns, before rejoining the British line. As she regained safety there was a sudden lull around them and they had to reduce speed and turn in a complete circle to avoid bunching up on the onrushing battleships, one of which thundered past their stern, towering over them, the men on her bridge peering down on them. Over the din of the sea and the guns they could hear bugles blowing somewhere aboard her.

'Swop you this 'un for that 'un, mate,' a wag on the forward gun screamed above the roar of water.

Despite the British losses, it was clear that the Germans were at last in real trouble. Endlessly the Grand Fleet stretched away to the horizon, with Hood's Third Battle Squadron, led by *Invincible*, further to the north. The German line lay in a shallow convex arc to the south. *Lion* had turned west-south-west now, to rejoin the line and lead her consorts in the van of the Grand Fleet. They seemed blurred by the mist and the Third Battle Cruiser Squadron, manoeuvring to join them, was barely visible. But the battle cruisers, for the first time able to see the German ships better than they were being seen themselves, were scoring hits now.

Talbot glanced round. It was already evening and the sky was growing darker, the visibility in the low cloud poorer now than it had been all day. Bright points of fire from the ghostly ships stabbed the gloom.

'The bloody sun will be gone soon,' he said. 'What there ever was of it. The Germans are going to get away.'

As he spoke the veil of mist in front split like the curtains of a stage. Clear and sharp, they saw Hood's battle cruisers silhouetted against the horizon and, as they watched, an explosion on *Invincible*'s centre turret lifted a great crimson flame to the sky. At the very top ship's plates were turning and tumbling, then the deep red faded and the pall of smoke merged into the smother and, as a shower of fine ash and debris began to drift down, they saw the two ends of the ship standing perpendicularly above the water.

'They said Jellicoe could lose the war in an afternoon.' Talbot's voice was harsh. 'It looks to me as though *this* is the afternoon.'

The light was fading rapidly as the destroyers pounded round to reach the battleships. There were only a few survivors clinging to the floating wreckage of Hood's ship; they were still cheering as the battle fleet bore down towards the Germans, then they were swept under by the vast steel hulls.

305

Kelly tore his eyes away. In the distance an unholy firefight was taking place and the German ships were being heavily hit. *Mordant* was rolling appreciably and he realised that the whole of the immediate area of the sea was heaving up and down in a confused swell created by the wash of two-hundred-odd ships all moving on different courses at high speed. The German battle line was struggling to turn away, hit constantly by the British dreadnoughts, and one of them was already on fire, her whole fore part ablaze.

The visibility grew worse until they could see only the flash of salvoes, and Talbot glared into the growing darkness.

'If we're landed with a night action,' he said, 'it'll be a proper Donnybrook Fair. Every night exercise I was ever on was pandemonium.'

The din seemed to be part of some heavenly battle, yet above it they could hear the thin sound of cheering across the darkening water as the great ships continued to thunder past them. Talbot was staring towards the German line, his expression tense, then he brought his fist down on the bridge rail.

'They're turning away!' he said. 'By God, they are! They're running!'

Red flashes and smoke ahead of *Mordant* indicated a separate conflict between destroyers and cruisers moving at the speed of an express train, but by the time they reached the spot it had all cleared except for a three-funnel cruiser, lying inert between the lines, the target for every British battleship which could not see her own target. The cruiser *Southampton* tore in to give the German ship the coup de grace but other Germans lying beyond the cripple opened a rapid fire on her and she turned tail and fled, zigzagging like a snipe.

Twilight was coming down on them now and the visibility was further spoiled by the low-lying clouds of smoke and cordite fumes which hung like a gloomy shadow over the sea. The British ships had worked to the eastward of the Germans by this time and were trying to edge into a semi-circle with the enemy in the middle. Then a few German destroyers crept out from the head of their line and began to make smoke. As the dense screen of oily black rolled along the surface of the water, they could see only the topmasts of the German capital ships.

'They're changing course, sir,' Kelly said, glancing into the dimly-lit binnacle.

'Sir!' Lipscomb appeared. 'Message from the flagship. "Where is enemy's battle fleet?" *Southampton*'s replying "Have lost sight."'

'Then, for God's sake, make a signal, Number One! Tell 'em we can see 'em. We're not here just to get involved in a life and death struggle with German torpedo boats. Give 'em their course and our position.'

But, as Kelly moved away and they raced along outside the smoke, four German destroyers emerged right across their bows. As *Mordant* jinked to starboard, the forward gun banged and there was a sharp glow and a flare of flame on the leading German, then all four Germans opened fire at once and *Mordant* was swamped in splashes that flooded the deck as they fell across her. There was a tremendous crash as a shell hit the forward gun and the whole ship seemed to stagger in its stride. Splinters slashed the bridge and funnel and hundreds more, blasted into razor-sharp slivers of red-hot steel, were flung into the W/T office to smash equipment and cut aerials. Then another salvo fell round them and the wireless office itself dissolved in a sheet of flame, and sparks flew upwards in a golden rain as if someone had taken a flying kick at a bonfire.

For a second Kelly seemed to be surrounded by a terrible noise and there was an agonising pressure on his eardrums and a searing pain over his right eye. A bright ball of fire exploded only a few feet away from his face like a blue-green flare, with yellow-white centre like phosphorous. Vaguely through the glare, he saw a man about to jump over the side, but he disappeared in the flash of the burst, and as the smoke blew clear he saw his lower torso and legs had vanished and the shoulders and chest were just turning slowly in the air before splashing into the sea. A panicking man running along the deck disappeared into a gaping hole where fire was roaring and his screams came through the rumble of the flames until abruptly they died.

Picking himself up, Kelly found that blood was filling his right eye and he couldn't see, and his nostrils were full of the stink of fumes. The burned and tattered body of a wireless operator lay sprawled among the wreckage. A second wireless operator was just dragging himself to his feet.

There was no point in asking if repairs could be made. There was nothing to make repairs with, and he brushed the blood from his eyes and stumbled towards the bridge. The ship was still moving through the water, smoke and steam escaping from her both midships and aft.

Vaguely, his eyes still dazzled by the icy-yellow glare of the shell-burst, he saw Rumbelo standing by the bottom of the ladder, with blood on his face.

'You all right?' he mumbled.

'I think, so, sir.' Rumbelo's voice came only faintly to his bruised eardrums. 'I was just dead lucky. I think everybody else's gone.'

The bridge was a shambles. What was left of it was splashed with blood and for a moment Kelly stood dazedly among the debris, waiting for someone to give him orders. Then it dawned on him through the shock of the explosion that had deafened and half-blinded him that the helmsman and Talbot were lying together in a heap, their bodies leaking blood. Beyond them, Heap was sprawled near the compass, and there was no sign of his head.

The binnacle was pitted with holes but the wheel seemed to be intact, and Kelly stared dully round him, still shocked but slowly recovering his senses. At last the completeness of the disaster struck him and he shook his head and forced himself to concentrate.

There was *no one* to give him orders, no one at all. It was he who was captain of the ship.

Six

It was dark as *Mordant* wallowed helplessly through the water but they could still hear heavy firing to the south-west where the horizon was lit by flickering lights as the German line was harassed by the light cruisers and forced further and further away from its bases into the North Sea. The thudding of guns seemed to be felt in every one of *Mordant*'s plates, as the flash, the display of searchlights, the glare of explosions and the blazing torches of burning destroyers marked the Germans' retreat.

Kelly jerked to life at last. Iron claws seemed to be tearing at his forehead.

'Rumbelo,' he yelled. 'Up here! Do you know the silhouettes of the German Navy?'

'Yes, sir.'

'Stand by the wheel then until we can get a relief quarter-master. Keep your eyes skinned.'

They were still moving ahead as Rumbelo swung their bows into the smoke, and thankfully, choking on the heavy fumes, they felt the relief as the shooting stopped. Then they were out at the other side into comparative peace and Kelly shouted down the voice pipe to reduce the revolutions.

The relief quartermaster appeared.

'Take the wheel,' Kelly snapped. 'Rumbelo, get Mr Naylor up here and ask Mr Hatchard to let us have a report on damage and casualties.'

As Rumbelo vanished, he stared around him. Below on the deck, a man covered with blood stood with his feet apart, swaying slightly, his head hanging, his eyes wild like a calf in a slaughterhouse. Kelly sighed. The big smash that the lower deck had been praying for, for two years, had certainly arrived. With his own eyes he'd seen four proud ships die, as well as several smaller ones, both British and German. Blood had been shed and lives had been ended, including that of Talbot, who had spent two weary, boring years staring at Scapa Flow, only to have everything blotted out for him in the first hours of the battle he'd waited for, like so many hundreds more dead men, over so many months. It was to be hoped that now the big ships had arrived, they would make all the slaughter of their smaller sisters worthwhile.

Naylor arrived, panting, white-faced and shaken, and Kelly lifted one hand to acknowledge him. 'Better act as my eyes, Sub,' he said. 'I can't see very well at the moment.'

'Shall I get the SBA, sir?'

'No, for God's sake, stay where you are. Let's stay at reduced speed until we know what we're doing. Make it "slow ahead" until we hear what the engine room's got to say.'

As they waited for Hatchard's report, the bodies of the dead were laid out on the port side near the wreckage of the after gun. The atmosphere seemed to stink from the heavy coal smoke from the big ships' funnels and the cordite and lyddite from the explosions.

'Where do you think the fleet's got to, Sub?' Kelly asked.

Naylor tried to look intelligent and knowledgeable. 'South-east by the look of it, sir.'

Kelly bent over the bridge rail, clinging to it grimly in his pain with one hand and holding to his eye with the other the towel he normally wore round his neck against the spray. He didn't bother to reply. He had merely been making conversation, trying to reassure Naylor. The wounded had crawled into the lee of the funnels in a pitiful attempt to find shelter, and they were now having to drag themselves back again as other men pushed forward with collision mats to cover the shellholes. Kelly struggled to lift his head, but he could hardly see.

'Where's the ensign?' he asked.

'Shot away, sir.'

'Hoist another, Sub. Got to look our best for the party.'

A flotilla of destroyers hurtled past in the growing gloom, dark shapes in the shadows, their funnel tops crowned with a vivid red glow so that a scarlet canopy seemed to hang over each vessel.

'No signalling,' Kelly rapped. 'Let's see who they are first.' As the ships flashed past, the last one fired a solitary four-inch shell at *Mordant*, which whistled harmlessly overhead.

'Some bloody gunlayer who was dozing and happened to wake up as they passed,' Rumbelo growled.

Hatchard appeared with Wellbeloved. 'Fifteen casualties,' he reported. 'Forward gun wrecked with most of its crew dead. Wireless office wrecked. Voice-pipes and electrical communications cut and steam pipes burst. There's also a fuel pipe fire but it's under control.'

'We've lost steam on Number Two,' Wellbeloved said. 'I can give you fifteen knots on the others.'

'How long before we can move off?'

'You can move off now, but give me a few minutes and I can give you full power on both boilers.'

'Make it fast. It seems bloody unhealthy round here.'

The engineer nodded. 'We shan't be long and then we'll give you all the emergency speed you want.'

The bridge had been cleared now. The wood and steelwork were scorched and pitted with holes; the canvas dodger, fluttering in ribbons, was splashed with blood.

The pain in Kelly's head seemed unbearable and the waiting seemed interminable but, after a while, he heard the thrumming of the boiler room fans, and a gout of black smoke was superseded first by grey then by a whitish, almost transparent gust of vapour.

The navyphone screeched. 'Both engines ready, sir.'

'Thank you.' Kelly looked round him. The North Sea seemed suddenly empty. 'Slow ahead together.'

A sick berth attendant arrived. He was very young and looked terrified. 'Christ, sir,' he said, peering at Kelly's face with a torch.

'What's happened to it?'

Kelly was standing against the binnacle, his face covered with blood. The sick berth attendant peered at him with a worried look on his face.

'You ought to be in your bunk, sir.'

'No.'

'A splinter's caught your cheekbone, sir. It's probably broken. It's also cut open the left side of your forehead. There's a flap of flesh hanging down over your eye.'

'That'll spoil my beauty, won't it? Fix it.'

As the SBA nervously struggled to adjust a bandage over his eye, Kelly's mind was roving ahead of their present situation. They still had the torpedo tubes and one gun amidships that would fire. As the SBA finished, he brushed him aside.

'Let's go,' he said to Naylor. 'Push her up to half revolutions. We'll find out what's happening before we shove our noses into it.'

As they headed south-west, steering by the remains of a patched-up chart, they passed the stern of a large ship sticking out of the water.

'What ship's that?'

It was impossible to tell and they circled the wreckage looking for survivors, but other ships had been there before them and they saw only floating bodies.

It was quite dark as they pushed up the revolutions again and searchlights began to criss-cross on the western horizon. On the port quarter a flash showed up over the horizon and a star shell hovered in the sky. Then another, greater flash followed and to starboard of it a great tower of flame flared up into the sky, died down and reared up afresh. The whole of the sea seemed to be rippling and flashing with fire. Then the searchlights, rising and falling like the antennae of a blinded animal, fixed their

313

implacable light on a group of distant destroyers rushing up the bright path of the beams. White splashes lifted all round them, then a lurid fire started in one of them and spread to a vast explosion of fierce white flame that made even the searchlights seem pale. Immediately the lights were extinguished and the attack died out, and everything was dark again, except for the glowing point of fire.

Higgins, the wardroom steward, appeared with bully beef sandwiches and cocoa, and they were eating quietly when Rumbelo muttered. 'Ships on the port quarter, sir.'

Kelly stared at them through his night glasses and there was a whispered discussion as to what they were. It didn't occur to them for a minute that it was the wing tip of the German fleet trying to break through the British line at its weakest point.

'Light cruisers,' Naylor said.

'Yes,' Kelly agreed. 'But whose? Ours or theirs? Challenge.'

As the signal lamp began to clack, coloured lights appeared at the fore yardarms of the other ships and a searchlight snapped on. A gun fired and *Mordant* rolled as a shell smashed into her above the waterline.

'Full ahead!' Kelly yelled as the solitary gun by the funnel crashed out.

The shell smashed into the opposing ship just below the bridge and seemed to tear her open even as Kelly rang for full revolutions and turned his tail to the Germans to present the smallest possible target. A second shell struck *Mordant* near the base of the funnel as they plunged into a bank of mist, riddling the metal, and Kelly spun round and fell as a searing pain scored across his back and the blast whipped away the bandage from his forehead.

Dragging himself to his feet, he saw the quartermaster had been hit. 'Take the wheel, Rumbelo,' he yelled. 'And let's have an SBA up here!'

Shells were still whistling past; as they emerged from the other side of the mist, they were illuminated once more by a searchlight and within two minutes a storm of fire swept the ship. The range was so close the German shots went high enough to burst on the upper deck, and round the super-structure of the bridge where all the flesh and blood was. An enormous blaze started just abaft the torpedo tubes where shell fragments had whipped across the deck and mowed men down like corn before a sickle. A second shell burst amidships and the fragments sliced across the waist like hail, scouring out the inside of the shield of the midships gun and igniting cordite charges.

The ship heeled as she turned away, empty brass cartridge cases rattling and rolling into the scuppers. The foredeck was a swirling mass of angry flames making an unearthly red glow in the darkness and giving a crimson tinge to the black smoke and white steam. A pillar of fire was roaring up the foremast from one blaze; a second reached above the top of the funnel.

Fortunately the German ships were more concerned with their own fleet than with doing damage and they thundered off into the darkness, leaving *Mordant* rolling on the swell, a wreck. The action had lasted no more than a minute, then they had plunged thankfully into a fresh bank of white haze. Staring back, Kelly saw a huge flare of flame rising beyond the mist, lighting it with a red glow.

Hatchard appeared, grinning. 'Torpedoed one of the sods,' he yelled. 'Let the whole salvo go. Couldn't miss. Thanks for turning away when you did.'

'I was thinking of my skin,' Kelly said shortly. 'Did you sink her?'

'Probably not, but she'll have an awful headache!'

'What about casualties?'

Hatchard's grin died. 'We seem to have lost the last of our guns, together with all its crew, I'm afraid.'

'Get a report from the engine room on their damage. They must have some this time.'

Hatchard stared at him. 'You're in need of attention,' he said.

'No, I can see now.'

Reports started coming to the bridge from other parts of the ship. Splinters had cut the freshly-repaired electric leads and steam pipes. Naylor appeared and, amid the deafening noise of steam escaping and the smoke and heat blowing back from the fires a few feet away, he had to shout to make himself heard.

'There's a fire amidships,' he stammered. 'It's the motorboat.'

'I can see it,' Kelly snapped, his voice diamond-hard. 'Put the bloody thing out!'

A splinter had severed the connection to the upper deck fire main and the flames were increasing.

'Let's have a good hose up here,' Kelly yelled and Higgins, the wardroom steward, appeared dragging one with him. 'Get up,' he was yelling at the wounded men. 'Get up and bloody help!'

Those who could dragged themselves to their feet, and a man with his clothes blown off and his skin hanging in strips led a file of blackened scarecrows away to the sick bay, one of them, with his ears charred off and burned from head to foot, dragged along by two of his shipmates. Lying by the funnel was a still-living gunner who had been ripped open by a splinter, his inside spilling out on to the deck, and the ship resounded with the mournful cry of 'Stretcher bearers.' A sailor who had lost both arms was begging his friends to throw him overboard, and all round the deck among the huge holes where fires flickered and grey smoke leaked men were vomiting with shock and disgust. A stoker trapped beyond a jammed hatch was burning to death, screaming his life out while his friends, who could do nothing to help him, could only try to shut their ears to his agony.

Naylor had already turned his attention to the fire by the foremast and Hatchard hurried to help him. There was no point in giving them orders or getting in their way. Hatchard had been in the navy long enough to know what to do. As the sick berth attendant who had arrived finished bandaging the quartermaster, he looked up at Kelly. He was a petty officer this time and was unimpressed by Kelly's rank.

316

'You've been hit, sir,' he said and turned him round without a by-your-leave.

'Good God, sir,' he went on. 'It's ripped your bridge coat, jacket and shirt, even severed your bloody braces! You're bleeding like a stuck pig.'

'Bandage it,' Kelly said.

The sick berth tiffy shook his head. 'Bandaging won't do any good to that, sir. It needs stitches. A lot of stitches. Your eye, too.'

He spoke with authority and confidence and Kelly longed to let him take over, but the pillar of flame was still roaring up the foremast and the ready ammunition for the midships gun kept exploding in a shower of sparks and shreds of blazing cordite. He noticed that the heat of the fire was strong enough to scorch his cheek and began to wonder what it would be like to be blown up. More than once that day he'd seen huge ships disintegrate and he wondered if *Mordant*, being smaller, would go more gently.

Then, beyond the struggling men, he saw the whiteness begin to go from the pillar of flame, and as it decreased, wavered, lengthened again, and finally began to die, he allowed himself to listen to the pleas of the sick berth tiffy. 'Right,' he said. 'Do as you like. Get the surgeon up here.'

'Sir, the doctor's dead. He was on deck attending to the wounded when that last lot got us.'

'Very well. Can you stitch it?'

'Yes, sir.'

'Put 'em in.'

As he spoke, Kelly was aware that he sounded like a *Chums* impression of a destroyer officer, brusque, rude and laconic. But it was chiefly because it was hard work thinking and harder still having to issue orders.

The sick berth tiffy frowned. 'Sir, I'll have to give you morphine.'

'No!' Kelly brushed him aside. 'Do it without or not at all. Save the morphine for the others.'

Hatchard appeared. 'It'll hurt like hell,' he said.

'Rumbelo can sit on my head and you can sit on my feet. I expect we'll manage. I'm not having morphine. There's no one else and nobody's putting me to sleep till I know we're safe. Let's go and see what's happened.'

Leaving the bridge, he stumbled over a body at the bottom of the ladder and Hatchard dragged it aside. Before he could reach the fire by the funnel, it wavered and died away and they were in darkness again, a strange darkness full of heat and smoke and the groans of wounded men. The deck was strewn with bodies so that he kept falling over them as he moved about, but by the aid of matches and torches the deck was searched.

'Keep those lights down,' Kelly ordered. 'We have no idea where the Germans are.'

He bent over a boy seaman torn by sickening injuries and covered with blood, splintered bones showing through his flesh. The boy smiled. 'It's no good worrying about me, sir,' he said. 'I can't feel much pain, anyway.'

The cooks who had closed up as sick berth attendants had rigged up a temporary operating theatre in the stokers' bathroom, using a table from the wardroom. The steel walls ran with sweat, but Wellbeloved had hung a cluster of lights from the shower and a bucket of water stood handy to swill the blood down the drain in the tiled floor. The sick berth tiffy had just cut off an unconscious stoker's hand at the wrist and was tying up the ligaments. He looked up as he saw Kelly but didn't stop.

'Know how to do it?' Kelly asked.

'I've seen it done before, sir. If I don't he'll bleed to death.' As the stoker was lifted off the table, Kelly lay down on it. The sick berth tiffy sounded apologetic.

'Sir, this morphine—'

'Get on with it!'

'It's going to be bloody painful, sir.'

'Just get on with it, for God's sake!'

Hatchard appeared. He seemed to pop up and down like the Demon King in a pantomime. 'Better drink this,' he said.

318

'What is it?'

'Rum. Nelson's blood.'

'I won't say no to that.'

As Kelly swallowed the raw spirit, it burned his throat and made him cough. The spasms seemed to tear at the wound in his back but he felt better at once and almost ready to have himself sawn in two. 'Who's sitting on my head?' he asked.

A cook with a bandaged head looked embarrassed. 'Me, sir.'

'I bet it's the first time you've ever sat on your captain's head,' Kelly said and was pleased to see the cook grin.

They stripped him of his shirt and he felt the cook put his hands on his shoulders and press down with a weight that drove the breath out of his body. Someone else lay across his legs.

'We'll do your eye first,' the sick berth tiffy said. 'Hold him.'

As he felt the jab of the needle, it was as if they were trying to pierce him through with a cutlass. Biting at his lip until it bled, he refrained from making a noise until at last a great groan broke away from him.

'Soon be finished, sir.'

They seemed to be sewing him up with marline spikes and wire hawser but at last the weight lifted off his legs.

'Sorry if it hurt, sir.'

Someone stuck a lighted cigarette in his mouth, then they poured iodine on his shrinking flesh, bandaged him and helped him into his torn clothing. For a while he sat still, recovering his breath, then he dragged himself upright with an effort.

'Since I'm here,' he said, struggling to keep his voice steady, 'I'll have a word with the wounded.'

The wardroom, its door splintered and buckled, was full of men, all lying very still and very white. One of the cooks was at work there and four stokers were just lifting the body of a sailor from the bench. There was a hole in the ship's side that admitted water which sloshed about their feet as the ship rolled, and in it swilled bloodstained bandages and debris. It was hard to move his arms but he managed to extract cigarettes from his pocket and hand them round. The worst cases were flash burns.

'How many?' Kelly asked.

'Twenty-three dead, sir. Thirty wounded. Some seriously. There may be more. I'm not certain yet.'

'That's a lot for a ship this size.'

As Kelly struggled back to the bridge, one eye and half his face hidden by a great pad of lint, cotton wool and bandage, the ship appeared to be a wreck. It had no guns and the torpedo tubes were empty, but Hatchard had already turned to rigging up temporary communications and Wellbeloved appeared, his face full of optimism.

'We're all right below,' he reported.

Rumbelo got the crew to muster under the bridge so that Kelly could tell them what was happening, and he tried to talk to them like a father, uneasily aware that most of them were older than he was.

'I suspect we're hardly in a fit state to try any more conclusions with the enemy,' he said. 'But we have both engines and we can manoeuvre. In case anything appears, I want all automatic weapons mounted and manned.'

As they dispersed, the destroyer began to move slowly through the black water, picking up speed as she went. 'Take the ship, Sub,' Kelly said to Naylor. 'At least you can see.'

A piece of heaving line round his waist to hold his trousers up in place of the severed braces, he stood on the bridge, clutching the rail. As *Mordant* lifted her forefoot, the horizon to the south was still lit by flashes and occasional searchlights.

'If they've called out Tyrwhitt from Harwich we must have cut them off from their bases,' Naylor said.

'*If*,' Kelly said. He had no great faith in the Admiralty. Pressed by the politicians in London who would be eager to protect the Thames estuary and the approaches to London, they'd be in no hurry to release the eager Tyrwhitt.

They were alone now. They had no idea where the Germans were, though the distant horizon was still full of flashes and the red glow of guns, and occasionally a bigger flare as some ship met its end. There was a strong suspicion growing in Kelly's mind as they drove westwards that this great battle for which the navy had been waiting for two years had not been the big smash that everyone had predicted. Over-caution, lack of training, foolhardiness, bad designs and damn bad signalling seemed to have snatched the victory from their grasp.

Occasionally they saw dimmed lights on the sea about them to show where darkened ships, more afraid than they were, crept past in an attempt to escape. Despite the wreckage along the decks, there was an atmosphere of satisfaction about *Mordant*, and despite their casualties, they had dealt some telling blows and had severely damaged one light cruiser.

Aware of a feeling of light-headedness, Kelly realised that his shoulders were growing stiff and that it was growing harder to stand upright. Someone brought him a stool and he sat down on it, clutching the bridge rail, his fingers knotted in his efforts to control himself. The sick berth tiffy appeared and once more suggested an injection but he shook his head. He was in command of a ship at last and he wasn't going to relinquish it easily.

Curiously, at that moment he thought of Charley and wondered what she would think. Sometime tomorrow or the next day they would learn at home that there'd been a tremendous battle and that the navy had lost several fine ships. He had lapsed into a dazed darkness of pain when Naylor touched his arm.

'Sir!'

A pointing finger jerked and in the blackness he could see the white glow of phosphorescence from the foam at a ship's forefoot. The two vessels were converging gradually and he had come out of his lassitude at once, alert to avoid a collision.

'I hope to God she's not a German,' he said.

Then, abruptly, as though she had not seen *Mordant* just off her quartet, the other ship turned to starboard right across their course so that there was no longer any hope of avoiding her.

'Searchlight,' Kelly snapped and, as the white beam of light leapt across the black sea, they saw at once that the other ship was a German torpedo boat, smaller than *Mordant* and carrying a large white number on her bow.

'It's a Hun!' Naylor screamed.

'Full ahead both!' Kelly said. 'Clear the forecastle! Stand by to ram!'

There wasn't a cat in hell's chance of missing. The German ship had increased speed and seemed to leap forward, and they saw white faces and a gun turning towards them and the flash as it fired. The shell screamed past and disappeared astern, and a second shell struck the bow a glancing blow, ricocheted downwards and exploded alongside, drenching them with water. Then *Mordant's* bows smashed into the German's side, just abaft the bridge, and Kelly was flung forward. As his body struck the bridge rail, a blinding stab of hellish pain rolled over him, and someone fell on top of him, knocking the breath from his body. The damaged foremast came down with a crash, crushing the searchlight in a shower of electric-blue sparks, and the battered funnel bent and fell forward like the hinged stack of a river steamer.

'Jesus,' someone said. 'Smack in the wardroom pantry! Right in the bloody breadbasket!'

For a second, Kelly decided he was dead and in hell as the German fired at *Mordant* with everything she possessed. All about him he could hear the grind and screech of tearing metal and wild shouts in English and German. Struggling to his feet, he dragged himself up to see the German ship lying below *Mordant's* bow, rolling over on her beam ends, and German sailors, their cap ribbons fluttering, running along the twisted decks.

'Full astern!'

Screeching and groaning, the two ships parted as *Mordant* backed off, her bows thrust upwards and buckled like a tin can.

'Like the cork out of an effing bottle,' a sailor below the bridge yelled exultantly.

The German was badly hurt, a great hole like a wedge of cheese carved in her side. As *Mordant* drew clear, Kelly saw two men standing in the opening among the torn metal, both of them yelling with fright, then the water rushed in and swept them away, and the German ship, released from the pressure, began to swing back, rolling to starboard as the sea engulfed her.

For a moment she straightened and a gun banged, but the barrel was cocked wildly askew and the shell screamed off into the air, then someone on *Mordant* opened fire with a Lewis gun and he saw men falling. The German began to heel over rapidly as she filled with water and, as they continued to back away, they saw her lay on her side, slowly as if she were tired, until the decks were awash, then she turned over, rolling a little as she settled, and finally disappeared.

'God,' Naylor said. 'That was quick!'

There were only about a dozen men in the water. They were dragged on board, dripping and gasping, two of them dying almost at once. To everyone's surprise, among them was Petty Officer Lipscomb, the yeoman of signals, who had been shot off the bridge by the collision. He was wearing two life jackets and was protesting he couldn't swim, but he did a record twenty yards to the side of the ship to yells of encouragement from the crew.

Twisted with pain, Kelly stared at the forepeak. It was lifted high and wrenched to starboard. Wellbeloved appeared along-side him, his jaw dropped, his eyes bulging at the wreckage.

'I think the next job,' Kelly said flatly, 'will be to get this damned ship home.'

Seven

Mordant sagged like a wounded animal as her frantic crew struggled to remove the debris of the mast and shore up the funnel.

The deck below the forecastle had been pushed back for nearly a quarter of the ship's length. A great stretch of steel had been peeled off and trailed its jagged edges in the water, while the cable locker had gone completely and the anchor chain hung down in a steel tangle like an old lady's knitting.

'What a bloody horrible sight,' Wellbeloved said.

The bow was now only half its original length with some twenty feet crumpled, twisted and forced bodily aft. Through the jagged holes in the plating, it was possible to look into the forward mess deck and see the stools and tables. The fore part of the forecastle deck had collapsed downwards until the stemhead was nearly touching the water, forming a vertical wall, over the top of which the muzzle of the wrecked four-inch gun protruded at an odd angle.

'Looks as if it were mounted on the edge of a cliff,' Kelly said.

'We'll have to be towed home stern-first,' Naylor observed.

'Who by?' Kelly turned with difficulty. 'Seems to me, we're all alone, Sub. Let's hope the mist holds and then, at least, the Hun won't see us creeping off.'

'*Can* we creep off?'

'We can try.'

It was now midnight and the flickering of flames along the horizon still continued with the glare of searchlights and the thunder of gunfire. Wellbeloved was already below, struggling with baulks of timber mattresses and rope to prop up the forward bulkhead. On that one bulwark of steel depended the ship's safety, and he and his men were struggling in waist-high water to strengthen it so they could move.

'We could wait for daylight,' Hatchard suggested. 'I dare bet there won't be any Germans around to sink us by then.'

Kelly winced at the pain across his shoulders. 'There probably won't be any of our ships around either,' he said. 'Not that we could call for help, anyway, because we've got neither searchlight nor wireless.'

Wellbeloved appeared. He was filthy dirty and soaked to the skin, his clothes clinging to his thick body.

'You can try her now,' he said. 'Dead slow.'

For a while they made way through the sea, but it was difficult to steer without any knife-edge to cleave the water. Plates were hanging loose and clanging and clattering as they moved, and with every yard they were shoving against the hundreds of tons of water that flooded into the open bows. Wellbeloved returned from a tour of inspection.

'Bulkhead's starting to go,' he said. 'Looks as if it might collapse. It's pushing the whole ocean in front of it. We're down by the bows and the oil tank's leaking into the sea.'

'What do you suggest?'

'Stop engines for a kick-off. It'll diminish the strain.'

'Right. And we'll adjust the weight to bring the bows out of the water a bit.'

Everything movable was shifted aft to lift the shattered bows, and the forward bulkheads were shored up by more spars, planks, mess stools and tables. The same was done to the top of the oil tank which was showing signs of bulging upwards, and the ammunition from the forward shell room was carried aft while the anchor chain was cut away and allowed to splash into the sea.

They finished the work as first light came to reveal the extent of the damage to the ship. The funnels that still stood, like the ventilators, were riddled through with hundreds of small gashes and the decks were slashed and ripped by splinters. All the officers' cabins and the charthouse had been set on fire and the navigational instruments destroyed, while there were three holes in the ship's side and the main topmast, charred and blackened by the flames, hung down over the wrecked searchlight. The rigging, signal lockers, everything, were a mass of torn steel and timber.

'Well, that settles it,' Kelly said. 'It seems we've *got* to get her home. We can't abandon because we've got no boats.'

A slight breeze had risen, as yet without malice but enough to ripple the water into minute corrugations, and as the temporary repairs were completed, they began once more to steam westwards. The North Sea looked grey and forbidding. There was no sign of the German fleet, just melancholy acres of dead men on the flat calm water, floating in their life jackets among the debris from their lost ships. All around them, over the horizon out of sight, other ships were also making their way home, ghostly in the mist, some of them wallowing under hundreds of tons of water.

Then they passed the wreckage of a German ship and bodies of drowned German sailors, including two officers lying across a spar, floating about with caps and clothing and pieces of timber among the smear of oil and scraps of charred hammocks; and finally a drawer full of seamen's documents and a raft with *Black Prince* painted on its sides.

Nobody spoke. Nobody had time to speak. Every movement of the sea caused *Mordant* to sway and groan and, as the wind freshened, she gave a little lurch and Wellbeloved stared anxiously at the scar in case it was lengthening to expose her flanks still further. Once it extended beyond an upright riveted rib he'd marked, yet another compartment would be flooded.

By this time Kelly's back felt as if it were in a straightjacket, and his fingers ached with being clamped to the bridge rail.

Wellbeloved appeared. 'We're making it,' he grinned. He looked exhausted and blackened with dirt, his eyes red-rimmed, his tongue pink in the hole of his mouth.

Below deck in an atmosphere stinking of scorched paintwork and burnt cordite, the first aid parties were still labouring over the wounded, and the dead were being collected and laid in rows on the stern. Their injuries were terrible. Some of them had been literally torn in half, or had limbs ripped from their bodies; some had been stripped naked by the blast. But the less injured were lying below on the mess deck tables now and those who could sit or recline were propped up with lifebelts.

Despite the groans of the burned and wounded, the spirit of the unhurt vas excellent. They were all exhausted and hungry because the galley had disappeared and they'd eaten nothing but sandwiches for thirty-six hours. Nevertheless, as they collected the empty shell cases and cleared the decks of wreckage, one of the torpedomen produced an accordion and began to play 'Keep the Home Fires Burning.'

'How about "Anybody Here Seen Kelly?"' one of the gunners shouted and, as he changed tunes, Kelly saw faces turned towards the bridge.

'Good old Ginger,' someone yelled. Kelly's face twisted into a grimace of a smile, and he lifted his hand in an acknowledgement that seemed to wrench at the stitches in his back.

'Rumbelo,' he said gravely, 'remind me to have it put about the ship that midshipmen and sub-lieutenants can be ginger but that when they reach lieutenant's rank they become red-haired, while a captain of a ship is *always* auburn.'

Rumbelo grinned at him, and he knew the bon mot would travel swiftly round the lower deck. It would do no harm. Sailors enjoyed a joke against their officers and it could only serve to bind them more tightly together.

Toward midday a zeppelin passed overhead, silently, like a ghost among the low clouds, and one of the reservists in the crew, a man with Egyptian ribbons for 1882 on his chest and a vast bottle nose, started firing a rifle at it.

'Why don't you fix bloody bayonets,' a derisive yell came from behind the wrecked funnel, 'and charge the bastard?'

At lunchtime they passed the bow of a destroyer sticking up out of the water, and soon afterwards steamed through an immense oily pool which marked the resting place of some great ship. During the afternoon Naylor announced that the dead were ready for burial. 'Shall I do it, sir?' he asked.

'No.' Kelly shook his head. 'I'll do it.'

With a relief helmsman on the wheel, Rumbelo prised his fingers from the bridge rail and helped him down the ladder while Naylor took his place. The service was held in the waist of the ship, the sagging topmast swaying giddily above them. Those men who could be spared from their duties were standing bare-headed in two lines, several of them wearing bandages.

'Rumbelo,' Kelly said. 'Stand behind me and make sure I don't fall down. Sound the "Still."'

The survivors had fallen in on the port side. The wail of the bosun's pipe broke the silence and a prayer book was pushed into Kelly's hand. He drew a deep breath.

'Forasmuch as it has pleased Almighty God of His great mercy to take unto Himself the souls of our comrades here departed...'

It hadn't been Almighty God who'd taken the souls of their comrades, he thought as he intoned the words, it had been the German High Seas Fleet and the dummies at the Admiralty.

As he finished reading, a murmur ran through the gathered men and as the bosun's pipe twittered the bodies disappeared, sliding from under the ensigns into the sea with hardly a splash. The water closed over them as though they'd never existed.

'Carry on,' Kelly said as he turned away. 'I'll need the names, Mr Hatchard.'

The bridge ladder seemed hundreds of feet high with thousands of steps and Kelly's legs were like lead. He felt Rumbelo's hand on his behind, pushing, and he made it with an effort. The place looked as if it had been through a reaper, with its wood and steelwork slashed by splinters and the dodger fluttering in rags.

'You should be lying down, sir,' Rumbelo grumbled.

'I know I should. But I'm not going to.'

'How's your back?'

'Stiff.'

'You look like death.'

'I feel like death. But I expect I can manage till we reach home.'

The barometer had gone down, and the sky looked threatening with the sun hidden behind a hard grey pall dappled over with lumps of dark cloud driving from the west on the rising wind. By two in the afternoon, *Mordant* was pitching to the motion of crisp little waves, and occasional wisps of spray came rattling over what was left of the bridge.

The motion was agonising and Kelly's fingers were white as he gripped the bridge rail.

Wellbeloved appeared once more, his face strained. 'That bulkhead's buckling and twisting like paper,' he said. 'And the shores are working loose. The boiler room bulkhead's not much better.'

Kelly made an effort to concentrate. 'What do you propose?'

'We'll have to abandon.'

'Not bloody likely. I'm taking this ship home. It's the first I've ever commanded and I'm damned if I'm going to let her sink.'

'You'll never make it. The minute you go ahead again, the bulkhead'll go.'

They seemed to be beaten, then Kelly remembered the trip he'd made into Surrey with Charley before he'd joined the ship and the way they'd climbed the Hog's Back in reverse because they couldn't make it any other way.

He grinned at Wellbeloved. 'Let's go astern,' he said.

'She'll sink.'

'She will *not* sink,' Kelly snapped. 'It's up to you to see that she doesn't!'

'You can't go all the way across the North Sea stern-first.'

'We can have a bloody good try!'

Wellbeloved's tired face cracked into a grin. 'I think you're barmy,' he said, 'But if you're game, so am I.'

As Wellbeloved vanished, Rumbelo looked at Kelly.

'You all right, sir?'

'I'm all right, Rumbelo.'

'How's your back?'

'Bloody painful.'

In fact, it was stiffening now and Kelly sat down cautiously on the stool they'd given him. His eye and cheek hurt like hell and the sick berth PO's stitching was dragging at the flesh of his back. He had to lean forward to ease his muscles every now and then and eventually, he knew, he'd set rigid, so he clung to the bridge rail, deciding that at least he'd set rigid in the right place. They'd probably have to prise him loose with a crowbar when they reached home, but that wouldn't matter much so long as they arrived, and the bleeding seemed to have stopped so that he had a feeling he was going to survive.

'We'll have something to tell them at home, Rumbelo,' he said. 'When we *get* home.'

'*If* we get home, sir. Pity it isn't better news. Still, I don't suppose they'll mind so long as we arrive. Biddy won't, anyway.'

'Why don't you marry the girl?'

'I might at that, sir. I've had about three of me nine lives already. How about you and Miss Charlotte?'

'Not old enough, Rumbelo. Got to wait until I'm thirty.'

'That's hard, sir.'

'No, it isn't. It's what makes admirals, Rumbelo, and I'm going to be an admiral.'

'When did you decide that, sir?'

'Just now.'

Rumbelo grinned. 'Does Miss Charlotte know?'

'I think she always knew.'

Wellbeloved dragged himself to the bridge. 'You can try it now,' he said.

'Right. Slow astern both. Let me know if she holds.'

The ship moved slowly astern. Getting home was going to be largely by guess and by God because they had no charts or compass and a stiff sea was getting up, but if they headed due west they were bound to hit England somewhere. In fact, *Mordant* steered much better than they'd expected and Wellbeloved popped up again alongside Kelly. 'I think she's holding,' he said. 'But, for God's sake, no faster.'

They were still staggering slowly home when darkness came again. The sea had risen a little and waves kept punching at *Mordant's* blunt stern.

'If it gets up much more,' Wellbeloved said, 'it'll remove everything aft and make the stern uninhabitable. We'd better have the storerooms cleared of food just in case.'

After sufficient food for the voyage had been salvaged, the stern portion of the ship was also abandoned and they set up camp for what was left of the crew amidships.

Wet, exhausted and weary-eyed, they watched through the second night. It was impossible to prevent water finding its way below and every gallon in the after compartment decreased the buoyancy of the ship. By next morning, the wind had increased still more and Kelly watched with anxious eyes as they punched into the waves, wondering if they would have to abandon after all and his boastful claims were going to be punctured. The forward bulkheads were bulging and parties of men were constantly kept at work replacing and wedging up the timber shores.

As the battered ship crept on, pushing her blunt stern into the sea, he clung to the bridge, aware that he'd changed overnight. He was in command now and he was behaving as if he were. He shivered, his body wilting under the strain of tiredness, pain and cold.

'Rumbelo,' he said. 'Go to my cabin and find me a scarf.'

Rumbelo disappeared. A moment or two later he was back. 'It's a wreck, sir. Water's coming through a hole in the side. I brought you one of mine.' As he fastened the scarf round Kelly's throat, he handed him the picture of Charley. The glass was smashed. 'I managed to salvage this, sir,' he said.

'Take it out, Rumbelo. I'll shove it in my pocket.'

It seemed to be a token of good luck. His last leave with Charley had been a period of mounting elation, with Charley behaving as though she might not live to see the next day; despite their new wariness towards each other, happy in a breathless but controlled excitement at everything they did together, her head tilted with delight at her own cleverness whenever she did something that amused or pleased him, wasting no time on irrelevancies, even the touch of her hand in his a perceptible caress. He'd never had anything but pleasure from knowing her and it seemed now that she might see them home.

The weather began to grow worse and they began to have trouble with the shorings and the plugs for the holes near the waterline and Wellbeloved appeared at a rush.

'You'll have to reduce revs,' he announced. 'The bloody ship's falling apart.'

'It is *not* falling apart,' Kelly said doggedly. 'I'm going to get her home if I have to swim underneath her to keep her up.'

During the afternoon, Rumbelo devised a mattress in the corner of the bridge and he snatched a fitful sleep, but he was on his feet again in the evening to fix their position. The first ship they saw was a trawler and Naylor hailed it and told it to stand by to escort them to safety.

To their joyous disbelief, May Island came in sight during the evening, then they saw the faint blue streak of the Scottish coast. Exhausted, unshaven, wet and hungry, they gazed greedily at the thin line of land.

'Thank Christ,' Wellbeloved said fervently.

332

A destroyer came hurtling out of the Firth of Forth to challenge them.

'Make with the lamp, Lipscomb,' Kelly ordered. '"Keep away from me. Your wash will sink me."'

The other ship cautiously moved round them, the men on her bridge eyeing the damage through glasses. At last she acknowledged and flashed back. '"Have ordered tug and hospital boat."'

When the tug arrived alongside, they were all snappy and irritable with reaction and fatigue.

'Prepare to be taken in tow by the stern,' the tug skipper ordered. 'Turn your stern to the sea and stop engines.'

A man with a lieutenant's stripes stepped aboard and to his disgust Kelly saw it was Verschoyle.

'What the hell are you doing here?' he demanded furiously.

Verschoyle smiled, clean, well-shaven and full of life. 'Come to take over,' he announced.

Kelly drew himself up. He was dirty and his face was grey with fatigue and covered with streaks of dried blood, and he felt as though he'd never be able to move his back and shoulders again. 'I'm in command of this bloody ship,' he said. 'I'm *staying* in command.'

Verschoyle studied the bandages under his torn clothes and peered at his one good eye beneath the wad of cotton wool and lint. Despite the battered ship and the weary men, there was something terrifyingly enduring in the spirit he saw around him and he realised unwillingly that it stemmed entirely from this man in front of him to whom he had once felt superior. For the first time in his life, Verschoyle was conscious of a feeling of admiration. 'Humility,' he said, 'was never one of your virtues, Maguire. By the look of you, you should be in hospital.'

'I'll go to hospital when we've finally made port and not before.'

'Do you mean to say you've been handling this ship all the way across the North Sea?'

Kelly gestured at the weary men with tired eyes and bowed shoulders moving about the waist of the ship. '*We* have,' he corrected. 'Me and these chaps.'

As the steel towing hawser was passed across, he suddenly realised whom he was talking to and the old dislike flared up.

'Why does it have to be you, anyway?' he demanded.

'That's what I was thinking,' Verschoyle said blandly. 'So the feeling seems to be mutual. Are you badly hurt?'

'I'm dying.'

Verschoyle laughed. 'You don't sound very moribund, and I can't imagine anyone ever being able to kill you. You'll be around for quite a few years yet to make a nuisance of yourself to the Admiralty, I'll be bound.'

Kelly was silent for a moment. 'I thought you were with Sturdee in *Benbow*.'

Verschoyle shrugged. 'Fell out. Had a few words. He's such a conceited ass. I was posted down here to *Queen Mary*. She left just before I arrived. Seems to have been quite a good thing for me.'

'You missed the battle. You don't reach flag rank without battle experience.'

'You'd be surprised. And, anyway, it wouldn't do me much good if I were dead, would it? They sent me and a few shore-bound types to help you chaps in. There are such a lot of you.'

Kelly glared at him from red-rimmed eyes. 'We'll manage without,' he said.

Verschoyle didn't argue. 'You always were a stubborn bugger,' he said.

Kelly stared at the grey northern coastline and drew a deep breath. 'Anyway, who won? If anybody knows, I bet you do.'

Versehoyle's face became bleak. 'God knows,' he said. 'It's hard to say yet. Before I left, I heard Jellicoe had reported the battle fleet available for action again at four hours' notice.'

'That's a lot of bloody good! There's nobody to fight. He let 'em get away.'

'Does seem a bit stupid, I suppose.' It was the keen, intelligent Verschoyle speaking now. 'We've been badly hurt. Arbuthnot's gone. Horace Hood, too. As well as around six thousand others. Only one of Arbuthnot's ships returned. The others are all sunk. And there are a hell of a lot of scars to be seen.'

'We got a few ourselves,' Kelly said stiffly.

'I'd say you *are* a scar. With bits of ship attached.' Verschoyle frowned. 'Men landing from *Warspite* were jeered at by the dockies.'

Kelly glared. 'I wish we'd had a few dockies in *Mordant* when we met the Hun. The bastards wouldn't have been jeering then.'

They staggered into the Firth, the waves lifting over *Mordant*'s stern. The battle cruiser force had long since entered but none of the expected flags had been flying to indicate a victory and no bands were playing. Some of the vast twelve-inch guns were cocked up in the air and mats covered their wounds, and it was a strange hushed place because even now no one was sure whether they'd won or lost.

Verschoyle moved restlessly in his clothes. 'Everybody's blaming bad visibility,' he said. 'To say nothing of interference from mist and smoke, lack of anti-flash precautions, inadequate armour, bad signalling and just plain bad gunnery.'

Kelly scowled. 'Nobody's mentioned the tedium of swinging round a buoy at Scapa Flow for so long every officer of spirit took all possible steps to get away, I suppose?'

'In the end,' Verschoyle observed, 'I suppose we can probably blame Fisher for it. He towered above everybody else but he split the navy from top to bottom with such effect that for over a decade no officer dared disagree or express an opinion on a naval matter in a mess, club, ship or even a bloody drawing room. And with his blasted dreadnoughts he put the whole navy out of date in a year because the Germans simply built better ones.'

Kelly was startled at Verschoyle's percipience. It was something that had begun to occur to him, too, but he was surprised to find Verschoyle agreed with him.

'We could have lost another six ships without worrying,' he growled. 'We've got enough building, and it'd have been worth it in the end if we'd wiped 'em off the face of the sea. But it didn't work that way. Someone was afraid to take the risk.' He drew a deep rasping breath that hurt his chest. 'One thing, we ought to have a better navy for the rest of the war. I would say the lesson's written into the soul of everybody with any brains who was there: you can't plan a naval battle from harbour, and if you don't seize your chances you'll never get 'em offered again.'

Verschoyle stared at him shrewdly. 'You know, Maguire,' he said, 'for the first time you sound like a bloody admiral. With luck you might actually make it. When I'm First Sea Lord I'll take pleasure in giving you some obscure command in the Far East.'

'Go to hell,' Kelly said, and Verschoyle laughed.

They reached Rosyth about midnight. They were towed stern-first down the reaches by the tug, the engines stopped, only the auxiliaries going to keep things turning. A few ships cheered them as they moved slowly past but not many because most of them were concerned with their own hurts and their own casualties.

'I'm taking you alongside,' Verschoyle said. 'The place's been astir all day waiting to help you chaps home.'

'Good,' Kelly said. 'The troops'll be able to get ashore. What there are left of the poor buggers.'

Another tug appeared and the captain started yelling irritably across the intervening water.

'If that bloody man doesn't stop yelling at me,' Kelly snarled, 'I'll turn a bloody machine gun on him. You'd better tell him so.'

Verschoyle passed the message as it stood and the tug captain stopped shouting abruptly. Slowly, watched by silent dockyard workers and sailors from other ships, they were nudged shore-wards.

'You'll be going into the basin,' Verschoyle said. 'As soon as we can clear it.'

Kelly nodded. He was limp from lack of sleep and pain but he couldn't imagine where he could go to rest. His cabin was wrecked. The captain's cabin was wrecked and the wardroom was still full of wounded.

'We'll have the injured lifted out in cots for the Queensferry hospital,' Verschoyle said. 'I think I can safely attend to that for you. You'll be going with them, of course.'

'I'm staying here.'

Verschoyle took a look at Kelly's expression and didn't press the point, and Kelly bit his lip, wondering if Wellbeloved's shoring would survive the last few hundred yards. It would be too bloody bad, he thought, if it collapsed and they sank just as they went alongside. Especially with Verschoyle on board, to laugh like a drain at his discomfiture.

The hospital drifter arrived. Kelly watched the wounded brought up and taken aboard. Verschoyle was no longer arguing with him and when a pinnace appeared with a message to say the basin was free, he simply passed on Kelly's orders.

As they were warped through the lock gates, watched by crowds of wharfies, men from *Warspite*, and survivors of *Warrior* in a mixture of uniform and civilian clothes, the heaving lines went ashore, dragging the hawsers and springs after them.

'I think you ought to go down now,' Verschoyle advised.

'Yes,' Kelly agreed. 'Perhaps I will.'

But as he spoke the dockside began to spin and the sky grew dark. His knees felt weak and his mouth felt like sandpaper. Little doors seemed to be shutting in his mind, one after the other, until finally the light began to disappear. There weren't many left to go now and when the last one shut he knew he'd know no more.

'I think I'll lie down,' he said, and as he did so he slipped quietly backwards into Verschoyle's arms.

Eight

Lying on his side, propped up by pillows, with a whole ward of other wounded men in white enamelled beds like a regiment of horizontal white guardsmen, Kelly stared one-eyed from under a great wadding of cotton wool and bandage at the grey sky through the hospital window. The nurse fussed round the bed, full of harsh good cheer and Scottish banter.

'Feeling better?' she asked.

'No,' Kelly said. 'Worse.'

'Don't despair. You'll be with us for a long time yet.'

His mother had been to see him but, with his grandfather appointed at last to a remount depot near Esher and in need of looking after and with the mare about to foal, she'd not stayed long. Kimister had also been. He'd looked faintly shamefaced. *Collingwood* had never been hit, and he'd never once been in the slightest danger and, looking at Kelly's battered face under the wad of bandaging, he'd had a feeling that somehow he'd shirked his duty. He'd brought the newspapers containing the Admiralty's communique. 'The German fleet,' it had said, 'aided by low visibility, avoided prolonged action with our main forces, and soon after these appeared on the scene the enemy returned to port, though not before receiving severe damage from our battleships.'

And not before dishing out a bit, too, Kelly thought.

In the lunacy of the moment the penpushers seemed to have gone off their heads. 'Glorious end of our cruisers,' one of them announced, but there seemed nothing very glorious about being blown up and reduced to ashes in a fraction of a second. Nor was there anything very glorious about badly designed ships taking men to their deaths, or bad gunnery and bad signalling practice allowing the Germans to get away.

It all seemed to have been so bloody pointless. A lot of lives had been lost and a lot of ships sunk to smash the Germans, and it seemed that the Germans hadn't been smashed after all – because of all those old duffers like his father who had lived by paintwork and brass and chucked their blackleaded practice shells overboard as they conducted their unrealistic exercises and behaved as if they were the lords of creation. It had been the boast that Britannia ruled the waves and that all other world powers were land powers. They'd never realised that battleships were meant to fight battles and throughout the hundred years of peace since Trafalgar they'd been resting on Nelson's laurels so that when the great moment came they'd not been up to the challenge.

The lost ships were known now – *Invincible, Queen Mary, Indefatigable, Defence, Warrior, Black Prince, Ardent, Fortune, Sparrowhawk, Tipperary, Turbulent, Shark, Nomad, Nestor* – to say nothing of those which had crawled or been towed home badly damaged. The destroyers alone had taken an awful hammering as they'd tried to screen their bigger sisters, and grief had come home to households all over the country. Menfolk had been snatched away in an overnight cataclysm which, for the relationship of dead to wounded, was not even matched by the slaughter the old duffers from Aldershot were inflicting on the army in France. Only a few survivors had been found in Norwegian and Danish coastal villages after being hauled from the sea by fishermen.

It was hard to find out the facts as far as the Germans were concerned. Perhaps it wasn't necessary. The gaps in the British lines were too depressing to make it important, and some sections of the press were already hue and cry after the Admiralty for 'making excuses'. No matter what had happened, they claimed, the German High Seas Fleet had been caught and allowed to get away. Even the fairest considered the outcome of the battle 'disappointing,' and claimed that the German Navy would have the assurance henceforth that it could cross swords with the British Navy and survive.

'Defeat must be admitted,' the *Manchester Guardian* said, and 'The result can't be regarded with satisfaction' was the *Telegraph*'s and the *Mail*'s view.

Kelly scowled. The Germans had fought well, but they'd been driven from the field and that was something. The Grand Fleet was still in control of the exits and entrances to the North Sea and although it had snapped at its gaoler, the High Seas Fleet was still in prison.

–

As Kelly looked up, he became aware of Rumbelo standing alongside the bed.

'Hello, Rumbelo,' he said. 'You all right?'

'I'm all right, sir. I managed to rescue some of your gear. Not much. But I brought it up for you. I wondered how you were and they said I could come in and see you.'

Kelly forced a smile. 'You deserve a putty medal, Rumbelo,' he said. 'For keeping me upright all that time. I bet your arms were aching.'

'They were a bit, sir. Actually, though, I don't think anybody could have pushed you over if they'd tried.'

'That's the best of having big feet. Are they giving you leave?'

'Yes, sir. I'm going down to Esher.'

'To see Biddy?'

'She said I could, any time I wanted.'

'Well, don't be a damn fool and stay at a pub. That room over the stable's there for you.'

Rumbelo grinned. 'Biddy don't approve of that, sir. She thinks it'd be wrong, without a chaperone.'

Kelly tried to shrug but caught his breath as the pain tore at his shoulders.

'There's no understanding women,' he said. 'How're the troops?'

Rumbelo's face fell. 'We were a bit bucked when we got in, sir,' he said. 'We thought we 'adn't done so badly, but the papers say we've been licked and that the admirals were just a lot of bloody fools. They don't seem to think much of the result and that's a fact.'

Kelly frowned. 'All those chaps in *Mordant* didn't die just to please the Hurrah Department of the *Daily Mail*,' he growled.

'It didn't come up to expectations, though, did it, sir? We had 'em stone cold and we let 'em get away.'

'Well, it wasn't exactly the glorious victory we were expecting,' Kelly agreed. 'Partial, perhaps, because they *did* run away, but it wasn't the big smash we've been looking forward to.'

Rumbelo shifted uneasily. 'They say they're after Jellicoe's blood, sir,' he observed. 'They reckon he threw his opportunity away.'

Kelly grimaced. 'It's always easy to be wise when you're sitting in an office in Fleet Street,' he said. 'All the same, perhaps we'd been waiting for it too long and the German taunts hurt. And, even if we didn't lose, there's still a bit of a loss of face.'

–

When Rumbelo had gone, Kelly stared at the wall for a while. The nurse tried to make him smile with her brisk clattery laughter and pawky humour, but he was in a stubborn mood and didn't reply. He wanted to be in a bad temper – the occasion seemed to demand it – and nobody was going to jerk him out of it. There must be something inside him, he decided, that would one day develop into the fuss and fury of the senior officer he'd made up his mind to become. He allowed her to give him a new injection in his backside but didn't yield an inch to her jokes.

'What's that for?' he demanded.

341

'Put you to sleep. They want you to have a good rest. Those stitches in your back are all going to have to come out. It's either that or a back corrugated like a rubbing board.'

Kelly glared. 'Oh, bloody charming,' he said. 'I'll enjoy that.'

She beamed at him. 'My, we are in a bad temper, aren't we?'

'Yes, we are.'

She laughed. 'Yon's a pity because there's someone tae see you.'

'Who?' Now that Kimister and Rumbelo had been and gone, Kelly could only think of Hatchard or Wellbeloved – or, for God's sake, not Verschoyle!

The nurse laughed. 'It's a lady,' she said. 'She says she's been travelling all night from London.'

Kelly tried to sit up but she pushed him down again. 'Young or old?' he asked.

'Young. Verra young. And verra pretty. A gey sight prettier than you anyway.'

Kelly glowered. 'Then why the blazes did you give me that bloody injection?' he demanded indignantly.

'So you'll go to sleep.'

'I don't want to go to sleep! Especially if she's come all this way to see me.'

'I don't think she'll mind. She said they'd taken a room at the George and that they'll be staying for a few days. All she wants at this moment is to see if you're in one piece.'

'And am I?'

'Oh, aye! Pretty well.'

'How long's she been waiting?'

'A few minutes.'

'Then stop your damned chattering and wheel her in.'

Charley came down the ward shyly, looking like a schoolgirl and conscious of the other wounded officers staring at her. She was dressed in pale blue, which made her dark hair seem darker, and she had a paper bag in her hand.

Kelly grinned. 'Grapes?'

'Yes.' Tears sparkling on her lashes, she sat at the side of the bed, her anxious eyes on what she could see of Kelly's face under the bandages. 'Mabel brought me. She didn't want to, but I made her.'

'Don't I get a kiss?'

Without a word she leaned over and kissed him gently on the cheek.

'That the best you can do?'

Cautiously, reaching under the wad of bandage, she transferred her attentions to his mouth and his hands came up and grasped her. She wrenched herself free.

'What's the matter?'

'I might hurt you.'

'I'm not made of icing sugar. How long are you staying?'

'A day or two.'

'Thank God for that! If I pass out on you, it's not because I'm dying, it's because that fathead of a nurse has given me an injection to send me to sleep.'

'It doesn't matter. I'll be here tomorrow. Do you think they'll let me sit here for a while if you do go to sleep?'

'There can't be much fun staring at a man snoring in bed. Unless you're in there with him.'

She blushed. 'I shall be all right. How are you?'

Kelly could feel himself becoming drowsy and he made an effort to stay awake.

'Fine,' he said. 'Or fairly fine. I'm not going to lose my eye and that's something, ain't it? And they've fixed my cheekbone. They're going to have another go at my back any day now.'

He noticed the tears in her eyes. 'What are you crying for?' he demanded.

She gave a choking sob. 'Kelly, your poor face!'

He managed a smile. 'Well, it was never much to write home about, and they say I shall be quite pretty again when they've finished. An honourable scar or two but nothing to mar my beauty.'

343

She drew a deep, painful breath. 'You hardly seemed to have left London when we heard about the battle,' she said.

Kelly sighed. 'I'd been there about nine weeks, Charley,' he said slowly, wonderingly, thinking about Talbot. 'Some people had been waiting for two years.'

'Mother says the war seems to follow you about.'

'She's probably right.'

Kelly's breathing was becoming steady and he noticed that the pain in his back was fading. Another minute or two and that bloody injection would have him asleep.

'Is that all?' he asked. 'I know that.'

She managed a shy smile, almost as if she were a stranger. 'I'm glad you're safe, Kelly.'

His smile was drowsy. 'That's the least I expect from you,' he said.

'When I heard there was a battle, I prayed for you.'

'It seems to have taken.'

'I'm so proud of you. I met Rumbelo outside. Did you know he and Biddy are thinking of getting married?'

'Good luck to 'em.' Kelly's voice was growing slurred. 'As neither of 'em seems to have a home, I suppose they'll do it at our place. Mother'll enjoy that.'

'Rumbelo was proud of you, too. He said the whole ship was proud.'

Kelly fought to keep his eyes open. 'Why?'

'Because you got them home. And because of the other thing, too.'

'What other thing?'

'He said James Verschoyle came aboard and told them you'd get nothing less than a Victoria Cross for what you'd done.'

Kelly's vision was hazy now and Charley's features were blurred. All he could see was a shy smile and dark hair, and a pale blue shape moving about in front of him. His heart felt full of warmth for her innocence and beauty and her belief in him, and he suddenly felt like crying. He swallowed, deciding that the injection was having a curious effect on his emotions, then what she'd said finally sank in and he gave a bark of cynical laughter.

'I bet that made the envious bugger bite his lip a bit,' he said cheerfully.

As his vision twisted, he managed another faint smile before his eyes crossed, then, his eyelids drooping and his head sagging into the pillow, he fell fast asleep.